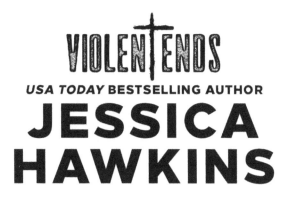

VIOLENT ENDS

USA TODAY BESTSELLING AUTHOR

JESSICA HAWKINS

I had a life, love, and future to ~~~
Until my ~~~

The devil has a name, ████████████████ my
wedding day, he w. ████████████████
standing at the altar. H ████████ ... queen. His
brother wan~~ ~~~~cue his princess.

Getting Cristiano to lose control becomes the name of the
game, and the stakes are life and death. But as truth and
lies blur, loyalty is tested, and our chemistry threatens to
reach the melting point, the prize grows less clear. Either
freedom no longer means what I think it does, or Cristiano
is as devious as everyone says, and he's mastered the art of
playing my mind.

All I know for certain is that nothing is certain.
And all you need to know? This is a love story.
But even love stories have to end.

1

NATALIA

The devil had a name—Cristiano de la Rosa—but from this day forward, I would call him *husband*.

The cozy church where I'd spent Sunday mornings over a prayer book with my parents stood still and quiet except for the echo of broken promises and ripped lace. Mid-day, sunlight flooded the pews around us, but only candlelight touched the darkened aisle.

In a sharp, tailored suit, my new husband stood before me, waiting for me to finish stripping off my wedding gown so he could thoroughly claim ownership before we'd even left the church.

Cristiano had forced my hand in marriage, and the man I'd envisioned spending my life with had agreed to it. Had *tricked* me into it.

"My new *bride* is shy." Cristiano smiled tightly, finding pleasure in the designation, likely just because he'd imposed it on me. "But I only required my brother meet two terms to validate this arrangement, and you've already broken one."

Cristiano had expected me to come to him a virgin, but

Diego hadn't delivered me that way. The implication was clear—would I break the second term, too? I couldn't. Cristiano had already invited me to walk away from all of this, but there would be a price for that, and the people I loved would pay it.

Consummate the marriage, or the Maldonado cartel would obliterate all of us.

"I'd hoped our first time might be different," I said, grasping for a way to change an inevitable outcome. He'd asked me to marry him when he could've dragged me down the aisle. He'd respected the ceremony, lassoing us in a show for our few onlookers. If there was a shred of humanity within him, I had to try to tap into it.

"As had I." He tilted his head, his eyes scanning my front, as if I was a puzzle to be solved. "But you chose to give your virginity to another. I was prepared to take you to bed and handle you gently, but it seems I no longer have a need for that." He stepped toward me, six-foot-five inches of suited muscle and dark beauty with a clean, masculine scent. "You *have* been thoroughly broken in . . . haven't you?"

I shivered as I slipped one arm through the wedding dress, mourning the beautiful, ruined lace my mother had worn to wed my father. "No," I whispered.

One thick eyebrow arched. "I'm sorry?"

"I haven't," I insisted. "Diego and I did it *once*. He was gentle. I'm not . . ."

"Broken?" he suggested. "Like a wild horse."

I turned away from his penetrating gaze as his black eyes danced. To sully the wedding altar, to slap God in the face, to force Diego to endure my ruination from the other side of the door—it was what I'd sold Cristiano in exchange for our lives. Not just mine, but my father's, Diego's, and anyone else close to the Cruz cartel. Men who'd protected my family, who'd *raised* families under my father, and who'd helped raise *me* after my mother's death.

I drew my other arm through its sleeve and pushed my dress down until it pooled at my feet.

Cristiano wet his lips, his eyes drifting to the ivory lingerie I'd worn for a wedding night I'd planned to share with Diego. Diego and I had made love, but tonight, I'd been ready to give in to the passion we'd been forced to bridle for years. *How naïve.*

Cristiano dipped his head. If I hadn't known better, I'd have thought it was in reverence. "Beautiful."

I shifted from one heel to the other. "You've seen me in my underwear before."

"In your bathroom, after the warehouse fire." He nodded, his angular jaw firming. "But I didn't let myself look at you this way. All I'd have seen was what I couldn't have." His broad chest expanded with an inhale as he raised his chin. "Now, all I see is everything I *own*. Every last inch of you, my darling."

My heart skipped. We'd been married mere minutes, yet he acted as if I was his possession. "Just because we're married doesn't make this consensual."

"As I've said before, you always have a choice. You can walk out of this church now and into my brother's arms. I'd ask you to stay, but I wouldn't force you."

As irritation flickered in me for his word play, I retorted, "But you *would* allow a rival cartel to exact revenge for the money Diego lost them."

"It cost me a great deal to call them off. More than Diego can ever repay." Cristiano shook out his wrist and adjusted his steel watch without breaking eye contact. "But as long as I have you, his debt is forgiven, and they won't lay a finger on you or anyone you love."

His solid footsteps resounded through the pews as he

circled me and stopped at my back. Perhaps he'd rip off my underwear the way he had my dress. I didn't care—unlike my mother's gown, they were worth nothing.

He parted my hair, drew it forward over my shoulders, and spread a hand against my bare upper back. "Not until this moment have I allowed myself to want you."

I swallowed dryly. Something new had entered his voice. Longing. Desperation. As if he'd been in need of something I was now offering. I waited for him to push me down, bend me over a pew, and conquer.

"How was he with you?" Cristiano asked quietly. "Did my brother destroy you, or did he leave me the pleasure of that task?"

"Diego was . . ." Words to describe the man I loved, once at the tip of my tongue, didn't come as easily now. He had betrayed me, but how thoroughly? If he'd been willing to trade me, was there a chance he'd also taken my virginity knowing what was in store for me? He wouldn't. He *couldn't*. Only a monster would do that, and the de la Rosa family already had enough of those. I'd known Diego practically my whole life, and I'd know if he was that evil. "He was sweet and caring," I continued. Even if doubt entered my memory of that night, I couldn't let Cristiano see that. Weakness was one thing I could no longer afford to show around him. "At least I'll know that kindness once in my lifetime, and I will cling to that memory every time I'm with you."

Cristiano chuckled deeply and lowered his mouth to my ear. "I look forward to watching you try. Your lips will know one word when I'm inside you—my name—and you'll feel only one thing—the pleasure I'm giving you."

I shut my eyes as the inevitable closed in. "Please make this quick."

"Never." Starting at my shoulder blade, he slid a finger

up under my bra strap. "*Quick* is not the way to fuck a woman like you, at least not until after I've thoroughly explored you."

I drew a small breath at his bluntness. What kind of torture would it be to have such a controlled, dangerous man explore me with his full attention? Sweet or cruel? A mix of both, I guessed. That wasn't the terrifying part, though. By the tone of his voice, he intended for me to enjoy my undoing.

He pressed his hands to my shoulders. "Stay here," he said before walking away.

I stared down the aisle toward the discarded pillows where we'd kneeled, which were backdropped by paneled, stained-glass saints. Our Lady of Guadalupe silently stared at me. I'd never given her my bouquet in exchange for her blessing of our union, but then, we didn't deserve it.

Some of the candles had gone out, likely with the way everyone had rushed out of the building with Cristiano's command to leave. Was Diego envisioning Cristiano shredding my clothing at this moment? The merciless way he'd use me? The fervor with which Cristiano had promised to take me after our first kiss as man and wife?

I hoped he was, and that each and every one of Diego's thoughts tortured him.

Any suffering he endured would never match my own.

This was *his* fault.

Cristiano's footsteps returned, and with barely a touch at my back, my bra popped open. He slid it off, dropping it on the ground. We were starting. My heart beat in my stomach as I anticipated his callused palms on my skin.

"Is quick really what you want? For me to tear through you hard and fast?" His voice deepened with unmistakable lust. "Or would you prefer I draw it out? Make you enjoy it? *Crave* it? What would be worse?"

I shuddered despite the warmth of the church. To enjoy it would be a betrayal to myself—a crime I had a feeling I'd commit. Already, my nipples stuck straight out, tingling in anticipation of his hands. Every time he touched me, my body responded—from our dance at the costume ball to his wandering fingers as he'd bandaged up my feet after the warehouse fire. But no matter the draw that existed between us, I would never admit to craving it. I'd sure as hell never ask for it.

What would be worse? I could comprehend pain, resistance, and hatred in a moment like this.

But to be pleasured by the devil and enjoy it? That felt like the highest sin.

"Get it over with," I said.

"I only ask out of curiosity," he said, pressing his hand to my back and guiding me forward. "It won't change the course of things. Now, my little butterfly, brace yourself on the pew."

I inhaled deeply, bent forward, and gripped the lip with both hands, offering my backside to him.

"What a sight," he said. "My imagination is getting the better of me. Maybe if you ask nicely, I'll sodomize you this way sometime."

Reflexively, I clenched my cheeks. I'd be naïve to think he had any limits, but my mind hadn't yet wandered to the sordid details. He made it sound as filthy as possible, so different than I'd ever heard.

Considering how he might use me, might violate me in such a forbidden place—my breath came short. It was what he wanted, to inspire fear. Being at his mercy in the most vulnerable ways possible, surrendering to him, was like falling at the feet of a hungry beast.

My body answered the thought with a sharp but pleasurable pang somewhere in my depths. *Oh, God.* What was wrong with me?

"*I suspect you'll even like the feeling of surrender,*" he'd said to me on the horse days earlier.

Could he have been right? Maybe I had the same dark nature inside me that he did, a craving to be bent to a man's will. But I wasn't an animal. I wouldn't allow myself to enjoy it just because it satisfied some carnal desire.

His first touch came as a grip around my ankle. "Lift your foot," he said.

I looked down between us and did as he said. Kneeling behind me, he held a black lace garment in his hands. "What is that?" I asked.

"Step into it," he instructed, waiting until I did. "Now the other foot."

He stood, sliding a long, floor-length dress up my body. The skirt fell to the floor with a small chapel train, almost like a wedding gown itself. "You're dressing me?" I asked.

"Regretfully."

"But . . .?"

He waited. I couldn't bring myself to finish the sentence. He'd sworn to defile me. Why wasn't he?

"We'll get to that," he said, reading my mind. "I quite like the idea of your thoughts running wild with all the things I'll do to you tonight—mine will be doing the same. By the time I put my hands on you, I'll have violated your sweet body every which way in my fantasies."

Another throb between my legs, harder this time. To cancel out my body's traitorous reaction, I challenged him. "You told me once you have no need to force a woman," I said.

"I don't." He zipped up the dress. "But, when I'm through with you, any shred of innocence, any scrap of the girl you were, will be gone—and that's a pretty thorough violation if you ask me."

"Why would you want that?"

"Because you're no longer someone's sweet, pure, naïve *princesa*. You don't live in the ivory tower anymore. You own it. You're going to learn to rule from it, because that's what it means to be Calavera royalty. And this dress is far more suitable for a queen."

Chills spread over my body with the threat and promise that I was one of them now. A Calavera. Like a crown, black lace turned me from eager bride to the cartel's first lady. The intricate bodice molded to my chest and waist, and the wide neckline stopped at the top of each shoulder, nearly baring them.

From behind, Cristiano skimmed his hands down the fabric clinging to my breasts and settled them at my waist. "The thought of nothing but lace between us all night is enough to drive me mad." Grit hardened his words, and the rawness in his voice vibrated in places that shamed me. "But I don't want any other men lusting after you. Perhaps I should warn them before we arrive that should their gazes linger, I will carve out their eyeballs."

"What men?" My breath came faster with his suggestive touch and graphic threats. "Arrive where?"

"I suspect they already know." Cristiano continued his thought, pressing his hips against my lower back and announcing his need. "After the trouble I've gone through to get you, and the sacrifices I've made, they won't question that what's mine is *mine*."

I was helpless in his grip, his large hands tightening around my waist, his erection strong against my back. Could there exist a certain kind of contentment in giving myself over to the inevitable? In submitting to a man who was so strong and sure of himself and his plans for me?

By the way his command made my heart race, I suspected there was some beauty to be found in resignation.

But I wouldn't give him the satisfaction.

I couldn't afford to remember that there was a time when I'd felt safe with him. Even eleven years earlier, as a scared little girl who'd walked in on Cristiano standing over my mother's dead body, I'd found an odd and unexpected sense of comfort in his arms later, as he'd carried me down into a pitch-black tunnel.

"You say what's yours is yours," I echoed back to him. "But I've heard the rumors about your men. Will you let them touch me? Use me? Tell me now so I know what to expect—do I belong to you or to the Calavera cartel?"

He ran one palm up my chest, his skin warm on mine, and loosely wrapped it around my throat. "Whatever happens, mark my words—you will love it."

No. The idea of serving multiple men made me want to run more than anything had up until now. And the suggestion that I'd enjoy it? Equally obscene and horrifying.

"I'm going to let go of you now. If I don't, I'll take you in God's house, and I may not be able to stop until dawn breaks."

He released me, leaving me breathless and confused. My legs shook as I stooped to gather my pile of things.

"Leave it all," he said. "My men will discard it."

I picked up the precious ivory lace of my abandoned wedding dress, running my bare fingernail over the long rip. "I want to bring it."

"You won't need it where we're going. Max already put your bags in the car."

"It was my mother's," I said quietly.

I looked up at him as I had eleven years earlier when he'd stood over her as she'd bled out. Over me. With blood on his pants and a gun in his hand. I remembered him as the most vicious yet protective man in my world.

His power and strength had only multiplied since then.

Pressing his lips into a line, he crouched and took the fabric from my hands. After gathering it and my bra into his arms, he stood. "Come."

"Where are we going?" I asked.

"Home."

2

NATALIA

Despite gray skies, there was no shortage of people in the plaza on Easter day. The scent of fried plantain filled the air as locals danced and filled their bellies with horchata and empanadas, and kids begged for candies, balloons, and toys from vendors.

It seemed as if the only person missing from the festivities was Diego.

A pair of black Land Rovers with tinted windows idled at the curb in front of the church. Cristiano led me to the second one, handed off my things to the driver, and opened the door to the backseat.

Getting in meant surrendering myself to Cristiano. Once inside, I was as good as lost to the world. My cell phone was in the bag I'd brought to the church and had been taken somewhere. I wasn't naïve enough to think I'd be getting it back any time soon, if at all. I squinted around the square. "Barto's supposed to pick me up any moment. He thinks he's taking me to the airport for my father."

"Then you'd better get in so he and I don't have a confrontation," Cristiano said. "Quit stalling."

I crouched to unbuckle the strap of one shoe. "My feet ache," I explained, furtively scanning the steps of the church and then the crowds for Diego. Laying eyes on him one last time wouldn't change my situation, but it didn't feel right to just leave.

"He's gone if he knows what's good for him," Cristiano said, calling my eyes up as he looked down on me.

Just like that, my entire life had been flipped on its side. Diego was nowhere to be seen, and his brother filled my vision and called me *wife*.

"Forget the shoes," Cristiano said, "and get in the car —and don't mention his name again, or so help me God, I'll—"

"You'll what?" I asked, standing. "Separate me from my loved ones and condemn me to a life I never wanted?"

He narrowed his eyes. What could he say? It was true. My fate was sealed.

I ducked inside before Cristiano could respond. He removed his jacket as he went to the first SUV and spoke to the driver. I fixed my gaze out my window, memorizing the town square. Until I saw Diego again, my last memory would be the defeat in his stance as Cristiano had ordered everyone but me from the church.

My heart sank. Diego had given me away. He'd had no choice—Cristiano had decided he'd wanted to unite our families, and his cartel with my father's, so he'd made it happen. Nothing could've stopped him.

But still. The person I loved, the man I'd been willing to defy my father to marry, had let me walk down the aisle to someone else. And not just anyone. His cruel, notoriously violent brother.

Was Diego sorry? How long had he known about this?

My chin wobbled, but I stilled it in an attempt to pull myself together. Fuck Diego for putting me in this position

—and fuck *me* for still trying to catch once last glimpse of him.

Cristiano tossed his suit jacket onto the seat next to me and slid behind the driver. "Why do you care where my brother is?" he asked, raising a partition between the front and back seats.

I turned from the window to Cristiano. "He was going to be my *husband*."

"Diego gave you up to save his own ass. He's not worth your time." Cristiano studied me as we pulled away from the curb. "You should be thanking me for stepping in."

Thank him? My blood simmered. Between our union and Cristiano's human trafficking business, I doubted there wasn't anything he couldn't justify to himself. "You left him no other choice."

"There's always a choice." Cristiano tugged at his shirt-sleeve, then held out his arm. "Do you mind?"

I looked at his hand. "What?"

"My cufflinks."

We slowly made our way through the square decorated with papier-mâché figures, multi-colored flags, and flower bunches. Men in sombreros and women costumed in tradi-tional ancient dresses with woven baskets on their heads moved aside, peering through the tinted windows, some of them tossing out angry words at our intrusion. We weren't supposed to be driving through here.

"You can remove them yourself," I said.

"But I'm asking you to."

Was an ask ever truly that with Cristiano? I heard the demand in his words. Hesitantly, I pulled his wrist to me and slipped the sterling silver bar of a grooved cufflink through its hole. "What would you have done in Diego's shoes? Or mine, for that matter?" I asked. "Although, I suppose you'd have to know love to truly understand the lengths you'd go to for it."

"I should warn you, each time you say my brother's name, a vision comes to mind. One I don't like. So unless you wish to provoke me, you won't speak his name again."

His cuff hung loose. He nodded at it, so I rolled it up, my fingers grazing a vein of his thick, dark-haired forearm. "What vision?" I hedged.

Once I'd secured his sleeve at his elbow, he shifted to give me his other hand. "If I vocalize it, it's likely to anger me. Not wise when you're trapped back here with me."

Diego's name could've called up a memory for Cristiano that haunted me as well. Eleven years earlier, Diego had accused his brother of murdering my mother knowing it would cost Cristiano his life. Diego had chosen justice over family, and in the cartel, betraying family was the ultimate sin. I could still see Diego clear as day, aiming his gun at Cristiano and me, and I wasn't even the one he'd wanted to shoot.

I removed the other cufflink, clutching both silver pieces in my palm. "I don't think I've ever seen a more composed man than you were in that church," I said to see if I could gain some insight into what made him tick. "Now you're angry. What changed?"

It was his turn to look out the window. Cristiano didn't have to acknowledge any of my questions, and that made answers precious. No matter the topic, anything could be considered a clue to the man behind the calavera mask. Who was Cristiano? What did a man as cold and callous as him fear? Desire? Love?

And why did I care?

Information. Once the only vice of a girl whose family told her nothing under the guise of protection, and later a burden when I'd wanted to forget everything to do with this life, could now be the thing that saved me. It would be easier to survive my enemy if I knew what he wanted. What he expected. What drove him.

Not just survive him, but maybe even escape him.

I was metaphorically chained to Cristiano by the power he held over the lives of the people I loved. I couldn't run. But that didn't mean there weren't ways to free myself of him.

I grazed a fingertip over the smooth skin of Cristiano's wrist, lightly enough to make it seem like an accident. "What made you angry?" I pressed.

He continued to stare out the window for a beat, then turned to me. "Jealousy is new to me, but I no longer allow emotions to overtake me, so I was able to conceal it in the church."

Jealousy? I schooled my expression to hide my surprise, both at his answer, and that he'd answered at all. Perhaps his response shouldn't have caught me off guard me, though. Cristiano had expected me pure. Was he upset that he'd gotten his brother's hand-me-down? Or was it simply the primitive urge of a husband who'd wanted to have his wife first?

He'd threatened to remove Diego's hands just for touching me—but what had Cristiano thought would happen? He'd walked into the middle of my relationship with Diego. He'd disrupted our wedding.

He'd *won.*

When he reached for my ankle, I sprang back.

"Is the ache from the shoes?" he asked, pulling my foot into his lap. "Or the cuts?"

My heart pounded as the hair on my arms rose. I could never forget that Cristiano could—and would—touch me at any moment. I shifted my back against the door so I was facing him. "The cuts have nearly healed."

"You had a good doctor." The corner of his mouth lifted as his big fingers struggled with the stiletto's delicate buckle. Days earlier, my fear of Cristiano had been overridden by how gently he'd tweezed glass from my feet. Instead of taking advantage of a situation, he'd helped me.

We cleared the town and accelerated down a two-lane highway, surrounded by desert on both sides as we barreled toward the storm clouds gathered ahead. I crossed my arms. "You're a doctor, captor, and husband all rolled into one," I said. "Lucky me."

"Say that again." He tossed my shoe aside and met my eyes. "I like the way that word sounds on your tongue."

"Captor," I said. "I'm your captive, and I have no doubt it brings you pleasure to hear that."

"Not that one. *Husband.*" He moved my foot a few inches over until my arch aligned with a bulge at his zipper. "You are my wife, and it brings me perverse pleasure to both say it *and* hear it."

My throat dried as he lengthened and grew against my foot. He was aroused, and I was at his mercy.

Rain pattered the roof as the sky darkened. "How long until we reach the Badlands?"

Cristiano wet his lips. "Another half hour or so."

I weighed my options. I had no idea what awaited me inside the gates. At least twice, he'd warned of taking me later. Better it lasted thirty minutes than through the night. If luck was on my side, maybe once would be enough for him to tire of me and move on.

"Just enough time to consummate our union," I said.

He stilled, blinking at me. "I'm sorry?"

I pushed through the instinct to shut my mouth. I could endure him for thirty minutes. And even if I couldn't, I'd have to find a way. "You said the marriage wasn't valid until we consummated it."

"Correct."

"Then the people I love aren't safe until the ink is dry."

He cocked his head, squeezing my foot as he ran a firm thumb along my sole the way he had after he'd removed all the glass from it. A sharp, delicious twinge pulled inside me, and I shuddered to hide that his touch tickled. "You're so eager that you want me to take you here the first time?" he asked, sounding genuinely curious.

"I want it done," I said.

"You cowered from me in the church."

"To be violated as Our Lady of Guadalupe looks on is heinous." I should've been more afraid of what I was asking. I was tempting the beast to defile me. But I tried to appeal to logic. The devil I knew was here, now, and the clock was ticking. "To be had in the backseat of a car,"—I swallowed—"feels truer than anything yet."

"Not in the least," he said immediately, curving a hand against the smooth black leather seat. "This isn't suitable for my bride."

"I'm not your bride—I'm your prisoner. You want to be my husband? It's too late for that. You will take me as your captive, not your wife."

He set his jaw and reached for my other leg. Instinctively, I pulled away at the thought of him taking hold of both my ankles, but the backseat didn't give me much room. He captured my foot and set to work freeing it from its satin confines. "You're speaking from anger," he said. "I understand. You feel betrayed—as you should. He traded you, but take comfort in the fact that *I* never will."

"Where's the comfort in that?"

"You'll learn to find it."

Though I faced him now with both feet in his lap, I turned my head away. "For my sanity, I hope I do."

My jaw tingled. *Trapped.* At least he acknowledged it.

But how literal would my captivity be? Momentarily, I'd forgotten to fear not just Cristiano but the place he called home. The Badlands had been described as dangerous, cultish, lawless—a wasteland for women and children. To add insult to injury, it was set against—but walled off from —the Pacific Ocean that sprawled from Mexico's west coast. And I would be in the center of it all.

"What are you thinking about that makes your toes curl?" he asked.

I flexed my feet, forcing myself to relax. I had to remember Cristiano was nothing if not observant. Even as a girl, I'd been the subject of his attention, which unfortunately meant he might know me better than I was comfortable with.

Having liberated my feet, he inspected the soles.

"Have you taken more bullets than drugs in your lifetime?" I asked.

He raised just his eyes. And a single brow. "Pardon?"

"That's the rumor about Calavera's leader."

"I have never taken drugs," he said.

"And bullets?"

"What do you think?"

"I think . . . yes. You have."

He squeezed my heel. "Good guess."

He seemed simultaneously amused and grave. I ran my tongue along the edge of my teeth. "Do you have a foot fetish?" I asked, just to see what he'd say.

"So many questions." He seemed to consciously flex his grip, as if he'd forgotten he was holding onto me. "Why do you ask?"

"First you cleaned my feet in my bathroom the morning of the warehouse attack, and now you're fondling them."

"I cleaned *you* in the bathroom," he said. "Now I'm

touching *you*. Maybe I have a Natalia fetish." He sat back in his seat but kept my feet where they were. "So, *la narco-princesa* is curious about my habits and fetishes. She must be wondering what awaits her in the Badlands."

How did a broken society function? If they were as devout to Cristiano as reported, what would they make of me? I didn't know much about his business, either, except he moved weapons and women. Virgins, everyone in this world knew, were valuable. If he hadn't married me, I'd be agonizing over the possibility of being sold. Maybe I *did* need to be worried about that.

I shivered and caught him staring at me. In an afternoon, Cristiano had already gotten what he'd wanted from me—the power two families and cartels afforded him. But at the end of a kingpin's long day of destruction, he was still a man, and he looked at me with a man's eyes. His gaze wouldn't release me, nor his large hands.

He would have me tonight.

It was all there in the way his eyes devoured me. I had to face the truth. I'd given myself to Diego on the promise that he'd be the only man to ever have me. Now, I was facing a lifetime of servitude to his ruthless brother.

I could not cower or run. Cristiano would get what he wanted. And one day, he'd tire of me.

A man like him was not made for one woman.

Having a wife would be more of an inconvenience to him than anything. I hoped, out of respect for our history, he'd keep me somewhere tolerable. That I'd be housed and fed decently as my father had done for him. That I'd be called to his bed when needed, and otherwise left alone. But I didn't dare expect anything.

Not after the things I'd heard.

What was it Diego and Tepic had told me? Rumors about Calavera's mistreatment of whores, and satanic practices that involved eating snails, sacrificing virgins, and chanting in tongues. Nobody could confirm nor deny what went down on the devil's playground, because apparently, no trespasser had ever lived to tell the tale.

Diego had promised to come for me. My father would try, too. But I couldn't depend on them against the all-powerful Cristiano. If I wanted out, I'd have to find a way from within—and until then, I just needed to hold on.

In the literal sense, too, it seemed. I latched onto the door as the SUV jostled when we pulled off the main high-way. Lush, green mountains rose from the barren desert, vibrant against the clouds. I knew the Pacific spread behind the mountain range. It was a trifecta of natural beauty, and it didn't surprise me he'd taken this particular town so he could erect his man-made hell.

He liked beautiful things, so he made them his.

"Do you get carsick?" he asked.

"Not usually."

"Good. It gets rough here. The roads leading up to the gates aren't paved."

"We're here already?" I asked.

"The distance from your father's house isn't great. It's the terrain that slows people down."

I gripped the side panel as we made our way down a rocky dirt road. "Why don't you fix the roads?"

"That would make it too easy to get in."

Or out.

My stomach dropped. Up ahead, stone walls rose from the desert like a fortress, sectioning off hectares of land that abutted the mountainside.

The Badlands. The designation made sense now. It was hard to get to, and anyone who made it in wouldn't be able to make a hasty escape.

A smirk ghosted over his features. "By the look on

your face, you've heard the rumors. I ruined this town—defiled, disgraced, and ran out its people. That I rule it with an iron fist." He slid his hand under the hem of my long dress, up my calf. "Maybe you can open that fist, Natalia. Turn it from iron to liquid mercury and sculpt it to your liking. As your mother once did with your father."

I ground my teeth together. "If I'm forbidden from mentioning Diego, then you should be forbidden from speaking about my mother."

I tried to pull my leg back, but he seized it. After a brief hesitation, he let go. "I knew Bianca well," he said. "She had influence—and a spine of steel to stand by Costa's side. You're not there yet, but you have it in you."

"She'd be horrified by what you've become. Of how you treat women. And by whatever you have planned for me."

Color crept up his neck until he looked away. I slid my legs from his lap and bent my knees to my chest, hugging them as we bounced toward iron gates several times taller than the men guarding them.

Silence settled between us as tires crunched dirt and rocks hit the bottom of the car. That was as much as he was willing to acknowledge my mother, it seemed. Or the brutal conditions that lay ahead. I'd find out soon enough what was true and what wasn't, but where there was smoke, there was fire. I could see the walls and gates for myself. They hid secrets, and people, and in this world, that could mean nothing good.

He was confused if he thought I'd ever develop a tolerance to treating humans like commodities. If he thought my mother would *want* that for me.

We stopped in front of a gate. The walls were thick enough that their stone housed checkpoints, as if we were crossing a border. Men with guns and clipboards stepped out as the gates opened inward.

Blocking my view was a grumbling semi. I craned my neck as we passed it. Men hopped out of the back and pulled down the door, and I glimpsed people in the trailer.

Who were they? Were they arriving or being taken somewhere? I *needed* to ask. But what would I do with the answer? I was as stuck as they were. I squeezed my legs more tightly to my chest and inhaled a breath to calm my racing heart as we entered *"las puertas del infierno,"* as Tepic had called them.

The gates of hell.

To mentally prepare myself, I closed my eyes and envisioned the worst—a scorched-earth ghost town, patrols with AR-15s nudging beggars and prostitutes along, heavy chains weighing down exits and people. Brothels and abandoned storefronts, warehouses of guns and drug labs, failed absconders hanging like examples from trees.

Medieval but effective.

When my curiosity became too much, I opened my eyes and looked out the windshield.

Envisioning the worst had proved futile.

Nothing could've prepared me for *this*.

3

NATALIA

It could've been Main Street in any affluent town. Clean and maintained buildings spread before us, tucked under the verdant, towering mountainside that would've shadowed the Badlands had the sun been out. This wasn't a ghost town—whatever the Calavera cartel had done to the people who'd lived here, the structures and homes had not only remained intact, but seemed to have been improved. Their red brick facades were bright, stucco white walls clean, and not a crack could be seen in the pavement or concrete.

It was in even better shape than where I came from.

No longer bumping and jostling, we started a slow tread as the road into the Badlands smoothed from potholes and rocks to paved roads and cobblestone. We drove down the wide, main road bordered by shops that went directly from the gates to the foot of the mountain.

I took my chin off my knees and released my legs to scoot closer to the window. Though the walls were high, the town was big enough that I couldn't see where it began or ended. Just beyond was the ocean, taunting the prisoners with salty air and the promise of an endless horizon they couldn't see. I wondered if anyone ever tried to escape that way, and how far they got.

Two young girls in t-shirts and shorts stood under a deli awning, watching us pass. They had plastic bags of groceries in their hands and umbrellas tucked under their arms. *Their freedom was stripped, but at least they're dry*, I thought wryly. Men on horses steered to one side, nodding at us. A group of women traveled as a pack and carried baskets of fruit on their shoulders; one smacked another on the shoulder as we drove by.

The rain started and stopped, and hardly a passerby didn't stop to stare as we drew closer and closer to green foothills dense with trees. I didn't know what to make of what I saw. Disoriented and slightly dizzy, I sat back in my seat.

"More than meets the eye?" Cristiano lowered the partition. Clouds darkened the sky, but the driver switched off his wipers as the rain became a drizzle. "You can see the house ahead," Cristiano said.

I didn't try to hide my curiosity. I ducked to peer through the windshield and spotted it instantly—a multi-story house built into the mountainside with white walls, a red terracotta roof, and crisp lines that offset curved archways.

"I can keep an eye on things from up there," he said.

I didn't doubt Cristiano had eyes everywhere.

It turned out the main road didn't go straight through to the base of the mountain. We made our way around the perimeter of a large plaza, not unlike the one we'd just come from, also anchored by a church. I wasn't fooled. Diego and Tepic had suggested the Badlands used storefronts and mundane businesses for money laundering. The church could've been a decoy for something else or just a cruel joke for false hope in a godless land.

People had set up stands in the same manner they had back home, though most were packing up their goods, and some stalls had been abandoned in the rain. A pair of children ran barefoot from booth to booth, jumping up and down with their hands cupped, tugging on the dresses of women who were boxing up everything from painted, wooden knick-knacks to talavera tiles to vibrant clothing.

"Begging for chocolate," Cristiano said.

"So sad," I murmured.

"Sad?" he asked. "They just want Easter candy."

Oddly, women wore colorful dresses and had decorated their stands with flowers, red, white, and green crepe streamers, and matching flags. With trash bins full of paper plates and plastic Solo Cups, it almost looked as if we were arriving at the end of an event.

"Pull over," Cristiano said, and the driver parked at a curb close to the square. Cristiano opened his door and strode toward a woman who was removing dresses from hangers and folding them into a crate.

When she noticed him coming, she stepped back, waving him away. He held something out to her, grabbed her hand and pressed it into her palm, then squatted before a yellow blanket displaying leather *huarache* sandals.

I had no idea what he was doing, but the woman clearly objected to it.

Cristiano headed back, his dress shirt dotted with raindrops. He slid in next to me and passed over a pair of brown leather sandals. "These will be more comfortable," he said.

I took them because I didn't know what else to do. Turning them over in my hands, I admired the detailed craftsmanship and high-quality leather. He stared ahead as we continued on and didn't look as if he expected a "thank you."

"These are well-made," I said. "They look expensive."

"Maricela is highly skilled. I've told her to charge more, but she refuses, so I gave her double."

"You paid her?"

"Of course." He glanced over as I ran a fingertip along the thin soles. "They remind me of the ones you were wearing . . . the ones you had as a girl."

Ah. Yes. I pinched the smooth leather strap. These were an understated, adult version of the woven *huaraches* I'd worn until the leather had been darkened by dirt and sun, and the frayed straps had started to come loose. "My mom hated them. She said—" I stopped myself. I'd been wearing those sandals the day I'd found Cristiano in her bedroom as she'd lain dying on the floor.

"What did she say?" he asked.

"Nothing." Cristiano didn't deserve to share in my past, however trivial. I bent over to pull on sandals like the ones I'd worn so ragged, my mom had teased that they were only a step up from bare feet. "It was nothing."

The car wound up the mountainside and turned onto the circular driveway of Cristiano's house. Upon closer inspection, the white, Spanish Colonial-style home had wrought-iron window grilles, and a stone walkway that led to a massive, arched, dark wood door. "You don't have a gate?" I asked as we parked. Anyone from town could hike up to his front door.

"Wait here," he said, taking his jacket from the seat and exiting the car.

I turned away from the house to peer beyond the cliff it sat on. Clay rooftops, stone buildings, greenery, and desert comprised the town. Businesses and activity gathered in the middle, around the main street we'd driven

down, and from there spiraled off pockets of neigh-
borhoods.

A slim woman with delicate, elfin features and long,
reddish-brown hair descended the front steps to meet Cristiano. He handed her his jacket, touched her shoulder, and
gestured to the car. She twirled her considerable hair into a
bun on top of her head as she nodded before walking to
the trunk.

Cristiano opened the door to the backseat and offered
a hand to help me out. "This is Jazmín," he said as I
unfolded from the Land Rover. "She'll see that your things
are handled."

The woman and I met eyes. She was indisputably
pretty and close to my age. How had she gotten here? I
studied her for any signs of mistreatment. In clean, pressed
black pants and a white button-down, and with no outward
signs of trauma, she almost seemed normal.

Jazmín bent her head toward me. "*Bienvenida, señora.*"

"I can get my own bags," I told Cristiano. "She doesn't
need to do that."

"Jaz has been preparing for you the last couple days,"
he said.

I tucked some of my hair behind my ear and straightened my dress. Even with the low-heeled sandals, the hem
just barely grazed the ground. "Why am I wearing this?" I
asked.

Cristiano glanced from me to Jazmín. "I apologize.
Natalia seems to have forgotten her manners."

My cheeks warmed. I hadn't responded when she'd
welcomed me, and she wasn't the enemy. "*Mucho gusto,*" I
said to her as she removed my bag from the trunk and
slung my mother's dress over her elbow.

Cristiano led me up the steps to the sturdy wood-and-
iron door. The tiled entryway had high ceilings with dark

beams and round-top windows that would've lit the space if the sun had been out. Instead, a chandelier made of wrought iron glowed above us and matched the railing of a staircase with blue and orange painted risers.

Jaz entered behind us. "We had to move everyone into the dining hall because of the rain." She gave him a small smile. "It's a little cramped, but they don't notice."

"Drunk?" he asked.

"Very. And extremely curious."

"I have no doubt," Cristiano said. "I'll give Natalia a quick tour on our way to the party."

I couldn't hide my surprise. "*Party?*" My life was falling apart, and Cristiano wanted to celebrate? "You can't be serious."

"Do you have any laundry?" Jaz asked me, readjusting the strap of my bag on her shoulder.

"I—what? I can unpack myself," I said, stepping toward her. "I'll just go to my room if you'll show me—"

Cristiano took my elbow and drew me back to him. "Jaz has it under control. I want you by my side right now. They've put a lot of time and effort into tonight. You'll make the rounds with me."

My lips thinned into a line. "You can't force me to enjoy a party."

He turned to block Jaz from my view and put his mouth to my ear. "Enjoy it or don't," he said quietly. "But you'll do as I say, and you won't question me in front of anyone again. Jaz asked you something. Answer her."

He straightened up again, and I was faced with Jaz's unreadable expression. The last thing I wanted was to be rude to someone who might be in an even worse situation than I was, but being thrust into a party an hour after my life had been ruined seemed cruel.

"My things are clean," I said to Jaz. I'd done all my

laundry at home before I'd packed. "Except . . ." I glanced at the ruined wedding dress hanging over her shoulder. Even if the delicate lace could be repaired, was there any point?

"Except?" she asked.

"Never mind. It's all clean." I cleared my throat. "Thank you."

"*De nada.*" Jaz started up a staircase, gripping the iron railing as she climbed the stairs over the front door. She cast me a narrow-eyed glance before disappearing through a rounded doorway.

"It will make my staff happy to know you're happy to be here," Cristiano said. "And when my staff is happy, so am I."

"But *I'm* not."

His posture eased with an exhale. He tipped up my chin until our mouths were aligned and he could bend and kiss me if he wanted. "Then fake it for their benefit."

I dropped my eyes to his lips when he wet them, then quickly turned my face away. "Why should I?"

"I already told you why. It makes *me* happy. And you want that." He guided my head forward and waited until our eyes met again. "But if that's not a good enough reason, then do it because I command it."

I had a feeling I'd get used to hearing that response. But if I had to endure his will, then he was also stuck with me. I didn't have to play nice when we were alone. "Fine," I agreed. "It'll be good practice anyway."

"For?"

"Faking what I don't enjoy."

He pursed his lips into what could've been a smirk. Before he could decide if he was amused or annoyed, footsteps sounded behind me, and Cristiano dropped his hand and stepped back.

The two guards that had stood by Cristiano's side in the church entered, and we proceeded down a hallway, past a long, wooden bench with muted cushions, to an airy living space that opened to a dining room—but as there were no people in it, it must not have been the one Jaz had just referred to. Though lines and curves anchored the tidied, Old World Spanish-style room, it was warmed by clay pottery over a stone fireplace, a gold-and-maroon tapestry covering one wall of the dining area, and trees in ceramic pots. Flimsy, sheer white curtains were drawn half-way, and windowed doors showcased a covered concrete patio with dining tables and couches, and a sizeable pool that rippled with occasional drops of rain.

The kitchen appeared more lived in—and less suited to Cristiano—with deep-orange walls, cornflower-blue shutters, and a green tea-colored wood table. A stout woman reached for a tray of hors d'oeuvres on the counter, and it was impossible not to notice the burn scars up and down her arms. She spared me a quick glance before she side-stepped a man in a chef's hat.

Cristiano gestured around the room rattling off names that went in one ear and out the other. My mind was at capacity for the day. "*Fisker* is the main chef," he added.

A blond, skin-and-bones man standing over a large pot nodded at me. "Fish stew?" he asked.

I looked to Cristiano, who asked, "Are you hungry?"

"N-no," I told Fisker. He didn't look healthy. Nobody in here did. Where had they come from? "But thank you."

Cristiano turned to exit but bent to whisper, "Don't let his gaunt appearance fool you. He was a fisherman in Denmark and knows food as well as any world-renowned chef I've met."

Cristiano nodded for me to follow, and we were moving again. Down another hall, past closed doors and small windows. I thought I detected the din of voices and music, but it wasn't until Cristiano opened one of the doors that a cacophony of singing, hollering, and mariachi overwhelmed me.

"Soundproof rooms," Cristiano explained the disparity in volume. "One of the best investments I've made in the house. The party can rage on while I—we—sleep. Or *we* can rage on while they dine."

His tone was teasing, but I doubted he'd meant it as a joke. He dipped his hand to my lower back and guided me down a small, dark passageway. We stepped through the doorway to the top of a staircase, as if entering a basement, and stopped at a half wall overlooking a subterranean dining hall. Distressed wood beams formed an X on the high ceiling, and candlelight sconces made shadows on white walls. Three long, sturdy picnic tables centered the room, where people ate from a restaurant-style buffet.

At one end of a community-style table, a group of women sat interspersed between children with plates of frosted cake. Their long skirts and dresses resembled what the women of my town had worn to church that morning. They sneaked bites of dessert from the children and laughed across the table from each other.

Cristiano urged me forward by my lower back, and though my hands were only figuratively tied, it still felt like walking the plank. "This is your home now," he said, removing his hand. "These are your people."

How did they get into this situation?

"They're just celebrating Easter."

I glanced back at him, not realizing I'd spoken aloud. "Easter?" I asked. "*Here?*"

"It's not as if we've left the country. We still have holidays here."

But anything beyond basic survival would be a luxury

for people being held and worked against their will. And they were, weren't they? The alternative was that they lived in the Badlands willingly. As one of Cristiano's victims, I just didn't see how that could be.

"Do you think people in distress eat cake?" he asked as if reading my mind.

Maybe, if it was the best they could make of a bad situation.

My heart fell. I should've been with my father, sitting down for an Easter feast now, or on a plane back to my friends and my life in California. Instead, I was surrounded by the lost and forgotten.

My gaze caught on an older man who glanced up and made eye contact. He lowered his beer mug to the table with a frown, and people fell silent in sections as they noticed us. The music stopped. Wide eyes stared. The number of women and children both surprised and saddened me. Mothers drew their children to their sides. Men stood straighter. They feared Cristiano, but their eyes were trained on me. Did they fear me too? Or was their fear *for* me?

"I can't be a part of this," I whispered.

"But you are."

"Why?" The intensity of their glares made me want to move behind Cristiano, which was ridiculous. *He* was who I wanted to hide *from*. "Why parade me around like this?" I asked under my breath. "You don't need me."

"You will learn all the things I need, and soon, I hope. But as of today, you don't know enough to say what I need." He kept his distance but spoke only for me. "Tonight, you'll meet your people, and they'll see they have nothing to fear."

"Fear?" I asked. "*Me?*"

A portly man raised a frothy ale and shouted, "Are the rumors true, *patrón?*"

Despite looking as if he'd just come from the fields, the man must've been one of Cristiano's inner circle to address him with such an informal term of respect.

"*Sí,*" Cristiano said, moving away from me. "I've formed an alliance that will benefit both parties."

An excited murmur moved through the crowd. The man banged the bottom of his mug on the table so loudly, I stepped back and hit Cristiano's body. He grabbed my shoulders and released them as if the lace had burned him.

Other men slammed their mugs and beer foamed over, dripping onto the tables as they offered celebratory shouts. "*¡Epa!*"

"It should be a prosperous year—" Cristiano started.

"Who cares about business," another said. "Who's the girl?"

Cristiano chuckled as if sharing an inside joke. "In order to make the deal, I've taken a wife."

I glanced over my shoulder at him, but he kept his distant eyes on the crowd as if I weren't there at all.

Though a few men and women smiled, and the children were mostly awed, some of the enthusiasm left the room.

"My bride will stay here with us out of convenience," he said, adding under his breath, "unwilling though she may be."

Cristiano started down the stairs, leaving me standing there alone. Up until then, he hadn't been so dismissive. He hadn't been dismissive *at all*. Not once since he'd turned up at my father's costume party. Even as I'd been forced down the aisle to him, he'd watched me with curious, hungry eyes. In the car, he'd shown interest and a modicum of warmth as he'd asked after the state of my feet.

And he'd claimed to be jealous. So he wasn't completely indifferent to me. Was he? Earlier, he'd claimed he'd wanted me by his side. Now, he didn't even seem to care if I descended into the party with him.

I hadn't realized the warmth of his attention until he took it away—especially in a room full of strangers.

Perhaps now that I was caught, I was little more to him than a product of the merger. And that was what I'd wanted, wasn't it? To be nothing to him? To be left alone?

The security guards were suddenly at my back, and my only paths were back through them or down the stairs. They looked even unfriendlier than him.

I followed Cristiano.

As I hit the basement level, a young boy ran up to Cristiano without any hesitation. I braced myself, though for what, I wasn't sure. Perhaps anger from Cristiano at being approached that way.

"*Mira*," he said, opening his mouth and pointing at his missing front teeth.

Cristiano stopped. "What am I looking at, Felix?"

The boy grinned wider. "I lost the second one."

"That's too bad," Cristiano answered. "You won't be able to eat any cake."

"Yes, I will," he declared. "I already had a piece."

A woman—Felix's mother, I assumed—took his hand to pull her son away. "*Perdón, señor*," she said to Cristiano as she eyed me. "He's just excited for the *el Ratoncito Pérez* to leave a gift under his pillow."

"Who wouldn't be? There will be one there tonight, Teresa," Cristiano said and looked to a member of his security team.

The guard nodded in acknowledgement, then limped away to speak into his two-way radio.

"*Gracias, señor*," Teresa said and thanked him again before turning her eyes on me. "She's beautiful."

"You need anything else from me for the project we discussed?" Cristiano asked.

"No." Teresa shook her head. "But it helps to see her for myself."

In any other situation, I would've demanded they not speak about me as if I weren't standing there. But I couldn't be sure who was friend or foe—or who worked for Cristiano and who was in my position.

Teresa guided her son away, and I found a sea of unreadable faces looking back at me.

"Eat, drink," Cristiano bellowed to them, gesturing at their tables. "Don't let us interrupt the fun."

The music resumed, and people turned back to their food, beverages, and conversation. It felt wrong to drink and sing. People almost seemed . . . *comfortable*. I could see that they were well-fed, and they acted as if they were safe. In some way or another, the people here must've been employees of the cartel and their families. Which made this the office Easter party.

Cristiano nodded at the buffet. "You should be able to find something to your liking."

"I'm not hungry." I crossed my arms over my stomach and hoped it wouldn't growl. To me, it just wasn't the time for tamales and cake. "What was that with the boy's mom? Some kind of code?"

"Code for what?" he asked.

"You expect me to believe that exchange was really about what the Tooth Rat would put under a kid's pillow? Did you just order someone decapitated or something?"

The corner of his mouth twitched as he led me to the

spread of food. "No, *mi amor*. Just handled. I'll do the same to you if you don't eat something."

My stomach was in knots. "Food is the last thing on my mind."

"What *is* on your mind?" he asked.

"I'm tired," I lied. "I don't see the purpose of being paraded around for people who don't seem to want me here. Is there somewhere I could lie down?"

"*Sí*," he answered. "My bed." Amusement flashed across his features. He was testing my limits. Trying to scare me.

"Fine," I said. "I'll eat."

"Good to know that threatening my bed works on you." He handed me a paper plate printed with party balloons. "While Felix and his mother are here, Eduardo will put a hundred pesos under the boy's pillow. I've also hired her for something personal, but it's nothing deceitful. Not as exciting as a beheading, just a small favor."

I eyed Cristiano for signs of sarcasm but was only met with a casual shrug.

A young man walked over, his arm extended in greeting. "*Felicitaciones*," he congratulated Cristiano, shaking his hand before turning to me. "*Y usted también, señora*. You make a lovely bride."

I couldn't tell if the man was mocking me by extending his congratulations to me as well—Cristiano had made it clear to all that this was nothing more than an arranged marriage.

"Doesn't she?" Cristiano remarked as if I were a prized pig, and barely glanced at me as he said, "Go make yourself a plate."

I understood his order for what it was—they needed privacy. Diego and my father had dismissed me the same way many times. In a way, Cristiano's true colors were a relief. This was the ice I'd expected to find in my new husband. It was a wonder he didn't melt in hell.

As I turned, Cristiano touched my arm, leaning in so only I could hear. "But stay close. I should be able to reach out and touch you whenever I please."

He returned forward, leaving me with his clean scent, promised heat, and a chill that raced down my spine.

Dusk encroached, and true darkness would fall soon. And when it did, Cristiano would touch me *whenever he pleased*.

4

NATALIA

S tanding over a hand-painted sink, with cobalt blue and white shiny tiles at my back, I stared at myself in a bathroom mirror, my wide, nervous eyes and pale face bathed with warm, honeyed light. Over an hour into the Easter party, and it was the first moment I'd had alone. Cristiano carried on conversations and shook hands as if I didn't exist, yet if I ever left his side, he'd reprimand me with a look or a clipped command under his breath to return.

I touched the dark circles under my eyes, and my new wedding ring caught the light. I inspected the small, meaningless diamond Cristiano had probably found in a pawn shop. Or, more likely, one of his men had been ordered to pick it up.

"In order to make the deal, I've taken a wife."

Literally.

How far back had Cristiano planned this? For Diego and me, the union had been sudden, but had Cristiano known my fate since the night of the costume party? If so, then he'd played with us—and I feared the game wasn't over.

Cristiano had admitted as much at his nightclub. This was all a game, and I had to play, or I'd lose.

But how did someone like me, with nothing except the clothes on my back, beat a man who had every resource available to him?

I had only one thing to offer—one bargaining chip.

I hadn't forgotten Cristiano's threat to Diego earlier.

"Envision me taking her with the same fervor on this, our wedding night."

I pressed my hand to my stomach as my insides wrenched. How long until Cristiano ended the party and took what he felt he was owed? I needed to prepare for tonight, mentally and physically. For me, sex was no longer about love. It was an exchange, and perhaps a tool I could use to make my time here bearable.

With a knock on the bathroom door, I opened it and met Alejandro, the guard who'd shown me to the bathroom and who'd also stood for Cristiano at our wedding. "*Don* Cristiano is asking for you," he said.

"Can't I use the restroom in peace?"

"It's been twenty minutes."

"Don't have the shrimp," I snapped at him.

I thought I detected a smile in his eyes, but he remained passive. "Noted."

He led me back through the house. In the kitchen, people continued to buzz, coming in and out with trays, though it seemed to me everyone had eaten plenty. Jaz stood at the sink washing dishes with her head down. Her bun sagged, and pieces of her red hair had come loose around her face. I'd thought she was young and pretty before, but as I studied her profile, I realized she was beautiful.

I stopped where I was, and without consulting Alejandro, I seized an opportunity to gather more information while Cristiano wasn't around.

I walked over to her. "Do you need any help?"

She looked at me with brown, startled eyes. "No. This is my job."

I rolled my lips together, glancing at Alejandro. "How long have you worked here?" I asked.

"Years."

My mouth fell open. She looked my age. "Is it . . . did you live here before? Are you being paid?"

"¿*Qué?*" Her gaze shifted over my shoulder to Alejandro. "I don't know what you're talking about."

"Where are you from?" I asked, touching her forearm.

She flinched back. "I'm from *here*. This is my home."

"Is there a problem, Natalia?" Alejandro asked behind me.

Everyone in the kitchen went quiet. The chef leaned against a counter and slurped stew from a bowl like a server on his dinner break. The scarred, elderly woman glanced at Jaz and me, and then quickly away.

I faced Alejandro. "I was asking for . . . aspirin."

Jaz turned off the faucet, yanked off her rubber gloves, and slapped them against the counter with a *thwack*. "I'll bring you some, *doña* Natalia," she said with obvious sarcasm and a glare before walking away.

"Come on," Alejandro said. "Jaz will find us."

I'd clearly upset her, and I hoped I hadn't gotten her into trouble. "How old is she?" I asked.

"Not sure. Early twenties?"

"But she's worked here years?" I asked. "Doing what?"

He frowned at me. "What do you mean? She's part of the household staff. Cooks, cleans—that kind of thing."

"But is there more that's . . . required of her?"

"Well, it's a big house," he said, his eyebrows drawn. "She helps keep the rooms in order, manages the land-scapers—"

"Never mind," I said with a sigh. I just didn't under-stand how such a young girl had come to work here, and whether she was in any kind of trouble. She didn't seem to be. So what was the truth about the Badlands?

Alejandro veered us away from the party and toward the living space we'd walked through earlier.

"Where are we going?" I asked.

He gestured in front of us. Some of the main room's French doors had been opened, and the scent of rain and wet soil drifted in from the patio I'd seen earlier, the pool just beyond. Cristiano sat at a round table with a group of men, his back to Alejandro and me, an ankle over one knee and a cigar in his hand. Alejandro continued outside and went to take the last open patio chair, leaving me in the doorway.

Cristiano drummed his fingers on the arm of his chair looking anything but bored. He almost seemed relaxed as he acknowledged Alejandro but didn't notice me behind him.

"It's all right," he said after a few moments of silence. "Continue."

"As I was saying, Cortez is demanding more from us than the buyer paid," the glass-eyed man said after a sip of his drink. *Max*. He'd brought me from the church garden to the wedding earlier that day.

"The shipment is invaluable, but he doesn't need to know that," Cristiano said. "Pay him a fair sum, nothing more."

Max nodded through a cloud of white smoke. "If he doesn't like it, he'll like the alternative even less."

I stepped lightly onto the patio so as not to draw attention. Though both Alejandro and Max knew I was there, it still felt like I was doing something wrong. But picking up even a few words of Cristiano's conversation could help me puzzle together what exactly was happening inside the Badlands' walls.

Cristiano placed both feet on the ground, leaned his elbows on his knees, and pointed his cigar at Max. "But make *sure* he understands that our payment is a courtesy I won't extend twice."

I held my breath, certain Cristiano would turn around and tell me to leave any moment.

"Next time we catch him transporting for BR," Cristiano said, "I'll *take* the shipment. Nobody gets paid shit. And I can't guarantee he'll walk out alive."

"Agreed," Max said.

Cristiano sat back in his seat. "Gentlemen, there's one thing you should know about my new wife: you should be even more alert than usual. She has been taught since childhood that eavesdropping is the only way to get information."

A few of the men chuckled as my cheeks warmed. He hadn't even looked in my direction—how had he known I was standing there?

"So you'll handle that then, Max?" Cristiano asked.

"*Sí, jefe.*"

Waiting to be dismissed, I folded my hands, and my knuckle caught on the diamond on my finger. It would take getting used to. It seemed blasphemous to wear it, a mockery of the marriage I could've had.

"What else?" Cristiano asked. "As much as I like you all, there's only one person I want to spend my wedding night with."

"There's the matter with Sandra," Alejandro said.

"Right. You think she's ready?" Cristiano puffed his

cigar, but he still didn't send me away. He knew better than to assume I'd leave my own, which meant he was allowing me to listen in.

Sweet, woodsy cigar smoke wafted toward me. Only Alejandro refrained from partaking. "She won't look this young forever," Alejandro said. "She can easily pass for fourteen."

"She's been going to Solomon about a year," Cristiano said. "She's ready. Put her on the corner."

I gasped, only mildly more shocked by Cristiano's suggestion than I was that they were talking business in front of me.

"If Sandra says she's too scared, send her to me," Cristiano added.

"You can't put a fourteen-year-old on the streets," I blurted.

Everyone except Cristiano turned to me. "She's not fourteen. She's eighteen."

"But you're trying to pass her off as underage?" I asked. "It's sick."

Cristiano finally looked at me. "Perhaps it was a mistake to let you stay. You're asking the wrong questions, and you don't have the stomach for this yet."

I pressed my lips together. He was giving me a choice, which was more than anyone in a position of authority had ever done before. I could stay and continue to gather information that might help me understand what was happening under this roof, or I could run and hide in my room.

As if responding to some silent signal, the men ashed their cigars, stood from their chairs, and nodded at Cristiano on their way inside. The one with the face tattoo and limp—Eduardo, I thought Cristiano had called him—was last to get up, hesitating before he shut the door behind himself.

Once we were alone, Cristiano turned to me. "Sit."

I obeyed, hoping it would earn me a chance to say my piece. Because despite being in a similar situation, or maybe because of it, I couldn't stay quiet when a young girl was being taken advantage of.

"I do have the stomach for this," I said as calmly as I could so he wouldn't get defensive. "But that could've been *me* on the corner. You protected me as a child once. Do you still have it in you?"

Cristiano eyed me passively. "What do you mean it could've been you?"

"If your father had struck against mine as he'd planned, he'd have left me an orphan. What do you think he would've done with me? Despite their pact with the other cartels in the area, including Papá's, your parents were secretly trafficking humans."

"I'm aware." A vein in Cristiano's temple pulsed as he glanced over his shoulder and into the house. "My father wouldn't have been as kind to you as I have been today. As I have been your whole life."

I swallowed. I couldn't deny that was true, but it wasn't a strong enough argument to justify what he was doing. "You're no different from him now, but you can still change."

He smashed his cigar into an ashtray. "You don't know what you're talking about," he said with a sudden sharp edge to his tone. "I'm nothing like him. I wouldn't exploit a woman, no matter her age."

"If that was true, I wouldn't be here."

He shot up from his chair, nearly knocking it over. "I didn't buy, sell, or trade you," he said, going rigid. "You're here willingly."

Willingly. Diego had used the same word. Was it a clue as to what justifications brewed in Cristiano's mind? He seemed set on believing I'd come here by choice. That he hadn't forced me into anything. Diego had told me all about how Cristiano had been so opposed to his parents' budding business in human trafficking that he'd gone as far as to enlist Papá's help to put a stop to it—even knowing there was only way to stop it.

My father had killed Cristiano and Diego's parents for sins similar to Cristiano's. Trafficking people. Exploiting young girls. Plotting against our family.

So what had changed for Cristiano? Why had he stood up to it back then, only to turn around and build an even greater empire on the backs of others? He'd obviously seen and done enough to turn him into a different man. One worse than his father if the rumors were true, and if he justified his actions by convincing himself that anyone came to him willingly.

The door opened behind us. "*Señor?*" came a small female voice.

We both glanced over at Jazmín as she stepped out with a decanter of amber liquid.

Cristiano smoothed out his dress shirt, rolled his neck, and sat back down, once again cool and unruffled. "Come," he said to Jazmín.

She brought him the bottle, and he refilled his drink, nodding at her other hand. "What's that?"

She passed him a pill bottle and set an Evian on the table. "For Miss Natalia," she said.

He furrowed his brows as he studied the painkillers. "What's wrong?" he asked me. "Headache?"

"Yes," I said, which wasn't a complete lie. By the end of the night, I wasn't sure what kind of pain I'd be in. The thought made me queasy and opened a door in my mind

I'd been trying to hold shut. How was I going to make it through this? I'd only had sex once, and it had been the complete opposite of what I was about to endure.

My chest started to cave, and I dug my fingernails into my palms, barely managing to keep from breaking down. That was probably what Cristiano wanted, to know the kind of power he had over not just my body but my mind.

"You barely touched your dinner," he said with a frown. "In fact, you look a little pale. You need to eat more."

"I can bring something," Jaz said.

I shook my head. "I'm not hungry."

"Bring us a little bit of everything," Cristiano said with a nod.

Jaz didn't move but bit her bottom lip and laced her fingers behind her back. "*¿Señor?*"

"What is it?"

"She was asking questions," Jaz said quickly, her eyes flitting toward me under her lashes. "About me and where I came from."

Cristiano scolded me with a look. "Why are you questioning our staff, Natalia?"

"They're not *my* staff." I set my jaw as frustration simmered underneath my skin. "I was curious, that's all."

"So ask *me*. What did you tell her?" he asked Jaz.

"*Nada*. Nothing at all." She shook her head hard. "I don't know her. I don't know who sent her. And I don't trust her."

"*Me?*" I asked.

"You trust *me*, don't you?" Cristiano asked her. "Do you think I'd bring someone here who was a threat to you?"

After a moment, Jaz slowly shook her head. "No."

"Natalia's only curious. Like you, she's also suspicious of those around her." He popped off the top of the bottle and shook two pills into his palm. "Can she take these or do I need to be worried you might poison her?"

My heart thudded in the ensuing silence until Jaz laughed. "If I were going to poison her, I wouldn't be so obvious about it."

He winked. "That's what I thought."

There was an easiness between them I didn't understand. She wasn't fearsome so much as . . . flirtatious?

"Jaz, please draw the curtains for us," he said.

"*Claro*. Of course," she said with a nod and returned back inside. A pit formed in my stomach as she shut us off from the rest of the house.

Cristiano opened the water bottle and handed it to me with the pills. I tossed them back quickly.

"Come here," he said.

"I am here," I said. We weren't a half meter apart.

"Closer." He took my hand and brushed his mouth against the back of it. "It has taken all my effort to keep my hands off you tonight."

Memories flashed across my mind—him cradling my face at the nightclub, running his roughened palms up my leg in my bathroom, encircling my ankle in the car. His touch so far had been callused but never cruel.

A thread of unwelcome desire tugged inside me at the idea that he'd been anxious to touch me again. What had stopped him earlier? Why did I care when I should just be thankful and let it lie? I didn't want to respond to his touch. I *couldn't*.

"Any closer and I'll be on your lap," I said.

"You've read my mind."

"You've ignored me tonight."

"I'm not ignoring you now." He stared at me expectantly. Now that we were alone, his full attention was back on me. I could see why so many people sought it. First, the boy who'd lost his tooth. Then, throughout the night, many people had approached Cristiano, vying for his time. He hadn't looked at any of them the way he looked at me now.

He tugged on my hand until I was standing, then pulled me across his lap. "This is where I like you," he murmured, hugging me against him. "Never question my attraction to you."

"What am I?" I asked, my heart rate kicking up as hardness pressed against my hip. "Something you stole from Diego? A way to hurt both him and my father?"

"*You*," he said, nuzzling my neck, "are my *wife*."

"You mocked me in the church, and you're mocking me now."

"I'm not." He slid a hand under my hair and ran his thumb up to my scalp. "You're mine. I wouldn't give you away, Natalia. I'm not my brother."

My heart missed a beat. The sting was fresh. Diego was both the person I would've called for comfort and the reason I was here. Perhaps Cristiano was right—Diego had given me away, along with my trust. But did a betrayal that deep slice right through my love for him? I didn't think it was that simple—I wanted to strangle him and then fall into his arms, anger and grief warring in me.

But I couldn't think of it now. When I had Cristiano's attention, mine needed to be on him. I had to play my cards close to my chest until I knew what Cristiano planned for me. He required all my energy and left me little to worry about Diego.

"At least Diego never held me against my will."

"You're not my prisoner." He massaged my neck. "You can leave when you like, but then the deal is off."

"You gave us your word that if I married you, we'd all be safe."

"Not only have we *not* consummated the marriage, but our arrangement was made in bad faith on Diego's part. I proceeded anyway, but my protection only extends to your family so long as it is mine. As long as *you* are mine. Leave me, and my obligations go with you. One phone call to the Maldonados is all it would take."

He wanted me. Even a dead person would be able to feel his need pressing against me. But it was there in his words, too. *Mine. His.* Diego had made a risky deal with one of the most powerful cartels in the country to transport their narcotics across the Mexico-US border, and he'd failed, costing them millions of dollars. Now, the only thing keeping them from retaliating against my father, his family, and his cartel, was my new husband. Cristiano. A man who had the means, the connections, and now, a reason, to keep the Maldonados at bay.

I tried not to give in to the feeling of Cristiano's strong fingers working my tendons. "Why?" I asked. "What do you want with me?"

"I want details." He put his mouth in my hair. "Tell me, Natalia. How was it with him? Where did you do it?"

I tensed. Surely, he didn't mean my night with Diego? "That's sacred," I hissed.

"Nothing you've done before me is sacred. As your husband, your secrets are mine."

"And let me guess—yours *aren't* mine," I said. "How is that fair?"

"I never said that. Ask what you like. I'll do my best to answer. But not until I've gotten my answers. Where did my brother dishonor you? Your bedroom?"

"Dishonor?" I snapped. "That's the height of hypocrisy coming from you."

"*Dishonor* is a gentle word for what he did." Cristiano curled a hand on top of my thigh. "He lied to both of us.

He broke my terms and stole from you in the most malicious way."

I took a breath, containing a shudder as I tried to keep up. "What do you mean?" I asked. "He lied to you, yes, but—"

"But nothing," Cristiano said. "You know the truth. When we made the deal, I'll bet my life you were still a virgin."

"He wouldn't . . ." My mind raced. I had trusted Diego all my life—I never would've opened up to him that way otherwise. Only two nights ago, he'd climbed up my balcony and into my bed. And this morning's wedding had not been spontaneous. "When did you make the deal?" I asked.

And I prayed. *Any time before Friday night.*

"After the warehouse burned," Cristiano said, "and Diego had no more options."

I turned my face away as my throat closed. *Friday morning.* I didn't want to believe it. Cristiano had more reason to play with my mind than Diego did to hurt me that way. To have traded me for his freedom was hurtful and cowardly, but to have come to my bedroom after having made this deal? Ruthless. Unforgivable.

When I looked back, Cristiano studied me. He'd given me this look in the past, one a student might give a complex math problem. He resembled his brother in that moment. Diego had worn the same frustrated expression trying to solve the Maldonado equation once it'd started to go wrong.

What had gone wrong, we'd find out, was Cristiano. He'd sabotaged Diego's deal by stealthily stealing, attacking, and burning the Maldonado's shipments before they'd ever made it near the border. If Diego had manipulated my virginity from me, then he'd broken my trust beyond repair. But that didn't mean I could believe a word from Cristiano's mouth, the man who'd orchestrated this entire plot.

"I've answered your question," Cristiano said. "Now answer mine. Where did he take from you? Your bedroom?"

Lights blurred together along with Cristiano's words. I barely heard what he'd asked. "Yes," I said absentmindedly.

"*Mmm.* That lucky piece of shit. I wouldn't have minded having you there, where you thought you were safest, where you slept and dreamed . . ." His hand slid up the lace covering my outer thigh. "Where you've touched yourself."

Everything sharpened back into focus. "How do you know that?"

"A guess, but I'm not wrong, am I?" I felt his smile against my cheek. "Did he warm you up at least?"

"Stop," I whispered.

"I will, once you tell me what I want to know. He betrayed you—don't protect him."

Protect him? It was my natural instinct. But did I owe Diego that anymore? "I'm protecting myself," I said. "Why does it matter how it was with him?"

"It humors me to know how he botched your first time, and what I'll have to do to redeem it."

"He didn't *botch* it. Far from it." Cristiano's arrogance fueled my anger. Both men had knocked me back and forth like a tennis ball. Despite my fury with Diego, he was turning out to be the easiest way to get under Cristiano's skin, and in that moment, I wanted that. I needed to hurt him. "He did warm me up," I said. "With his mouth. And it felt *amazing.*"

"Amazing?" Cristiano repeated, sounding amused. "A

trip anywhere is amazing until you've been to the moon. Then what?"

"We had sex," I said, and amended, "*amazing* sex."

"And you didn't bleed," he said.

"No, but I had an orgasm, which I much prefer."

His grip on my thigh tightened, and he shifted under me. "Did you?" he asked. "Or are you making that up?"

"You told me not to lie to you—that's the truth. I didn't even know I could get so wet, and it took practically nothing for—"

"Enough," he snapped, his lip curled. "Did he use a condom?"

"Yes," I said. "Or no. I guess we'll find out in a few weeks. Will you want me then, baby and all?"

He took my chin, turning my face to his. "Watch your step. You're entering dangerous territory, my love. Condom or no condom?"

I'd never seen Cristiano unravel, and it hadn't taken as much as one might think. His breath came fast, his eyes dark. I knew without knowing—few saw this side of him and lived. It should've scared me. It did. But it was equally electrifying to drive such a powerful man to the edge so quickly and keep him there.

"Tell me honestly," he said, "and in exchange, I'll invite your father for dinner tomorrow night."

Tears instantly filled my eyes. *Papá*. I would've done anything to see him in that moment. "My father?" I asked. "You'll let me see him?"

"No doubt he has questions."

"*Questions?* He'll be worried sick!"

"Then I'll bring him here and show him he has nothing to be concerned about." He flexed his fingers against my thigh. "That you're in good hands. Unyielding hands. That is, if you tell me what I want to know."

I swallowed. "We used a condom."

Cristiano's expression eased slightly. "Smart girl."

I hadn't realized I'd sunken deeper into his lap until the door opened again, and I vaulted forward.

"*Ay*," Jazmín said. "*Perdón.*"

"It's okay," Cristiano said, beckoning her while keeping his eyes on me. "But discretion, please, Jaz."

"Yes, yes," she said, hurrying to the chair. "The curtains are still closed."

"Good." Cristiano took a plate from her, and she disappeared as quickly as she'd arrived.

"What're you hungry for?" he asked. It sounded like a threat.

I surveyed the serving plate with fried chicken, rice, beans, plantains, and more. None of it sounded appetizing when my stomach was nothing but nerves for what was ahead.

"Dessert?" He slowly forked off a pale-blue frosted bite of Easter cake and held it up to me.

"You already announced our marriage," I said. "Why are we hiding behind curtains?"

"Eat," he said.

Tit for tat. Indulge his questions, and I'd get to see my father. Eat his food, and I'd get my own answers. It was enough to get me to open my mouth and let him feed me a bite.

"It won't be possible to keep much from Jaz," he explained. "She's everywhere. But while you and I get to know each other, I prefer privacy. People are curious about you." He nuzzled under my ear. "As am I."

His breath tickled my neck, and I cursed my body as it warmed, threatening to arch into him, my nipples pebbling. It came as no surprise a man so adept at manipulating people's minds could also do the same to a woman's body.

He offered another bite, and I leaned in to take it.

"You're pretty when you eat." He thumbed frosting from the corner of my mouth and licked his finger. "Not like me. I went through a period where food was hard to come by, and if I didn't fight to eat, I might not eat at all."

My heart panged at the thought of anyone going hungry until I realized the cause of his struggles. He'd fled the home he'd known for eight years, ours, because of his involvement in my mother's death. I didn't care how many *sicarios* he brought me—unless we could go back in time, I'd always believe his guilt before his innocence.

"You have plenty to eat now," I said, pursing my lips. He didn't deserve all that he had.

"I do." His voice rumbled as he added, "And I'm voracious, *mariposa*. I take big bites. I eat like I won't get another meal. I gulp down the finest wines and unwrap my candy fast, lick and suck until I get to the sweet core,"—he nipped the shell of my ear—"because I'm greedy for the juicy center."

I shivered, reading his words perfectly. I'd once envisioned Cristiano like an animal fending predators off his spoils. I had no idea what was to come, but I knew I'd be his feast, his candy, the frosting he licked clean. Tremors of dread mingled with a craving to be devoured as Diego had promised but not delivered.

Shame washed over me. What prey harbored even the smallest hope of being caught?

Stupid prey. *Senseless* prey.

Cristiano would have his way with me and discard the carcass.

"If my brother warmed you up with his mouth," he

said, "I will make it my new life's mission to set you on fire. Are you ready for our wedding night?"

"Why do you think I wanted the aspirin?" I asked.

He drew back as if I'd slapped him. A second time. "Meaning?"

"You can make me sit on your lap and feed me sweets, but it doesn't change the fact that you'll push me down on a mattress later and take what you want."

After a moment, he released his hold on me. "I'm not making you do anything," he said. "Sit where you like."

It almost felt like a trick, and perhaps it *was* a mind game. As long as we didn't consummate the marriage, I'd be on edge knowing he could call things off at any moment. That was, assuming Cristiano was even true to his word. I stayed where I was, deliberating as my weight rested on his large wall of a chest.

Neither of us moved until he said with an edge to his voice, "Go now, *mariposa*. If I'm not forcing you, then you're pressed against my cock *willingly*, and my control slips fast."

I stood quickly. I wasn't sure what I wanted, but slipping control was enough to scare me off for now.

He pulled a chair so close that it wasn't a far cry from sitting on his lap. I took the seat, and he passed my plate over. "I'm not the one who forced you into this marriage," he said, all the rumble, grit, and sex in his voice gone. "I tried to warn you about Diego."

I paused with a bite halfway to my mouth. "You manipulated him into a position where he'd have to give me up or lose his life."

"Is that what he whispered in your ear at the church— that I stole you from him?" Cristiano asked.

What other explanation was there? There was no question that's what had happened. Diego had given me away, but Cristiano had stolen me as well.

I put the fork down and pushed the cake away. "He didn't have to whisper anything. I know what I know—neither of you are innocent."

"And you decide what's true, do you?" he asked. "You don't have even a shadow of a doubt that I killed your mother, so it must be true."

I choked a little, barely managing not to cough. If that *wasn't* true, then it would turn Cristiano from a murderer on the run to an innocent man fleeing persecution. I refused to believe that. Cristiano was the last person who deserved my sympathy. "Yes," I said. "I still think you murdered her."

"You want to believe it, because you want to believe the worst in me. You'll excuse Diego anything. Imagine how you'll feel if none of it is true."

"I have eyes and ears. You were standing over her with a gun and blood on your clothes, ready to make off with the contents of her safe." I could admit to myself that I had shreds of doubt as to whether he'd done it. But how would being falsely accused have shaped the man he was today? It still made him a wild card—but one with an axe to grind. And it still didn't excuse the business he ran now. Emotion bloomed in my chest, and I channeled it into anger. "You'll put a young girl on the street," I accused, my voice rising. "That's the lowest of the low, and it can never be forgiven."

"I agree," he said coolly. "But you refuse to listen to my side or to see reason." His jaw firmed as he nodded at my plate. "Eat your cake, Natalia. Live in that world where Diego is a prince. When you want answers, and you've got the guts to face them, let me know." He stood, took out his phone, and said with finality, "When you're ready for the truth, I'll be here."

I jerked my head up. "That's it?"

"What's it?" he asked as he typed.

"I can go to bed?"

"You sound disappointed."

Ending the night now meant I'd wake up and go through all of this again tomorrow. He would devour me—it was inevitable. The sooner we got it over with, the sooner I'd know my family was safe. "I told you—I want this done."

"Don't worry. It will be done. I don't need you to believe me to fuck me." Narrowing his gaze on me, he slid his phone back into his shirt pocket. "But I intend to take my dessert in the bedroom."

5

NATALIA

N ight had fallen, covering the town like a blanket. Out front, freedom spread in every direction from the precipice on which Cristiano's home sat. But even in the dark, I could feel how abruptly it stopped at the Badlands' gates. A light flickered here and there to the soundtrack of a hooting owl but it was otherwise silent and the horizon black.

"Put a smile on your face," Cristiano said as we stood in his driveway, waiting to see off the next wave of guests.

On the patio, he'd been unable to keep his hands off me, but now, distance was all he seemed capable of. I was once again invisible until I was a nuisance or had done something wrong, like frown.

I forced my mouth into what I hoped looked like a smile when an elderly couple exited the house, the old man walking on a tilt. His wife took both my hands and rushed out a goodwill prayer as Cristiano helped her husband down the steps. Nobody seemed to have cars except Cristiano himself—once they left, they descended into the night on foot.

After the final guest, Cristiano held open the front door for me. This was it. We were alone, and there was no more time. I entered the house to the *clink* of dishes from the kitchen. Lingering smells of fish stew and baked goods lent me no comfort. As I trailed behind him, Cristiano glanced over his shoulder, as if ensuring I hadn't made a break for it.

In the kitchen, cleanup had begun. Staff members in rubber gloves and aprons filled the dishwasher, topped plastic containers, and scrubbed the ovens.

"We'll continue to eat like kings for a few days," Cristiano said, and some people laughed. "Everyone raved about tonight's fare, Fisker. Well done."

Applause filled the room as I hovered in the doorway, trying desperately to piece the scene together. Nobody seemed distraught. Either the staff members were resigned to their situations, or like tonight's guests, they supported, benefitted from, and profited off Cristiano's business.

Even beautiful Jaz had something quietly ugly and fearful about her, like an elegant cat that purred to lure you in, then used its claws on you. She sat on a countertop, feet dangling, watching me as she dried dishes and slid them onto the top shelf of a cabinet.

As Cristiano spoke to a man who looked like a butler, I inched toward Jaz. "Can I have something to drink?"

She gestured around the kitchen. "It's all yours. There's filtered water from the fridge or bottles inside, along with soda, beer, and anything else you want."

It wasn't mine. Just because I'd married Cristiano didn't mean I had a right to anything in his home. I opened the fridge and found a sparkling water I hoped would settle my nervous stomach.

I took a few long sips. Fizz bubbled up my chest, and I

pressed my hand to my chest, trying and failing to conceal a burp. Everyone but Jaz laughed—even Cristiano.

An embarrassed smile crossed my face. "Excuse me."

"Jaz," Cristiano called across the kitchen. "Please show my bride to her bedroom."

She cocked her head at him. "Her . . . bedroom?"

He nodded once, and Jaz sighed, conveying her disappointment. Perhaps she, too, had thought he'd toss me in a locked cell and forget about me. Or maybe she knew what was to come, and it was jealousy that plagued her. It didn't seem like a stretch that there could be more to their relationship than employer and staff. That didn't sit right with me—that Cristiano would abuse his power that way, then flaunt it in front of the household and me. And if he was an unfaithful husband—did I care? Was there any chance he *wouldn't* be?

Cristiano took the dish in Jaz's hands and popped it on the top shelf. "I'll finish this," he said. "Go."

Jaz shrugged as she hopped off the counter and gestured for me to follow. "Come on."

"I'm sorry if I made you uncomfortable earlier," I said as we climbed the staircase. "I was just trying to help."

"We don't need your help," she said.

So I was coming to find out. The question was why? I glanced at my interlaced hands. "And if I need yours?"

As we hit the second floor, she dove into an exaggerated curtsy-bow. "I'm at your service, *doña* Natalia. We all are. It's our jobs."

"I hope we can be friends." We continued up to the top floor. "Coming from university, where I knew lots of people and had rarely a dull moment, I'm afraid I'll get lonely."

Jaz didn't respond. I'd been willing to give up all that so I could have Diego, but now I had neither him nor that life. And how would I fill that hole in my chest? As night closed in on me, all that I'd lost did too. But I couldn't let it weigh on me tonight. I had to be strong when Cristiano called for me later.

At the end of a hallway, Jaz used her shoulder to shove open a heavy plank door with iron hinges and hardware that made me feel like I was boarding a pirate ship. A breeze passed through the dark room, fluttering the white gauzy curtains of an elevated, four-poster bed. Only the moon shone through arched doorways that opened to a balcony. Jaz flipped a switch and warm light bathed the thick white walls and red-clay Saltillo tile. A weathered, leather chest sat at the foot of the bed across from a sitting area with a red velvet couch, russet-colored coffee table, and stone fireplace.

I turned in a circle. The room paralleled the rest of the house with dark wooden support beams that cut across a white vaulted ceiling with an antler chandelier as a center-piece. "*This* is my room?"

"*Sí*," Jaz answered.

As far as jail cells went, it was undoubtedly the most luxurious one in existence. I removed my sandals, picked up the hem of my dress, and made my way to the balcony. I hadn't even scratched the surface of the bedroom's magnificence. As I neared, the world spread out before me.

Stars shimmered like a city in a black sky that bled into the horizon and became the ocean. Waves crashed below. A refreshing sea breeze misted my face, almost delightful enough to make up for my circumstances.

The house had been built through the mountain, desert and town behind us, jungle around us, and nothing but ocean and sky before me.

"But it's so wonderful," I said to myself. I lived on a

bluff, directly over the water, and had never seen anything like it. "And so big."

From my balcony, it was nothing but ocean and sky. And a long drop to the small strip of beach below. I stared down into the darkness as I once had into a tunnel.

There's always a choice, Cristiano had told me more than once.

There was always a way out.

"It's the master," Cristiano's deep, contented voice answered behind me, rumbling through the beauty of this new world like thunder. "If you're thinking of jumping, don't. You're forbidden."

I turned and braced myself against the short, stucco wall. A cream and brown woven hammock big enough for two swayed in one corner with the breeze. "I'm *forbidden*?"

"Rule number one in my home," he said, his hands in his pockets as a sinister smile tugged one corner of his mouth. "Don't die."

Jaz was nowhere in sight—it was just the two of us. "Why do I have the master?" A knot formed in my stomach as the truth hit me. "Where do you sleep?"

"In the master." His smile broke free and slid over his face. "Where else but by my wife's side?"

But I wasn't his wife. I was, at best, the product of a merger and a convenient mistress, and at worst, a slave to his every whim. Someone to call to his bed when he wanted and to send away when he was finished. What exactly did it make me if I wasn't that? What would compel him to sleep by my side each night when he didn't have to?

With a gust of wind, I hugged myself and walked by him, back into a flickering room. The nights were cooler by the water, and Jaz had lit the fireplace and iron candlesticks on the mantel. "I assumed . . ."

"What?" he asked. "That our marriage was for show?"

"Yes. I mean, no," I said carefully, trying to slow my racing heart. "I know you have certain expectations of me. But there's no need to encumber yourself with a true wife. I don't expect us to sleep in the same bed after we . . ."

"After we what?" he asked, not bothering to hide his amusement.

He wanted to make me uncomfortable by forcing me to say it, but I wouldn't let him. I turned around, lengthening my spine. "I figured I'd go back to my room after you fuck me."

He inhaled deeply, fisting his hands in his pockets. "There is no *after* I fuck you, Natalia," he said. "I'm always fucking you. I should like to be able to roll over and be inside you. To slide down between your legs at your request. To unwrap your pussy and suck on candy at all hours of the night."

My skin pebbled with the alarming conviction in his voice. His filthy mouth was fit for a devil, and I had no doubt it would be just as bold between my legs. Ashamed by the way I quivered at the thought, I kept my back stick-straight. "Most men would be happy to take what they want and send their whore away. I'm fine with that arrangement."

"I'm not." His dress shoes clapped the terracotta as he stepped into the candlelight. Gone was any inkling I might've had that his bullishness was for show, or that he acted so profanely just to frighten me. His desire for me showed in his face and in his ragged words. "In case you haven't figured it out, I'm not most men. You're my wife, not my whore, and don't ever call yourself that in or out of my presence again. Every night, you will eat at my dinner table. And every night, you will sleep in my bed."

"Every night?" I asked, my voice breathy even to my own ears.

"*Every* night," he replied on a growl.

"Until you grow bored of me."

"You may wish for that," he said with furrowed brows that made it hard to tell if he was teasing. "But don't count on it."

I swallowed. Just like my confusion over his interest in my virginity, I didn't understand what would possess him to shackle himself to me when he had the luxury of freedom. The sex, I understood, even if the heat between us continued to bewilder me. We were matched enemies, and that ensured a modicum of respect between us, however small. Walking that fine line between hate and admiration only seemed to kindle our sexual attraction. But I could be both curious to explore that explosive spark and also *not* want to sleep with him.

I'd only planned to give that gift to one man.

My plans didn't matter anymore, though.

There was no denying Cristiano when he'd been stoking the embers between us since he'd returned into my life as a haunting calavera. Except then, our chemistry had been harmless.

But a true marriage? It couldn't be. I'd play a dutiful wife for others as I'd been forced to tonight. I'd placate Cristiano while I listened and watched for opportunities to get myself out of this situation. But what was the purpose of pretending in private that I was anything more than his plaything?

"Forever is a long time to sleep next to someone," I said.

He prowled closer until we were toe to toe. "As you'll grow used to the heat behind the gates of Hell, so will you come to enjoy sleeping by my side—and the safety it affords you."

"Safety from whom?" So far, I'd only lamented what had been stripped of my old life, and feared the dangers that came with being in Cristiano's grip—but I'd not yet considered any outside threats that came with this new one. "Who do I have to fear more than you?"

"I don't want to find out. Where you sleep is non-negotiable." He raised my chin with his knuckle. Candlelight danced over his face, creating shadows around his eyes much like the dark circles he'd painted on as a sugar skull mask. "In my bed, you'll be safe, Natalia—and in my bed, you'll be *mine.*"

The crackling fire was no match for what sizzled between us. Alarmed, I took a step back, and he came with me. A dance with a complex man who had many faces. Earlier, he'd been cold and distant. Now, he was no less hard, but somehow equally warm. I couldn't fathom him so attentive and serene outside this room. For a man as controlled as Cristiano, there was something alarmingly thrilling about getting a side to him others didn't—and to unpeeling his layers. "Are you so insatiable that you need me to be within reach all the time?" I asked, embarrassed by the rasp in my voice.

"Oh, *yes*," he said as if it were a threat.

"You can have any other woman," I said. "Those you can't charm, you can take. Why me?"

He circled me as he had in the church, and my breathing sped. But *unlike* then, when I'd been too stunned to keep up, I turned my head and watched him until he disappeared behind me.

The hairs on the back of my neck stood up as I felt his eyes on me. He would touch me any moment. My body would respond. It already was, my legs unsteady, my heart racing as my mind wandered to a thought I'd had before—what it might feel like to be trapped beneath such a strong body with broad shoulders that shielded us from the world as I took all he had to give.

And he had much to give, I was sure—even before it suddenly pressed into my backside.

He wrapped his arms around my middle, enclosing me in a strong, warm embrace. We faced a floor-length mirror framed by hand-painted talavera tiles that I hadn't noticed before. Cristiano towered behind me in the reflection, hugging my back to his front. His massive hands slid up my stomach and cupped my breasts through the black lace.

"Why you? See how perfectly they fit in my hands?" he asked, watching my face. "They were made for me."

Cristiano was hot and cold, ignoring me one second—and the next, so hopped up and hungry that I felt like a drug he needed in order to stay upright. The only other thing that seemed to take him from zero to sixty was a certain trigger word from my mouth. Cristiano held all the control in our relationship, but I had to grasp it where I could. "They fit that way in Diego's hands, too."

He snarled near my ear, squeezing my breasts until the place between my legs shamelessly throbbed. "I know you only say that to anger me, and it works. It makes me jealous as a dog. Before you were mine, I hated the thought that you were his. Now that you belong to me, it's enough to drive me insane that he had your heart and your pussy first."

The room threatened to spin as my emotions ping-ponged between anticipation and trepidation at being at the mercy of such a powerful and hungry man. To know I'd soon submit, and to have him grow harder against my backside. This was it—what it had all been leading up to.

He moved one hand up my neck, jerking my face to the side and my mouth up to his.

"Kiss me," he said.

With our mouths centimeters apart, I fought the infuriating urge to close that small space between us. "No," I said.

"No?"

"You'll have to take it from me."

"There are many women who'd like to be standing where you are."

"I know," I said.

He flinched as surprise crossed his features. "Do you?"

"You're handsome, rich, and powerful. I'm sure many have spread their legs for you. And I'll spread mine, too. But I'll be wishing someone else was between them."

He tightened his grip on my face, holding me still as he lowered his mouth to mine. "I've endured many years of disappointment and suffering, Natalia. I can take a lot. But if you're going to provoke me in this way, you should know —I'm not sure I can control my response."

His warm breath caressed my lips as I swallowed his harsh words. As soon as he'd spoken them, I understood that was what I'd been trying to do—test his control. And if *he'd* meant to scare me, it was working.

Or maybe it was something other than fear that made my heart pound.

He grazed the bridge of my nose with the tip of his. "The thought that he has had you before me means I will work twice as hard to erase him. To claim *you*. Now, don't keep me from that another moment." He nearly bared his teeth. "*Kiss . . . me.*"

"No."

He took my mouth, plunging his tongue deep as mine lashed back at him. He slid a hand between my legs and cupped me through my dress, sending bolts of pleasure crashing through me as he rubbed me in the exact spot to make my knees buckle.

I didn't realize I'd shoved my hand in his hair until he groaned and growled. He held me in place and thrust his hips into my backside like a bull ramming a fence that detained him. Cristiano was going to fuck me. I'd known it for hours, but now it was happening. And my body was already giving into him, grabbing at him, yielding for his bruising kiss, growing wet under his firm grasp.

He turned me around, cradled my face, and devoured my mouth again. I fisted his shirt, pulling him closer as he walked me backward.

I gasped for more. For him.

And then in shock.

What was I doing? Minutes in Cristiano's arms, and I was surrendering? It couldn't be. The bastard didn't get to take and take with no consequences. He didn't get to win in every way. He'd succeeded in tearing Diego and me apart, but he would never *have* me.

I released his shirt and dropped my hands to my sides. The pulsing heat between my legs remained, but I ignored its demands and slackened my jaw. Cristiano curled his fingers into my hair, kissing me harder.

There was no point in fighting—our terms had been agreed upon. But if he was going to consummate this marriage, it would be with the understanding that I didn't want it.

That was our reality. If I let myself escape into a fantasy and enjoy this, I'd be playing his game—and losing.

And if he thought I wanted this, he'd never see himself for the monster he was.

He drew back, his breathing labored. "What is it?"

My dry throat made my response hoarse. "Nothing."

"What did I tell you about lying to me?" He squeezed my arms, bringing me to the tips of my toes until our mouths nearly touched. "Don't deny me, Natalia. You want this. I need it."

Need. To be needed by a man as dominant and typically dispassionate as him was a heady feeling. It inspired my unsettling—and dangerous—impulse to obey his orders. He made it too easy to fall under his spell. I had to douse any embers of passion between us and detach in order to come out physically and emotionally unscathed.

Sex couldn't always equal intimacy. I'd thought I'd had that with Diego, only to find he'd broken that trust. Sometimes sex was an exchange of the world's most valuable currency—power—and it was the only playing field where I rivaled Cristiano.

I tilted up my mouth and put my tongue in his with the same enthusiasm I'd show a brick wall.

He didn't kiss me back. "What are you doing?" he asked.

"I vowed to obey you." When his grip loosened, I wriggled free and backed away toward the bed. "That's what I'm doing," I said, removing my wedding ring to set it on the nightstand.

"Put that back on."

"As you wish." I replaced it, sat on the edge of the mattress, and lay back.

"I asked you what you think you're doing," he said slowly. "Answer me."

"Do you want me a different way?" I spread my knees and stared up at the ceiling as I gathered my dress. "This is the only position I've known."

"Never mind what I want. What do *you* want?"

"We have a contract. You brought me here, so take what you've bought."

"Did you sign anything?" he asked.

"I took vows before God. Before you. It's my duty—"

"Stop."

I parted my lips and took a breath. A breeze passed through the room and the fire roared in response. Cristiano was known for taking what he wanted. He'd declared he would many times. He'd made it clear sex was non-negotiable.

And yet he kept his distance. It was my unwillingness that stopped him. That puzzle piece snapped nicely into place. If he needed me to want this before he proceeding, that gave me something I could use against him.

"Close your legs." It took me a moment to register his order. With his face turned toward the fire, he fixed his collar. "I said close them."

I dropped the hem of my dress and sat forward, bringing my knees together. "Why?"

He smoothed out his shirt. "Go to bed."

I almost couldn't believe it had worked. He could be stopped. Victory rushed to my head like alcohol, and for a moment, I was high. I'd won.

Except, I hadn't.

Reality came crashing through. Until the people I loved were safe, I hadn't won.

"My protection only extends to your family so long as it is mine. As long as you are mine. Leave me, and my obligations go with you. One phone call to the Maldonados is all it would take."

"Wait," I whispered as he turned and walked to the door. "Wait!"

He didn't.

He reached for the handle, and I jumped to my feet. Cristiano wouldn't guarantee anyone's safety until he'd had me in the most carnal way. We would consummate the marriage regardless of what he or I wanted—I'd make sure of it.

Now, I knew how to stop him—but I'd always known how to start him up.

I ran across the room, my bare feet slapping the tiles until I stopped short. "Please."

He froze.

"You can't go," I said, grabbing his bicep with both hands to pull him away from the door. "We had a deal."

He arched an eyebrow. "I changed my mind."

I tugged him toward the bed with me as I repeated, "Please."

With a lazy blink, the same desire he'd worn earlier returned to his face. He'd told me once I would beg. He *wanted* me to beg. My dignity had been stripped away in the last twenty-four hours. My virginity had been stolen, my love rejected, and I'd been forced to my knees before God to pledge my obedience to the devil. What more did I have? I was the only person who could keep Cristiano's wrath at bay.

And I knew what he needed to give himself permission.

Only one word—*please*—had warmed his demeanor just now.

I dropped to my knees. I wasn't begging for sex but for the lives of my father, everyone who worked for him, and any innocent person who'd pay the price of Diego's deal. I had no idea how far the Maldonados would go, and I wasn't going to find out.

"Please what?" he asked.

"Consummate this marriage as you promised you would."

His chest heaved. "I don't like the word *consummate*. Choose another."

"I . . ." My throat thickened. I doubted he meant *make love*, and whatever shred of dignity I retained wouldn't allow me to call it that anyway. "Fuck," I said. "Fuck me, Cristiano."

He seized my bicep, urging me to my feet and spinning me around. "You're willing to take whatever I give to save Diego?" he asked, hauling my hips back and making his erection known as he walked us toward the bed. "This is what you want?"

What I *didn't* want was to admit that my quaking was just as much born of desire as it was fear. But I had to if I was going to break his control. "I want this."

He fisted my hair and bent me over the lip of the bed. Despite the fire's warmth, I shivered. Cristiano's dominance finally matched his threats, and it was as thrilling as it was terrifying. He held me down as metal *clinked*, and his zipper *purred*. He pushed my dress up over my ass and pressure weighed against the crotch of my underwear. I gripped the comforter, fighting warring urges to push him off and gyrate against him. I thought I'd wanted gentle, but gentleness had deceived me.

I wanted the monster.

Break me so I can break you. What would it do to him to lose control? To look himself in the mirror tomorrow knowing deep down he'd taken me against my will? I would soon find out.

He closed his body over my back, his mouth in my hair. "This is how you like it?" he asked, pinning my hands to my sides. "Answer me."

"Yes."

He thrust, and my damp underwear pressed against my opening as he begged for entry. "No other woman has ever gotten me this hard. I could break right through your panties. Maybe my brother put his dick in you and moved around, but I'm going to wreck your pussy and show you what it truly means to have your virginity taken. To have it *destroyed*."

Ohh, God. I sucked in a breath. In any other moment, his words might've confused me, but now that I was poised to be thoroughly shaken and ravaged, I understood what I'd experienced before him was simply a tremble. "Whatever you command is yours," I said through gritted teeth.

He groaned in my ear. "You thought what he gave you was an orgasm? Child's play. When I'm through with you, you won't even remember my brother's name. You will clench on my cock so hard, you'll suck me dry. I will show you,"—he thrust again—"how a man fucks his wife. How an animal fucks. So tell me. How do you want it the first time? Like an animal or as my wife?"

I needed him to fill me, to rid me of the confusing, *consuming* ache between my legs.

I needed him to break me once and for all so I could hate him for it. So he could hate *himself* for it.

"Animal," I said.

"I see," he said evenly. "The beast scares you in the light, but not only do you crave it after dark . . . you become it. I'm not surprised—I knew it all along." He released me and stood, taking his heat with him. "That's why you've soaked the tip of my cock right through your underwear."

I began to shake, trying to connect his words to his actions. With a *zip*, the moment disappeared into thin air. I glanced over my shoulder to find him doing up his pants. "Why are you stopping?"

"I told you once," he said, buckling his belt, "I have no need to force myself on a woman."

My body flushed as I became acutely aware I was still baring my ass to him while he was fully dressed. "But I told you I want this."

"You lied."

"I won't fight you," I said.

"You should. You should fight *anyone* who touches you against your will. Diego tricked you into sleeping with him —I won't do the same, no matter how hard you pretend to beg for it."

I scrambled into a sitting position, pulling my knees to my chest. "But what about our deal?"

"Indeed," he said, his eyes wandering over me as he walked backward. "What about it?"

He turned and left the room. The silence following such chaos was deafening, and I covered my mouth as a sob ripped through me. I'd stooped to a level I never thought possible, and Cristiano had still managed to make me feel even lower. He was right. In the dark, my desires were shameful. I'd wanted him to follow through with his threats.

But he was also wrong. My begging for the beast hadn't been pretend. What kind of animal did that make *me*?

And in the end, I'd failed. Cristiano claimed he wouldn't force himself on a woman, but he would. It was only a matter of time before he did, and until then, we were all still in danger. If he thought walking me down an aisle, filling my stomach with world-renowned cooking, and lying with me on the finest sheets made him anything different than a captor, then there was no question he was a master at justifying any sin to himself.

And I might be in the best position to show him who— and what—he truly was.

6

NATALIA

B right light flooded my dreams. I'd been on an airplane soaring through cotton-ball clouds, headed somewhere that wasn't here.

In Cristiano's bed.

I cracked my lids as Jaz yanked apart the white curtains and opened the door to the balcony. Sunshine, warmth, and ocean air filled the room as waves crashed through the silence.

Cristiano hadn't come back to bed until well after I'd cried myself to sleep. I barely remembered the mattress dipping with his large body. With as riled up as he'd been, was there any question what had kept him out so late?

I sensed the bed was empty now, but I still held my breath as I checked over my shoulder. He was gone.

I sat up against the headboard, rubbing sleep from my eyes. "*Buenos días, Jazmín.*"

"Oh, *perdón,*" she replied without inflection. "I forgot you were here."

"What time is it?"

"Late. *Don* Cristiano is waiting for you downstairs." She

disappeared into the closet and called, "He sent me to get you dressed."

"I thought you forgot I was here," I said.

She didn't respond. It didn't matter. I was going to see my father today, and together, we'd find a way to fix this. We had to. If Cristiano respected my father as he claimed, then this was his chance to prove it.

"What do you want to wear?" Jaz asked. Hangers scraped in the closet. "You don't have much."

"I was only planning on staying in México for two weeks," I grumbled.

"The rain has stopped." Jaz returned from the closet with my jean shorts. "It's pretty warm today—" She stopped short and screamed.

I whipped my head around, following her gaze to the patio. Under the grand arched doorway, backlit by sunlight, stood the tall, muscular silhouette of a man with a gun in each hand.

My heart jumped into my throat as I scrambled to Cristiano's side of the bed and Jaz lunged for the top drawer of his nightstand as the man stepped into the room.

Broad chested with dark, spiky hair, a wide jawline, and impeccable posture, I recognized him instantly. Relief filtered through me. I laid eyes on a friend, not an enemy.

Jaz yanked a semi-automatic from Cristiano's drawer, racked the slide, and leveled it on him.

"It's okay, Jaz," I rushed out.

Footsteps barreled down the hall. Cristiano burst through the bedroom door in a suit and tie, his gun raised. "Barto," he said, cinching his eyebrows a millisecond before his jaw clenched. "What the fuck—"

"Don't take another step." The head of my father's security team, a man who'd been blindly loyal to my parents since I could remember, aimed both pistols at Cristiano. "I've been hearing for *years* about Calavera's impenetrable walls and top-notch security." An uncharacteristic grin crossed Barto's face. "Yet here I am on my first try."

Cristiano's knuckles whitened around the grip. "How?"

"You forget, I grew up with the same training you did," Barto said, walking forward when Cristiano did. They stopped before their extended guns touched, eyeing each other—Cristiano, in his tailored suit, aimed his pistol at Barto's chest, and Barto, in head-to-toe black, kept both of his on my new husband's head.

Though the two men were similar in stature, Cristiano had both height and muscle on his former comrade. Apparently, they were matched in other ways, though—Barto had pulled off the impossible feat of breaching my gilded cage's security system, and I was secretly cheering him on. He'd been Cristiano's closest friend at the ranch, and my father's number one since my mother's death, after Cristiano had vacated the position.

"What'd he tell you, Natalia?" Barto asked, keeping his eyes on Cristiano. "That you'd be safe here with a whole town to protect you? I've disproven that completely, and I'm sure I don't need to tell you—it's the people within its walls you need to fear."

"Get in the closet, both of you," Cristiano ordered Jaz and me over his shoulder.

"Barto won't hurt us," I started. "He—"

"*Now.*"

"Not until you put your guns away," I snapped at Cristiano. Leveling my voice, I tried my luck with Barto. "There's no need for them. *Please*, Barto."

With obvious reluctance, he made a show of lowering one gun. "Now you," he said to Cristiano.

Cristiano followed suit but didn't completely holster his gun until Barto had put away both of his.

Jazmín kept hers raised until Cristiano said, without turning around, "*Está bien*, Jaz. I'm good."

Once we'd crossed the room and entered the walk-in closet, she hugged the gun to her chest while I stayed at the doorframe where I could see and hear everything.

"Is it true?" Barto asked.

"It is," Cristiano said instantly. "We're married."

"You'll pay for it, you know."

"I'm sure you hope that's true, but you're in for disappointment." Cristiano crossed his arms over his chest. "You're threatening what's mine, Barto. And just because it has been mine less than twenty-four hours, don't think that means I won't protect it fiercely."

Barto shrugged. "A man who calls his wife 'it' has no regard for her."

I stopped just short of shouting my agreement. Finally, I had a true ally on my side.

"We'll handle this as Costa sees fit," Barto said. "But I see his only daughter in the bed of a man she has hated for over a decade, and I can only assume you forced yourself on her. For that alone, I hope Costa locks *you* in a room with someone who'll repay the favor."

"Are you offering?"

"Fuck you."

"Fuck *you*," Cristiano said. "You know me better than to think I'd hurt Natalia."

Barto snorted, his posture easing marginally from his militant stance. "You're not the person I knew. You're a stranger, and I don't trust you. Costa wants to give you a chance to explain. Me? I'd have already put a bullet in your head."

"You would rather she belonged to Diego?" Cristiano asked, arching an eyebrow.

Barto narrowed his eyes, shaking his head. "We're not talking about Diego. You've interfered with Costa's family. For some reason, he wants you alive, but he'd believe that you attacked me and I had to defend myself. Especially with Natalia as my witness."

"Good luck getting her to lie for anyone but Diego," Cristiano muttered.

I pursed my lips. It wasn't exactly the time to passive-aggressively raise grievances. "I think I'd make a concession in this case," I offered.

Cristiano clenched his jaw. "Get back in the closet."

"Change, Natalia," Barto said. "You're coming home."

"She's my wife. Where she goes, I go. Costa is invited here." Cristiano turned his head over his shoulder while keeping Barto in his sight. "Tell this brute of a bodyguard, Natalia."

"It's . . . true," I conceded. "Cristiano was planning to invite my father over today."

"Forgive Costa if he's lost any reason at all to trust the man who might have murdered his wife," Barto said.

Barto still believed Cristiano was guilty. Or was it that he was beginning to waver in that conviction? Barto generally didn't use words like *might* or *maybe*.

"He wants to see you both at the house," Barto said. "Now."

"Where he, or Diego, or anyone can try to ambush us?" Cristiano straightened his tie. "Costa can come to me."

"Diego isn't there," Barto said.

Where was he? I refrained from asking, knowing any mention of Diego from me would change the entire tone of the conversation, and not in my favor.

They stared at each other, distrust radiating from each of them, an interloper and a kidnapper in a standoff. We were going to be here all day.

I exited the closet, approaching them slowly, like I might a pack of wild dogs, and touched Cristiano's back. He stiffened, his tensed muscles only reinforcing the obvious power beneath my hand. "Please, can we go?" I whispered. I hoped Papá wouldn't need any convincing to get me out of this marriage, but on my turf, I'd have a better chance of making my argument. "Your problem is not with my father."

"Nobody will try anything," Barto said. "You have my word."

Cristiano kept his eyes on him and sniffed. "It holds no weight."

I spread my hand on Cristiano's back to see if I could get him to relax. "It does to me," I said gently.

After a pause, Cristiano's shoulders eased. "Given he's family, I'll extend Costa the courtesy of going to him." He raised his chin. "You going to tell me how you got in here?"

"It could've been an inside job." Barto's mouth twitched, as if resisting a smile. "Do you trust your team?"

"With my life. I know you didn't have help from in here."

"Maybe I did." I'd never known stoic, dependable Barto for an antagonist, yet he clearly enjoyed having caught Cristiano off guard. "Or maybe I bypassed all your security measures, your walls, your guards, your team, all on my own."

"Then I'd suggest you come work for me," Cristiano said. "If I trusted you wouldn't knife me in the back."

"Then you have more sense than I thought," Barto said, and to me, "Go on and change, Natalia."

"You don't tell my wife what to do. You're lucky to be standing here after you broke into my bedroom. Any man who steals a look at my wife in her nightgown should enjoy the view. It'll be the only thing to comfort him on his way to hell."

Barto's lip curled, but he didn't move. "I've seen her in her pajamas more times than you ever will."

Cristiano stepped forward. I grabbed the back of his shirt as he looked Barto in the eye. "There will be no second warnings. Next time you enter my home, you're dead."

Barto's eyes shifted to mine. The determination in them both comforted and concerned me. Was it that he believed Papá would get me out of this? Or that he couldn't? Was Barto just reassuring me he'd never give up?

Cristiano and my father were each bullheaded—neither would back down until he got what he wanted. The question was whether Cristiano wanted me in this life as much as my father wanted to keep me out of it.

And whether what *I* wanted mattered to either of them at all—or if it ever had.

Cristiano let me tug him back. "Get dressed," he said under his breath. "Be quick."

I ducked back into the closet, where Jaz already had an outfit ready. "He should've killed him on first sight," she muttered, holding out a pair of lightweight jeans. "I don't know why he didn't."

"They trust each other, despite how it looks," I said as I drew my nightgown over my head. Neither man would've lowered his weapons and left himself vulnerable in the presence of a true threat. Jazmín, for instance, didn't know Barto at all, and if the way she kept a gun in one hand was any indication, she was prepared to send him to the grave before she ever gave him a chance to officially meet her.

"Who is he?" she asked.

"He works for my father. He and Cristiano used to run security together. Barto has never forgiven himself for my mother's death," I explained quietly, "even though he wasn't even in town at the time." I hooked myself into my bra. "He won't let anything happen to me."

"*Cristiano*, you mean," she said, frowning. "*He* won't let anything happen to you."

Right. Jaz was living in denial if she thought he was the hero here.

As I stepped into the jeans, she took a few steps toward me. "If this is some kind of trap . . . you won't get away with it. I promise you that."

I froze, staring at her. "If what's a trap?"

"You. Here. The marriage. All of this."

"*I'm* the one who's trapped." I balked at her. "Why can't you see that? I'm the victim, just like you."

"I'm no victim." She tilted her head at me. "You expect me to believe you're innocent? He's been acting different ever since we heard about the abrupt wedding. You think you can sit on his lap or touch his back, and he'll do whatever you say? I see what you're doing—using sex to get your way."

I blinked at her, racking my brain. "What are you talking about?"

"You can control a man with your mouth, but not by telling him what to do. Cristiano caves because he wants to believe he's found what he's looking for in you. I know better. I know all the tricks, *puta*. I had to learn them to survive."

My eyes widened. Tricks? *Me*? The accusation caught me off guard until the truth hit me—she was right. Cristiano showed me a different side when we were alone. And he *had* heeled just now when he'd agreed to go to my father's. More than once the night before, too, he'd been reduced to basic needs and desires I knew I could fill.

The pieces I'd been collecting fell into place. I hadn't purposely tricked Cristiano into anything. But I was more powerful than I'd realized.

None of that made me a whore, though. I was a survivor, just like Jaz.

"You and I are on the same side," I told her. "But if you can't see that, then we're opponents of your own making." I snatched my t-shirt from her, suddenly regretting I'd trusted her enough to undress in front of her. "And it's *señora de la Rosa* to you," I leveled at her as I pulled on my shirt. "Call me a whore again, and I'll have Cristiano throw you out."

"He would never," she said without an ounce of doubt.

I had far less confidence, but that didn't mean I couldn't fake it. I tipped my chin down. "Who do you think he'd choose?"

"Me, if he's smart. And he is. Smarter than you. We may be forced to wait on you," she said, "but we don't trust you. He lets you in his bed and drops his guard, but rest assured, if ever I come in here and find you've betrayed the man we consider our savior, you won't make it off the property."

She left before I could tell her to get out.

7

CRISTIANO

As we drove up the tree-lined road to the Cruz house, Natalia's father came into sight, his wrinkled face set in a scowl and his arms crossed over his chest. Waiting at the top of the front steps under the porch, he was tall enough to reach up and touch the metal sconce over his head.

Or rip it out and beat me with it.

If I hadn't known him almost twenty years, I might've been intimidated.

We parked on the rustic, Tuscan pavers Bianca Cruz had not only picked out but helped install herself—the way she'd painstakingly overseen every remodel or addition to this house.

As I exited the SUV, Costa raised his chin. "You'd better have one hell of an explanation, de la Rosa." Natalia jumped out of the car before I could get her door. Costa kept his eyes on me as he extended one arm to her. "Come here, *mija.*"

Natalia went to her father, looking up at him with big, hopeful eyes. "Papá."

"Did he hurt you?"

"No, but—"

He nodded shortly at me. "Talk. Fast, before I draw my own conclusions."

I stuck my hands in my pockets and sauntered up the front steps with Max at my back. Barto took his position by Natalia. She should be by my side now. I'd grant her and Costa this time to adjust, but I'd never been known for my patience. "Our houses are one now," I told him.

"If this is an effort to take over the Cruz cartel—"

"Not a takeover. A partnership." I glanced at Natalia. Once, it'd been part of my job to keep an eye on her. Now, I was finding it hard to look at much else. And as time went on, it seemed, she looked back with a little more defiance. And a little more familiarity. "If not for me," I said, "Diego would be dead."

"A sacrifice I'd be willing to make in exchange for my daughter's safety," Costa said.

"Then talk to him," I said. "But Diego didn't only jeopardize his own life. He put you, your cartel, and your daughter at risk. Until I stepped in. So you can thank me."

"He *has* thanked you," Natalia said, her cheeks beautifully flushed, her hair slightly undone, "by not wringing your neck for kidnapping his daughter."

Boldness agreed with Natalia. It always had, even when she'd demurred from it. But that didn't mean I'd step back and let her accuse me of *more* crimes I didn't commit. "Kidnapping? I didn't drag you down the aisle." And I wasn't the one who'd dragged *her* away from the door when *I'd* been trying to leave the room the night before.

God reward me for my restraint when my dick had been painfully hard against her underwear and begging for relief . . .

I cleared my throat and returned my eyes to Costa. "I've kept her alive. I've kept her safe."

Costa's eyebrows lowered along with his register. "And she wears a ring."

I nodded once. "A condition of our arrangement."

"Look at your daughter, *don* Costa," Barto said. "She's terrified."

Natalia cowered against her father. It was for show. Not since we'd left the church had she shown true fear. Even when she'd trembled against my body the night before, there'd been determination in her voice. One could even detect a hint of submission in the way she'd fallen against me during our kiss if one was looking for it.

And I was *always* looking for it.

Even if Natalia had been experienced enough to fake her arousal, she had no reason to. The kiss in the church, and then later in our bedroom, had swept her off her feet. She was right to be afraid of that, but she'd be wrong to deny it.

"I found her in his bed," Barto continued, "and seeing as she's hated Cristiano since the day she discovered him standing over Bianca's body, I can only conclude the worst. Will you let him get away with that?"

"Never. Cristiano will explain himself, believe me," Costa said, still staring at me. "I want her out of this life. What gives you the right to keep her in it?"

"I make my own rights." Now wasn't the time to assure Costa his daughter was safe from me—well, for as long as she resisted. Once she allowed herself to ask for what she wanted, I couldn't guarantee there wouldn't be some carnage, all of which she'd enjoy. "I'm not the one who put her in danger. I pulled her out of it. The Maldonados are no longer a threat, but that can be undone."

Natalia glanced briefly to the top floor of the house—

Bianca's old art studio—and I followed her gaze. She and Diego had spent time there as children, hiding from Bianca, playing when Diego should've been working.

Costa turned, steering Natalia into the house. "Go wait in your room. I'll talk to Cristiano and work this out."

"What? *No.*" She pulled away, looking up at him. "I'm not going to sit around while others decide my fate. That's how I got into this in the first place."

If she hadn't been trying to escape me, I might've applauded her. Natalia had been bent to the will of others since before Bianca's death, but it had only grown worse in the years after. Diego, her father, Barto and his security team—and even myself. We were all guilty of it. But as a kid, she'd stood up to me, a man with a reputation that would terrify most girls, with nothing but grit and determination on her side. And her White Monarch.

She had it in her to rise to the job of cartel queen, but the steel spine that ran in her blood needed space to grow. And encouragement.

"She should be present for this conversation," I told Costa as I followed them into the foyer.

"Of course. But let's you and me speak first." Costa kissed the top of Natalia's head when we reached the door to his study. "Go on upstairs."

"Let me rephrase," I said. "She *will* be present for this conversation."

Natalia turned to me, her light, purple-blue eyes wide like saucers. It was all the thank you I'd get from her, but I wasn't expecting anything more. Natalia had been a precocious and smart child who'd found a way around the rules and limitations put upon her. She wasn't anyone's pawn, but she'd let herself fall into that role for my brother.

Diego, who'd put his hands on her, knowing she was my future wife.

I tried not to think of it, because that was exactly what Diego had hoped to achieve by fucking her—to get under my skin.

Not to ease Natalia into her first time, and not to claim her for any romantic purpose before he released her. But to have something over me I could never get back.

Costa turned to face me, his chest out. "You're telling me what's best for my daughter?"

"No. I'm telling you what's best for my wife. She's no longer to be kept in the dark about this world, her life, or our cartels. She's in it now, as Bianca was."

Costa's expression pinched, and his eyes narrowed on mine as he seemed to read me like a book. He ushered Natalia into the study, but turned and lowered his voice so only I could hear. "You don't know what you're getting yourself into, son."

"I don't follow."

"Bianca never should've married me. Don't you think I knew that from the moment I set eyes on her? But I did. Marry her. And I don't have to tell you how much I loved her." He glanced into the study, and I followed his troubled gaze to Natalia. "I did all that knowing what the outcome could be—so some would say I got what I deserved. I worry for Natalia's fate as I did her mother. But I also wouldn't wish my pain or guilt on any man."

Costa was worried I'd get my heart broken, was he? Coming from anyone else, I would've laughed in his face. But the old man had gone through the worst of it, and he was protective of those he loved. Given our history, and mine with Natalia, it hadn't taken him five minutes to see that something flickered in me for his daughter. But he didn't need to warn me of the danger of attachments.

"Would you go back and change it if you could?" I asked.

His eyebrows sank. He took a step closer to me, each of us rising to our full heights, then nodded into his study. "Inside. Now."

Costa stood before Natalia and me like an emperor looking to make a head roll. With Max and Barto competing to guard the door, I stayed by Natalia's side, forming a united front with her, even if she didn't want that.

"Let me see if I have this right," Costa said. "You kidnapped and married my daughter without my permission, and in exchange, you're keeping the Maldonados from eliminating every last one of us."

"That's Diego's version of the story, so it's not entirely accurate. But the outcome is nevertheless the same—Natalia and I are married."

"Give me one reason I shouldn't have it annulled and put Natalia on a plane back to California."

I glanced sidelong at my bride. "I think that reason will mean more coming from Natalia herself."

Her eyes flitted up to mine, as if I'd called on her to recite the North American Free Trade Agreement. In Costa's bright, sunny office, her irises appeared violet. "Cristiano has agreed to cover Diego's—the Cruz cartel's —debt," she said, and turned back to her father. "Without Cristiano, the Maldonados are still a threat to all of us."

"Natalia understands this is greater than me and her. With this union, you and I are family. Our loyalty is to each other. You have my protection, not just against the Maldonados, but against anyone who dares cross us." I smiled tightly. "That would've always been true if I hadn't been forced from this home. We're stronger together."

"There were other ways of merging," Costa said.

"This way, we're respected as one family. With the exception of Diego, of course." I put my hands in my pockets and shrugged. "Thanks to me, the Maldonados have pardoned Diego. But he has not been pardoned by me—or you."

Natalia swallowed. "What do you mean?"

"We're partners now." I glanced from her to Costa. "Together, our families will accomplish great things. But Diego's no longer my family or yours. He has nothing left —you will cut him loose or the alliance dissolves."

"Diego has nothing left but this cartel," Natalia said flatly, as if she were concealing any emotion she might have about that.

Smart, but frustrating for me.

"A prison of his own making," I said, eyeing her. "I promised to let him live, nothing more."

"Despite his flaws, he's been loyal to us," Costa said. "Why would I cut free a good man?"

Anger simmered below the surface. I'd been treated like a criminal for eleven years, and Diego was *loyal*? He was *'a good man'*? "If Diego is a man, then I am a god," I said, "and which would you rather have protecting your family?"

Costa grunted, leaning his hands on his desk and looking over my shoulder at Barto. "Against Diego's advice, I welcomed you back into my life," he said, shifting his eyes back to me. "I trusted a man I wanted dead for over a decade. Since then, you have taken my daughter, stripped your brother of everything, and attacked my cartel as I sat across the dinner table from you."

I took a pack of cigarettes from my pocket and offered it to Costa, but he shook his head. "Regarding the attacks on your houses and tunnel, I wish it could've been different," I said. "It was necessary, and I'll repay you."

"You killed my men."

"A cost of doing business." If I were in Costa's shoes, I'd have security marching up here now to take me away, but he'd never been as sentimental about his army as I was mine. He treated his men better than most, but taking Diego and me in was the closest he'd come to forming attachments—and that had been at Bianca's urging. "I owe you a great debt—"

"You could let me go—"

"Not *that* great." I cut Natalia off and resisted from smirking, simply because Costa wouldn't see the humor in it. "But I will do what I can to mitigate the loss of good men. As far as the rest, you can place the blame where it belongs—on Diego."

"He said you'd say that," Barto spoke from behind us.

"He took a risk working with the Maldonados." I picked a cigarette and the lighter from the pack. I generally only indulged in smoking at the club, but I was feeling accomplished these days. "If Diego's deal had gone well, he would've made another and another until he'd eventually failed and put you all at risk. I just . . . sped things along."

"You don't know that he would've failed," Natalia said heatedly.

"I do. He wants more. He feels he's owed. That blinds him, and that's how mistakes are made." I winked at her. "If you can't see how I've protected you, consider my interference a preventative measure."

"Owed?" Costa asked. "What for?"

At one of the study's long, wide windows overlooking Bianca's garden, I lit my cigarette. She'd put a lot of work into the backyard, the roses especially. I pushed the window open wider, sat at the sill, and faced my new wife. My budding rose. "Diego's grievances against this family run deep, but I don't blame you for not recognizing that. He's a master of disguise and manipulation."

She glared at me. "Some would say that was you."

"He was never the loyal charge you thought him to be," I said, tearing my eyes from her to look at Costa. "I don't relish being the one to break that to you."

Costa came around his desk. "What're you saying?"

"I came to you as a boy when I was lost and in need of help," I said. "You brought me to this very room. We formed a plan. You trusted me then, and I'm telling you to trust me now. Diego never forgave us for what we did."

Costa drew back. "For your parents?" he asked. "That was years ago. He was—what—eight at the time?"

"He has seen it as a betrayal ever since. I set it in motion, but you aimed the gun, and you pulled the trigger. We each watched our mother and father die by your hand."

"Against Bianca's advice," Costa mused, walking to one of the other windows and looking out. "I did that to ensure you boys understood that even though I was taking mercy on you, I was the boss, and I was not to be fucked with."

I took a drag. "He has fucked with you. And me."

"Bianca warned me that could happen. She never worried about you," Costa continued, glancing at me, "but your brother . . . she wondered if seeing that had irreparably scarred him. I called her paranoid."

Natalia's eyebrows met in the middle of her forehead. "You never told me that."

"As I said. I thought it was bullshit, so after her death, I didn't give it much thought."

Out the window, I tapped ashes from my cigarette. "He sees us as responsible for the loss of his parents, his family's business, and perhaps most importantly—his legacy."

Costa returned to his desk, but sat against the front of

it this time, crossing his arms over his chest. "He blames you too?"

I nodded once. "He never forgave me for it."

"How would you know?" Natalia asked. "You weren't here. He was. He stayed by my father's side for almost twenty years."

"Diego is loyal," I agreed. "To himself, and his needs. Staying here suited him." I raised my eyes to Costa. "He's always been good with strategy, hasn't he? He knows when short-term sacrifice equals long-term gains."

I knew Costa was thinking of how Diego had convinced him to work with the Maldonados, despite the risk involved. The business they would've gained from such a prolific cartel would've set them up for years to come—if not for me, of course.

Natalia's defense of my brother was weak at best. She was listening to what I had to say, but until she could grasp the full meaning of it, her default was to act defensive.

But the doubt was in her. She was beginning to see the truth about Diego. As I tended to and nurtured her distrust, it would grow, and her devotion to him would shift easily. I just needed to cultivate a weak trait of my own to get us there—patience.

I studied my cigarette, considering the best way to word what came next. I raised my eyes to Costa. "Diego's plan was always to earn Natalia's love so he could use that against you to take your business."

Costa's response rumbled through the room. "That's a bold accusation."

He could call it what he wanted. It was also the truth. I'd waited longer than I would've liked to tell him that, and yet, it was Natalia's reaction I watched for. A flush worked its way up from the collar of her tight little t-shirt. Her nipples hardened when she was angry—interesting. Where would she direct her wrath?

"He said he didn't care about the business—he just wanted to save enough money so we could live comfortably," Natalia said, her jaw working back and forth. "He said we were going to California."

"I'm sure he also said he'd marry you." I inclined my head toward her left hand. The small ring was missing a diamond fit for a queen, but that was on its way. "And that he'd love you. Protect you. Yet here we are."

Her sexy lips twitched in frustration. "How can I believe a word you say?"

"Don't, then," I said, and looked to Costa. "Believe your gut. Logic and reason. Believe a man's motivations when he shows them to you."

Costa massaged his jaw, lost in thought. "How?" was his only response.

I brushed ash from my pant leg. "Diego lied to Natalia as part of a greater plan to make her love and trust him," I explained. "Then, when it came time, he'd ask her to choose. You or him." Natalia's face reddened. I did so enjoy when she flushed and blushed, such a desert rose . . . and I looked forward to watching her bloom under more intimate circumstances. "She would've chosen Diego."

"You don't know that," she said immediately.

"You chose Diego the moment you agreed to marry him against Costa's wishes."

She shut her eyes briefly. "*Papá*" wouldn't take kindly to this new information.

"What's he talking about, Natalia?" Costa asked. "Is that true? I'm sure it's not." His thick, graying eyebrows fell nearly to his chin as he leveled a glare on her. "Diego knows better than to propose marriage to my daughter. And she knows better, too. Don't you, Natalia?"

She turned fully to him. It didn't surprise me that she took a small step back in my direction. Suddenly my protection didn't sound so bad. "We had no choice," she said. "It was all we could think of to save the family. The Maldonados were closing in—"

"Get to the point," Costa barked. "When Cristiano says you agreed to marry Diego, what does he mean?"

A beat passed, and I resisted from jumping in. This was a battle Natalia had to fight, even though she wouldn't win. "Just as it sounds," she said quietly but without wavering. "It's the reason we were at the church on Sunday."

"How? Diego said Cristiano ambushed you after Mass."

"He did." She touched her ring, then stilled her hands, drawing up straighter. "But everything was already in place, because Diego and I had planned to do the ceremony right after. Quickly. Because the Maldonados—"

"Fuck the Maldonados. Are you telling me you were going to go behind my back when I *specifically* told you to stay away from Diego?" He took heavy, deliberate steps toward her. "When I forbade you from even *seeing* him again?"

"That's why we had to do it," she cried. "I knew you'd say no, and Diego told me it was the only way to save the family. If I'd come to you first, we might not even *be* here right now."

Costa and I met eyes over her head. "See what I mean?" I asked. "As soon as Diego realized he was in too deep and that I could make it all go away, his first thought was what—or whom—he could trade for his life."

"I just assumed that he . . ." She spoke to herself, her eyes on the floor. "He never actually proposed. I just assumed."

"Because he never intended to make you his wife," I

said as gently as I was capable of. "Only to make you *mine*."

As the level of his deceit settled onto her slender shoulders, I had warring urges to gather her in my arms and hunt down my snake of a brother so I could bring her his head. It bothered me to acknowledge that in this moment, especially with Costa looking on, distance was probably what she needed most.

She bent her head briefly, but picked it back up to meet her father's blistering gaze. "If you had listened from the start, I wouldn't have had to go behind your back."

"Then I suppose it's a good thing Cristiano was there!" he bellowed.

Even Max flinched, and I couldn't help a small laugh—the man had faced down far scarier men than Costa, but never an irate father.

Natalia whirled to me, fire blazing in her eyes. "Do you think this is funny?" She jerked a hand back at Costa. "Tell him, Cristiano. We were all in danger."

I looked to the back of the room—not to Max, but to the second ever invader to make it inside my home. The first, an overeager and overqualified *Federal*, was now on my team. Even though Barto and I had been tight-knit comrades once, I'd be a fool to trust him with sensitive information. "Privacy, please," I said to both men.

Max stepped to the door instantly, but Barto waited for Costa's signal before leaving the room.

Once the three of us were truly alone, I spoke to Natalia. "The threat was against Diego for the millions and millions he'd cost the Maldonados. Of course, that threat extended to the Cruz cartel. Costa knows that. It's why he was sending you away."

She glanced at her father. "I was doing what I thought—"

"But." I cut her off, and silence fell over the room as my audience waited. "Diego lied about the danger you both were in. I told him I'd make a deal with the Maldonados to protect you. To protect everyone but him. He was the only one who'd pay the price."

Natalia's face paled as she shook her head. "No. I don't believe you."

"In a final, desperate attempt for his life, he offered you up as my bride," I said.

Costa walked up behind Natalia as she began to shake, her fingers curling into balls. He placed his hands on her shoulders. "Why would you accept, Cristiano?"

"Our families would unite," I said. "We'd both become more powerful. You have a better infrastructure for distribution within México than I do—"

"Your business brings in far more than mine," Costa said evenly. "There's more to it than that. So why?"

My eyes drifted from his down to Natalia, whose gaze burned with anger. But for once, it wasn't directed at me. She had every right to feel enraged. I was, too, for her. In moments like these, stripped down, she was the young girl I'd silently protected from the wings. I saw the headstrong, smart woman she had become but which had been blunted by Costa, Diego, and a sheltered life in the cartel. I saw Bianca in her, as well as a woman I didn't deserve, but one I hadn't hesitated to take. And now that she was my wife, and I had decided I could—and would—keep her, I saw our future.

Costa leaned back on his heels, looking between us. "I see," he said, even though I hadn't responded.

"Diego promised he'd get her to marry me of her own free will, and she did, Costa. I didn't kidnap her. I gave her a choice—she made it."

Natalia's shoulders fell. Either she was still processing

the depth of Diego's betrayal or she was realizing that this deal was done, and Costa wouldn't save her.

I was torn. As I willed her to get back up and fight for what she wanted—always, no matter what—I also hoped this was one battle where she'd stand down. I would make her a good husband. And in order to get Costa on my side, I was willing to use all the tools I had to convince him of it. Without his blessing, I'd be forced to choose between the wants of a man I deeply respected and my own.

Costa had always known me to be a good man, even when I'd stood accused of murdering Bianca. If he'd ever truly believed I'd done it, I'd be rotting six feet under right now.

"Natalia knows she's free to walk away at any time," I said. "But if she does, I'll have no more stake in this fight. I'll be forced to walk away, too. I won't send anyone after you, but I can't promise they'll stay away." I glanced at Natalia, shifting on the windowsill. "As I've told your daughter, my protection extends to your family as long as it's mine. And that will remain true when threats like the Maldonados or Diego are nothing but an afterthought."

"And if we refuse?" Costa asked.

I flicked my lighter open and closed, darting my eyes between the two of them. "If I hadn't stepped in, Diego would've pulled off his deal with the Maldonados and made another, building his fortune. Knowing your objections, he would've convinced Natalia to marry him in secret by promising her the world—or in this case, promising to get her *out* of this world."

She took her bottom lip between her teeth, and I had to look away so I wouldn't be tempted to take her sexy, plump lip between *my* teeth.

"Once he'd secured her hand," I continued, trying to gauge Costa's reaction, "and her undying love and loyalty, he would've gone to you with an ultimatum." I paused, then returned my gaze to my wife. "If you didn't hand over the cartel, he would turn Natalia against you."

"I wouldn't have betrayed my father like that," she said. "And I wouldn't stay here and run the cartel with Diego."

"You would've protested . . . at first," I said, nodding. "But he works a long game, Natalia. And the proof stands before me." I tilted my head. "You agreed to give up your life in California. To marry Diego behind Costa's back. In time, there's nothing you wouldn't have done for my brother."

She shook her head. "That's not true."

I squinted at her with one final drag. "Once you were willing to do anything Diego asked of you, then *Costa* would have to do anything Diego asked of *him*."

"You make it sound like I'm just a pawn," she said. "I have a mind of my own."

"Just imagine if he'd gotten you pregnant."

She snapped her mouth shut.

"The leverage he would've had over you . . ." I inhaled a deep breath through my nostrils, more agitated at the idea than I would've thought possible.

And that motherfucker had come close.

Thank fuck for condoms and Natalia's good sense enough to use one—but she'd better believe I'd be inquiring after her period starting now.

Costa squeezed her shoulders with a dark chuckle. "Fortunately, that's not possible for a virgin."

"She's not a virgin," I said.

Natalia's mouth dropped open. "You *asshole*."

Costa flexed a fist as a much greater tide of anger rose in him than in her. I'd known Costa a long time and it had once been my job to read his moods, understand the things he didn't say, and anticipate his needs. He had a temper.

He cast her side and marched at me. "Tell me how the fuck you consummate a marriage with a bride who wants nothing to do with you."

"I haven't," I said, meeting his eyes, waiting for understanding to dawn. "You have my word—the marriage hasn't been . . . made official."

Costa's neck corded, another swell of rage overtaking him. He looked over his shoulder at Natalia. My mind flashed back to days earlier, when he'd found out she'd spent the night with Diego and thrown her to the ground. It would be the last time in my presence.

He paced toward her, seething. "Diego? He did this?"

I flicked my cigarette out the window and got to my feet, ready to intervene if necessary.

"*We* did this," she answered solemnly, her posture stiff. "I was there too."

"Is this a joke to you?" He blew by her and slammed his fists on the surface of his desk. "How could you let him?"

She flattened her palm to her breast as her chest stuttered, her confidence clearly shaken. "Because I *loved* him," she said, her voice breaking.

"Only because he manipulated you," I said.

"And what about *you*?" she accused, whirling to me. "You've gotten everything you wanted while taking my chance at a happy life."

With a deeply buried pang of guilt, my control slipped. "Then go."

Surprise momentarily flashed across her face, followed by resignation. She wanted to keep making me the bad guy. To make me into my father. I wasn't him, and I wouldn't let her reverse all the work I'd done to make sure of that.

"I warned you about this," Costa snapped at her.

Her chin wobbled. "I thought I loved him—maybe I still do. I don't know, Papá. He hurt me."

"*Qué chingado*, that motherfucking *bastard*." Costa swept his hands over the desk so everything in his path went flying. "I told you if he broke your heart, I'd kill him, and I don't make idle threats."

"I'm as responsible as he is." Natalia swiped a tear away, taking a breath. "It was my choice to make—you couldn't have stopped it."

Costa ignored her, turning to me. "I will ask you this once. By marrying her, do you have my daughter's best interests at heart?"

"Yes." I took a few steps so I could look him in the eye. "And no."

He frowned. "Excuse me?"

"I've always sworn to protect your family. If I hadn't been in the wrong place at the wrong time during Bianca's murder, I would've been here by your side every day the past eleven years." I paused. "I'll make it up to you now and deliver on my promise to Bianca that I'd protect her daughter—even against Diego."

Costa shook his head. "Bianca had her concerns about him. Though she accepted Diego into our family, she suspected he was hiding something, or that he resented us, and I knew the feeling—I had that same instinct. But his words and actions were always loyal, for so many years, and he never gave me reason to turn him out."

"He's clever that way. And he has something I don't— great patience," I said. "But that may be the only thing. I've got him beat in most other ways and now that your family is mine, your enemies are mine. Do I think Natalia deserves this life? No. But I do think she's made for it."

She flinched almost imperceptibly. It was a lot to take in; she needed time to process.

Costa's rage ebbed, but I knew it sat close to the surface. "I want Natalia to be with someone who loves her, treats her well, and protects her."

"Did Bianca have the same concerns about me that she did Diego?" I asked, because I had complete confidence how he'd answer.

"You know she didn't," Costa said. "She trusted you and thought you capable of great things."

With the word *great*, Natalia looked crestfallen. "You said you didn't want me with a good man, but a great one," she whispered.

Costa turned his head over his shoulder to her. "I did, yes."

"Then Bianca would support our union, as should you," I said, reluctantly peeling my eyes from her. "As long as Natalia's under my roof, you have my word I'll do my best to see her loved, treated well, and protected, as you've asked of me."

"Then under your roof she will be. But if I hear a whisper of harm against her, you will have a father's rage to deal with, and I don't think I have to tell you what that means."

"Understood."

I could practically hear Natalia's teeth grinding from where she stood, any despair vanishing. "You talk about me—my virginity, my *mother*, my past and future—as if I'm not in the room." She whipped her eyes to me. "Both of you."

She had been knocked down in this fight, but she struggled to get back up. Now that Costa had acknowledged her as my wife, I knew he'd take my lead. I nodded for her to continue, silently encouraging her.

"I have been traded between families, and brothers, even by my own father." She paused for a few deep breaths, struggling not to cry as she addressed us both. Her forearms tautened as she made fists and pressed on. "You can't tell me who to love, and you don't get to shame me for sleeping with Diego when it was *my* choice. It was my mistake to make."

Tension I hadn't even realized I'd been holding drained from my muscles. I exhaled through my nose as her words etched themselves into my mind. She knew she'd made a mistake. This early on, that realization was the best I could hope for. She may have been holding strong to the shreds of what she thought was love for him—I couldn't fault her that. It would dissolve and fizzle, because it was never real. But for her to acknowledge that Diego had betrayed her meant she'd soon be strong enough to push him out of the way for good.

And I'd be standing in his place.

"I am not your pawn," she said. "You can move me around, buy me, sell me, berate me, but you won't break me. I've known the greatest pain a woman can—first losing my mother, and then having my heart pulverized and my love violated so ruthlessly. But I haven't broken yet, and I won't."

She stormed out of the room and slammed the door behind her.

She was hurting, but I wouldn't pity her. She'd been bent but not broken, as she'd said. It was necessary in order for her to come back stronger and one day take her place as my queen.

Because now, there was no question she would be.

Costa had been my biggest obstacle in the way of this marriage.

Natalia was mine now, and nothing could change that.

For every door she slammed, I would open another. I'd pursue her. I'd break down that defiance until I found myself in her sweet core. She would cross over into the darkness. And I'd be waiting with open arms.

Costa pulled a box of cigars from his desk. "You say my enemies are yours," he said, picking one out. "But yours are also mine. And I've heard rumblings."

Belmonte-Ruiz. They were coming for me, and they had every right to. I'd been fucking with their business for a while now, but I'd gotten more aggressive lately. Before I'd ever known it would put Natalia and Costa at risk. It was a train I couldn't stop, and one I didn't want to.

"What you've heard is most likely true," I said, approaching the desk. "I have it under control, but I'm happy to bring you up to speed."

"Do." Costa slid the box of cigars toward me before cutting his own. "Tell me everything."

"There's only one thing to tell." I held up a cigar to the light and ran it under my nose with a long inhale, indulging in the ripe cherry and tobacco aromas. "I'm going to bring Belmonte-Ruiz down."

8

NATALIA

T he doors and windows to my mother's art studio had likely been shut since Diego's and my last visit. I hauled open the heavy curtains and let sunlight into the still and quiet room. Cacti and brush dotted the vast desert surrounding the house—a stark contrast to the mountainous, verdant, sea-misted landscape of my new home.

The familiar, dusty vista of my childhood did little to soothe me. Two men I'd trusted more than anyone, and one I barely trusted not to murder me in the night, had completely and utterly failed me. I'd had to fight simply to be in the room as Papá and Cristiano had discussed the trajectory of *my* life.

If I wanted out of my marriage, I couldn't rely on anyone else. What did getting out even mean? I couldn't run, so I'd have to step into the ring with Cristiano and pull no punches. Escape couldn't be physical, so it had to be mental. Emotional. In order to know what it would take to win against Cristiano, I had to *know* Cristiano.

When the door opened behind me, I closed my eyes. I

didn't have to turn to know it wasn't Cristiano—the air in any room shifted entirely when he entered.

I'd chosen the art studio on purpose. If Diego was in the house, he would find me in here, the room my father and his staff rarely entered.

"*Princesa.*"

I'd know Diego's voice anywhere. A confusing mix of anger, love, and hurt flooded through me—along with hints of relief. I realized I'd thought there was a chance I'd never see him again.

I turned around. Aside from dark stubble, he looked no better or worse than he had the day before. Our wedding day. His golden-brown hair swayed past his ears as he strode across the room.

Before I could process anything, he'd gathered me in his arms. "I knew you'd come up here, my sweet Natalia," he whispered. "Costa sent me to the ranch, but I couldn't stay away knowing you were here." He kissed my cheeks, nose, and forehead. "Hardly any time has passed since I've drunk from your lips, and yet I feel a painful thirst."

He pressed his mouth to mine. The familiar feel of his kiss comforted me. It would've been so easy to sink into. A day earlier, I would have. A day earlier, I had. But everything had changed.

More than ever, I wanted to ignore reality, but more than ever, I couldn't. And Diego was to blame for that.

I put my hands on his chest and pushed him away. "Drink from somewhere else, you . . . you lying, manipulative *bastard.*"

Diego's eyes widened as my own shock hit. I'd never called him anything close to that before.

He raked a hand through his hair and made a fist. "Natalia. I know you must be angry—"

"You tricked me." My heart pounded as I drew on the

strength I'd started to find in my father's study just now. "I showed up at the church like a fool thinking I was walking into eternity with you. I gave you my *virginity*."

"I know—let's just slow down," he said, taking my hands and bringing them to his mouth. "Please. You have every right to rail at me, but first, I just need to know if you're okay."

His lips warmed my knuckles as they had many times before. Before, when we were shy and new at this. Before, when we'd had to hide our developing love from others. Before—when I had been his. That mouth had soothed mine, had formed words I'd never forget, and now . . . lies I'd never forgive.

"Don't." I yanked my hands back and turned my face away. "I can't even look at you."

"You know I had no choice—"

"There's always a choice." Cristiano's refrain was bitter on my tongue because I hated to admit it was true. Diego'd had more of a choice than I had. He'd put his life and the lives of the people I loved on my shoulders. "You chose to make a risky deal. You chose to trade my freedom for yours." A vision washed over me—Diego climbing up the wood lattice to my bedroom. I'd been so scared he would fall. Now I wondered if it would've been such a bad thing. "You came to my bedroom and stole *everything* from me."

"*Tali.*"

I stepped back from him, resisting the pained way he said my name. "You don't even deny it."

He shrugged helplessly as if lost to some higher power. "I was scared if I told you what was going to happen, you'd make me leave, and we'd never get the night we deserved. I had no idea if it would be our only chance to—"

"So it's true." I'd hoped Cristiano was wrong, though

I'd suspected he wasn't. Hearing how Diego had plotted to deceive me made my skin crawl.

He swallowed as tears filled his eyes. "Forgive me."

"How can I? You made one of the most important decisions of my life for me. And I'm not even talking about the wedding." A wave of grief rolled through me. "You hurt me."

"I know."

The man who stood in front of me had never given me any reason not to trust him—until now. He'd wanted to know if I was okay? It was a simple question I'd answered countless times before. Too simple. Physically, I was unharmed. The last twenty-four hours had been a whirlwind of emotions from fear and anger to curiosity and even unwelcome desire. My request to Diego should've been straightforward—help me break free of Cristiano's chains. But as my expectations of the Badlands had been wrong, so was my trust in Diego also weaker than it'd been the day before.

I crossed my arms and moved to look out one of the glass doors. "You don't get to care how I am anymore."

Silence filled the room as Diego's eyes burned into the back of my head. "But you are okay," he said, as if it'd just dawned on him. Relief threaded his voice. "He didn't consummate the marriage. I knew he wouldn't when we made the arrangement."

My first reaction was to doubt him, but curiosity got the better of me. I glanced over my shoulder, and then turned to face him. "How could you have possibly known?"

"I put two and two together. He insisted you come to the church willingly. That extends to his bed as well." Diego massaged his jaw, looking to the side as if thinking over his next words. "Cristiano can't see himself as our father. He has twisted and manipulative ways of justifying his actions—even to himself." He paused and met my eyes. "You have to stay alert at all times, Natalia."

There was no other way to deal with Cristiano. Having a conversation with him was on par with navigating a chessboard. "I know that," I said.

"Do you?" He peered at me. "Because he's already coming between you and me."

"*You* came between you and me," I said.

"That's what he wants you to think. Who benefits most from a divide between you and me? Between Costa and me? I warned you Cristiano would try to do this."

I swallowed audibly. I'd always believed anything Diego had said. That he'd had my best interests at heart. Now, I questioned all of it.

But Cristiano had fed these doubts in my head. I'd be a fool to think he wouldn't play with my mind just like Diego would. Neither brother was innocent.

"He'll tell you I took your virginity to get back at him instead of the truth—I wanted one night with the woman I love. He'll say I plotted against your family." Diego was most handsome when he was pained—or acting like he was. His eyebrows met, wrinkling his bronzed forehead as he scrubbed his hands through his hair. "Fuck. If Cristiano can kill your mom and convince Costa he *didn't*—I wouldn't even be surprised if he tried to pin that on me, too. Just like he blames me for all the hardships he endured after he had to flee from here."

I had to look back out the window to keep from giving into him. With his serious, pouty frown and disheveled hair, still in the rumpled clothing he'd worn the day before, he was made to look tormented.

Cristiano *had* said, or insinuated, some of the things Diego accused him of. I doubted Diego's words now more than ever, but that didn't mean I trusted Cristiano, either. Who could I believe? At this point, I couldn't even put my fate in my father's hands.

"Cristiano said Papá and I were never in true danger— that he was willing to make a deal with the Maldonados so only *you* would pay the price."

"Of course he did. A convenient lie." Diego didn't even seem ruffled, as if he'd expected such a brash accusation by his brother. He approached my back, gathered my hair in a hand, and moved it over my shoulder before running a knuckle down my spine. "Please turn around. We don't have much time together, and I don't want to waste a moment not looking at you."

I closed my eyes. "Don't touch me."

"I have a plan."

I hadn't known I'd been expecting those words until he voiced them. I glanced at the ground, inhaling and exhaling through my nose. Diego had a plan—sure. But for long had it already been in play?

I suspected Cristiano would tell me it was time to join the game if I had any chance at winning. Diego's deception stung worse because I'd loved and had planned a future with him, but I had to recognize that things had changed. I could mourn the loss of him another time. Now, I needed to get my emotions in check, or else they'd consume me, and I'd never get my freedom back—from any of them.

I turned to meet Diego's soulful green eyes. "There's my girl," he said, smiling as if the past few minutes hadn't happened. He took my hands, slouching as he studied them.

This time, I didn't pull away. If Diego was as smart, cunning, and patient as Cristiano made him out to be, then he likely had either knowledge or a plan that could help me dissolve this marriage. Whether that meant finding a way to get Cristiano to lose interest in me or bringing him down from the inside, there had to be a way out.

Diego ran a thumb over my wedding ring. "It was my mother's."

I drew back. I'd assumed it was meaningless. "Are you sure?"

"Yes. I'm surprised he kept it." He frowned. "It means nothing to him, and it has no real value to a man of his wealth."

"Maybe it's sentimental," I said.

Diego squeezed his hands around mine. "He had her *killed*. I prayed to her, to Bianca, to my dead ancestors to keep you safe from him." He clenched his jaw. "My prayers have been answered. You remain mine. Your heart, soul, and body."

I wasn't his. Not anymore. It hurt for me to admit that, but his betrayal had been too thorough. It was also liberating in a way. I had only myself to look out for now. "Belonging to Cristiano leaves no room for anyone else," I said. "You must know your brother has a possessive side."

"But you *are* mine, first and always. It's written right here on my body." Diego shifted our grip to expose his small tattoo, our initials along the inside of his ring finger. "You're what I want, Tali. Try to hold my brother off. Make sure he knows you don't want to sleep with him, and he'll keep his distance."

"What do you *think* I've done?" I asked, slipping my hands from his. "Begged him for it?"

Except, I had. And I might've rubbed it in Diego's face if I wasn't so ashamed of it. That not only had I begged for *my* life, but also for the life of a man who'd traded me, who'd used me.

But worst of all, I had fallen into Cristiano's kiss.

Nearly melted at his touch. And then begged for his destruction. His desire had incited my own.

I'd felt Cristiano's carnal need against me more than once, and it was undeniable. Diego might think Cristiano would wait, but there was a line, and Cristiano would cross it. The question was who would be in control when he did —him or me?

"I'm sorry. You're right." Diego wet his lips, glancing at mine as if there was a chance in hell I'd give in to a kiss. "I'm soothed by the fact that I'm still the only one to have you. And if all goes according to plan, I will be the only one."

I lifted my chin. I wanted to know the plan. Not because I thought he'd be successful, but because any information was power—and if I was going to save myself, I'd need all the power I could get, wherever I could grab it. "How are you going to get me out?"

His mouth slid into a smile. "All those snooping skills you've been honing will finally be put to good use."

My scalp prickled. "I can't snoop in Cristiano's house. If he catches me . . ." I didn't need to finish my sentence. A leak in any cartel would be plugged and sealed as fast— and as ruthlessly—as possible.

"You're as stealthy as anyone I know. I need you to look for information on a cartel."

"The Maldonados?"

"No, not those hotheaded idiots—although, continue to ask Cristiano about them. It will distract him." He inclined his head, growing more serious. "The Belmonte-Ruiz cartel is more organized. They know what they're doing."

Belmonte-Ruiz. Was that the "BR" Cristiano had mentioned on the patio the night before?

"Tali?" Diego ducked his head to catch my gaze. "Do you know something about them?"

I hesitated. Cristiano had trusted me with information our first night together—a privilege I'd rarely been afforded with Papá, and one it had taken me years to earn with Diego. Even though Diego had finally confided in me about the Maldonados, it was clear now, given my current situation, there was just as much he *hadn't* told me.

For the first time, I didn't know where my loyalty lay. It wasn't with Cristiano, but that didn't mean it was with Diego.

And I didn't need to be told that anybody outside of a cartel was an enemy to that cartel—and anybody who fed enemies information might as well be dead.

"I've never heard of them," I said, and it wasn't a complete lie. "Who are they?"

"I've told you Cristiano and the Calaveras are deeply entrenched in the sex trade," Diego said. "His cartel has been ambushing and stealing Belmonte-Ruiz shipments."

"Shipments?"

"People."

Blood drained from my face. That aligned with what Cristiano had said the night before—that payment was a courtesy and next time, he'd take the shipment. I was disgusted but not surprised he'd referred to *people* so callously.

"Why would he do that?" I asked. "And how is he getting away with it?"

"He's hard to get to. Hard to bring down. That's where you come in. If you confront him, he'll just spin it some-how." Diego got a cigarette from his shirt pocket, then seemed to think better of lighting it. "Play dumb, but act smart. Listen. See. Hear. And report back to me what you find so Belmonte-Ruiz can do the dirty work."

I shook my head. "I'm not doing anything until you tell me exactly who they are."

"Belmonte-Ruiz?" He stuck the cigarette behind his ear. "The most successful traffickers of forced laborers and sex slaves in the country."

The contents of my stomach turned over. "Why would I want to help them?"

"You don't. But they have more reason than anyone to bring Cristiano down. He's costing them money and resources and making them look like fools." Diego glanced over his shoulder and lowered his voice. "Nobody on Cristiano's team can be bought. Trust me. They're loyal dogs. But you're in a better position than any of them. Be my eyes and ears on the inside, and I'll handle getting Belmonte-Ruiz the information they need to take out Cristiano and his business—and to free you."

Diego wanted me to snitch. I didn't need Cristiano to tell me not to go through his things and not to repeat anything I'd heard. Anyone who'd grown up around here, no matter how sheltered, knew that narcs were one of two things—undiscovered or dead.

If Diego was willing to risk me getting caught going through Cristiano's things, that told me two things.

Whatever he felt for me, it wasn't selfless, and that meant it wasn't love.

And that this wasn't a plan to save me, but to save himself.

"And then what?" I asked, to see what he'd say.

"And then we go to California like we planned."

I would've laughed if it didn't hurt so much. I'd wanted California and that life with Diego more than I'd wanted anything except my mother back. California seemed like a distant dream now, though. And if I was honest, it felt *wrong*. The perfect life I'd had there suddenly and starkly contrasted with the dire fates of the women whose lives were being played with by warring cartels.

Diego checked the door again and reached into his back pocket. "Come here, Tali."

Curious, I inched closer to him. He hooked a finger into my waistband and tugged until we were face to face. "Diego," I warned. If Cristiano caught us like this, we'd both be dead. "I told you not to touch me. I don't want you to."

"I know you're scared of how my brother will react, but don't lie and tell me you don't dream about our night together."

Even before all this had come to light, I hadn't thought about the sex we'd had much at all—I was too busy trying to survive. And now, thinking of it only made my mouth sour. "I don't think about it. I can't."

"Then maybe I need to refresh your memory," he said quietly, lowering his mouth to my cheek. "We could steal away into the closet for a kiss."

His hot breath on my cheek made my heart pound. It wasn't exciting. It felt calculating, as if he were trying to get something from me. And even if I'd wanted to have a few final moments in fantasyland, the thought of Cristiano bursting in kept me firmly rooted in reality.

"He will cut off your hands," I said to Diego, trying to take a step back.

"Wait." He kept his finger hooked in my belt loop. Reaching between us, he slipped his hand into my pocket, where he deposited something rectangular. "You'll need this so we can stay in touch. A burner phone."

"Diego, I can't," I said, swallowing as my nerves flared. "Cristiano will find it."

"Then make sure he doesn't. I've disabled the ringer. Delete any text conversations we have immediately. And if he does find it, it won't reveal anything. It has only one number in it—mine. It's saved under your dad's name, though."

"He'll never buy that."

"You're smart and resourceful. Convince him, Tali. I've seen how he looks at you, and you don't even realize the power you have over him. Over both of us." He cupped my cheek, thumbing the corner of my mouth. "If he's about to find the phone, if his hands wander somewhere you don't want them—redirect them. Use his desire for you against him."

Diego was woefully naïve when it came to his brother's prowess. Cristiano could not be misdirected or distracted when he set his mind to something. And if I were going to use my sexuality against anyone, it would be on *my* terms. Not Diego's.

"I believe in you," he said. "I'll do everything I can on my end to make Cristiano pay for putting you in this position."

With one hand on my cheek, he slipped the other around my waist and leaned in.

I pulled back, trying to wriggle free. "Stop," I insisted. It felt strange to deny him when only days ago, I'd have done anything for a few minutes alone with him. "I told you not to touch me."

"That's Cristiano talking, not you." He tilted my chin up, waiting until I met his eyes. "You're only giving them what they want. First your father, now my brother. They're determined to keep us apart."

"Determined?" I heard behind me. My heart leapt into my throat as Diego's eyes shot over my head. Slow, controlled footsteps echoed through the room. I closed my eyes, knowing what I'd find when I turned around.

Knowing how bad this looked, and that *I* would pay the price, not Diego.

"*Determined* is not the right word," Cristiano said. "Try resolved. Hell-bent. Try this—I'll stop at *nothing* to keep you two apart."

With deliberate movements, I pushed the phone as deeply into my pocket as it would go. I didn't even want it, but I couldn't let Cristiano see it.

I turned around. Everything about Cristiano was buttoned up—not just his suit jacket and perfectly knotted tie, but his tense frame and locked jaw betrayed his discontent.

"We were just talking," Diego said.

"That's not the way it looks to me." He kept his eyes on Diego. "Come here, Natalia. Behind me."

Leaving Diego's side would expose him to his brother's wrath. *Good.* It was becoming apparent that Diego would use my body as his shield as long as I let him, but Cristiano used himself as mine now—just as he had that morning with Barto.

I went to Cristiano, whose dark, endless eyes bored into mine a moment before he shifted them back to Diego. "And what did you talk about?" Cristiano asked him, dark, sinister amusement lacing his words as he moved in front of me. "The weather?"

Diego smirked. "We spoke of the impossible."

Cristiano didn't stop until they were face to face. "I'm not in the mood for riddles."

"I said there was no way you'd pleased her more than me," Diego said, lengthening his spine. "And she said you had. That she'd never been so satisfied as she was on her wedding night because her groom never touched her."

"*Diego*," I said, covering my mouth. I had shared that in

confidence. I was already going to be in trouble—why make it worse for me?

Cristiano grabbed Diego by the shirt. "I hope those ten minutes alone with her were worth it. Now tell me which hand you'd prefer to lose."

"Enough," came a bark from the doorway. I turned as my father took a few measured paces, his expensive loafers silent on the wood floors.

Cristiano released Diego with a shove.

"Cristiano has *attacked* me." Diego fixed his collar, looking to me for backup. I wouldn't offer it—not to either man. "He has attacked your family," he continued, "and proven what I've known all along—he isn't the man we once knew."

"None of us are," Papá said, pausing at my side.

In that moment, they were two wards of the cartel, standing before their fed-up *jefe*.

Papá sighed as if he carried the weight of the world on his shoulders. "When night falls, I'm alone in the dark with only my character. The choices I've made, if I've kept my word—and whether I've stayed true to myself and my instincts."

I looked up at my father as lines crinkled around his eyes. He wouldn't end this. The deal was done. He was the man in my life, but today, my trust in him had eroded just a little.

Cristiano gave a satisfied rumble from his chest. "What do your instincts tell you, *don* Costa?"

Papá looked between the both of them. "Leave my home. And don't return."

I didn't have to see which brother his eyes had landed on, but my nerves flared nonetheless. A day ago, I would've fallen to my knees and begged my father to pardon and

forgive the boy I loved, but Diego's sins were too great—
and his betrayal had cut this family too deep.

"I am not the enemy here, Costa," Diego said, a
tremor of panic in his voice. "You're alone at night
because you lost your wife. We may never have hard
evidence Cristiano was behind it, but you know in your
heart he was."

"I know in my heart that he wasn't," my father said.

He'd said it before, and his mind was made up. I
hoped, for my sake, he was right.

Diego narrowed his eyes. "You seem to forget Cristiano
blew up one of our tunnels and killed a number of our
men at the warehouse last week—an attack which almost
took Natalia, too."

"A nearly inexcusable offense," my father agreed. "But
one you're guilty of as well, since you made the deal in the
first place. Cristiano has promised to make it up to me."

"I'm not the enemy," Diego repeated with conviction.

"No?" Papá asked, fisting his hands. "You never planned
to fuck me over? Never thought about it?" His body seemed
to grow bigger beside me. "Never wondered what it might
be like to back me into a corner—and use my daughter to do
it,"—his voice boomed so loudly, the windows nearly shook
—"and break her heart and *fuck her* when I explicitly told you
to stay away?" He thrust his finger at the door. "Get out!"

Diego's jaw looked painfully tight as he stared at us.
Hearing my father talk about me that way, my cheeks
burned with the heat of a thousand suns, and I wished for
a trapdoor to open up and swallow me.

"You nearly got us all killed," Papá said evenly, but no
less threatening. "You went behind my back and tried to
take Natalia from me."

"And I failed." Diego seethed more quietly than my

father. "But Cristiano succeeded. He's the one who's fucking her now—in more ways than one."

Cristiano turned his head, looking cool and collected, but his neck corded. For a moment, I thought he might make good on his promise to remove one of Diego's body parts.

"And that's no longer your concern," my father said. "My instincts—and those of my beloved wife, God rest her soul—tell me this is where you and I part ways, Diego."

And that was it—Papá's word was the final one. Barto waited by the door, and Diego was forced to walk through his past—by his brother, his benefactor, and his lost love— and toward as uncertain a future as mine.

"May God protect you when I can't, my love," Diego said softly to me as he passed. He glanced over his shoulder at Cristiano. "And may He protect you from the devil—as He has me."

I was beginning to learn it wasn't God's job to protect me, and it certainly wasn't Diego's. Even Papá hadn't been able to reverse this. The job was mine. I wanted to go back to the way things were—to fall into Diego's embrace and believe that he'd fix this. To let my trust in my father over-flow as it always had. But they had both failed me, and the sting was fresh. Neither had given me any reason today to believe he wouldn't fail me again.

I was on my own.

9

NATALIA

Taking the terrain at a higher speed than we had yet, I jostled in the cab of Max's pickup truck on our way back from my father's house. We sailed over rocks and potholes right up until we entered the gates of the Badlands and Max slowed down.

Cristiano had taken two calls during the ride home, neither of which had offered anything of value with his monosyllabic responses.

When Max parked out front of the house, Cristiano spoke his first words to me since we'd left my father's. "Wait there."

As he came around to my side of the car, he removed his jacket and undid his cuffs. He opened my door, rolling up his shirtsleeves and looking expectantly at me.

"What?" I asked.

"You will always sit in the car until I come to the door for you. It's a show of respect."

"You can't command respect," I said. "It has to be earned."

He took my waist and spoke low in my ear as he lifted

me from the truck. "Put your claws away. I'm the one showing *you* respect."

"I'm not a dog." My feet landed in the dirt. "You don't have to train me to stay until you tell me to come."

"Only time will tell," he said.

I wasn't on my feet two seconds before Cristiano spun me around by my shoulders and yanked my back against his body. He wrapped an arm around my front and something cool and flat pressed against my neck.

I lost my breath entirely, my body registering a millisecond before my mind that he was holding a knife. He knew. He'd seen Diego press his lips to mine. He'd seen him slip the cell phone into my pocket.

"Wh-what are you doing?" I managed.

"I'll tell you what I'm *not* doing," he said, his voice pure grit and gravel in my ear. "I'm not standing here shaking like a leaf, letting panic overtake me. That's what *you're* doing."

"Why?" I choked out. "Why are you doing this?"

"Does anyone need a reason to hurt you? Scare you? Touch you against your will?" He marched me forward to the lawn in front of the house. My heart pounded painfully as I felt the phone against my hip with each of our long strides.

"I'm sorry," I pleaded.

"For what?"

"For betraying you."

He paused, and I could've sworn I felt *his* heart beat against my back. "When did you betray me?"

"Diego touched me, but I told him not to. I tried to stop him."

"And you think I'd punish *you* for *his* gutless actions?"

When I swallowed, my throat moved against the blade.

I was afraid to even speak. I sure as hell wasn't going to nod.

"*Do something*, Natalia." When I didn't respond, he growled. "I said fucking *do* something."

Tears filled my eyes. I didn't know what he was asking. Did he mean something sexual? But I was firmly in his grip. I'd made a grave mistake dropping my guard with Cristiano for even a moment. Now, we were going to consummate the marriage as I'd wished—but with a knife to my throat.

I closed my eyes and moved my hips back against him.

He inhaled a sharp breath and threw the knife on the ground. "If that's your move, then I won't say no." He laid a heavy hand on my shoulder. "Get on the ground, face-down, so I can fuck you."

"No," I cried, my throat protesting. "Not like this."

"You're grinding against my dick, Natalia. What did you expect?" He tried pushing me to my knees. "Get down or fight back."

"I c-can't," I said. "I can't fight you."

"Then I'll teach you how," he said, releasing my shoulder and stepping away.

I clutched my throat, whirled around, and backed away as a tear slid down my cheek. "*What?*"

"I wanted to see what you'd do in that situation, and I have to say, Natalia—I'm sorely disappointed. You wilted like a flower. I thought you were a survivor."

"Fuck you." The unbidden words rasped from me as tears built in the back of my throat, but I wouldn't take them back. "What's the matter with you?"

"I could've beaten you. Raped you. Slit your throat. And you didn't even try to stop me." He picked up the knife, wiped the blade along his pants, and sheathed it.

"Nobody should ever be able to touch you against your will, Natalia."

"You're the only one who would," I shot back.

"And you stand there and let me, trembling and freezing up the way you did last night."

I gritted my teeth, anger overtaking my fear. "What am I supposed to do?" I accused. "I'm half your size. You're probably five times stronger than me."

"Yet I possess the same weak spots you do, *mamacita*. You just need to know where they are." He looked almost amused as fury burned through me. With a smirk, he said, "Show me the self-defense moves you learned after I stole you away into the tunnel you eleven years ago."

"What are you talking about? I don't know any."

"As I suspected." He shook his head at the ground. "Your father threw you on the ground. Diego tried to kiss you earlier when you told him not to. And me? I don't have to tell you I could've done any number of things to you back in that tunnel—as I could right now. What's it going to take to get you to fight back?"

I shuddered as I stared at him, but not just with after-shocks of fear. He made me sound completely helpless while conveniently ignoring the circumstances. "I may never even *see* Diego again," I sniped at him, "so you don't need to worry about him touching me."

"Fuck him. This isn't about Diego. It's on you." Cristiano's chest rose and fell a little faster as he cracked his knuckles. "It never occurred to Costa to teach you how to sever a brachial artery or handle a handgun? It never occurred to *you* to learn to defend yourself?"

I removed my fingers from my throat, but the ghost of the cold metal blade remained. "I *did* defend myself. I left this life. You're the one who brought me back in."

"If your father had ever upset the wrong people . . . don't you think they'd have been able to track you down in California? Did you think that precious, flimsy bubble you created for yourself would keep you hidden? You don't know the simplest self-defense. Can you even operate a bottle of pepper spray?"

"Is there more to it than point and spray?"

"For fuck's sake, Natalia." He ran a hand through his black, normally smooth hair. Now that he'd disheveled it, it stuck up. "Given the malfunction rate, taking a few minutes to learn would behoove you."

"I was doing just fine until you took me." I scowled. "Why are you teaching me this?"

"Do you think I want a wife who'll crumble the moment an attacker puts his hands on her? I need you to fight back." The edge to his voice faltered as he added, "I need you to save yourself and come home to me."

I drew back. Cristiano wanted to arm me . . . but did he not realize I could use what I learned against him? There was almost something *romantic* in his response, and despite the heat, a shiver worked its way through me. "What if I *am* home?" I asked. "Barto got in."

"Believe me, I'm aware. I wasn't planning to work on this with you so soon, but today was enough to open my eyes to the fact that I can't be everywhere you are all the time."

That was why he'd reacted so aggressively, then. And scared the shit out of me just now. Not that I was about to admit that I probably wouldn't have taken this little lesson so seriously otherwise.

He widened his stance and looked down his nose at me. "First, you have to change your mindset. You're in control of your life. You *can* take down an attacker of my size. With a knife to your throat, you might get cut, you'll likely get hurt, but you *can* fight for your life and escape. Come here," he said.

"No."

"Get your ass over here *now*."

I took a moment to catch up and process what was happening. Cristiano was *actually* going to teach me this. How to fight. How to protect myself. That was something nobody else had ever given me. Not even Mamá. Protection had always come from someone else. But as this morning had proved, I couldn't always rely on others. That put me at risk. And Cristiano, apparently, wasn't having it.

I exhaled and stalked toward him until we were toe to toe. "Now what?"

"Turn around."

When I did, he carefully enveloped my shoulders and drew my back against his front. He positioned the sheathed edge of the blade to my neck again. "Show me how you'd fight me off."

I grabbed his forearm and pulled, but he didn't budge.

"You can't compete with my strength," he said, "so don't try."

"Then I'd kick my heels into your shin or aim for your groin."

"Don't tell me," he said. "Show me. It's how you'll learn."

I stomped on his foot, but his shoes must've had steel toes for all the good it did. He just laughed. I couldn't angle to kick him, so I bucked my hips back into his groin.

"You're moving too much," he said. "Either you just slit your own throat or gave your assailant a hard-on."

Without thinking, I pinched the skin of his forearm between my teeth.

"You're a biter," he said. "I sort of suspected you might be . . ."

My tongue flickered over his skin, tasting salt. To my horror, my nipples tingled. I removed my mouth to see I'd left a red mark.

"Usually," he said, "your chin would be locked by my forearm. I'm just not holding you as tightly as I would if this were real."

"Maybe you should," I said and mimicked, "How else will I learn?"

"Relax, Rocky. We'll get there. I'm just walking you through it now." He strengthened his hold. "If you were ever in this position, it'd likely be a planned attack. But not necessarily. Given what we do, your attacker could easily be drunk or high—his pain tolerance will be elevated, and he won't be fazed by a nibble, or, depending on what he's on, something as severe as a stab wound."

"I wouldn't 'nibble' an attacker," I said. "I was demonstrating on you."

"Next time you demonstrate," he said low and gravelly in my ear, "feel free to sink 'em in. I've been looking forward to unleashing your wild side."

"That makes one of us," I muttered.

I felt his silent laugh against my back as he straightened. "If you're going to rely on inflicting pain, you'd better not miss, and you'd better not be half-assed about it. If you go for the eyeballs, gouge them. If you bite, draw blood."

I shuddered. "You're going to teach me to gouge out someone's eyeballs?"

"No. Max is," he said. "He's an expert at it."

"What a weird expertise," I said.

"How do you think he got his glass eye?"

I shuddered. "Yuck."

"Yeah. Anyway, the point is—if you try to hurt the assailant and fail, you'll only anger him." Cristiano repositioned the knife under my jaw. "Listen. You don't want the blade to go sideways or up, or else you're dead. So what does that leave?"

"Down."

"Right. Now, the weakest part of me within your reach is my wrist. Sneak your hands up—slowly," he added as I followed his instructions, "so I don't know it's happening. If you can create some kind of diversion—asking random questions to distract him, for example—that helps, too."

I slid my hands up the front of my body. "Have you ever been to Disneyland?" I asked.

He barked a laugh, and I seized his wrist. "Not yet," he said. "Now pull down, away from your throat."

"I just did that. I'll never be able to budge you."

"That's why you have to know a man's weak spots. My forearm is a bar—you won't move that, but with practice, you *can* move my *wrist*."

I didn't see how that was possible, but I tried. I focused on the weakest part of his wrist until I'd drawn the knife a short distance away. "Like that?"

"Yeah. Now trap my forearm with your right shoulder, and rotate—no, don't twist," he corrected. I resumed my original position and tried again with less *twist*, and more *rotate*. "This is where you leverage your body weight," he said. "Always put your body into it. Rotate toward me."

Since Cristiano wasn't using his full strength, I was able to keep a hold on his wrist and turn into him, contorting his arm at an unnatural angle so the knife was now aimed at his side. "Then you'd stab me," he said. "Keep going."

I glanced up at him. "Stab you?" I asked hopefully.

He raised an eyebrow at me. "No. Keep *rotating*."

I reversed under his arm, bringing his wrist with me until he was forced to bend at the hip, and I was standing over him.

With his face inches from my hip, I suddenly remembered the phone. My heart, already thumping, began to pound as his eyes shifted.

How would I explain it if he found it? Would he even give me a chance to?

My mouth dried as possible punishments ran through my head. Cristiano had earned his nickname, *El Polvo*, for a reason. The Dust. He'd poured sand down the throats of those he'd deemed deserving of a slow, painful death—and no doubt he'd find a certain poetic justice in that particular fate for a snitch with a big mouth.

"Wrestle the knife from me if you can," he said.

I released my breath finally, praying I could get upstairs soon and stash the burner.

"But if not," he added, "at the very least, you can knee me in the face and run away."

I released him. "You'd catch me."

"I would, yes." One corner of his mouth quirked as he straightened. He looked almost comical in a loosened tie, wrinkled dress shirt, and slacks, with sweat dotting his hairline. "But we're going to train you so *nobody* can catch you, *mariposita*."

"Who's we?"

"Solomon, Alejandro, Max, me. We all fight differently, so you'll learn from each of us." He unknotted his tie and slid it off. "Your main goal is to incapacitate the attacker long enough to run away," he said. "You're tall but skinny —we're going to build up your strength so you can fly. Solomon will teach you to assess the situation and make a quick decision—outrun him, stab him, or knock him unconscious. It'll depend."

"Kill him?" I suggested.

"If that's what it takes," he said grimly.

"Who's Solomon?"

"Our resident expert on martial arts. As former Israeli military, he's got experience in street fighting, Krav Maga, Muay Thai, and more." He sniffed, wiping his upper lip on his sleeve. "Let's try again."

"Are you sure you're up for it?" I asked. "I'm not the one breaking a sweat."

He scowled. "I weigh twice what you do, and the sun is fucking strong today."

I shrugged, not bothering to hide my amusement as I turned my back to him.

As his arm surrounded my shoulders, and he pressed the knife to my skin, he said, "Natalia?"

"Yes?"

"If we're going to keep doing this, don't wiggle your hips. It won't do either of us any good if I develop a conditioned response to holding a knife at your neck."

As his meaning registered, I flushed and glanced at the ground. "I *didn't* move my hips."

"Maybe it's a subconscious way of physically preparing yourself, but either way, make it stop." He raised the knife, forcing my eyes up. "Be stealthy," he said, "but don't hesitate. You're not grabbing my wrist—you're yanking it. Use speed, leverage your body weight to bring it down."

"Cristiano?"

He shifted behind me. "Hmm?"

"Did you know, according to Jewish folklore, a pomegranate has exactly six-hundred-and-thirteen seeds?"

"What?" he asked. "I—"

With his wrist firmly in my grip, I rotated, and this time, while we were tangled, I poked the sheathed blade into his ribcage. "Bang, you're dead," I said quietly.

His eyes met mine over his shoulder. A moment in our shared history passed between us. I'd just repeated back to him the words he'd said to my nine-year-old self in my parents' closet before he'd whisked me away down the tunnel.

"Who knew pomegranate trivia could save your life?" he asked, and I was grateful for a reprieve from the gravity of the memory.

"The name Solomon made me think of it." We separated, and I was surprised to find myself out of breath. At least I'd have more than enough free time here to get in shape. "Supposedly King Solomon had his crown modeled after a pomegranate. Thank you, religious studies," I said. "Can I see the knife?"

His eyebrows rose. "Not yet."

"Afraid I'll hurt you?"

He removed the knife from its leather case and showed me the fine, smooth edge that ended in a sharp point. "You'll hurt one of us if you try."

"So that's it?" I asked.

"For today, yes. It's an introduction to get comfortable with panic. If we reenacted this for real, you'd be dead before you even registered what was happening." We briefly met eyes, and he added, "I don't want that, so you'll have to learn how to stay calm and practice these moves until you know them with your eyes shut." He turned the blade, and it caught the light. "When I'm not here to practice with you, Alejo or Solomon or someone else will."

I squinted up at him. In the sun, his coal-black eyes were closer to the color of coffee beans. "You don't want me dead?" I asked, testing out how it felt to tease him.

He put the knife away and wiped his hands on his pants. "Of course not."

"Just trapped." My humor faded. I glanced beyond the cliff, out toward the Badlands' gates.

With a knuckle under my chin, he gently turned my face back to his. "I want to make sure you're prepared," he said. "At some point, you may find yourself in a position where you'll need to defend yourself."

I'd *already* found myself in that position. "What makes you think I wouldn't use what I learn against you?"

Searching my eyes, he lowered his hand back to his side. His demeanor shifted away from its rare lightness— espresso beans darkening to pitch black. "Dinner will be served shortly." He turned toward the house. "Wash up."

10

NATALIA

inner will be served shortly. Wash up.

D Like any other command from Cristiano's mouth, he'd ordered it nonchalantly and with no room for argument.

It wasn't nonchalant to me.

Balanced on the edge of his bed after our impromptu street fight, I waited for him to vacate the shower. Since the day before, I'd been married off, shuttled to a new home, shuttled back to my father's, told this was my new life, and held at knifepoint.

And now, Diego was trying to turn me into an information mule. I'd wrapped the phone in a bra and shoved it to the bottom of my overnight bag until I could decide what to do with it.

Use his desire for you against him, Diego had said.

Wiggling my hips against Cristiano had been enough to get his attention. It was becoming obvious it was important to him that I be willing, but I was sure his patience had a limit. A perverse side of me wanted to tempt him just to prove that he was no better than his father or brother. That I was here because I had to be, and that he'd fuck me against my will with no more thought than he'd give to fucking me against a wall.

But did I have the guts?

I tiptoed to the bathroom, careful to stay out of view. In the mirror, I could see the hazy outline of his bronzed, naked form through the steamed-over shower door.

He flipped off the water and stepped out before I could retreat. "Well, well," he said, nude and dripping on the bathmat.

My face burned. I was mortified, but for some reason, I didn't want him to know it. I fought my instinct to run and hide in the closet and held his gaze instead.

I could face him.

Just as long as I didn't look down.

He grabbed a towel from a hook and came around to face me, scrubbing it through his hair. "How long were you standing there?"

"I just walked in," I said.

"Two minutes earlier, and you would've gotten a show."

He wrapped the towel around his waist, and it was then I realized I'd been clenching every body part that could be clenched—teeth, fists, ass cheeks. I urged myself to relax. "I don't know what that means."

"I'm not used to sleeping next to a woman I can't touch," he said. "It makes things a little hard . . . *¿Comprendes?*"

It took me a second, but inexperienced as I was, I understood. It literally made *things* hard. "Because you have no privacy?"

"The physical contact we just had downstairs isn't helping."

My heart thumped. I'd felt it, too, but I wasn't about to

admit it. And I'd been right. His patience was too thin for him to wait for me to be willing.

Not that I ever would be, I reminded myself.

"Good to know holding a knife to my throat turns you on," I said.

He arched an eyebrow and went to the mirror, inspecting his stubbled jawline. "Shower's all yours. There's a towel on the counter."

I picked it up, went to the closet, and closed the door so I could strip down. I found a deep drawer with a hamper in it, dumped my clothing inside, and secured the towel under my armpits before returning to the bathroom.

Still wrapped in his own towel, Cristiano stood in front of the mirror and shaved up under his chin. His back was not only tan and smooth but very broad. I wondered if he lay down, whether it could fit two of me. I'd never seen anything like it, the way his muscles rippled beneath the surface, the embodiment of his capabilities, his weaponry —his power.

"You . . . you won't look, will you?" I asked, pulling my towel tighter.

With his head tilted back, he lowered just his eyes in the reflection. "If I do, I'll have to jerk off again, and the shower's occupied."

I frowned. "In a house this size, surely you can find somewhere else to . . . do that."

He rinsed the razorblade. "Is that an invitation to look?"

"No."

"Why shouldn't I?" he asked. "You belong to me."

"I don't belong to anyone."

"You're Natalia de la Rosa. You bear my name. You've said vows in front of God."

"That doesn't make me your property," I argued. I

didn't know why I bothered when he was clearly *trying* to get under my skin. "Are you *my* property?"

His eyes had moved down to my bare legs. "Sorry, what?" he asked.

"Selective hearing," I mumbled, opening the shower to turn on the water.

"It's cute," he said.

I glanced back. "What is?"

"How you're worried I'll only *look* at you."

He was capable of so much more, as he'd proven out front. I was no match for his strength, and no matter how he trained me, I never would be. As if my feet were made of lead, I suddenly couldn't move. "You said you wouldn't force yourself on me."

"I did say that." The razor scraped his skin. "But I can change my mind, can't I."

It was a statement, not a question.

A reminder.

A threat.

A bluff?

If Cristiano had wanted to take me, there would've been no better opportunity than our wedding night. He could've dominated me if that got him off, or given himself permission if he'd needed it once I'd begged him to get it over with.

But he'd held back.

If he truly thought of me as property, he would've staked his claim on me. I was the one in command, and I suspected he knew I was nobody's property.

I dropped my towel. He froze, keeping his eyes on mine. My heart pounded as I bared myself to him. As I showed him my body on my own terms. As I demonstrated for him that I retained a small measure of control, no matter what he said or did.

It wasn't until I'd turned and stepped into the shower that I released a massive exhale. The last man who'd seen me that way had turned around and passed me off like a baton. I'd shown Diego much more than my body that night—I'd exposed *all* of myself and had held nothing back. At least, the self I'd been days ago. I hadn't been enough. And I was pretty sure that was a good thing.

I shook as I stood under the stream of water, but at least I still stood.

But the problem with testing Cristiano's control was that I didn't know what might break it. Once he crossed the line, then I'd know where I stood. I'd know for sure who he was. I'd know my place here. His restraint put me in a frustrating limbo.

He talked a big game, but so far, he'd only smiled when it came time to bare his teeth. I needed him to break. To show his true colors.

I couldn't beat a monster I didn't know.

———

At dusk, the back patio glowed with strung white lights, and a square, candlelit table set for two. I'd found my way here on my own since Cristiano had disappeared while I was in the shower, and I hadn't seen Jaz since that morning.

A temperate evening with an air of romance suited the long, floral, strapless dress I'd bought in Mexico City a few summers earlier. I'd found it hanging on the back of the closet door after my shower. Cristiano sat at the table, an ankle crossed over one knee as he scrolled on his cell phone. His shoulders were as high as his eyebrows were low. This time, he definitely didn't sense me standing there. I'd snuck up on him—a first.

I recognized the tableware as fine china and silver, impeccably set in the organized manner my mother had tried to teach me as a girl. A bottle of white chilled in a marble wine cooler.

"Are you expecting company?" I asked from the doorway.

The frown he'd been wearing disappeared as he slipped his phone into the pocket of a white, linen dress shirt open at the collar. His eyes drifted over my dress. "*Hermoso*. It's beautiful."

I smoothed my hands down the front of the dress. "The staff does all this for you?"

"For us." He stood and pulled out the chair next to him. "Sit."

I walked by him to the seat across his instead, to the only other place setting. "It seems someone prefers me to sit here."

He reached over and grabbed the corner of the placemat to slide it next to his. "Yet I have the final word."

In all things, I was sure. I took my place beside him.

"Wine?" he asked, drawing out the frosty bottle of Sauvignon Blanc.

My mouth watered for a taste—not of the alcohol but of an escape. A way to dull my senses. But I had to be sharp as a tack to keep up with Cristiano. "No, thank you."

"It's French. Or would you prefer something of the Russian variety?" His eyes twinkled the way they had the night at the club, when he'd pulled two shots of chilled Siberian vodka from nowhere.

"I find myself suddenly on the wagon," I said.

"*¿Qué significa?*" He made a face. "What does it mean?"

"Sober," I explained.

"Ah. Probably wise, but I hope you don't mind if I partake." He poured himself a glass and didn't bother to look, smell, or swish before taking a gulp. "That was quite a show earlier," he said, examining the glass. "I don't know whether to thank you or spank you for it."

My breath caught in my throat. "Why would you spank me?"

"You thought it would rattle me. And it did. I enjoyed it, but that doesn't mean I condone it."

"It was only fair. You showed me yours, I showed you mine." I put my napkin on my lap, averting my eyes. "Now we're even."

He snorted. "Hardly. You didn't even look."

"You don't know that."

"If you'd seen what I've got to offer, you'd either have dropped to your knees to give thanks—or fainted."

I gaped at him. "Your arrogance knows no bounds. Diego was—"

"Nothing compared to me." His mouth slid into a sinister smile.

"Such humility," I mocked.

"I know when to be humble and when it isn't necessary. In this case, I know what I have." His eyes drifted over me. "But I have yet to know my own wife. Though I'm certain she has no reason to be humble, either."

"I'm not a piece of meat," I said.

He picked up his knife and scraped the blade across the tongs of a fork as if sharpening it. "*Bon appétit, ma chérie.*"

Hunger glinted in his eyes, but not for food. It wasn't the first time I'd pictured him devouring me like an animal.

The chef stepped onto the patio and set down a plate in front of each of us. "*Escargot à la Bourguignonne* in garlic-herb butter. Enjoy."

I frowned at the dish, confronted with the first of the many horrible rumors I'd heard about the Badlands. "Are these . . . ?"

"*Escargot*," Cristiano said blankly. "Have you been to France?"

"No," I said, wondering how a half-dozen snails had made it onto my plate. Tepic had warned of satanic rituals like this—but compared to what my mind had conjured up, this was fairly ordinary. I couldn't help it—I started to laugh.

"What's so funny?" Cristiano asked. "Snails are a delicacy in France."

"I know. It's just . . . I heard these rumors about Calavera."

He used a two-prong fork to remove the meat from its shell and dip it into the sauce. "Well?" he prompted.

I pinched one between my tongs. "I heard your cartel is like a cult."

"What's that got to do with snails?"

"You eat them and other strange foods, then you speak in tongues, sacrifice virgins, and throw rotten fish at whores."

Cristiano chewed, nodded, and didn't deny any of it. "I suppose to people who'd never been outside of México, likely those spreading these rumors, foreign foods like drunken shrimp, bratwurst, bird's nest soup—or snails— would seem strange."

"So that's all there is to it?" I asked. "What about the other rumors? Are they true?"

"I know when to keep my mouth shut." He swallowed and sat back in his seat. "So if I address them for you, you give me your word what I tell you doesn't leave this house."

My laughter faded. Suddenly, I wasn't sure I wanted to know. Surely not all the rumors were as innocuous as French food. That would mean facing the truth about my time here.

"Oh, no," he said, shaking his head as he read my

expression. "You don't get to back out now. Tell me you can keep my secrets. I intend to have all your secrets, too, so it's only fair."

I thought of the mission Diego had charged me with. If I accepted, from this point on, I'd be passing along sensitive information I'd been sworn to keep. At least last night, I hadn't yet agreed to anything.

So who had my loyalty?

After today, there could be only one answer. Me. I was loyal to myself. I couldn't trust the reasons why Diego wanted the information, but I wasn't going to kneel for Cristiano, either. Nor would I give up the phone just yet. As of now, it was my only communication with the outside world.

I glanced at the table and back up. "You have my word."

"Fisker—*oye*," he called out. "How many languages do you speak?"

The chef sauntered onto the patio wiping his hands on a dishtowel. "Fluently? *Cinco, señor.*"

"So that's Danish, Spanish, English . . .?"

"German and Swedish. And some French." He turned to me. "You look surprised, *madame*. But it's very common where I come from, and in the Badlands too."

"My men are from all over the world. They speak everything from Russian to Chinese to Swahili." Cristiano gestured at Fisker. "In how many languages can you say snails?"

"In more than I speak. *Escargot, snegle, caragols de terra, slakken, caracoles*—"

"This is Natalia's first experience with them."

"Ah, but you requested them?" he asked Cristiano, who nodded. Fisker turned to me and added, "Butter is the key. Dip generously."

Cristiano dismissed him with a "*Merci.*" When we were alone again, Cristiano said, "To an uncultured ear, some languages, especially all at once, might sound—"

"Barbaric," I finished.

"But what's *barbaric*," he said, "is the Scottish wedding ritual I partook in last year."

I glanced up, my eyebrows cinched. "What was it?"

"Our Scotsman found himself a lassie, and in his super rural part of the country, they have some outlandish customs. The bride and groom are blackened with soot, feathers, and more, and paraded around the night before the wedding to ward off evil. We then covered the bride in the worst things we could find, like dead fish, sausages, and curdled milk . . . and tied her to a tree."

My jaw tingled as he sat there chewing his food like it was no big deal. "That's disgusting," I accused. "How can you allow that?"

"Should I judge someone else's culture? They have their ideology, and she was a willing participant. Some people might find it strange that you and I were lassoed."

"No one more than me," I muttered.

He chuckled. "The happy Scottish couple was married right here on the property, and they're expecting a son next month."

"So how do people know what happens in here if nobody has lived to tell the tale?"

"Rumors find a way, and that's not true, anyway. People can leave any time they want, but most choose to stay."

I didn't know enough yet to say if that was true, but why *would* they stay?

"And drones," he added. "We capture or shoot them out of the sky on a regular basis, but occasionally I'll allow one to spy on us—if I think it helps."

I was almost afraid to ask. "Helps . . .?"

"Let the people talk," he said, waving a hand. "That's my logic. What the idle mind conceives is far worse than what I can do. If people want to believe we have no internal compass for right or wrong, and that we'll brutalize intruders who would do us harm, I won't correct them."

I blinked. Either he was fucking with me or he was fucking with the world. "You *don't* brutalize intruders?"

"Who'd do us harm?" he asked, sucking his teeth. "Of course we do."

I narrowed my eyes. "What about the virgin rumor?"

"Well." He dipped another snail. "That I'm not sure about, although I have some ideas where it started."

I studied him a moment, then finally gave in to the aroma of garlic and butter and picked up a shell. I followed his lead, extracting the meat and dunking it in the sauce. It looked even slimier drenched in melted butter. I stared at it, steeling myself to put the creepy crawler in my mouth.

"Are you sure you don't want wine?" he asked with a hint of a smile.

I tested the snail with my tongue, but all I tasted was the flavoring. "I'll have a little," I conceded.

Cristiano eyed me as he poured Sauvignon Blanc into my glass. "I chose this meal for a reason."

"To rattle me?" I asked, mimicking his earlier accusation.

The corner of his mouth twitched. "No. It's a tribute to your mother, actually."

I froze with the tiny fork in front of my mouth. Hearing anyone talk about her was enough to catch my attention, but walks down memory lane were few and far between. Diego hadn't known her very well, and Papá could be stingy where emotions were involved. Cristiano was one person with actual memories who I'd never been able to talk to about her. "What?"

"The meal I had prepared for you tonight is one Bianca made for me once, start to finish, after a trip to Paris with your father. I had snails at your house—imagine the reactions of my brother and the others at the ranch when I told them *that*."

I could only imagine. Diego had often shared rice and beans from a community vat. "Was I there?"

"Yes, but you were too young to remember."

Sadness tugged at my heart as I shook my head. "I *don't* remember."

"There's probably a lot you don't."

As much as I wanted to hate Cristiano and anything to do with him, the food before me took on new meaning. I put it in my mouth and chewed, and though the gelatinous consistency was unnerving, it wasn't nearly as gross as I'd thought. With warm butter and garlic, it resembled seafood.

"Imported from California," Cristiano murmured. "Like my young bride. I look forward to teaching you about the world."

I had to stop from warning him his arrogance was showing. Perhaps the women he normally dated weren't very worldly, but he knew my parents had liked to travel. "I've been places," I said smartly. "And I've spent more time than you in North America. I can show you some things, too."

"Of that I have no doubt." His gaze darkened. "But I have fourteen years on you—and believe me, I intend to use them."

Fourteen years, several countries, and likely countless

women in his repertoire. How was *I* the one who'd ended up here? "Do you have other wives?"

His eyes nearly fell out of his head before he bellowed a laugh. He seemed more and more relaxed as the night went on—more than I'd ever seen him. Was it the wine, or something more? "That would make me a polygamist," he said.

"It wouldn't surprise me."

His smile faded instantly, and he blinked his gaze toward the pool a few moments. "Fear not. You are my one and only," he said and cocked his head as I glanced at my plate. "You look disappointed to hear that. Do you want me to keep other women?"

"I'm sure it doesn't matter what I want," I said. "You didn't come to bed until, like, three or four this morning I think. When you left the room, you were suitably . . ." And without warning, I lost my breath remembering the ravenous way he'd trapped my body, whispered in my ear, and probed the aching spot between my legs. He *must* have gone to see another woman—and how had he treated her? With the same hot and cold regard? Had he pretended she was me? Had he *wished* she was? "It doesn't take a genius to figure out where you were," I finished.

"And where was I?"

"Is there a brothel in this 'town'?"

"I don't pay for sex."

"Maybe Jazmín then," I said. "She's beautiful, and very loyal to you, it seems."

Cristiano rubbed his jaw, watching me. "I must say . . . if you're wading into the waters of jealousy, I quite like it. I like it very much."

"Jealousy?" I mocked. "That a man who would rape me probably raped someone else instead?"

"Jealousy," he said in a corrective tone, "of a woman

who doesn't want her husband with anyone else. Even if *she* doesn't want him."

I picked up my drink and took a sip that half drained it. "A tribute to my mother," I said, shaking my head into the wineglass. "What a crock of shit."

"I beg your pardon?"

"I think you made all that up about my mom to toy with me."

The pocket of his shirt lit up with a call. When he made no move to answer it, I said, "Your phone is ringing."

Fisker stepped onto the patio with our next dish. "Duck confit," he announced, delivering an aromatic, beautifully presented duck leg with caramelized apples in front of me.

Cristiano sat back in his seat, his eyes suddenly glued to me as he reached into his pocket and appeared to send the call to voicemail. "Don't wait for me," he said. "Go on."

I started to say it was impolite to eat until he'd also been served—but who cared about manners at a time like this? Politeness was almost a form of capitulation, of following rules set by someone with more authority than me. I picked up my fork and knife and took a bite.

The rich, tender meat and crispy skin instantly transported me to my past. I'd eaten this before at my mother's dinner table, right before she'd passed. "This is familiar."

"I suspect you haven't had it since childhood," Cristiano said.

I looked up at him and took longer than necessary to chew so I wouldn't have to admit I'd jumped to conclusions. Maybe he *was* taking me for a walk down memory lane—but why? Another mind game?

And to what end? To make me feel safe?

Even if it was a game, memories of my mother were more temptation than I could resist—they'd always been hard to come by. In the years following her death, my father had grieved fiercely but privately. At some point, that had changed, but it had always been rare to find him in a state that he could open up about her. Most other adults who'd known her weren't the sort a young girl would pepper with questions.

How much did Cristiano remember? How much was he willing to share?

And what would each revelation cost me?

"She made this for you?" I asked.

"Everything Fisker will serve tonight, she made." He looked down on me in a way that made me feel like he was imparting wise advice. "Who cooked for you in the years before you went to boarding school?"

"The staff or myself," I said. "But Papá wasn't this adventurous. We mostly stuck to regional dishes. Things he grew up on."

"I figured as much."

It was strange to think Cristiano had figured anything at all. "You wonder about my diet?" I asked with a hint of a smile.

"Mostly how things were after her death. After I left," he said. "What do you remember about her?"

I frowned at him. "What do *I* remember?" I asked. "A lot. More than I can say by dessert."

"Then tell me about dinnertime."

Studying him, I used a napkin to pat sauce from the corner of my mouth. I wasn't sure what he was getting at, but maybe my memories would trigger his. "She hummed when she plated the food. That's how I could tell when it was time to eat." I could still remember the tune, though I never hummed it aloud. It took me to a simple yet blissful point in time I'd never be able to get back to. "She always served herself last. I think she was lactose intolerant because I remember her getting stomachaches if we had cheesy meals, and she never liked ice cream."

"Sometimes she brought *queso fundido* to the ranch," Cristiano said.

"With chorizo." I smiled sadly and took a sip of wine. I wanted these memories, but they were also little knives in my heart. What hurt the most was the time we'd lost. I would never completely know my mother, the kind of woman she was as an adult—the friend she would've been. Seeing her through others' eyes was the best gift I could receive.

I hoped Cristiano understood I was grateful, even if I couldn't bring myself to show it. I suspected he did. "Why did she like you so much?" I asked.

He paused as if caught off guard, and it took him a moment to answer. "I like to think she and your father were both great judges of character."

"I like to think that, too, which is why their regard for you is so confusing."

His mouth parted with surprise before he breathed a laugh. "Bianca took me in. I owed her my loyalty, and she knew she had it."

"What kind of man turns his back on his own family to fight for their enemy?" I asked.

"Listen . . . I don't pretend to be moral in any way. Much of what I've done is inexcusable. But some things are so vile, they can't be forgiven."

"I agree," I said, raising my chin. If he had stopped his parents' descent into human trafficking, how could he excuse himself for the same crimes?

"She trusted me," he continued after a moment.

"But why?"

"It's not hard to gain someone's trust; it's just too easy to lose it. I tried to be there when she needed me. I never lied. I was forthcoming. When she and your father disagreed, I didn't automatically side with him. I told them what I thought was right. I always did with Costa, even if I knew he wouldn't like the answer."

I glanced toward the kitchen as Fisker brought Cristiano a plate. He dug in before the chef had even turned his back. "What did you and Papá disagree on?"

"Not a whole lot, but I remember once," Cristiano said, gulping down a mouthful of fowl with wine, "he wanted us to light up a location. He thought it housed two gang members responsible for a drive-by that took out some of our men. He was trusting his gut, but I was trusting mine, too. Despite his order, I wouldn't move until I had proof."

Though Cristiano was as calculating as Diego, it was in a different way, and I couldn't quite put my finger on why. Most men around here shot first and aimed later. "Why not?"

"Costa was right—the men were in there. But I was right, too. There were also women and children in the house who would've paid the price if we'd attacked."

Maybe that was it. Diego looked out for himself, and Cristiano looked out for others. Which was nice and all, except that nobody seemed to be looking out for me. Diego had acted in his own best interest by offering me up, and Cristiano in his by taking me.

"Weren't you so noble, then?" I asked, sitting back. "And I suppose you feel that Diego and I forced you into a life you'd once looked down on."

"Only as much as I have forced this life on you."

So what did that mean—we were even? Hardly. Even if he'd been wrongly accused and pushed out of the cartel, at least he'd had his freedom. "Do you still think you're the voice of reason?" I asked, my temper rising. "Did you think if you cornered me, you could then convince yourself that you had *saved* me?" I rolled my eyes. "Maybe you hoped I'd see it that way, too."

A server I didn't recognize cleared our plates as we stared each other down.

"Did you roll your eyes at me?" It was a warning more than a question. Cristiano grabbed a toothpick from a tin and stuck it in his mouth. "You're certainly brave for someone who thinks I'm capable of murder on a whim."

That image of him didn't match the man sitting in front of me, who'd restrained himself many times over in the weeks since he'd returned. Who was he? How long until he showed me? I was rolling my eyes and sniping at him because I was *frustrated*. "I think you still need me, so you're playing nice," I said. "I just don't know why, or for how long."

"I never needed you."

The cutting words snipped at my already short wick. "Then why am I here?" I retorted.

"Because I wanted you."

My heart thumped beneath his suddenly darkened gaze. All playfulness evaporated from between us and in its place was whatever inexplicable charge had existed the night of our costumed dance. Of the morning he'd bandaged my feet. Or of any time since I'd arrived when I'd been under his spell.

"I told you that merging our families through marriage wasn't my idea. I have no *need* for you and your family. Only desire." He relaxed into his seat again and chewed on his toothpick. "I took you, yes. The idea of having you as my bride appealed to me for several reasons. But now, I can't imagine things any other way."

11

NATALIA

As Cristiano paced by the pool on a call, I rationed what remained of my wine. I picked up the glass. Backlit by the turquoise pool, it glowed ethereal blue. It was tempting to drown myself in the wide, generous wineglass after the day I'd had, but I had to be smart.

I'd wasted too much time being gullible. I'd hated Cristiano for his elaborate plan to get me to the Badlands, but it was Diego who'd orchestrated the whole thing. Forty-eight hours earlier, I would've sworn on my mother's grave it wasn't possible.

But I knew it was the truth.

As I tilted my glass, watching the translucent liquid pool to one side, I recalled something Diego had told me before we'd slept together.

I'd have to be willing to promise him anything to get him on our side. Even if I don't mean to keep those promises.

Now, thanks to Cristiano, I was thinking like Diego. If he were here now, he'd spin the tale in his favor. He'd tell me he'd promised Cristiano the world to get him to agree to help us, but that he'd planned all along to free me once the coast was clear.

I righted the wineglass. Two more sips, I decided, but then I'd stop. I doubted I'd get tipsy after the snails, duck, mixed salad, and cheese, but I wasn't taking any chances. Reading a man like Cristiano required my full, unadulterated attention.

Especially when *I* had *his*.

I drizzled honeycomb over blue cheese, impressed by the meal we'd just eaten. Recreating world-class fare my mother had made might've been a way for Cristiano to distract me from the truth of my situation—but the walk down memory lane was welcome nonetheless. It was as close to time spent with her as I'd get.

Cristiano made his way back to the table, tucking his phone into his shirt pocket. "I have to leave town for the next couple days, so we're going to go over some things."

And of all people, I had brash, taciturn Cristiano to thank for my night with Mamá. Not that I would.

I swiped my index finger through the remnants of honey on my plate. "Rules?"

"If that's what you want to call them."

"You already told me the first one—don't die."

He slid his chair from the table and sat. "Be kind and courteous to the staff. It's not their fault you're here, and they just want to make you comfortable—that includes Jaz."

"I have no problem with Jaz." I drew a sad face on my plate, then sucked honey off my finger. "She has a problem with me."

"She's, ah . . . protective."

I didn't miss the way he stared at my mouth or momentarily lost his words. This was what Diego had meant by redirecting Cristiano's attention where I wanted it to go. "Protective of . . .?" I asked softly.

He inhaled and looked away—which made it hard to mesmerize him into spilling his secrets. "Of me. And herself. She wants to be here, if that's what you're getting at."

"Why?" I asked.

"Gratitude." He dipped his head, his eyes darkening. "And, of course, reparations."

A sense of unease worked its way through me. Was Jaz indebted to him somehow? Or he to her?

"Courteousness should be obvious," he said, "as should this—you're to stay on the property."

"Are these just the rules while you're gone?" I asked.

"They're the rules until I say they're not."

"So I'm confined to this house for my foreseeable future?"

"Correct. There's plenty to keep you occupied here."

"Such as?" I asked.

"There's a game room, movie theater, indoor pool. Just let one of the staff know what you want to eat. If we don't have it, they'll procure it."

Hanging out with a staff who was paid to be here didn't appeal to me. I missed my friends. It felt strange to wonder about companionship when the day before, I wasn't even sure I'd have a proper bed or a warm meal.

He leaned back in his seat, drumming his fingers on the table. "Anything a girl could ask for, and I suspect it's still not enough. We also grow fruit, vegetables, and flowers out back if that interests you."

"My mother liked to garden," I said, but of course, he'd know that. I'd never tended my own, but I'd helped as a kid, and it'd been a long time since I'd sunk my hands in fresh soil. "That's something, I guess."

"Landscapers maintain it, but you can help as long as you stay between there and the house."

"Who will I talk to?"

He winked. "You can always call me."

"I don't even want to talk to you when you're here."

"No?" He gestured away from the table. "You're free to go up to our room."

Our room. He was mocking me. I stood, and he eyed me as if he knew my next move before I did. Perhaps he did. He'd called my bluff. Cristiano's company wasn't ideal, but it was preferable to being alone. The more time we spent together, the more likely he was to open up. Learning as much as I could about him and this place could only be valuable. Somewhere, somehow, I was going to figure out how to pull the pin that would implode this cartel like a grenade—or at least its leader.

Cristiano had spent an entire day with me when he surely had better things to do, and I couldn't fathom that would happen very often, so I had to seize what time I had.

I sat back down. "Arguing with you is more stimulating than staring at a wall," I reasoned. "Barely."

"Every day, you'll continue learning self-defense," he said, resuming our conversation. "That should keep you busy." He ran his tongue along his front teeth and added, "But I suppose I could also arrange to have one of your professors brought here if you'd like."

My jaw dropped. I could never forget for a moment the all-powerful reach of a kingpin in this world. "Oh my God. You can't just keep . . . *taking* people," I said, blinking rapidly. "Especially not an American professor. It's not right—it's unfathomable."

He set his elbow on the table and massaged his jaw. "I—"

"People have lives and families and—and dreams and

goals." A fleeting vision crossed through my mind—palm trees in the wind, coolers of beer on the California beach with my friends, even all-nighters at the library before finals. And that all had amounted to what? The same life I'd had as a child. Occupying myself in a big house while keeping one eye over my shoulder. Losing all that was bad enough. Now, I was putting others at risk? "That professor could be a mother or father. Do you have any idea the uproar—"

"For Christ's sake, Natalia." He sighed heavily, dropping his face into his hands. "I didn't mean I'd *kidnap* him. I'd make him an offer to come and teach you." He glanced up. "I'd *pay* him. A far superior salary to what he currently makes. At least double—whatever it took."

I scoffed to hide my laugh at how wistful I'd become over his suggestion. "Oh."

"*Oh*," he echoed. "Not everything has to be done with brute force."

"And I'm sure a professor would feel perfectly comfortable turning away someone like you from his doorstep."

He rested his hands on the leg crossed in front of him as his mouth turned down. "What does that mean, 'someone like me'?"

"You're twice the size of some men. Anyone would be right to feel intimidated by you."

"You don't."

"*Of course* I do."

"Not really, though," he said. "Is it because you grew up around me?"

I gaped at him only a moment, then shut my mouth. I wasn't going to indulge him in a conversation about how scared or not scared of him I was. That was just another way for him to exert power. Since I didn't care for the direction of the conversation, I changed it. "How do you know Barto won't break in again?"

His knuckles whitened around his shin. "Max and I are taking care of it."

"You know how he got in?"

"We have video."

"So you know?"

He narrowed his eyes. "We're still reviewing it."

That was a *no*, and I could see it bothered him. I sipped my wine, using the glass to hide my smile. "Are there cameras outside the house?"

"Of course, and after Barto's little show, we'll be installing more as soon as possible. Inside and out."

"So you and your men can watch me at all times of the day. I'll never have any privacy." My jaw tingled. "Perverts."

"We're not per—it's for your own safety." He inhaled through his nose and flexed his hand a couple times. "No man will ever lay eyes on your naked body again."

"What if I strip down right here in the middle of the patio? You're telling me there aren't cameras here?"

"You wouldn't, but my team knows when to look away anyway. You have my word."

"Your word doesn't exactly mean much," I pointed out.

"Then consider that shielding you from them isn't for your peace of mind. It's for mine. If Max ever looked at you, he knows I'd remove his other eye."

"Why?" Now that my basic needs had been met, I could focus all my attention on the man in front of me. Who he was, what drove him, what held him back. That would only help me navigate whatever was coming my way. "You've told me I'm only yours, and you haven't even touched me. Why do you care what happens to my body?"

"Because I'm selfish and possessive over what's mine."

"This home is yours, and you share it with others. You invited half the town here last night."

"And you think I should invite half the town to your body?"

He'd never. I pushed the unbidden thought away, irritated I'd assume there was any horrific thing Cristiano wasn't capable of. Maybe he'd been possessive, and even protective, since he'd returned to town—but that didn't mean I was safe with him. "I thought when I came here, I'd be treated like your other women."

"What women? I don't own anyone else," he said, wetting his lips with a hint of a smile before it vanished. "How are women around here treated?"

"Worked, passed around, sold."

The flash of irritation over his face told me more than words could—I'd poked at something he didn't like. His brows lowered. "We don't treat anyone that way, no matter their age or sex."

"Just me then. How many women have you sold?" I asked. "Is that why you go to Russia?"

His eyes shuttered. "I'll answer your questions in time, I promise. But not when you're on a mission to malign me."

"I'm not," I said, relaxing into my chair as I ran a fingertip along the rim of my wineglass. I still had a sip left before I'd cut myself off. "I'm genuinely curious."

"This isn't a two-sided conversation." He tracked my hand with his eyes. "You won't listen to reason now."

I sighed and told the truth, hoping sincerity would gain me *something*. "If you're hurting women, or anyone, I won't be a part of it. Not even as a bystander. And children?" I asked. "Do you take them, too?"

He slid his drink away by its stem, wine sloshing against the glass. "I don't take anyone."

"You took me," I challenged.

"That's not true."

"I wasn't willing, and we both know it." I picked up on the irritation in his voice, but I had a feeling getting to the bottom of it would teach me something important about Cristiano, especially if he didn't want me to know. "If you'd take one person, you'd take others, and how is that different from smuggling people like weapons or narcotics?"

He inhaled audibly. "Marrying you is *not* equivalent to human trafficking."

"Why not?" The cracks in his composure sent a thrill through me, spurring me on. "It's playing with a human life."

"That's enough," he ground out through clenched teeth. "What right do you have to question me when—"

"True, prisoners don't generally have many rights."

He rose to his feet and his palm slapped the table. "You don't know the *first* thing about my business, and you haven't made any honest effort to learn. You see what you want to see and believe rumors without substantiating them. I won't indulge that behavior."

Despite the menacing way he towered over me, triumph surged through me. Finally, an honest reaction. One that gave me more insight into this man. The fact that this was a sore spot for him confirmed what Diego had said.

Cristiano was just twisted enough to believe he was different from his father. He considered himself the hero of his story.

"Another rule that may need reiterating," he started.

"I already know what you're going to say." *Don't question me. Don't snoop. Mind your own business.*

I'd heard it in one form or another as long as I could

remember, but this situation was different. My life and my future might depend on my ability to learn my surroundings—and the man standing in front of me—inside out.

He arched an eyebrow, regaining his composure. "Please—enlighten me."

"All the regular cartel stuff. Don't touch anything of yours, don't explore the house or eavesdrop or talk to the staff."

"You can do all of that," he said.

"Really?" Let's see if he felt that way when I tried each of them while he was away.

"You're free to roam and to talk to whomever you want," he said, "as long as the person is comfortable with it —which Jaz was not the night you got here."

I continued my list, ticking off items on my fingers. "Don't challenge you—"

"I invite you to."

"—or drink your two-thousand-dollar-a-bottle liquor—"

His eyebrow quirked. "Costa's rule no doubt."

"—and don't share sensitive information or repeat anything I hear or see—"

"Well." The air shifted as something cold passed over his face, and he inclined his head, leaning over me. "Sensitive or otherwise, *no* information leaves these walls. None. That's not a rule, it's a way of life, and I'd assumed it would go without saying. You can eavesdrop all you like because I know you understand—opening your mouth would be a death sentence."

I hadn't told Diego anything, but my throat still constricted thinking about the phone upstairs. I laced my fingers in my lap, squeezing them together as I held his gaze. "I wouldn't."

"And none of those are what I was going to say

anyway," he said, smoothing his hand down the front of his shirt. "You will be at my dinner table and in my bed every night. Even when I'm not here. If ever the day comes when you're missing from either, I'll assume you're gone."

I blinked up at him a few times, recalling his same words from the night before. "That's a rule?"

"It's *the* rule, sweet butterfly," he said. "If you're not at my table or in my bed, I'll have no choice but to assume you left."

"I can't even step off the property," I pointed out.

"Can't and shouldn't are two different things. I haven't chained you to a post. If you want to leave, you'll find a way—as those who are whip smart and resourceful tend to do. You've been honing those traits since childhood."

To my dismay, I blushed. Whip smart? Resourceful? Papá hadn't thought so. More like disobedient and sneaky. Or stealthy, as Diego had called me.

Cristiano set one hand on the table next to me and the other on the arm of my chair. No, he hadn't chained me up, but his body trapped me now. A powerful frame that acted as a reminder that my *husband* could flip at any moment and take what he wanted from his wife.

"I don't think I need to repeat myself," he said, "but I will so there's no confusion. If you fly away, so does my protection. I said I wouldn't set the Maldonados, or whoever else holds a grudge against your family, on the people you love—but I've been known to change my mind."

I'd grown too comfortable today. My stomach fluttered with fear but also with a sense of satisfaction. *This* was more like it. Now, he was treating me the way I'd expected, and it made more sense than serving me a four-course dinner garnished with memories of Mamá.

His threats weren't idle. I'd always known of his ruth-lessness. But for some reason, he seemed to be holding back with me, and that only confused my time here. Hoping to provoke him to see if he even *knew* how far he'd go, I asked, "What does it mean to change your mind?"

By the way his bloodless knuckles curled on the table, my prodding worked. "Let's work through this, shall we? I could set them loose like a rabid dog in a chicken coop. They'd snap the old rooster's neck—that's *Papá* to you— and tear chicken-shit little Diego limb from limb. They'd definitely knock Barto off his high horse and obliterate all the men who'd ever breathed a word near your father, including townspeople. Maybe even Pilar. Definitely your mother's family at their farm north of here."

I stilled. It made perfect sense that Cristiano knew of them—it'd been his job to once—but it disquieted me nonetheless. I'd never met my mother's parents since she'd chosen cartel life with my father and had severed ties to keep them out of danger. But they'd always been in it, emotional leverage in the shadows, and they likely didn't even realize it.

"But what about you? How would you fare without my protection?" Cristiano continued. "Such a beautiful girl who can't fight . . . they would find you. Easily." He ghosted his knuckle under my chin. "You've accused me of many things. What was it? Worked, passed around, sold? You were worried I'd invite half the town to fuck you." His dark eyes reflected the cool blue of the pool as he passed them over me. "You must understand, Natalia. They would do all of that and worse. And never forget that I could, too, with less than a snap of my fingers."

I'd hunched back into my seat, cowering from him, but when my attention snagged on one word, I straightened. "Could?" I asked. "Or would?"

His eyes drifted down to the strapless neckline of my dress. Instead of answering, he said, "Don't give my staff any trouble while I'm away, and we can take out the horses when I return."

Cristiano would go all the way up to the line, but something kept him from crossing it. He had the power and inclination to treat me however he wanted, or at least scare me so badly that I never stepped out of line. And he had the reputation to back it up. But he wouldn't. Why not? What was that raw place in him I'd touched when I'd equated my being here with human trafficking?

"You have horses?" I asked.

"You already met mine, remember?"

How could I forget being forced onto a saddle and stolen away from a burning warehouse while the love of my life had been inside. Or that confusing mix of relief and safety as I'd submitted to the things I couldn't stop— the wind in my hair, Cristiano's body cocooning mine, the sound of hooves pounding the solid ground as the desert had spread out before us.

My most unbearable memories of my mother were those of laughing and riding free on our horses. Nothing took me back to those days like the smell, sound, and *feel* of riding a horse. I worried if I ever took the reins again, I'd keel over from a broken heart. I looked away. "I don't ride. Not anymore."

"Then you can stay in the house while I go."

I jerked my head up and met his glittering eyes. "You're a dick."

Still bent at the hip, he removed his hand from the table to pinch my chin between his thumb and forefinger. "Not yet, but I can be if you like. Perhaps as payback for slapping me in the church in front of my men, I ought to gather the staff out here and spank you for your attitude. Now, *that* would make me a dick."

"You won't," I said.

"How do you know?"

Because that would be over the line. "You just gave me your word you'd never let anyone lay their eyes on me," I challenged, "and I'm pretty sure that includes my bare ass. But maybe I'm wrong. Maybe you'd like to let Alejandro take a swat."

"Go upstairs," he bit out before I'd even finished my sentence. "You'll find a closet full of new things, all in your size. Don't touch a single garment." He paused to let me connect the meaning of his words to his fiery gaze. "Take off your clothes and wait for me in bed."

My heart skipped. He sounded more serious than he had yet—and more menacing, which was welcome. We both knew what he was, but he hadn't fully stepped into the role yet. A captor, rapist, and monster with heroic restraint had kept me on edge more than anything.

Whatever he was, I was ready to face it. I shoved my seat back from the table, took one last healthy gulp of wine, and marched upstairs.

In the closet, I slammed the door. Each hanger had been filled during our meal—floral summer dresses, beaded ball gowns, silk blouses in every color of the rainbow, wool slacks. T-shirts and jeans piled to the tops of each shelf. The stilettos, pumps, sneakers, and sandals lining one wall were so dazzling that I had to force myself to look away so I wouldn't lose focus.

I wasn't here to play dress up. To fall into the role of wife and keep house. I was something much uglier—a captive who'd been bestowed with a closet of beautiful things but had been sent to bed with nothing.

My dresser drawers were filled with satin and silk, lace,

rhinestones, and scalloped trim. I stripped down and rifled through *his* drawers instead for the most unattractive thing I could find.

He wanted me naked in his bed? He'd have to look me in the eye as he stripped me of *his* clothing and *my* choice.

I pulled on his sweatpants, knotted the drawstring as tightly as I could, and threw on a matching black sweatshirt.

As I whirled around to march out of the closet, I stopped cold. My wedding dress hung elegantly on the back of the door, clean and pressed on a cream, padded, satin hanger. I approached it slowly, with bated breath, as if it might dissolve beneath a sigh. I ran the ivory lace through my hands and removed the hanger from its hook to turn it, inspecting the back. The lace that had ripped in a clean line along the column of buttons had been repaired, and the damage was barely noticeable. Somebody very talented—and very *fast*—had fixed this. But why?

Was it possible Cristiano had felt a shred of remorse upon discovering this had been my mother's dress?

I saved the thought for another time. Right now, I couldn't think of any decency that might be buried under his cold demeanor.

With a sound in the next room, I replaced the hanger and walked out of the closet.

Cristiano unbuckled his watch by the bed. He glanced briefly at my outfit, then back down. "We'll have to work on your listening skills," he said, his watch clattering on the nightstand.

I continued to my side of the bed and slipped between the sheets before turning my back to him.

But within seconds, he was standing over me.

I stared forward, avoiding him as he took his time

unbuttoning and removing his shirt. As he discarded it, I caught the shadowed ridges of his abdominal muscles.

"Look at me."

I was afraid I'd lose my nerve if I did, but when he reached out, I flinched, rolling onto my back as I raised my eyes to him.

"Let me list all the things you think could stop me but wouldn't," he said, peeling the top sheet away from my body. "Sweatpants. Your period. Diego. Your father."

He ghosted the back of his hand down the front of the sweatshirt. I didn't even have to feel it to sense his hand stop at the tie of my pants.

"I know what *will* stop you," I said.

"Tell me."

Cristiano wanted to test me. I could play that game, too. He wasn't the only one who could take us to the edge, but would he push me over . . . or pull me back at the last second?

My heart raced as I let one leg fall open. "Yours."

His gaze darted to my hand as I placed it on the inside of my thigh. "My what?" he asked hoarsely.

Diego had been right about one thing—Cristiano had somehow convinced himself he was different from the other unforgivable people in this world who played with human lives. He'd played with mine, and he didn't get to ignore that. "Your father."

He froze as if a chill had fallen over the room—while *my* body continued to warm. Even though he towered over me, it felt as if I was the one looking down on him. A shadow passed over his face, and his jaw firmed, its angles sharp enough to cut glass. But nothing sliced as deep as words. "What did you tell me once?" I asked. "Nobody thinks they're a monster?"

He swallowed with a quick nod.

He hadn't even touched me, but his magnetic hand continued to hover. I resisted the urge to lift my hips to meet it. "You run the same business your father did on a much larger scale. Somehow, you've justified that to yourself, but if nobody else will tell you, I will. You *are* your father."

He made a fist, veins winding like vines around his dark forearm. I let my eyes travel up to the solid, thick muscles of a powerful bicep. *Tense* muscles that looked as if they were on the verge of exploding like his temper. "You're wrong."

"I don't think I am." And as someone from his past, how did I fit in? Cristiano could've had anyone in his bed, but he'd chosen me. Maybe it was only that I meant something to Diego. But perhaps it was more. He'd watched me grow up. He'd protected me from people like him.

His long lashes lowered. The promise of his father was enough to scare him off, I was sure. He unfurled his hand, flexing it. I left my leg open, expecting him to withdraw but tempting him to give in to the darkness behind his eyes.

He stretched his long fingers and brushed the stiff fabric. Reflexively, I grabbed his wrist. I'd called his bluff, and he'd called mine right back. Realizing he was going to touch me, a thread of desire yanked inside me. Hands the size of my head that had wrapped around men's throats, and had both commanded artillery and cradled me as a baby—they wouldn't relent until they'd made me feel terrifying things, like euphoria. Bliss. Or worse, connection. What if Cristiano made me feel so good that I began to crave—or *need*—a man I was supposed to fear? Already, I had the unsettling impulse to pull his fingers down so he could soothe this new ache when I should've pushed him away.

With lightning speed, he flipped his hand to capture *my* wrist.

I exhaled a soundless gasp. My helplessness was instant, along with a new, deep-seated yearning to submit. Being in his firm grip turned the gentle pulse between my legs into an angry throb. He could overpower me without much effort. And I wanted it. Every heated look, every restrained touch, and each inciting, sizzling word he'd uttered in my ear since he'd come back into my life suddenly culminated inside me, demanding relief.

I lifted my hips just enough to draw his eyes back to them.

He released my wrist, my skin prickling with the loss of his heat. After rounding the bed and unbuttoning and removing his pants, he climbed under the covers next to me.

Warmth spread through me. My nipples tingled as I waited for him to roll over and be inside me like he'd promised he would.

Promised? He'd meant that as a threat.

But I wasn't scared. I was turned on, and he wasn't doing anything about it.

That was it?

After what felt like minutes of nothing, I moved my head over my shoulder. Silence. Then, for the first time in this bed, I turned to him.

On his back, he had his eyes on the ceiling, but they drifted to meet mine.

All pretense evaporated, and I bit my bottom lip.

He licked his.

The small distance between us nearly crackled with heat.

And yet, Cristiano somehow remained cool. Just like our wedding night, he'd made me admit the worst to myself—that I wanted it. All so he could assert his dominance by leaving me on the ledge alone.

"I knew you wouldn't do it," I said, acid on my tongue, and turned forward again.

Suddenly, he was at my back, his mouth at my ear. "Tell me something, sweet Natalia." He reached over me, took my hand, and pushed it past my waistband, down the front of my pants. "What filth runs through your mind when you touch your pretty pussy? What do you fantasize about?"

Unable to hide my sharp pang of desire, I sucked in an audible breath. "Not you."

Over my underwear, he used my own fingers to apply pressure to my clit. "I already know that," he said, heat gathering beneath his touch. "Because you need permission to go into the darkest corners of your fantasies. I can give you that."

He held my hand there but didn't move. He wanted me to scrape the barrel of my mind, and he knew I wouldn't do it on my own. Just the thought, just hearing *pussy* spill from his lips, my stomach filled with butterflies. I chased the feeling, pushing my hips against my palm, and was rewarded with a rippling ribbon of bliss.

"Getting fucked by me doesn't scare you. You're only afraid you'll enjoy it. And that afterward, you might want it. And that you won't be able to resist *asking for it*." He met my next thrust, pressing my hand against the pulsating knot between my legs. With the thrill it inspired, I bit my lip to contain my whimper. "That's why you won't call yourself my wife. It's easier to play my captive. Follow that path, in the privacy of your mind. I will you to. See how long it takes you to come."

I slipped into that rare and mystifying sense of safety I'd

found with him before. I'd been in more precarious situations with him than this one, and he hadn't hurt me. I'd known he wouldn't. I trusted that instinct now, closed my eyes, and let myself fall into pleasure's tightening grip. Nobody would know if I wondered how it would feel for Cristiano to turn me over and press me into the bed. Nobody, not even him, knew that I was grinding against our hands as I fantasized about opening to him. About how completely and brutally he would fill me, even though it was wrong on every level.

"I can sense your disappointment that I haven't broken you in yet—but I will." His hips pressed against my backside, and this time, I couldn't hold in my moan. The size and solidity of his erection was intimidating but not surprising—what caught me off guard was how it answered a primal, unwelcome need inside me to receive him. "You'll take me in each one of your three holes," he continued, urging his hips against my ass so I was stuck gyrating between my hand and his cock. "I like that your holes *could* belong to anyone—but they don't. They belong to you. My wife. That pleases me to no end."

I groaned an ugly and guttural sound I'd never heard from myself as my arousal reached new heights. If Cristiano viewed my body as property, that meant no part of me was off limits. In that raw moment, I was more turned on by what I didn't know than by what I did. I'd only thought of him on top of me, breaking me in—not all the other ways he could ruin me. A blissful feeling spread through me, his seduction as quick and ruthless as it was slow and mounting.

"How does it feel to hear me defile you, Natalia?" he breathed in my ear.

"Call me Natasha," I said, the name he'd used in the nightclub. Natalia was his past, his bride, his future, but

Natasha was just his toy. It would be easier for both of us to think of me that way.

But he said, "No, *Natalia*." He gripped my hand more tightly and my fingers stroked my clit as we moved together. "*Your* pussy and *your* ass will stretch to fit me, and it will be *your* sweet, pouty lips that suck me sloppy—until I explode down your throat."

My body shook with an impending explosion, his hot and profane mouth putting my climax within reach.

He removed the sweet, pulsing pressure against my clit and used his index finger to swipe mine against the crotch of my underwear. Missing the weight between my legs and taken aback by how wet I was, I sucked in a breath.

"I suspect I'm the first man to soak your underwear clean through." He withdrew both our hands and brought them to his mouth to suck on my dewy finger. "*Mmm*. My first taste of heaven. I imagine it will inspire a thirst so deep, even drinking from you every day wouldn't satisfy it." His chest rumbled against my back. "I wonder if the same will be true when an angel like you drinks from the devil," he mused, as if perusing a menu and trying to decide on a lunch order. "Will you come to crave it? Or will you do it just to please me?"

Adrenaline pulsed in me with the blood rushing through my veins. "Or will I spit it out?"

He answered with a sinister chuckle. "You think you can only drink from your mouth?" he asked. "I will spill myself into all your holes, and I won't relent until your body has drunk every last drop I have to give. Until you're mine through and through."

I was going to climax just from his words. I *needed* to. The ache firmly rooted in the depths of my tummy cried for more. I tried to put my hand back down my pants, but he lowered it to the bed, pressing it into the mattress in front of my eyes. "Final rule," he said in my ear. "Your orgasms are mine. You will not come until you ask for it. Until I stick my cock in you and tell you to."

He rolled away as shudders of pent-up frustration quaked through me. I opened my mouth to protest, but what could I say? Was I willing to ask for it? That was what he wanted. And I had no doubt—once I asked, he'd make me beg.

His breathing evened out within moments, and he fell asleep as if it were nothing at all, leaving me wide awake and alone with my thoughts.

As need vibrated in me, my longing for release became so agonizing, I almost wished I'd just broken down and asked.

That I'd begged for my own destruction.

12

NATALIA

The cicadas' song vibrated the heavy air. Sweat trickled from my temples and under my breasts as I stood on dry grass, trying to mirror Alejandro's stance as he droned on about the importance of stability during a fight.

If my self-defense lessons with Cristiano were equal parts terrifying and exhilarating, the ones with Alejandro were downright yawn-worthy. He was lucky he was so easy on the eyes, because he spoke in a monotone, without inflection. And he never got too close to me.

Cristiano was such a master of diversion that a few nights before, I'd forgotten to feel relieved that he was leaving town and I'd get some measure of freedom from him. For days, I'd mostly just read by the pool, watched TV or movies, and snacked.

The air was thick, as if polluted and dirty, even though I hadn't seen one car within the Badlands' walls aside from those in Cristiano's flock. A need for relief weighed on the sky. Things seemed desolate, as if it hadn't rained in years, even though it just had.

I massaged my side through a cramp. My period had just started, and even though I was bloated and disgusting, everything seemed to turn me on since Cristiano had left me aching.

The more I tried not to think about him turning my own fingers against me or the orgasm he'd denied me, the hotter I got. That uneased throb spurred me on, and as my hormones went haywire, each day I *wished* Cristiano would return and finish the job he'd started. One firm touch between my legs had inspired all kinds of things in me, but when I'd tried to replicate it in the shower the next morning, it'd simply felt like touching two body parts together. No fire, no easy walk to the brink of pleasure.

Cristiano had demanded ownership over my orgasms, and it shamed me how easily my body had complied.

"Natalia?" Alejandro asked, pausing with his hands hovering in the air. "Are you paying attention? Adjust your back foot inward a bit."

"This would go a lot faster if you just arranged my legs the way you wanted them," I said.

Either he blushed or he was getting a sunburn. He looked away and continued his narration on how to protect my liver from a potential strike.

Alejandro wore a long-sleeved shirt despite the heat, and I wondered if it was due to the raised, pink skin peeking out from his collar. I'd first noticed his scars in the church as he'd stood by and watched Cristiano marry me. "You look hot," I told him.

"It's pretty humid," he agreed. "I think we're in for another storm."

Every person in this house had a story that could help piece together the mystery inside these walls. The chef had served me politely enough, and Jaz had reluctantly helped me around the house, but nobody wanted to talk to me.

Alejandro's scars might tell his story best of all. "Why don't you take off your shirt?"

"*Ay.*" He widened his eyes. "Have you met your husband?"

"Sometimes I wonder," I said to myself. "But what do you mean?"

"He'd wring my neck. Cristiano's become a jealous bastard."

I coughed a laugh, shocked. Would he call his boss a bastard to his face? For the first time, a thought hit me— maybe he would. Maybe they were actually *friends*. I hated to admit that would explain the easiness between Cristiano and his staff much better than the story I'd concocted— that Alejandro's and the others' loyalty and respect had been forced on them.

"Maybe if it was Eduardo training you with his pot belly and limp." Alejandro snickered. "But I've had my fair share of female admirers, and Cristiano knows it."

I laughed at his unexpected confidence. "You're about as humble as he is."

"I'm not bragging, just relaying the truth."

I bit the inside of one cheek as I glanced at the edges of his scars. "Can I ask what happened?"

"Um." He scratched behind his ear. Maybe it was forward, and none of my business, but he'd actually been acting friendly, unlike others. "I've had them since child-hood. I was an orphan, and not a very happy one."

"I'm sorry," I said. "Are they from your foster parents?"

"The keepers of an orphanage. They seemed welcoming enough in the beginning, but looks are deceiv-ing, Natalia."

He said it as if imparting wisdom. I was surprised he'd said it at all. Even though Cristiano had said I could ask the staff questions, I'd assumed Cristiano had put some kind of moratorium on most topics. "How did you end up here?" I asked.

"I grew up near Tijuana." He wiped his sweaty temple with his shoulder. "Once I was old enough to run away, I went wherever I could to make ends meet. I met Cristiano in Bolivia when I was nineteen, and he took me under his wing, so to speak."

"How?" I asked. "Did he live there?"

"No, he was there trying to start a business."

"What business?"

"The Calavera cartel," he said as if it was obvious. "It was a small operation then, but I didn't have much else, so I joined the cause."

The cause. Sure, if he thought the fortune they all made off their business dealings was a worthy movement. "You mean you worked for him."

Alejandro shrugged. "When Cristiano learned my story, he asked if I could fight. I'd never been formally trained, but I'd picked up plenty of moves on the street. Within only a week of knowing him, he brought me to meet others like me. Friends that would become family."

Others like him. A shiver worked its way down my spine. Was Cristiano's "small operation" in Bolivia to lead the lost and desperate into a life of their choosing, or of servitude? "Do you mean other orphans?" I asked, picturing Cristiano as some kind of savior in disguise, looking for workers the way my father had brought boys to the ranch.

"No—well, not exclusively." He reached his hands toward the sky, exposing a sliver of his washboard abs. "Mind if I stretch? My joints are stiff, which is why I'm pretty sure it'll rain tonight." I gestured for him to proceed. Whatever he needed to keep the conversation going. "I was talking about Max, Eduardo, Jaz, Daniel, Solomon, Fisker —you know. The others."

The misfits Tepic had mentioned. I couldn't very well call Alejandro that to his face, though. I nudged the toe of my new, ultra-fancy performance sneakers in the grass. "I don't understand."

"Those of us who had no one." He linked his hands and turned his palms up before bending to one side. "Society cast us aside and forgot about us. Our families turned us out or sold us." His forehead wrinkled with a frown. "Hasn't Cristiano explained this to you?"

"No . . ." I didn't want Alejandro to stop talking, but a pit formed in my stomach. Would he get in trouble for revealing things he wasn't supposed to? "I'm not even sure he'd like us talking about it."

"Never said not to," Alejandro said, stretching the other way. "Cristiano is discreet given his position, but inside the walls, he's more of an open book than you'd think."

"You're joking," I deadpanned.

"No, *señora*."

"Don't call me that," I said. "It makes me feel old. I'm only twenty."

"That may be, but you're married now, and no longer a *señorita*."

"Just because a book is open doesn't make the story true. I don't know what's fact and what's fiction. Cristiano married his enemy's fiancée," I pointed out.

"I know. I was there."

"So why would he tell me anything or let me into all of this? He doesn't trust me as far as he can throw me."

"I'll bet he can throw you pretty far. Have you tried asking him anything about the cartel?"

"A little. He explained some of the rumors, like the rotten fish and the snails thing."

Alejandro opened his mouth as if to respond but just blinked at me. "Huh?"

"Never mind. It's the other stuff that he hasn't explained, and I'm sure I asked . . ." Hadn't I? Cristiano's fuse had run out quickly when the trafficking had come up. He'd accused me of believing hearsay, of not entertaining both sides of the story, and he *had* denied some of his practices, but not given me an explanation for them.

"Have you asked what we're about, though?" Alejandro asked, cocking his head. "What we're doing?"

"I know enough. You deal in arms, and you traffic women and children."

He stepped back as if I'd shoved him. "Those are the rumors, yes, but . . ."

"What? Am I wrong?" Why wouldn't I assume the worst in Cristiano when he'd forced this life on me? Even if there were shreds of decency in him, that didn't make him decent. "Isn't that what you guys do? Isn't that what you did to me?"

Alejandro's jaw slackened. "Is that . . . is that how you feel?"

Raising my eyebrows, I crossed my arms. "Why wouldn't I? You were at the wedding. You saw."

His eyebrows drew together as sweat dripped down his temple. He swiped it away with his sleeve and turned his face away, shaking his head. "Jesus, Natalia . . . I mean, you should really ask him about all of this. Don't let him off the hook until he explains what we do here."

"You just told me we're allowed to talk."

"We are," he said. "But it doesn't feel like my place to explain. When Cristiano gets back, try putting aside what you've heard and go in with an open mind."

"Will it change the fact that I'm here against my will?" I didn't expect an answer, but I wanted Alejandro to see things from my side. I sighed. "Forgive me if I find it hard to keep an open mind."

Alejandro glanced at the ground, looking uncomfortable. "I get it, I do. But if you could just *try* . . ."

"If you think this is about anything other than Cristiano's need for power and control," I said, "you need your head checked."

"I *do*," he said, squatting to tie his shoelace and then glancing up. "I mean, the first part . . . not the head check. Cristiano is a control freak. He needs to live in that space —he's a provider and a guiding light for more people than I can count. Sometimes, it's destructive. But in some cases, it can save lives."

"Destructive," I repeated, frowning. "Do you know what I gave up to be here? I *loved* someone else. I had a future with him—"

"Diego's a piece of shit."

My mouth fell open. My reflex was to block the insult, to defend the man I thought I'd marry, but even hearing his name lit a fire inside me, and not the kind it used to. Diego *had* done awful, unforgivable things, but that had nothing to do with this. "The point is, now I'm here, spending my days wandering around a house that isn't and never will be, mine. I'm learning how to defend myself in case anyone, including my 'husband,' tries to hurt me."

Alejandro rose slowly, a frown tugging the corners of his mouth. "He wouldn't hurt you, not ever."

"He already has."

"How?" he asked. "You tell me right now if Cristiano has put his hands on you. I would kill him. He may be rough around the edges, but he's making an effort."

Taken aback by the vehemence in his voice, I scoffed. *This* was making an effort? Cristiano had held a knife to my throat in this very spot. He'd pointed a gun at my head as a child and had left me in the dark to fend for myself. A week ago, he'd almost killed me in a warehouse fire.

But then he'd carried me from a burning building and bandaged me up.

And though he and I had been alone two nights, only arousal—and a demanding need—had resulted from his hands on me. So, no. Maybe he hadn't inflicted any physical violence or force on me, but still.

"I meant emotionally," I said.

"I'm sorry for that," Alejandro said. "I've endured physical and emotional abuse, and they're equally painful in different ways."

He spoke evenly, but the pain of his past came through anyway. Suddenly, my plight didn't seem as severe. "I'm sorry."

Shrugging, he nodded toward the house. "Come on. We can pick this back up tomorrow. Cristiano wants me to show you the cellar."

"A wine cellar?" I asked. "Why?"

One side of his mouth curved, and a deep dimple dented his cheek. "It leads to the panic room. If you ever hear the alarm go off, that's where you go."

I blinked at him. "How big *is* this house?"

"It's designed for a kingpin," Alejandro said. "And a kingpin needs a place to go if and when shit goes down."

"Then why doesn't the property have tunnels?" I asked since my father had commissioned them in his house.

Alejandro arched an eyebrow. "Who says it doesn't?"

It was a relief, finally, to have someone treat me normally. Jaz couldn't seem to stand me. Eduardo, the other guard from the wedding, had a face tattoo and seemed largely unapproachable, and the rest of the staff had kept their distance.

Alejandro and I walked back side by side. "Are you married?" I asked.

He laughed. "No. It's not easy to meet women in this life."

"Do you want to?"

He scratched the back of his neck. "Yes. But I prayed to God many times for a family, and he gave me one. *This* one. My devotion lies with Calavera and Cristiano always."

I didn't understand how somebody so cruel could command loyalty from so many people, but Alejandro seemed to be proof it was possible. He had a genuine air to him, and I believed him when he said he wasn't in a bad situation.

I followed Alejandro back into the house and through a multi-car garage I hadn't yet seen. We passed a Jeep with mud-splattered tires, a sleek, black Mercedes-Benz G-Class, and a monstrous Ford F-150—and that was only in the first section of the garage. "How many cars does one man need?" I asked.

"They're for cartel use, and they're how we get in and out. We have another garage off the premises where we keep the good stuff. McLarens, Audis, etcetera."

Well, I supposed there had to be *some* spoils in exchange for the risks they took. Alejandro opened a door to a staircase and flipped on a light. "I'll meet you down there," he said, pulling out his two-way radio. "I'm going to have one of the guys run this like a drill so it feels real. I'll let the staff know so nobody freaks out."

"How will I know which alarm means to go down there?"

"There's only one," he said. "Trust me—you'll know."

I descended the stairs into the cellar. Stacks of wine bottles lined the walls, some behind glass in refrigerators that emitted a warm glow. I walked the perimeter of the room until I reached a steel door that must've led to the panic room. I tried the handle and was surprised to find it open.

I stepped into the dark and tried a switch. Fluorescent lights hummed to life overhead. The large concrete box had clean, gray floors, a windowed office, and multiple doorways. Industrial washing machines and dryers sat against one wall. Boxes and crates were piled next to a row of bicycles. Definitely not the panic room, but still not a place I was sure I was allowed.

I glanced over my shoulder and walked in, peering into a large closet of cleaning supplies and equipment. I was about to move on when I noticed transparent bins of women's sneakers and sandals, separated and marked by size, stacked almost to the ceiling. I flipped on the light to see what was in some smaller tubs piled in another corner.

My jaw tingled as my eyes adjusted to what was in front of me.

Assorted sizes and colors of bras and underwear.

What the fuck?

I made my way to another doorway. This one led to a whole other room, as big as Cristiano's bedroom. Metal shelving lined the perimeter, stocked with more folded pants, t-shirts, and sweaters than a person could ever need. Even stranger, I realized as I picked up a pair of jeans, it was only women's and children's clothing.

Countless boxes were labeled in Spanish for tooth-brushes, toothpaste, hairbrushes, and other toiletries. Down the center, on a long metal slab of table, travel-size toiletries were grouped like some kind of assembly line. At the end were boxes of plastic zippered bags stocked with everything from shampoo and conditioner to cotton balls to aspirin bottles. Like toiletry bags I'd pack for a trip.

It made no sense. I'd expected to find a museum of

body parts—and I still did—but this was more akin to a drugstore.

Drugs. It hit me. People smuggled narcotics in all sorts of creative ways. I picked up a tube of toothpaste, cracked the seal, and squeezed some out. I smelled and tasted it, but there was nothing suspicious about it.

I broke open a plastic toothbrush, half-expecting something like cocaine to come spilling out. But as far as I could tell, it was just a regular toothbrush. Frustrated and confused, I threw the evidence of my snooping into a garbage can and left the room, glimpsing more boxes, this time with packaged food like trail mix, nut bars, and dried fruit.

Was this some kind of processing center for the women and children Cristiano trafficked? And if so, where were they? Surely he kept them somewhere else in the Badlands . . . but then why hadn't I seen a single one?

I turned to leave and came face to face with a whiteboard that took up half of one wall. It was divided into four sections—*Missing*, *Taken*, *Found*, and *Belmonte-Ruiz*.

I covered my mouth with one hand as my eyes roamed over myriad photos of women and children taped to the board under each section. The images had names scrawled beneath them except each column also had a subsection titled *No photo*.

I ripped off a printout of several stapled pages that had been taped to the board. Thumbnail photos filled each page. Some faces had been crossed out in red.

A door slammed, and I dropped the dossier. Footsteps on the stairs had me hurrying back into the cellar as quickly as my heart raced.

Alejandro jogged down the steps and stopped short at the base of the stairway. His eyes drifted from my head to my toes.

He knows.

Surely there were cameras everywhere, and that included down here. Someone had seen me snooping.

Alejandro was a friend, though—wasn't he? As he tilted his head, my mouth went dry as a desert. Maybe the sun peeked through the clouds. Maybe its warmth was inviting. But that didn't mean it couldn't also scorch you.

I took a step back as Alejandro took one forward.

His mouth twitched into a friendly grin. "Ready to panic?"

13

CRISTIANO

I leaned in the doorway of my spacious dining room as my delectable wife, completely oblivious to my presence, licked the tongs of her fork between bites of Black Forest cake. Her dark hair curled around her shoulders and arms, encircling her like dying black roots.

It'd been a few days, but my desire for her burned just as hot as it had in our bed. Back in her presence, I could sense my emotion overtaking my reason. How to stop it? And why?

Because attachments were dangerous. They blinded men. They exposed us. They hurt us. I'd learned that lesson early. And now, I'd relearn it. I wanted to trust Natalia, but I couldn't yet. I'd thought to get what I wanted from her, I had to give the same. A safe space to speak the truth. It was the first thing I'd asked of her after we'd said our vows—honesty.

And my honest reaction to my security system picking up the signal of an unauthorized phone in Natalia's things while I was away?

A deep-seated need to remind my wife whom she answered to, and that I'd been a far kinder and more generous husband than I needed to be.

Natalia Cruz—Natalia de la Rosa—was a handful. And she was a problem. She'd proven herself untrustworthy just by having the phone, not to mention all the system breaches it could cause.

But the bigger problem was that Natalia put me at odds with the one person I feared most—myself. I'd married her for purely selfish reasons. The things I wanted to do to her were everything I stood against. Everything I hated. They were part of a past I'd overcome.

I prided myself on having a code.

For her, I'd broken it.

Would I go even further than that? I'd resisted her the other night, but just barely. She knew my patience held on by a tenuous thread, and when tugging on it got her no reaction, she yanked on it.

The right thing would be to set her free—but the moment I'd let myself think of her as mine, I knew that wasn't possible.

Did keeping her cancel out anything I'd accomplished the past several years?

Did my urges to defile her undermine those I'd helped?

Her fear both excited and calmed me. Her tears were mine to collect and soothe. Her pussy was mine to devastate and worship. And lick and explore and fuck. All in due time. But what did it make me that I wanted to do it now? That I had taken her in the first place and wouldn't let her go?

She might never come around. I was not a patient man. I never waited for anything anymore. I took. If my self-discipline with her faltered, I worried I'd enjoy it, and that would make me as bad as those I sought to take down.

That made me my father.

But not even that knowledge was enough to make me walk away.

I strolled into the dining room, staying on the rug to mute my steps. When I reached her back, I wrapped my hands around her neck.

She froze in her chair. *Wrong reaction, little girl.*

After a moment, she tilted her head back all the way and met my eyes upside down.

"Haven't you been training with Alejo?" I asked.

"He talks too much."

I nearly laughed at the unexpected response but managed to maintain my composure. Her safety wasn't a game. "Excuse me?"

"He won't let me practice." Her throat constricted against my palms as she swallowed. I refrained from tightening my grip around the slender column and shifted my focus to the chocolate frosting at each corner of her mouth. "I think he's afraid to touch me," she added.

"Then he's smarter than I give him credit for." I lowered my mouth to her forehead for a kiss. I wanted more. Was it so much to ask that a husband could kiss his wife's lips? I moved down her cheek, but the tension in her body remained.

She'll come around, I reminded myself. It was no victory to take from someone who didn't want to give.

But then again, I'd been suffering for my lust for some time.

I slid my hands under her chin, tilting her mouth up to mine. She parted her lips for a gasp—or a sigh?—and clearly fought to keep her eyes from fluttering shut. One flicker of my tongue and I'd get that chocolate right off her lips.

I hoped she'd been stewing in her own juices since I'd left her wanting in our bed.

I hoped at that moment, she was questioning the wetness between her legs.

I reached by her and plucked the cherry off the top of her cake. Straightening, I popped it into my mouth, discarding the stem on her plate before I fell into the seat next to her. "You weren't going to eat that, were you?"

She scowled, wiping her mouth with a napkin as she picked up her plate and stood. "I'll just have to get another slice."

I smiled. "Be my guest."

I watched her until she'd disappeared into the kitchen. Who was I kidding? My attachment to her was already forming. It was hard to avoid that when she'd been under my protection as a child. Now that she was a woman, and my wife, the affection I'd once had was something else entirely.

Her vulnerability was also mine, though. She was my responsibility. Was I doing everything I could to ensure her safety? A week ago, I hadn't known I'd be bringing her here. Now that it was more than the staff and me in the house—now that I was more exposed—it was time for a full security check-up.

Max and I had come to the conclusion that the only way Barto could've entered my bedroom that Monday morning was by scaling the cliff beneath my balcony. It seemed impossible. The beach below the house acted as a port and had its own robust defense in place, yet they'd never seen him. We'd inspected every camera and triple-checked each passageway in and out of the house to no avail.

While security had always been the top priority in the

Badlands, it was also important to me that townspeople felt welcome and could take shelter in the house if they ever needed to, no questions asked.

But with Natalia under my care, and with a target on her back as my wife and Costa's only daughter, it was becoming clear I'd have to take greater measures to protect the house.

Max had begun meeting with ex-military to get us up to date on biometric technology—fingerprint scans and voice and facial recognition, and new steel-fortified, bullet-resistant doors with automatic locks. I'd learned hand-to-hand combat and marksmanship as a boy growing up in a cartel, but I'd learned what it meant to fight for my life on the streets. I hated that I needed all the latest gadgets to protect myself and my people. I'd installed a large, open balcony in the first place so I could taste freedom at all hours of the day and night. I didn't want to board myself up in a house. But I couldn't be everywhere all the time.

I'd laughed Max out of the room when he'd tried insisting on installing cameras in my bedroom. If I needed men watching me as I slept, then I deserved whatever attack was coming to me.

But Natalia was in my bed now. I wanted the ability to lay eyes on her at all times if need be.

At the very least, I'd have to go overboard on our wing of the house and in the bedroom.

Natalia returned, not with cake, but with two plates full of food. She set one in front of me, avoiding my eyes as she sat. "You didn't eat dinner yet?" I asked.

"I was going to skip it."

In lieu of another multi-course dinner, I'd asked Fisker to prepare two balanced meals since we weren't staying long. I'd assumed Natalia had already eaten hers.

"I can appreciate cake for dinner," I said carefully, trying for amenable where I could afford it, "but the chef says you had mostly salad, wine, and dessert while I was away."

"You're keeping tabs on what I eat?"

"I want you to build strength." If she noticed the pomegranate that I'd requested on her plate, she kept it to herself. I pointed my fork at her food. "So, eat your chicken. What else did you do while I was away?"

She took a bite. "I'm sure you watched from your ivory tower. I can't imagine it was very entertaining, seeing as I mostly just wandered around the house."

"You're bored. Noted." She needed company, and I'd get her some, though it might be a reminder she should be careful what she wished for.

"Alejandro showed me the panic room." She hesitated, presumably deciding whether to ask about what she'd seen downstairs. "I saw what was in the basement. That . . . that warehouse room."

I chewed, pleased with her honesty, even though it didn't make up for the phone. I'd already known she'd snooped, but I hadn't expected her to bring it up herself. "Great, isn't it?" I asked. "It's like a mini superstore down there."

"How can you joke about something like that?" Her eyebrows cinched. "What was all that? And the whiteboard with the pictures? I want to know what goes on under this roof."

"All you have to do is ask, Natalia. You don't need to sneak around. This is your home. You can go where you please."

"This is *your* home."

"And you are my wife. What's mine is yours. I trust that whatever you see, you'll view with an investigative eye and an open mind." I paused to let that sink in. She'd seen quite a bit down there, and based on the other rumors she'd brought to me, I had no doubt her mind was running wild with potential scenarios. I tilted my head. "I trust you in our home."

At least, I had.

"I haven't done anything to earn that trust," she said.

"You haven't done anything to break it . . . have you?"

She drew a short breath. I'd have to teach her how to perfect—or even begin to hone—her poker face. I knew she was thinking of how she'd stashed a phone Diego had surely given her. *I* was. Diego was the last person I needed knowing about the goings on of my home, because he wouldn't hesitate to use them against me.

"No, I haven't," she said finally. "So how do you explain the food, clothing, and toiletries down there?"

"They're for the women who arrive here. To make the transition smoother. Whether they choose to stay or go, there's always an adjustment period. Most of them have nothing."

She picked up a glass of water and peered at me over it. "But you're why they have nothing. Aren't you?"

I sighed and rubbed the inside corners of my eyes. If she would just ask before insulting me, I would answer honestly. But she continued to dig her heels into her assumptions, and she'd have to dig herself back out once she learned the truth.

It was my own fault she chose to think the worst of me, but that didn't make it any easier to hear.

"If there's any kind of abuse, I won't live here," she warned.

That tone was new, not quite an accusation, perhaps even cracking the door open to a real conversation. But it was too hard to resist watching her get riled up. "Where will you live?" I asked. "In the stable?"

She pursed her lips, reminding me of the petulant child I'd once known. That fiery attitude she'd had before Bianca's death was returning, and I didn't mind the burn. In fact, knowing me, I was pretty sure I'd be sticking my hands into the flame anytime the opportunity presented itself.

After a bite of chicken, I said, "Going downstairs into the panic room must've brought up some old memories, no?"

Her answering silence spoke volumes. I wasn't wrong, but I was probably the last person she wanted to open up to about the day I'd locked her in a closet with me and threatened her life before Bianca's body was even cold. But who understood better than me? We'd both stumbled across the body. We'd both loved and respected Bianca. We'd both descended into the darkness together.

"It was fine," she said, but her body language told a different story. Her shoulders rose nearly to her ears. "Alejandro made me feel safe."

Safer than I did. I ignored the jab and continued my thought. "I think about that day a lot. Especially lately. What it must've been like for Bianca. For Costa, when he got home. And for you."

Had she talked through it with her father or a therapist? With Diego? All of it—every last detail? It was a heavy burden to carry, watching a parent die.

"Why were you so cruel that day?" she asked, her posture easing with her tone. "I was covered in my mother's blood. I was in shock. And you had no sympathy." She picked up her water again, and I noticed she'd pushed her wine away. "You made me think you were going to kill me," she said, glancing into the glass. "Or worse, take me with you."

I needed no reminder of the things I'd said. I didn't regret any of them. It'd contributed to getting her out of there and off to California. I only regretted that I hadn't scared her off Diego. "My life was on the line, Natalia. You and Diego were accusing me of murder. I was scared, too. But I was also angry. You ferociously defended Diego, but not me."

"I was *nine*," she said. "All I knew was what I saw."

"I *wanted* to frighten you," I added quietly.

She took a breath. "You succeeded."

"I don't think I did." But given the night I had planned, I might. "I've been watching you closely ever since my return—as closely as I did when you were young."

"You watched me then?"

"Of course. I was responsible for your life. And in a world as grim as ours, a child like you was a ray of sunshine in the dark." She'd had a laugh that'd made murder and mayhem bearable. And Bianca had trusted me around Natalia. Nobody else would've left me, a hitman with a long rap sheet, alone with their kid back then. Now, I was responsible for rays of sunshine all over the Badlands. "If anything had happened to your parents, I was supposed to get you out of the house and take you somewhere safe."

"She told me once to go to you in an emergency," Natalia said, slackening against her chair. "But you didn't take me. You left me in the dark."

"I couldn't take you where I was going. Not as a fugitive. It would've been kidnapping." My chest tightened. In the seconds before I'd left her down there, she wouldn't let go of my neck. I'd scared her so badly, she'd actually wanted the monster. "At least in the tunnel, you were stowed away until Costa could get to you."

"Like a doll on a shelf."

An action figure maybe, though she had yet to own the role. "I don't see a timid girl who was broken by her mother's death," I said. "I don't see a porcelain doll who needs to be shelved for her own protection."

She took her entire bottom lip into her mouth, seemed to think as she bit down, then released it. "What do you see?"

"A woman trying to break through the restraints placed on her—including the ones of her own making. I understand why you went to California—I'm glad you did. You needed the distance and protection from this world. But you're not a girl anymore. Losing your mother the way you did is no longer an excuse to run away from the life you were destined to lead. I have forced your hand, but in time, if you're the woman I think you are, you'll come to see that you're right where you belong."

She blinked her gaze around the main room, her eyes drifting from the still fireplace to the pottery above it. But she understood I was talking beyond the literal. I could practically see the wheels turning in her head. "And where do I belong?" she asked.

A sense of pride gathered inside me, tinged with a lust for the devotion I'd always wanted from her. "Next to me," I said. "At the head of the Cruz-de la Rosa empire."

"What if . . ." She glanced at her hands fidgeting in her lap. "What happens if I'm not the woman you think I am?"

"The same thing that happens to anyone who's not cut out to rule. You'll fall in line, or you'll perish."

"Then I'll perish," she said without inflection but raised her eyes to look upon me with renewed fire. "If you think for one *moment* I will rule a cartel responsible for bringing horror to human lives, then you *will* learn what I'm capable of."

I couldn't help my smile. That was exactly the woman I thought she was, and I looked forward to bringing out this ferocious, protective side of her. "I hope I do."

"I won't stand by your side if you inflict pain and slavery on others. If you wanted that, you should've chosen a different wife. If I find out the rumors are true, I will stand in your way at every turn. I will not fall in line."

If, if, if. Her accusations were yielding as doubts crept in. Pride and lust surged through me again. This time, the lust was more carnal. The impulse to spar with her, to see just how close I could bring her to falling in line. And the pride was that of a husband watching his wife grow. "Spoken like a true queen. This is the Lourdes in you," I said, referring to her regal second name. "But how long would you hold strong to your ideals? You promised to obey me. I don't need to remind you that defying me could bring danger on your family."

"Yet you do remind me quite frequently."

I had to stifle my chuckle.

"What would *you* do?" she asked. "Would you choose the right thing over family? If it meant saving countless lives?"

"I already did." My amusement vanished. "And I'd do it again."

"But that doesn't make any sense. You turned your father in because he was involved in human trafficking. But he never took it as far as you have."

"You don't know that, do you?" I asked, my tone verging on snapping. I wanted to be patient with her, but it got under my skin when she compared me to him so easily without verifying anything that she assumed was fact. At some point, I needed her to realize that she was doubting and maligning me without evidence, while I saw nothing but potential and goodness in her. And even if I was her own personal beast, I was still nudging her toward a better version of herself. "You've made a lot of assumptions and accusations, Natalia, but not once have you asked about the specifics, or even generalities, of my business."

She smacked her water glass on the table. "I'm asking," she said with a frown, as if I hadn't just invited her to.

I stuck a toothpick in my mouth, somewhere between wanting to teach her a lesson and trying to be patient with her. One minute, her curiosity allowed her to listen, the next, she was obstinate for no reason. "Then I will show you."

But not until she ate. I'd already finished my meal, and she'd barely taken three bites.

I shifted to take a velvet box from my back pocket and stuck it squarely on the table in front of her plate.

Her gaze bounced between the box and me. "What is that?"

"Your wedding ring. Teresa made it. Remember Felix, the boy with no front teeth? His mom."

"But I already have one. It's—oh. I see." She glanced at her hand, then slid off the ring I'd put on her finger in the church and placed it in front of me. "It was your mother's. You must want it back."

That wasn't why. My mother's ring had been a stand-in. It wasn't good enough for my wife. I'd found it amongst Bianca's jewels, the ones I'd recovered for Costa over the last several years. It meant nothing to him so I'd pocketed it, meaning to melt it down. It'd come in handy, but now I could get rid of it. I tossed it aside, opened the little box, and slid it closer to her.

Her eyes widened. "Cristiano. This is . . . *enormous*."

Indeed it was. I'd explained to Teresa what I'd wanted, but she'd insisted on meeting Natalia before creating it—to capture her personality, apparently. Who needed personality when you had a big, fat rock to back up your confidence? I'd wanted something bold. A jewel fit for a queen. I'd told Teresa to recall the biggest diamond she'd ever worked with—and then find one double the size.

Natalia would wear my ring, a piece of jewelry so heavy, she'd feel the weight of me at all times.

"Is it real?"

I arched an eyebrow, suppressing a laugh. "Natalia, for fuck's sake. Of course it is."

She gave me a minx-like smile—she was messing with me—then slipped on the emerald-cut diamond set in a diamond band.

I picked up the box. There was more inside—a two-tone, gold-and-silver ring with a fine, almost invisible pearl inlay strip around the center, engraved inside with our wedding date and one word.

Mine.

I passed it to her, and she slid the rings together to form one. She spread her fingers, peering at them. Would she recognize why I'd chosen it? She placed her splayed hand on the table, admiring it in silence.

She only raised her eyes to watch me push on my ring. My band matched hers, but without the pearl and with a different word inside.

Yours.

I was a married man.

I didn't wait to hear what she thought about it. She wasn't in a place to thank me for anything yet, and if she was going to tell me she hated it, because it didn't come from Diego, I was in no mood to hear that.

"You haven't touched your fruit," I said. "In Greek mythology, pomegranates are the fruit of the dead."

"That was true for Persephone," she said right away.

Ah. I wasn't expecting such a smart comeback. Between us, we seemed to possess a wealth of knowledge on tempting berries. "If you see her time in captivity as a death sentence, then yes. Some would be willing to die in order to become the queen of hell, though." I sliced my pomegranate open to get to the juicy red center. I couldn't wait to sink my teeth into Natalia, too. "*Es un delicia inigualable.*"

A matchless delight. Her cheeks pinkened as she watched me scoop out the seeds. "Jaz," I called, and she appeared in the doorway. "Pack Natalia a bag. We're not staying here tonight."

Jaz nodded. "Yes, sir."

Natalia stilled, her palm still pressed to the table. Her fingers curled. "We're not?"

"You said you were bored." My tone dropped, making it sound like a threat—and I was fine with that. "We're going out."

"Out?" She met my gaze. "Where?"

There it was. The slight tremor of fear in her voice that she tried to hide. It did something to me, owning that fear. That was at least one thing Diego had never gotten from her. Perhaps he'd made her quiver, but *I* could inspire the deepest tremble. I would make her shake.

I'd make her beg.

Natalia jumped up before I could answer. "*Wait,*" she called across the room, but Jazmín was long gone. "I can pack my own things."

"Sit and finish—you'll need the energy," I said. "Jaz will do it."

The phone wouldn't last another night.

With an audible swallow, Natalia lowered herself back into the chair. "Where are we going?"

"To *La Madrina*. You remember my nightclub?" I allowed myself a smile at the way her spine lengthened. "But first, I'm going to introduce you to the Belmonte-Ruiz cartel."

14

NATALIA

In Cristiano's closet, I quickly dug through the bag Jaz had just packed while Cristiano showered. During his absence, I'd gotten my hands on a sewing kit and stitched a secret pocket into the lining for the phone. I tore through her precise folding and the tops she'd rolled into neat, tidy torpedoes until I felt the weight of it in my palm and breathed a sigh of relief.

"All there?"

I jumped at Cristiano's voice behind me, then tucked the phone back into place, piling clothing on top of it. "Yep."

I turned around and darted my eyes away. I didn't think I'd ever get used to the way my heart skipped seeing him in just a towel—all the trim, powerful muscles that lay in wait beneath his clothes. The fact that his body had pinned me to the mattress several days ago made me want to sneak another peek when it should've made me desperate enough to throw myself over the balcony just to escape. I'd never felt that kind of firm, promising weight on me, not even with Diego. And it made my insides tighten with desire.

I was a traitor to myself and my gender.

And Cristiano was a smirking jerk who seemed to read my mind.

"We'll leave in ten minutes," he said. "Wear the same black dress you had on the night you came to my club."

But it was so *short*. So revealing. I'd only worn it around Cristiano knowing Diego was nearby. And we were meeting the Belmonte-Ruiz cartel, a thought that immediately dried my throat. I was supposed to meet sex traffickers in a skimpy dress? "I don't think it's clean," I lied.

"Even better. Put on the dirty little dress you wore for me that night." His pupils dilated as he looked me over. "We can roleplay what would've happened if you'd come up to my office like I'd asked you to."

"What if there are people I know at the club?"

"Doubtful as it's out of town. But you don't need to worry about that. You won't be seeing anyone I haven't arranged for you in advance." He turned his back to me. "I don't like surprises."

My eyes drifted to the carpet. "And yet a life in the dark is nothing but surprises."

"At least it's not boring, eh? Now, where's that dress?" He discarded his towel on a chair and surveyed his extensive suit collection. "I want to watch you squeeze into it."

I lost my breath at the sight of his ass. I could've flicked a quarter at it and ducked as it ricocheted right back at me. Smooth with bronze, concave cheeks, it had more definition than his top-of-the-line TVs.

I slipped out of my robe and took one of the last clean pairs of underwear from a drawer.

"Leave them," Cristiano said.

I froze. "But I'm still on my period."

He grunted his disapproval. "How much longer?"

"A few days probably." I proceeded to pull on the most unflattering underwear I had. "I found tampons in your bathroom. You must spend a lot of time with women to keep those handy."

"Jaz put them in there for you," he said.

I slipped into my dress, feeling his eyes on me. I'd been told on enough California beaches that I had a good ass, but it wasn't the product of the gym. I never worked out, though that would have to change if I were going to continue with the self-defense classes.

"Is there a fitness center here?" I asked.

"I'll get someone to dust it off."

I looked over my shoulder at him. "You don't use it?" I hadn't meant to sound so surprised. He wasn't beefy by any means, but muscles like his went way beyond genetics.

"Nah. Get my exercise in other ways. You can't design a better glutes workout than squatting outside a drug lab with binoculars for eight hours. Nor can you spar with friends like you can fend off enemies. Sharpens reflexes. Builds muscle." He winked. "And stamina."

I stared at him, trying to decide if he was exaggerating. "I never thought I'd have a killer for a husband," I muttered.

"What do you think Diego is?"

The question caught me off guard, but it was warranted. "He may have killed, but he isn't a murderer at heart."

Cristiano snorted. "You still believe that?"

I supposed I couldn't. If he was willing to lie and deceive so thoroughly, then it was likely he'd also created himself a new persona.

"And how about you, *mariposa*?" he asked. "Are you a

killer? If I ask you to knot my tie, will you try to strangle me with it?"

I turned as he tucked his dress shirt into his pants. "If I thought I could get away with it," I responded wryly.

"I'll take my chances." He stepped toward me, took my waist, and lifted me onto the island in the middle of the closet. "Do you know how?"

"I learned when I was nine."

He spread my knees, and my dress rode up as he settled himself between my legs. He smelled of the same soap I did and the cedar shampoo in his shower. "Nine?" he asked.

"My father taught me how to do Diego's tie for my mother's funeral."

His Adam's apple bobbed as he swallowed. "I see."

As I pulled the wide end up, he lifted his chin and kept it there even after I'd looped the tie and tightened the knot.

"Give me your hand," he said. When I did, he brought my fingers up and pressed them gently to the hollow of his neck, under his Adam's apple. "Remember I said we all have the same weak spots?"

"Yes."

"This is one. The trachea—or windpipe. If your attacker ever exposes this to you, hit him here."

"I would think higher." I moved my hand up to his Adam's apple. "Wouldn't this be worse?"

"No." He stretched his thumb away from his other four fingers to show me the webbed curve between them. He held it to the middle of my throat and squeezed. "If *I'm* attacking *you*, there's no chance in hell you're going to be able to strangle me."

"You'd be surprised at the strength that comes with a rush of adrenaline."

"Natalia, I can crush a skull. You're not going to win

unless you're strategic." He contracted his hand even tighter. "See how much effort it takes? Do you feel anything?"

"Not really."

He lowered his grip, pressing his palm into the base of my neck, and immediately, I was choking. Alarms fired in me, my hands flying up to grab his forearm just as he released me. "You felt *that*," he said.

I moved my fingers to my throat as my heart pounded, the terrifying sensation lingering. "Right away."

He took my hand, spreading it into an L-shape the way his had been. "It has the same effect on me that it does on you. You can hit someone there—hard—to incapacitate or disorient them, giving yourself time to run or do more damage."

He slid his hand under my jaw and pressed his thumb and index finger into the sides, where I'd been taught to take my pulse. "These are your carotid arteries. You can strike them to do damage, but if you have a knife, even better. Cut both of them at the same time."

My throat constricted, and I struggled for my next breath. Cristiano had an unsettling obsession with throat-related murder. "At the same time?" I asked. "How?"

"Don't just stab your assailant in the neck. Stab through it."

I inhaled sharply with the gruesome mental image, but also—I could barely admit in the depths of my mind—embarrassment that his savagery was a turn-on. His hand was hot and tight around my neck. I wrapped mine around his wrist, not to pull him off this time, but to try to channel the utter strength he held against an opponent. A beat passed between us. "How many men have you strangled?" I asked softly.

"Are you asking if the rumors about *El Polvo* are true?"

"I know they are. Diego saw you pour sand down a man's throat until he choked to death."

"I did." He spoke without inflection or emotion, his hand loose around my neck.

"What did he do to deserve that?"

"I'll tell you what he didn't do. He *didn't* kill me first— and that's what matters." He grazed his thumb under my jaw. "Such a pretty, slender throat," he said, his eyes drifting down. "I'll bet there are many who'd love to get their hands on it."

"You're the only one who has."

He looked pleased by that, even though I hadn't meant to flatter him. He dipped his head but kept his gaze on me. "And I'm the only one who ever will. That's my promise to you."

A threat . . . or a promise. He'd be the only one to keep my fate on a precarious edge.

"You don't have to worry about the sand," he said, moving his mouth closer to my ear. "That would be such a waste. A throat like yours would bruise and tighten and succumb so beautifully under a man's hands."

A shiver prickled down my spine as cords of fear and desire tangled in me. I couldn't stop swallowing. "How many women have you choked?"

"With my hands? None."

"But you've strangled some?" I asked.

"No." His crow's feet deepened as he suppressed a grin. "I was being suggestive, but I'm glad to see it was lost on you. I assume that means mine will be the first cock you gag on."

A gasp sucked the air from my lungs with the delicious, maddening pull I was coming to expect between my legs whenever he spoke about dominating me.

"And before you accuse me of abusing a woman's

mouth," he added, bracing his hands on both sides of me until our mouths were close, "I'll let you in on a secret. Some women love it. They shouldn't call me *El Polvo*. They should call me *El Gallo*."

"The rooster?" I asked at the same moment it clicked. The *cock*.

"More women have willingly choked on my rooster than men have been forced to eat my dust."

Of course, Cristiano de la Rosa's attempt at a joke would be both sinister and provocative. I didn't laugh, mostly because I was too focused on trying not to picture the look that would cross his face the first time I took him in my mouth. Would he become even more domineering when I kneeled for him? Or would I steal his control?

"How many men have you killed?" I asked.

"Countless."

"How many women have you been with?"

He searched my eyes. "Tell me why you're asking, and maybe I'll answer."

"I want to know if I'm one in a long line of many, or if you intend to take our vows seriously."

He went uncharacteristically silent, as if racking his brain for a response. "And how would you feel if I promised the rooster belongs to you and only you?"

"I would feel that the rooster was in for a long nap. And that he perhaps should not bother waking at all, as he'll be in for great disappointment."

The corner of Cristiano's mouth twitched into a lopsided smile. I, too, almost smiled. *Almost.* At his sudden playfulness, in part, but also because there was something appealing about Cristiano never taking another woman again.

Not even me.

My hardwired female instinct saw the romanticism of

keeping a wild man, but even as my fantasies wandered, the angry, bitter part of my brain wanted to torment him with our vows until death did us part.

"We should go," Cristiano said. "Everyone's waiting."

"Everyone?" I asked.

He took his blazer off a hanger and wrapped it around my shoulders. "Wear this until we're alone again."

I put a hand on his chest before he could help me down. "Wait."

With our faces inches apart, dark, nearly black eyes, looked back at me. Nose to nose, I could see their deep brown color and slight amber flecks.

"Hmm?" he asked, staring at my lips.

His skin warmed my palm, even through his shirt. I imagined all the strength under my hand aimed at anyone who tried to come at him. At me. At *us*.

"Your knot is crooked," I said. As I adjusted his tie, a tiny black spot in a sea of white fabric caught my eye. I ran my fingertip over it. "There's blood on your shirt."

"That's why I chose it," he said gravely. "I don't want to ruin a second one."

———

A kilometer outside the gates of the Badlands, Cristiano parked in the driveway of a large, freestanding garage.

This, it seemed, was the everyone who'd been waiting for us: two SUVs, a Dodge Ram, an Audi, and a couple of shoddy Hondas—all black with tinted windows.

Cristiano stepped out of the car and joined a circle made up of some of the men who'd been at the Easter party. I knew better than to follow or even open my door until Cristiano came for me. Instead, I watched from where I was as a very young blonde girl in a denim skirt and a tank top exited one of the SUVs.

Cristiano gave her a once-over before circling her.

I knew that walk. That stare. That scrutinization. He'd done it to me on our wedding day before he'd ripped off my dress.

As she kept Cristiano in her sights, Max approached her from behind, grabbed her elbows, and yanked her down onto her knees so she crumpled like a ragdoll.

She thrashed, threw her head back, and he released her as he keeled over. Jumping to her feet right from her knees, she turned and kneed him in the face so he fell back onto his back.

She put a foot on his chest in triumph, then backed away.

Cristiano smiled as he helped Max off the ground, then slapped him on the back and nodded at the girl before she got into one of the SUVs. The rest of the men dispersed into other vehicles that left the garage.

Only Cristiano remained, looking in my direction. As he walked over, he signaled for me to lower my window.

"Who was that girl?" I asked when Cristiano neared. "Where are they taking her?"

He stuck an arm on the roof of the car and leaned into the car. "If you want answers, come with me." He straightened and called over his shoulder as he walked away, "But you might not be ready. If you're not, Eduardo can take you home."

When Cristiano had mentioned the Belmonte-Ruiz cartel, all sorts of scenarios had run through my head, most ending with me in the trunk of a car. But we'd come this far without Cristiano hurting me—or letting me get hurt. And I was finding that being in the dark was far worse than anything I'd learned yet. I held fast to the instinct that he'd keep me safe as I popped open the door and exited the car.

My spiked heels stuck in the rubber garage floor, but I wobbled along to one of the Hondas, where he opened the trunk and handed me a bulletproof vest. I'd seen plenty in my lifetime, but I'd never worn one.

"What's this for?" I asked, holding it with both hands.

"What do you think?" He shot me a grim glance. "Still want to come?"

I put the vest on under the blazer and pulled back my shoulders to keep from slouching beneath the weight.

Moments later, we were pulling out of the garage in the Honda. The first in a line of vehicles took off in the opposite direction of the Badlands, and we followed.

"Why are we in this car?" I asked.

"To remain inconspicuous."

It wasn't a long drive, but Cristiano's silence made it seem that way. With permanently furrowed eyebrows, he focused out the windshield, only breaking his concentration to speak into a two-way radio.

As darkness spread around us, I glimpsed a side of him I'd expected to see more of—the determined security team member I'd known as a girl. It was how I knew we were heading somewhere important, and in this world, that was usually synonymous with dangerous. There was an allure to seeing him in his element. I could picture him wearing the same grave expression in the bedroom as he found ways to exert his dominance. Maybe he was this serious, too, each time he'd had to jerk off because he wouldn't let himself touch me.

He could control my body, but he couldn't control his own. The thought made me shiver with a heady mix of lust and control.

Cristiano cursed as we took a pothole too fast. He

slowed the car as the pavement became uneven and we entered an unfamiliar neighborhood. Dim, yellow street-lamps barely lit the people sitting along a chain-link fence on upside-down crates, smoking and watching us.

"Where are we?" I asked.

"Get down in your seat," he ordered.

I slipped low enough to appease him but continued watching through the window as we turned a corner onto an unlit street. As we passed an alley, a flame lit a ghoulish-looking face and disappeared.

Cristiano parked, turned off the engine, and lowered his phone between his knees to send a text. "The side panels and windows are all bulletproof. The car looks like shit, but it's secure and runs well," he said absentmindedly. "Nobody should get close enough to try anything, but you may hear gunshots. Try not to scream."

"That's like asking you to look approachable or gentle —it's just not the natural way of things."

He stopped typing to look at me sidelong. "You had gentle. How was it?"

My cheeks warmed as I slouched against the car door. How could he *possibly* know what it'd been like with Diego? But he was right. It was gentle. Satisfying. Pleasant.

Nothing like being told I was going to get my mouth fucked and throat choked.

I bit my lip a little too hard and forced my eyes back out the window, ignoring his question. A woman walked down the street, her blonde hair as impossible to miss as the moon in the sky. "Cristiano, look," I said. "Isn't that the girl Max was just fighting?"

He shut off his phone and stuck it in a cup holder, sinking down with me. "That's Sandra. She's Estonian."

She sat on a bench and took out her phone. I'd never been here, but it didn't take a genius to see this wasn't a good neighborhood. She should be paying attention to her surroundings. I balled my hands in my lap and surveyed the area. "Why is she so far from home?"

He sniffed. "Her aunt sold her to Brazilian traffickers when she was thirteen," he said. "Unfortunately, we only got her out a couple years ago, so she was forced into prostitution for a while."

My stomach dropped. *That* was a betrayal unlike any I'd ever heard. What Diego had done to me paled in comparison. "Her own aunt?" I repeated, my nose tingling.

"People get desperate. The weak ones break." He touched my hand. It took me a moment to realize he was trying to uncurl my fist. I opened it, and his warm palm took mine. "Young, light-skinned, light hair—she's easy bait, but this is the first time we've put her in the field. The important thing is that she wants to be here. To help."

It took me a moment to adjust to the simple act of holding his hand. Was it for comfort? I checked myself before reacting to the word *bait*, remembering what Alejandro had said about trying to keep an open mind. Cristiano had also said *help*. I relaxed my hand into his. "Is she the eighteen-year-old who looks fourteen?"

"Yes."

I closed my eyes. "I'm trying not to think the worst, Cristiano."

"And what's the worst?"

I glanced over at him. "That *you're* prostituting her now."

"I've spent a fortune on girls like her." His eyes grew distant as he looked at her with obvious affection. "It's why I've worked so hard to earn it. They're worth every penny."

Again, I had to work to read his ambiguity so I

wouldn't jump to conclusions. He'd told me earlier in the week that when I was young, he'd tried to scare me. I sensed he was doing that now. "What do you mean?"

He squeezed my hand. "Sandra has intimate, inside knowledge of these operations. Sad but true. Just by sharing what she knows, she has helped us free more than twenty girls—and more tonight, we hope."

My heart began to pump, and I felt the rush of blood in my veins. "I don't understand."

His two-way radio went staticky, and a voice came through. "*Hay viene un hombre.*"

Someone was coming. Cristiano stuck a baseball cap on his head. I started to glance over my shoulder, but he grabbed the back of my head and shoved my face into his lap. "What—"

"Suck my dick like your life depends on it," he said. "Or at least pretend to."

"Cristiano—"

"I shouldn't be making jokes—this is serious. Stay down. He's about to walk by." He curled his fist against my scalp then smoothed a hand over my hair. "Do you know this area?"

My irritation with talking to his zipper dissipated as uneasiness settled in. "No."

"It's a forgotten neighborhood. The next one over is a hotbed for trafficking, but law enforcement in both is owned by Belmonte-Ruiz, and they're paid to look the other way. Every person we've seen is either a drug addict, dealer, or prostitute, and they're *all* spies for BR. We have to blend in, or we'll stand out."

"Fortunately, playing your whore isn't too much of a stretch," I said, even though I was near purring by the way he stroked my hair.

His hand stilled. I doubted he even realized he'd been

petting me. "In that case, if you have any impulses while you're down there, feel free to indulge them."

Your curiosity is an affliction. Papá's words continued to haunt me into adulthood.

With Cristiano, my curiosity was as strong as ever. He was an enigma. My favorite part of business school had been case studies of the inner workings of companies— their mistakes and triumphs. Here was one right in front of me. Nothing about him added up. Nothing about *him and me* added up. Not only could I stomach being this close to him, but I felt safe here, as I had the other times I'd sought solace in him when *he'd* been the one to put my life in danger.

Was it because he hadn't shown me cruelty yet? Or was it that I knew, instinctively, he never would—no matter what evidence I mounted against him?

"How much longer do I have to stay down here?" I asked.

"He's gone. I just like having you there."

I sat up quickly to glare at him. In his black baseball cap, he looked younger, slightly less menacing, and he almost verged on . . . boyish. "I thought you weren't making jokes."

"It wasn't one." His eyes shone, but he didn't keep them on me long, shifting them to the blonde instead. "The Belmonte-Ruiz cartel has been tracking Sandra since we put her on these streets a few days ago. They know she doesn't have a pimp yet, or she'd be working a street in the next neighborhood. Hopefully they'll pick her up tonight."

A small tremor of panic worked its way through me. "But you won't let them take her, will you?"

The man who'd passed our car earlier approached Sandra, and after a quick exchange, she handed him a lighter. With a few drags of a cigarette, he said something, and she smiled.

"He just complimented her looks," Cristiano said. "Sometimes they grab girls. Other times, though, the girls go willingly."

There was that word again. *Willingly.* I was beginning to think Cristiano thought it meant something different than the rest of the world.

"They're lost and looking for connection," he said in an instructional tone. "Protection. Could be that they come from a shitty, abusive home and this is one way out."

Sandra fidgeted with her hands in her lap.

"Anyway, this guy?" Cristiano continued. "He's feeling her out."

An SUV rounded the corner and crept toward them. The smoker said something, laughed, and nodded discreetly at the car. Sandra turned her head over her shoulder, and her grin vanished as she shot to her feet.

I sat forward as she took off in a sprint, but Cristiano shoved me back into my seat. "Don't call attention, for fuck's sake."

The man flicked his cigarette away and ran after her. "But you have to do something," I hissed.

The SUV reversed, trying to catch up with her, tires jumping what was left of a crumbling curb before the car screeched onto the sidewalk to block her path.

"Cristiano," I said more firmly. "*Do* something."

Cristiano said nothing. Did nothing. The man grabbed her, and she struggled against him. Suddenly, he howled like an animal, jerked, and fell, clutching his leg. The driver bolted out of the car and stopped at his partner's feet, his face scrunched in confusion.

Sandra whipped a knife from under her skirt, raised it over her head, and plunged it into the top of his neck.

I covered my mouth to conceal my gasp, but it filled the car.

"See how she stabbed *into* his spine, not through?" Cristiano asked. "I hope you're taking notes."

My stomach churned violently as I watched blood spurt everywhere. The man who'd approached her on the bench writhed on the ground, trying to yank what looked like an arrow from his leg.

A third man I hadn't seen ducked out of the passenger-side door and crept along the side of the car that was hidden from Sandra.

"Fuck," Cristiano said, grabbing his two-way and barking into it, "Now. Go!"

The blood was excessive and I hadn't seen that much of it since my mother's death. The thought, the sight, made me woozy, my jaw tingling as bile rose up my throat. The third man snuck up behind Sandra until she whirled. He smacked her across the face, and she stumbled back, tripped over the smoker's foot, and landed on her back.

The man jumped on top of her with a pair of handcuffs, wrestling her wrists to the pavement.

Cristiano sat forward. "Come on," he said in a way that sounded as if he was cheering her on.

A Honda screeched around the corner, followed by a convoy of speeding cars. They skidded to a halt in the middle of the street, distracting the man long enough for Sandra to knee him in the balls.

"Yeah," Cristiano said, hitting his palm against the steering wheel triumphantly.

As my attention darted between him, Sandra, and everyone else, my head began to swim, but I narrowed my eyes, focusing on the scene in front of me.

As men from the warehouse swarmed out of the cars,

Sandra's attacker released her wrists. She punched him hard enough to send blood and teeth flying.

She shook out her hand, and gold flashed in the head-lights. She had a ring on every finger—thick, heavy bands and gems. Not even brass knuckles. Just rings.

I glanced at the massive diamond on my finger. Earlier, I'd regarded is as stunning and elegant—if not over the top. Now I saw it as a potential weapon.

Just the motion of bending my head to look down made me feel queasy, so I raised it again, trying to ward off the sick feeling.

Cristiano unbuckled his seatbelt and tossed the hat aside. "*Stay,*" he ordered. "Or so help me God, I'll leave you here tonight."

I shrank down in my seat but kept him in my sights as he marched across the street, rolling up his shirt sleeves. The menace in that one move, in the way he exposed his veiny, hirsute forearms, made sweat trickle down my temple. Who could ever stop Cristiano when he was hell-bent on anything?

One thing I knew—it would take more than physical force.

A man like Cristiano could only be brought down through mental and emotional warfare—carefully chosen words, intimate, deliberate touches, manipulations and schemes so subtle, he would never see them coming.

But as far as what he was walking into now? I wasn't worried for his safety, though I was surprised by how vehe-mently I wanted it—especially if the alternative was him getting hurt and me having to fend for myself.

By the time he reached them, Max had the smoker and the third attacker on their knees by the curb. The man with the knife in his neck *had* to be dead.

When Cristiano reached them, he squatted to face the

first man who'd approached Sandra. They exchanged words until Cristiano seized him by the neck—or was it his *trachea*?

Cristiano released him and circled the two men. He stopped behind the smoker, accepted a machete from Max, and decapitated him in one clean slice. I covered my mouth to hold in my scream as the body slumped over, bleeding and convulsing.

Vomit rose up my throat, and I swallowed over and over to force it back down.

I wanted to look away, but I forced myself not to. I'd wanted answers, and I was getting them. I wasn't sure what they meant yet, and perhaps I'd regret having them. But I was beyond the point where I could turn a blind eye.

Cristiano moved behind the last one and paused. I held my breath as I waited for him to send the last man's head the same way of the smoker's.

But Cristiano passed the machete back to Max and gestured for Sandra to take his place. She didn't hesitate— just sliced her blade across the man's neck, leaving him a bloody heap with the others.

I'd heard the rumors, but I'd not yet seen Cristiano in action. He'd delivered death without hesitation—and faster than it would've taken me to cross the street to him.

That was the vicious killer I'd grown up with. The man who'd stolen me out from underneath his brother. That was also the man whose tie I'd fixed earlier, who'd just made a crude joke, who'd served me duck confit over a bed of precious memories.

That was my husband.

And he'd been right—I wasn't ready.

I put my head between my knees and retched.

15

NATALIA

Black, vomit-splattered pavement blurred with tears as I emptied my stomach again. The car door had been opened, and a hand had gathered my hair into a too-tight ponytail, away from my face.

"You puked *in* the car and somehow managed to avoid *your* shoes," Cristiano said, wrapping my hair around his wrist. "Mine weren't so lucky."

I wasn't sure if I was crying in response to the vomit or for what I'd just seen. I looked past Cristiano's blood-splattered pantlegs. Max had a bound-and-gagged woman over his shoulder as he hurriedly transported her from the back of the attackers' SUV to one of Cristiano's. Eduardo did the same with a different girl. "Where are they taking them?"

"Got it all out? We have to move," Cristiano said. "Get up."

"I can't," I said, the words grating from my raw throat.

"*La policía* will be here soon," he said. "And as I told you before, they're not on my payroll. Either they'll find an abandoned car and a pile of vomit or they'll find an abandoned car, vomit, and you." He took my elbow. "Let's go."

I let him yank me out of the car as Max shut the doors to his SUV and climbed back behind the steering wheel. Blood and guts painted the broken pavement.

"They're taking the girls somewhere safe," he said, dragging me along.

Disoriented, I tried piecing the scene together. "Then why are they still gagged?"

"So they don't scream and fight. If Belmonte-Ruiz sends men after us, or if law enforcement shows up, it'll get ugly. We need to go *now*. You're walking too slow."

He ducked, hauled me over his shoulder, and carried me to the Audi.

After settling me into the passenger's seat and securing my seatbelt, he removed his shoes, went to the trunk, and returned with a fresh pair.

Within seconds, we were speeding away.

I gripped the door handle in an attempt to quell my uneasy stomach. "During the Easter party, you said you weren't going to pay for another shipment," I said. "You were going to take it instead."

"That's what I did."

He rescued them?

That would change everything. *Everything*.

It would mean he wasn't a monster at all—at least not to them. Only to me. "I don't understand."

"Belmonte-Ruiz is the leading sex trafficker in the country—one of the top in Central and South America. They're not easy to get to, so I interrupt them where I can."

"Like you did to Diego?" I asked, trying to relate everything together. "You sabotaged him to force him into a position where he'd be vulnerable."

"Pretty much. Nobody who traffics for Belmonte-Ruiz is safe from me. I try to intercept shipments or in this case, hit their own men on a small job." Cristiano steered into the next lane with one hand on top of the wheel. "Basically, the Calavera cartel doesn't traffic people."

"Then what *do* you do?" I pleaded. "Help me understand. After everything I've heard, I don't get why you'd help anyone."

He set his jaw, staring forward. "Because you came in here with your mind made up. You saw what you wanted to see, but it's time to open your eyes."

"You're asking me to believe that all this—this . . . that everything I've seen—the women's clothing in the basement, Sandra as fourteen-year-old bait, and the rumors about the Badlands—it's all . . . it's . . ." Overwhelmed by confusion, I put my face in my hands, shaking my head. "That's not what this world is. If you steal from another cartel, you die."

"We've been hitting Belmonte-Ruiz for months, and I'm still standing," he said. "And they aren't the first cartel we've brought down."

"But all those people in the Badlands," I said. "The gates—"

"Are to keep those who'd hurt us *out*. That's all."

"When we drove in, I saw people in the back of a semi."

He shifted in his seat, frowning. "It was headed south. We were taking people home—Guatemala, Brazil, Chile, wherever. It's not like we can just send them on their merry way once we excavate them from bad situations. They need help to get home and get acclimated. And we have to be stealthy about it because of the circumstances." He ran a hand over his mouth and rubbed his jaw before glancing over at me. "The Badlands are full of slaves and whores, Natalia. And laborers, misfits, and ruthless people."

I looked back at him, meeting his eyes a second before he turned them back out the windshield. "That's what I've been saying all along," I said.

"I never denied it. You were just looking at it from the wrong angle. It's not a prison. It's a sanctuary. They're not abused. They're rehabilitated."

Holy shit. A coat of goose bumps sprang over my skin. Why had it been so hard for me to see it? Why was it hard now to admit that it made sense?

Because Cristiano was still my captor. My bad guy. He'd done the opposite of all this to me—so how could I be expected to see him as anything else?

"What about me?" I asked. "You can't get angry that I assumed everything I'd heard was true. *You took me.*"

His nostrils flared as he swerved into the next lane and took a turn too fast. I braced myself against the door. The Audi's smooth hum filled the silence until Cristiano smacked his palm against the steering wheel. After a few moments, he spoke calmly. "It would seem you're the one exception."

Of course I was. *How convenient.* Cristiano got to be a hero to everyone else while keeping me locked up in his house. I crossed my arms and leaned into the corner. "I see. And Sandra? Is she also an exception?"

"No." He stopped for a red light, and I registered my surroundings. We were almost at *La Madrina*. "She's had two years of therapy and rehab, including one of intense physical training—twice as hard as what you've been doing. She wanted to see those men suffer." His grip tight-ened on the wheel. "She understood that the best way to help was to draw them out. There were about a dozen pairs of eyes on her, ready to spring into action if she needed help." He snickered. "Well, eleven and a half if you count Max."

I didn't laugh. "Where are Max and Eduardo taking the other girls?"

"To the Badlands. There's a team there to receive them. Clean them up, feed them, set them up in a safe house with whatever they need while they adjust. That's the purpose of the toiletry kits you saw." He blew out a sigh. "Then we learn who they are and where they came from."

I fingered the unfamiliar, obtrusive diamond on my hand as I eyed him. "And then?" I asked softly.

When the light changed, Cristiano hit the gas and turned in the direction of the club. "We try to get them home. If they don't have a home or don't want to return—like Sandra—then we have good, fair work and modest housing for them in the Badlands."

My heart sank as the truth of the situation over-whelmed me. These women had been in the worst situations imaginable. Cristiano and his team had saved them. I had not only doubted him, but accused him of unspeakable things. Considering the lengths he went to in order to help, my character assassination must've been shitty to receive.

My throat thickened. "They stay willingly?" I asked, feeling smaller than ever.

"Yes. They have jobs and pay rent like anyone else. Because after what they've been through, many of them want to *be* anyone else."

I wrinkled my nose. "You . . . charge them *rent*?"

"You don't miss anything, do you?" A half-smile slid across his face. "Working gives them a sense of purpose. The Badlands are a safe place for them to do it. I don't need the rent money—I put it back into the community.

But none of them came here for a handout. Most like to feel like they're contributing."

I shifted in my seat, grateful for the dark cover of night to hide the range of emotions surely playing out on my face.

How could I have missed all this?

How were girls and boys and *humans* enduring this every day, and why weren't more people helping?

I looked down at my hands. Had I made a terrible mistake treating Cristiano with such disdain, even though he was still guilty of his crimes against me?

"What about the men?" I asked. "Where are they from?"

"All over—and right there. Many of the residents who live within the walls were there when we arrived."

"The town you plundered, raped, and pillaged."

"That's the rumor, yes. And I thank you not to dispel it, since it keeps our reputation intact."

If Cristiano hadn't said something similar at dinner a few nights earlier, I might not have believed him. But it seemed he not only appreciated his bad reputation—he needed it to continue the work he did.

"We needed a town in a strategic location with natural security like the ocean to protect our backs, the mountain over our heads, and the flat desert to see anyone foolish enough to approach. We found that, and we took it." He flexed his hand on the wheel and leaned an elbow on the windowsill. "But we came to the townspeople with respect," he said. "We worked out an amicable deal with those who wanted to stay and compensated those who didn't—all with non-disclosure agreements, of course."

It was like a fairytale, and I wanted to believe it. But regardless of what Cristiano had done for others, there was one person who wouldn't get a happy ending.

As he pulled into the lot behind *La Madrina*, the tires tread over a track to a sliding gate. He parked, exited, and helped me out before taking my bag and his suitcase from the trunk.

"We're sleeping here at the club?" I asked, removing Cristiano's jacket and then the bulletproof vest.

"*Sí.*" I tried to take my duffel from him, but he hoisted it over his shoulder. With the cell phone tucked into the bag's bottom, I probably didn't need to worry, but Cristiano seemed to know all. He had yet to punish me for anything like snooping or snarky comebacks and barbed words—but if he thought I'd used the phone at all to get in touch with Diego or *anyone* outside this cartel, his threats would no longer be idle.

"Opening your mouth would be a death sentence."

He turned to me. "Leave the vest. Put your jacket back on. I won't have club rats ogling my wife."

It didn't much matter what I wore. We used a private entrance in the back and rode upstairs in an elevator reserved for him and his team.

We walked out of the elevator and across a carpeted hallway that thumped under my feet. He unlocked his office and held the door open for me. It was an extension of his club—sleek and black with shiny surfaces and gold hardware. Computer monitors with surveillance footage made up the wall behind his desk. A bar cart in one corner held decanters, glasses, and spirits in varying sizes. I went to the floor-to-ceiling window overlooking the club. Aqua, turquoise, and seafoam green lights splashed over the patrons and made shimmery, squiggly lines on the dancefloor.

"Tonight's theme—*Bajo el Mar*," he said.

"Under the sea." So many people, and they probably

had no idea they were being watched. "How long did you spy on me before you made your presence known?"

"Long enough to know you were looking for me. Long enough to fantasize about stealing you away to my office."

"And here I am." I turned to face him, wondering why he'd brought me here. Was he planning something? Or was a change of scenery supposed to be a gift to me? The spot of blood I'd seen on his shirt earlier was now one of many. "You wore a tie just to murder a man?"

"No. I wore it to murder three." He dipped his head with a sinister smile. "How about a drink, *mi amor*?"

How easily we slipped back into our roles—Cristiano in control, and me trying to make sense of things and even anticipate his next move. "You don't have what I want."

"I own a bar. Try me."

"Coca Light."

He cocked his head. "Of course I have it."

"Warm," I said. "That's the only way I like it."

He paused. "I'll have them put it in the microwave."

Despite my uncertainty over what was happening around me, I almost laughed. "I mean unrefrigerated."

He winked and kept his eyes on me as he picked up his desk phone and placed my order.

I glanced around the dimly-lit office shaded blue by the ocean theme. "Do we sleep on the couch?"

"We can if you like. It'd be cozier."

"What's the alternative?"

"I have a bed on the next floor."

I raised my eyes to the ceiling as if I might be able to see through it.

I could barely feel the vibration of the music below. "It's so quiet in here."

"The walls are soundproof so the noise doesn't disrupt

me while I'm working. As are the walls upstairs." He grinned. "So you and I don't bother the patrons."

Another attempt at humor. But also, perhaps, a threat. Maybe outside the Badlands, there were no rules. Maybe willingness was more subjective here, in a dark club, where he'd tried to get me up to his office before. Could everything he'd told me tonight be canceled out by the fact that I was the exception?

Could I appreciate that he was a savior worthy of praise and loyalty, but also hate him for making me his only victim?

I had to keep my eyes and ears open. I admired the things he did, but to me, he was still the same man he'd been before the past couple hours. I couldn't take the chance that if I gave in and saw him as something other than the devil, I might stop fighting for my freedom.

I stared at him, utterly perplexed at the puzzle before me. This was exactly what I'd feared. Not knowing whether to hate him or to feel something else entirely.

"I need to change my tampon," I said.

He blinked at me, opening and closing his mouth. "I— I can send one of my employees out for some. Did Jaz not, uh, pack some for you?"

An ember of delight sparked in me as he stammered. Even the most composed man in the world could be derailed by menstruation. "I have some," I said. "I just meant I need to use the bathroom."

"Ah." He nodded at a closed door to his left. "Through there."

I hesitated. "Are there cameras in there? I don't want an audience."

"For God's sake, Natalia. No. I don't surveil toilets."

My pleasure grew at the offense he took. It wouldn't hurt to remind him that while he called me his wife, I was still his prisoner, and that even when he treated me well, he was only the hero in his own story—not mine.

I picked up my bag and started across the room.

"Leave that," he said.

I paused. "What?"

"The bag," he said evenly, and with no room for argument. "Put it on my desk."

My heart thumped once. I looked back at him. All teasing had left his face, and his dark demeanor had resurfaced. What did he want with the bag? I feared the answer was obvious. "I need it," I said.

"No, you don't." He nodded in front of him. "There."

Inhaling through my nose, I carried it to his desk, setting the bag down slowly. I wanted to protest more, but that would raise a red flag.

I took a tampon from the inside pocket and glanced up, trying to gauge his shift in mood. There was an indisputable hardness in his eyes that hadn't been there a moment ago.

Could he possibly know about the phone? And how?

Leaving the bag felt more like surrendering it, but I had no choice. If he knew enough to search the bag, then he knew what he was looking for.

My gut smarted as I made my way to the bathroom.

I had the distinct feeling that the hero had left the building.

16

NATALIA

Compared to the nightclub below, the marble full bathroom off Cristiano's office was eerily quiet. I stood at the door, steeling myself to face the possibility that Cristiano had found the phone Diego had given me. I'd uncovered things about Cristiano tonight I never could've imagined. Good things. But I didn't have him pegged in the least. He could still flip on a dime.

I exited the bathroom and found him towering over his desk—and the contents of my overnight bag.

"Coca Light, warm." He nodded to his bar cart, which held a glass of soda that must've been delivered while I was in the bathroom.

I took a sip hoping the carbonation would soothe my stomach—uneasy from both my earlier nausea and my current nerves—but otherwise kept my eyes on him.

"You know," he said, his eyes shadowed by heavy brows, "Diego was standing right about where you are now when he figured out the truth."

My fingers tingled with alarm. "What truth?"

"I cannot be bought off or dissuaded from getting what

I want. Whatever I desire, I find a way to take it." He opened the top drawer to his desk. "But my brother proved me wrong."

I spun the giant rock on my finger and moved closer to the door. "How?"

"He gave me you. And in exchange, I let go of something I'd wanted for a long time. But I don't have you, Natalia. Not yet. Not the way he did."

When he glanced down into the drawer, I quickly scanned the items on his desk for the phone, but it wasn't there. "I could've told you that before I walked down the aisle," I said. "I could've saved you the trouble."

Cristiano took out a gun, and my back went straight as a rod. He'd found the phone—there was no question now. Holding the 9mm up to the light by its pearly white grip, silver and gold flashed.

I stepped forward, my heart pounding as I recognized the White Monarch. I looked down at my rings, and it clicked—the reason they'd felt so familiar. The two-toned metal and pearl inlay wedding band complemented the gun. All it needed was a big, fat diamond in the middle.

The last time I'd seen the White Monarch was in the moments before it'd blown out a *sicario's* brains. "Where'd you get that?" I asked.

"When you pulled this on me eleven years ago, my life didn't flash before my eyes—yours did. The child I'd protected since before she could walk had turned on me. You know what else I saw?"

He didn't wait for my answer.

"Your loyalty to Diego. You offered yourself up in his place. I saw Bianca in you that day. Your mother would've followed your father to the grave. You risked your life for my brother's. I admired that." Still holding the gun, he leaned his hands on his desk. "And I *hated* it."

I pulled his jacket closed around me. "Why?"

"I already told you—because *I* wanted it. I'd pledged my loyalty to your family, and that included you. But in a moment, it all vanished into thin air. Nobody would risk their life for me, though I had for them, over and over." He unknotted his bloody tie and discarded it on the desk. "So I left, built a steadfast cartel around me and made my own family," he said, undoing the buttons at his throat. "Why, then, is it not enough? Why do I still think about that moment you pulled this on me?"

"Is that why I'm here?" It wasn't the answer I wanted as to why he'd married me, but it was an answer nonetheless. "Some elaborate scheme for revenge on a scared nine-year-old girl?"

"No, *mi corazón*. My scheming is done. It didn't go the way I'd planned—Diego's still alive—but only because he knew what I wanted, even when I didn't." He gently slid the gun across the desk. "Just when I was about to throw him to the dogs, he stood where you are now and offered something I couldn't take on my own."

I released a breath I'd been holding. "Me."

He nodded once. "You."

"You could've taken me at any point. You didn't need Diego to do it."

"That's where you're wrong."

Because Cristiano wouldn't *let* himself take me. He'd needed Diego to give me. Maybe he'd thought that my loyalty was part of the bargain, but something like that couldn't be forced.

"Diego is more cunning than you think," he told me. "I didn't even recognize my own want for you until he showed it to me. I'd never let myself think I could have you, so it was never an option in my mind. Diego gets credit for pinpointing a weakness and exploiting it. But he doesn't get to keep any part of you."

"Of *me*?" I asked. "He doesn't have me. He doesn't have *anything* anymore."

"You can't be loyal to both of us, Natalia. It'll get one of the three of us killed, and it won't be me."

"He *doesn't* have me." Cristiano had to know that— didn't he? Feeling short of breath, I walked a few steps toward him and steadied myself on a chair. "But neither do you. Do you honestly think loyalty can be demanded?"

"Yes. So tell me—who are you loyal to, Natalia?"

After this past week, the answer came easily. "Myself, and no one else."

A vein in his forehead ticked, and he nodded at my bag. "Where's the phone?"

My heart stopped, even though I'd known where this was going. "Diego gave it to me," I said, focusing on keeping my voice firm and steady. "I didn't ask for it."

"Where is it?" he demanded.

I swallowed as his patience ran thin. "Sewed into the bottom."

He rifled through his drawer and slammed a pair of scissors on the desk. "Get it out."

As I approached, he jerked his desk phone to his ear and punched a single digit.

I could see that I'd angered him—but did that mean what he'd said it would? Since I'd arrived, he'd been all bark and no bite. He'd warned me leaking information would lead to death—period. But Cristiano wouldn't kill me.

I hadn't shared any information. I was only guilty of accepting and hiding the phone.

He wouldn't hurt me, I told myself.

What then? How would he punish me for hiding the

phone? Did he have it in him to lock me away, chain me, starve me? The answer was easy—yes, he did. He hadn't gotten where he was without ruthlessness. Torture, destruction, and murder. And you didn't torture, destroy, and murder without having developed some degree of detachment from people.

He'd lavished beautiful clothing upon me, fed me the best food, and surrounded me in comfort. He'd kept his distance, as had his men, warned away from touching Cristiano's "things." He was teaching me how to fight them —and him.

He'd liberated women and children, mostly, I realized in that moment, without credit since he'd been underground until a couple weeks ago.

He wasn't a rapist or an abuser. But he *was* a murderer.

And I?

I was his one exception.

He leveled his eyes on me as he held the phone to his ear and waited. After a moment, he spoke into the receiver. "Send Scratch upstairs with his equipment."

My stomach dropped. *Equipment*?

He shoved the contents of my bag onto the ground and picked up the little black phone. "What did you tell him?"

"Nothing," I rasped through my dry throat.

Cristiano swiped swiftly and expertly before holding up the screen to show me the one saved number. "*Padre*. You expected me to be so fucking dumb that I'd believe this phone was from Costa?"

"No," I said.

"You don't even call him that. You call him *Papá*. Tell me how you still believe Diego cares for you when he put you in this position."

"I don't," I said, "but even if I did, I take responsibility for my own actions."

"Oh, yes," he said. "You will."

The hair on the back of my neck stood up. Cristiano had only been this cold to me in the company of others. His iciness, paired with the mention of *equipment*, sent a chill down my spine. "I didn't share information," I said as panic tightened my chest. "You have my word."

He resumed looking through the phone. "If there were texts, you've deleted them, but one of my tech guys can easily recover them. Tell me honestly, Natalia. What information did you give him?"

"Nothing," I swore again.

He slipped the phone into his shirt pocket and came around the desk. "If you're conspiring with him against me—"

"I'm not—"

"Let . . . him . . . *come for you*," Cristiano intoned, raising his voice. "I am *not* him. I won't let you go so easily."

"Easily?" I exhaled. "What would you have done in his shoes?"

"For the woman I claimed to love? Built an army to protect her or died by her side. But I wouldn't give her to another man, especially one I knew to be dangerous. And I won't let him have you."

The stark confession, which came so easily to him, shocked me. Did a man like Cristiano even *know* love? Did *I?* I'd been the one stupid enough to fall for a phony like Diego. *I'd* been the one begging him to flee with me, to die with me if it came to that. And he'd refused. Words meant nothing anymore—only action did. Now, I stood before his brother, who was turning out to be the complete opposite of what I'd thought.

Cristiano continued around the desk until he was standing over me. "He'll have to kill me if he wants you back."

I tried to hold my shiver at bay, but every inch of me was vibrating with adrenaline, both from Cristiano's frightening threats . . . and his exhilarating promises. "I imagine he wouldn't be the first to try."

He snorted. "Not hardly. *Pero todavía estoy aquí.* I'm still standing before you, so you can guess what happened to those who failed. As I told you once before—betrayal can only be treated as a life or death matter."

He was trying his best to scare me, and though it was working, I wouldn't give him the satisfaction of knowing it. I raised my chin. "Are you going to hurt me?"

"Don't you think I should?" He stood in front of me, blocking me from the exit. "If you were a man in my cartel who'd gone to the enemy, what the *fuck* do you think I would do to him?"

I gripped my neck. *El Polvo.*

"Exactly," he said.

"I *didn't* betray you. I swear it."

"Are you certain?"

"*Yes.*"

"But you're wrong, naïve girl."

I gritted my teeth. "I'm telling the truth."

"I know you are. But the phone synced with the Wi-Fi at the house. And that may mean nothing to you, but it means a hell of a lot to me, my security team that works very hard to secure our town, and to Diego—an enemy. And I assume *all* my enemies enter *every* situation with the worst of motivations. Especially him."

My hairline began to sweat. I'd already known this was bad, but it was much worse than I'd thought.

"He could've gotten access to sensitive information." Cristiano's lips pressed into a bloodless line. "He'd have known your whereabouts anytime the phone was on. He could be standing outside the door right now, ready to ambush us, thanks to his ability to track us here."

None of this had even occurred to me. I shook my head, at a loss for words. "I didn't know."

"It doesn't matter. You knew enough not to bring the phone into my house, and to cut off that line of communication. You did it anyway, knowing what it could cost you. You broke an unspoken rule that I *did* speak." His pupils seemed to eat his irises—completely black eyes with not a single fleck of light to be seen. "You fed information to an enemy."

"Not on purpose," I said, battling against a rising wave of dread. I looked to the gun. I'd thought loyalty couldn't be forced, but maybe I'd been wrong.

"You haven't learned your lesson, even though Diego so brutally taught it to you," he said. "So I ask you again. Who are you loyal to?"

I didn't want to show fear, but I couldn't help it. Cartel law was no joke. I'd been shielded from it, but I was no longer someone's innocent daughter. I was *in* this life now for better or worse. And I wasn't going to cower.

"My answer is the same. Myself," I said, mustering all the conviction I could, even as I wrung my trembling hands in front of me. "Every man in my life who means anything to me has broken my trust—even you."

"I can't break promises I never made," he said coolly. "Deceiving me has consequences, but when the going penalty is a slow, tortured death, I hope you'll find this punishment more than fair."

With a knock, Cristiano looked over my head and called through the door, "*Espérate.*"

He'd told someone to *wait*. "What are you going to do?" I asked, glancing back.

"You wanted to be a captive. You wanted me to impose

my will. That's what I'm doing."

My heart stopped. "Who's at the door, Cristiano?"

"Scratch. Best tattoo artist in the region. You're a member of the Calavera cartel now—and you're going to own it."

A pit formed in my stomach as I looked between Cristiano and the door. "You're going to—to *brand* me?"

"You're already branded, sweetheart, but this way, there'll be no question."

My heart pounded. Cristiano was going to put his mark on me. Permanently. There would be *no* mistaking who I belonged to with the Calavera name inked on my body. It was barbaric, possessive, and it was making my breath come fast. Part of that was anger that he could be so callous—but *most* of it was something else. Something deeper. Murkier. Cristiano hadn't even officially claimed me yet, but he wanted to tell the world who I belonged to.

And that spoke to an inky darkness in me I'd been trying not to give in to for as long as I could remember. It nudged the basest of my desires awake, just like the ones Cristiano had whispered in my ear on only my second night in his bed.

"I won't relent until your body has drunk every last drop I have to give. Until you're mine through and through."

The tender place between my legs responded to the claim of ownership now just as it had that night. Why did I want to be dominated like this? Why had I never known it until Cristiano?

I'd struggled for control since I'd stepped foot into the church. I was terrified but also tempted to let go, just for a little, just to see how Cristiano would respond.

"There *is* another option," he said, tilting his head.

I released a breath, but disappointment tinged my exhale. Why? My body wasn't his property. But if ever there were a man who could own a person in every way, it would be Cristiano. And he'd picked me to be his. He'd married me, brought me into this cartel, and he was going to fuck me, no question. He'd decided I was his, so I was. What would a tattoo mean or even change?

But I wasn't as easily fooled as I used to be. "Another option" would only cost me in some other way. "What is it?"

"One last chance to pledge your loyalty to your husband. But now, I want you to do it on your knees." He walked around to my back and cleared my hair from my neck. After a soothing squeeze of my shoulder, he grazed his hand down and very gently molded his hand to the curve of my ass. "You will beg my forgiveness, you will promise *never* to betray me again—and then, I'm going to let you off with a warning. But not before I put you over my knee and punish you with a spanking."

I inhaled a sharp breath, my ass cheek already stinging with his promise. His enormous hand heated my skin while barely touching it—with only the *thought* of him exerting his dominance.

My legs threatened to buckle. Which was exactly what he wanted—to prove he could get me to my knees, and then that he could get my body to betray me by making me enjoy my punishment.

I was wet already—but he'd known I would be. I hated that he did, especially before I did. Getting spanked and enjoying it was a form of capitulation all on its own, but that he also wanted me to beg? And to mean it?

They should've been easy demands to meet. Swear to keep his secrets, plead him for mercy, and receive a punishment that terrified me not because of the pain it might inspire, but because of the pleasure it definitely would.

I *had* betrayed his trust. I'd put him, Jaz, Alejandro—

the entire household, the entire town—at risk. I understood. He couldn't let that slide.

And any fool could say and do what was necessary to save her own life. If my mother was watching, God rest her soul, she would understand. Any idiot could see that being taken over one knee like a petulant child was a thousand times preferable to a permanent tattoo.

But my spine lengthened instead of bowed. It occurred to me that was what Cristiano had been teaching me to do. To show strength and fight back. And I'd warned him I'd use it against him.

"No," I said.

"I beg your pardon?" he asked against my hair.

Submit on my knees or learn what it meant to have my loyalty forced. I'd wear the tattoo like a badge of honor. I clung to the deep-seated knowledge that even though Cristiano'd had plenty of opportunities to hurt me already, he hadn't. "You can shove me down, but I won't beg."

"You put my men at risk, along with every single person in my household."

I bowed my head. "Then do what you have to do."

His hand disappeared from my backside. "If you're trying to provoke me, you won't like the result."

Except, I *wasn't* just denying his loyalty to prove he couldn't demand it. And my trust in him would never be absolute just because he'd kidnapped me. I was hit with the realization that there was a deeper, more powerful reason holding me back.

I could never willingly let Cristiano have me in the ways he demanded . . . and it had nothing to do with his actions over the past few weeks, or with Diego.

"You want my devotion and my loyalty, but they're based on trust and respect," I said calmly over my shoulder. "I have neither for my mother's murderer."

"I already *brought* him to you," he said through his teeth. "I hunted your mother's murderer. I put him on his knees and handed Costa the gun. For closure. For Bianca. For *you*."

Maybe he was right. Maybe with everything I'd learned about him tonight, I should've known with complete certainty that he wouldn't have hurt my mom on purpose. And perhaps it'd been an accident, or perhaps he'd given the *sicario* access, or perhaps a million other possibilities. But as long as I had even a *shred* of doubt, I could never fully trust Cristiano.

I turned to face him. "I can't know for sure."

"*I* can. I *do*. I'm not her murderer. She didn't die because she was shot in the stomach—she bled out. Do you know how long that takes?"

I blinked at the ground, unprepared for this argument. "Several minutes," I said, having looked up as many details as I could remember over the years.

"At the very least. Could be ten, fifteen minutes—or more." He took my arms and drew me close. "What fool would stay at the crime scene that long? I walked in moments before you did."

"You were cleaning out the safe—"

"All the money in the world is useless if I'm dead."

"It doesn't matter. Don't you see that?" I wriggled free of him, backing up until I hit his desk. "Even if the *sicario* wielded the gun, someone else gave the order—but who?" I asked. "As long as I have questions about your involvement, I will doubt you. A wife cares for her husband in sickness and health, she lies with him willingly—she loves him. I will never do any of that for a man who could have killed my mother."

The skin at his collar reddened as his chest expanded

with an inhale. He turned his head over his shoulder. "*¡Adelante!*"

As the door opened and heavy boots pounded the floor, closing in on us, my nerves flared—but they were anchored by a shameful thrill of excitement. Cristiano knew how to make me enjoy a spanking, I had no doubt. But he would never suspect being marked this way spoke to a terrifying —and utterly confusing—desire in me.

I tried to see around him, but his shoulders were too wide.

A bald, lumbering man with a chest-length red beard and a black bag over one shoulder stepped into my peripheral vision. He pulled on a glove. "Where do you want it?" he asked in a low, rumbling voice as rubber snapped against skin.

I could feel that same sting, Cristiano's big hand landing squarely on my ass, spanking me into the submissive role he knew would leave me wet.

But I wasn't going to beg for anything.

"Turn and face the back of the room," Cristiano said to me.

As I did, my eyes landed on the White Monarch he'd left on the desk.

He noticed it, too. We exchanged a look before he slid it outside my reach.

My trust in him would never be absolute—and it seemed the reverse was true, too.

From behind, he slid the lapels of his jacket to my elbows, trapping me and exposing my upper back. "Last chance to say mercy, *mariposa*." He spoke quietly so Scratch wouldn't hear. "Tell me you've learned your lesson. I warned you once. No lie, no betrayal will go unpunished. Say mercy, and I'll turn that sweet ass red in return."

He wanted an out, but not for me. He'd walked right

up to the line, and now he expected *me* to pull him back so he wouldn't cross it. So he could sleep easy at night knowing he wasn't his father.

He was. And I'd be the one to prove it to him.

I met his burning gaze over my shoulder, and I could see that no part of him doubted I'd concede my loyalty and my dignity. "I won't beg for anything, even your forgiveness, and I won't be willingly bent over your knee as punishment."

He drew back. It gave me a secret thrill to surprise him. Now, the tables were turned, and *he* had to decide what to do. "Careful, sweet girl. The thought of spanking you until you're dripping wet turns my dick to stone. But my cartel's name on your skin? I'll truly own you then, and I don't think I need to tell you what that means."

Heat pulsed in me. I didn't need to be told because I felt it, too. His hand would only dominate my ass for tonight, but the act of permanently marking me said ownership in a soul-deep way.

"Give me a reason to do it, and I *will* take it," he warned.

"Take it."

He searched my eyes, perhaps looking for any doubt or reservation. After all, I had to be willing, or I suspected he wouldn't go through with it. His expression eased as he tilted his head and seemed to find the answer in my gaze— one that pleasantly surprised him.

Cristiano wanted my loyalty, and as with anything else he desired, he would take it.

But that wasn't enough. He would make sure the world knew it.

He'd make sure I never forgot.

I belonged to Cristiano now, and I'd have it permanently stamped on my body for all to see.

NATALIA

The butterfly stung. I peeled back the bandage on my shoulder. Orange wings shimmered iridescent within black windowpanes. Slightly whimsical and a touch artistic, I was grateful to see it was a tattoo I would've chosen for myself, although until tonight, I would've balked at the script, sugar skull, and red roses inked around it.

In the mirror of Cristiano's bedroom on the top floor of his nightclub, I read the tattoo reflected back at me over my shoulder.

Calavera Cartel.

Yes, I'd agreed to it, but that didn't change the fact that the asshole had branded me like I was cattle and sent me upstairs to bed like I was a petulant child. I'd tried to sleep, but I was drunk on a cocktail of emotions. A bitter aperitif of adrenaline, anger fizzing like soda water, an infuriating sweet-and-sour clash of irritation, and worst of all—secret excitement from Cristiano's absolute arrogant and unapologetic claim over me. I was sure he couldn't wait to pluck off the cherry garnish and slice clean through it with his teeth. And it would be irreversible when he did.

Cristiano liked permanence—no room for question. An entire town nobody could take from him, a Catholic marriage to bind our souls, a tattoo to remind me of my place. Or was it a warning to others? Nobody else would get too close to me when they saw who I belonged to.

When we'd danced at the costume party, my fury was aimed as much at myself as at him for my unsettling attraction to a man who'd so flippantly come on to me while knowing I was spoken for. Not many men would take another man's woman, then threaten to *remove his hands* if he touched her again.

I was angry at myself again, this time for the secret thrill that came with being staked by a man as wild and hard to pin down as Cristiano. Could the thought of it both make my pussy flutter with excitement and *also* piss me off? Could I have both allowed it to happen *and* use it to prove he was a bastard to decorate my body like a wall in his home? He had no right to assert his dominance in such a permanent, irrevocable way, even if it aroused the hell out of me.

And like splashing alcohol over a wound he'd created, he'd done it an hour after I'd learned he was an *advocate* for women.

I was the *exception*. The one captive. Keeping his dick in his pants allowed him to convince himself he was different. That he was a protector. That he'd made up for his father's sins.

No monster thinks of himself that way. He's just living by a different code than yours.

Frustration over my traitorous reaction, and with Cristiano himself, simmered close to the surface. I needed somewhere to direct it. I knew just the man to receive it. If

Cristiano's definition of evil was a man who liked his women helpless, then I'd hold up a mirror and show him the reflection of a soulless beast.

I turned away from my naked body. The black and gold bedroom on the top floor of *La Madrina* looked like the kind of bachelor pad you'd find in a nightclub. It shared the same soundproof walls and one-sided window as Cristiano's office so he could look out over the dance-floor in complete silence. I imagined him standing here, choosing a woman, and having her sent up to him. And the thought of him touching someone else, putting his *mark* on someone else, made me even more eager to rail at him.

Surely the playboy mini-mansion was woman-friendly for the many guests it saw. I found pink disposable razors, a blow-dryer, lavender-scented deodorant, and a black satin robe in my size on the back of the bathroom door.

The bedside clock read one in the morning, and once again, I was alone. He was a hypocrite to demand I sleep in his bed while he came and went as he pleased. Every day he asserted more dominance over me, and tonight, he'd taken control over my own body. But I suspected neither of us completely grasped the power I possessed.

I slipped into the robe, leaving my shoulder uncovered as I cinched the sash around my waist. Descending the staircase to return to his office, I was unsurprised to find Eduardo out front, his back straight and hands crossed in front of him. Even as I approached, he kept his eyes trained forward, as if I were Medusa, and one look would turn him to stone.

If only.

I reached for the door handle, but Eduardo blocked me from it.

He held his two-way radio to his mouth. "Your wife is here."

"*Uno momento*," Cristiano responded and cleared his throat.

Another power play, making me wait to see my own husband. I folded my arms over my chest and muttered, "Asshole."

"He's not," Eduardo said, his voice quiet but sharp.

I balked at him. "Excuse me?"

He rubbed his face over the tattoo darkening his cheek. "You're lucky to have his protection and affection."

"*Lucky*? You were in the church when we married. You know the truth of the situation."

"The truth is, he's our leader. He puts all of us before himself. He puts *you* before himself. And *we* reciprocate— but do you?"

It was, in much subtler words, the same threat Jazmín had leveled at me my first morning in the Badlands.

"If ever I come in here and find you've betrayed the man we consider our savior, you won't make it off the property."

The office door opened and a petite, slender blonde in skinny jeans stepped out. Her damp hair made wet spots on a white t-shirt. She waited for me to move so she could pass, but I was too stunned. My already sizzling anger boiled over. I didn't *want* to move. He was seeing another woman in the middle of the night *while I was upstairs*? Regardless of our arrangement, he was my *husband*. Her eyes sparkled as she ducked her head and went around me with a small smile.

Eduardo grunted what sounded like a laugh.

"Come in, Natalia." Cristiano called my attention to where he stood at his desk in a white, ribbed undershirt. His gaze drifted down my body as he picked up a tumbler of alcohol. "I thought I told you to go to bed."

"I'm not a child," I said.

"Then don't make me spank you like one, or that

tattoo would've been for nothing."

My insides tightened with a rush of desire, but equally potent mortification ripped through me as Eduardo listened on. On some level, I must've believed Cristiano when he'd said there was nobody but me, because now, the blow of seeing a woman exit his office had turned my feet —and possibly my throat—to concrete.

"Eduardo's standing *right there*."

Cristiano sighed. "I can see to it that to him, you're only one of my prized possessions. Like a car or watch. That my men hear nothing, see nothing, touch nothing, and wouldn't think of you as a female."

I gaped at Cristiano. "He thinks of me as a *car*?"

"He might, if he knows what's good for him—but would you like me to enforce that on him?"

I slammed the door to the office and walked in. A white terrycloth robe, far too small for Cristiano, had been discarded on the couch. "So every other man should see me as nothing, but you can enjoy your whores whenever you feel like it?"

Cristiano's eyebrows dropped, disturbing his normally unreadable expression. Confusion played over his face like film slides. "I see. Earlier she was a victim, now she's a whore? What changed?"

"What are you talking about?"

"That was Sandra," he said, shuffling some papers to one side of his desk. "The bait from earlier."

I glanced from the robe to his bare, muscled arms. "You're *sleeping* with her?"

He scoffed. "God, no. She showered, and I changed shirts because we were both wearing another man's blood. Well, several men's."

"What was she doing in here then?"

"What are *you* doing in here?"

I didn't answer, because I wasn't even sure I knew. He had tattooed me and sent me away—and didn't seem to hold any remorse over the extreme punishment. I wondered if he'd every truly thought I'd beg. And then, let him spank me—even if he suspected I wanted it.

I'd thought, maybe foolishly, I could turn Cristiano against himself. That I could gain a measure of control and freedom—not by escaping, running, or petulance, but by luring out his demons so he could no longer hide from them.

If I was enticing enough, could I undermine his work, his willpower, and his self-control, and *finally* get him to cross the line?

He ran a fingertip along the rim of his glass. "Sandra was here to discuss a top-secret project," he conceded when I didn't answer.

A large ice cube melted in another glass on his desk. "Have you cheated on me?"

"Is it cheating if you don't care?" he asked. "Although it seems you might at the moment."

"It makes me look stupid."

"To whom? As I said, my men see nothing, say nothing, think nothing about you." He set down his tumbler. "You shouldn't be down here. I sent you upstairs for your own good."

"Why? What will you do? Call Scratch back?" As if given life by my acknowledgment, my exposed *mariposa* tingled. "Go ahead. Mark me once and you might as well mark me everywhere."

"I intend to, just not with ink."

"Another baseless threat."

"Baseless?" He whipped his undershirt over his head, every muscle in his arms and torso flexing as he pulled it off. "Careful, Natalia, sweetheart. You tempt me."

I bit down on my lip at the embodiment of his power, surprised that my first thought was how elegant and sensual such profound and brute strength could be. *My* strength didn't lie in my muscles, but I wanted to prove that it didn't make me any less powerful. I stepped toward the desk. "But you're a master of resistance."

"Not tonight." He balled up his shirt and tossed it on the couch with the robe. "I haven't had so many sleepless nights in a row since I was on the street. My willpower isn't as strong as it has been."

"That explains the girl."

"All it explains is why I sent you away." He heaved a sigh and his eyes drifted to the paperwork and laptop in front of him. "Believe me, I wish your accusation were true," he said, rubbing the bridge of his nose. "To care so little that I could be buried in someone else's pussy right now."

I clenched my teeth, stemming jealousy at the thought —and then satisfaction that he'd resisted something he clearly wanted . . . for *me*.

"Especially when you stand there looking like you came here to fuck." His expression turned pained. "I need it, Natalia."

An answering ache between my legs caught me off guard. It was becoming clear that each time he voiced a need, my body's primal response was to question how I could fill it.

I couldn't imagine him asking *anyone* for what he needed. As he'd said before—he *took* what he wanted. He didn't ask. So what stopped him now?

I took another step forward, and he moved back.

This was where my power lay. Tonight, his weakness was on display. Perhaps because he'd thought I'd gone to bed and had naïvely let down his guard. I forced words from my mouth before I could chicken out. "What do you need?"

"You're the one who came to me," he said. "So I ask you *again*—*why* are you here?"

"It's hard to change the tattoo bandage when I can't see it that well." A small fib. I raised my chin as I delivered a jab just to irritate him. "Although, if it gets infected, maybe they'll remove it for me."

"Anyone else in my position would have killed you in a *heartbeat* for putting his livelihood and team in jeopardy—I shouldn't need to remind you of that."

"I shouldn't need to remind *you* that kidnapping me didn't make my loyalty automatic."

"It's your duty as my wife." He pressed his knuckles to the surface of the desk. "We're family now, and family comes above almost anything else."

"I'm not your family just because you put words on my skin. I'm not your property, either."

His eyebrow rose in challenge. "You're both."

I breathed through my urge to rage at him. That was why I'd come down here, but I needed to be smarter . . . to keep my cool the way he did . . . and to find and employ the *right* weapons, not the obvious ones.

He'd told me once I'd have to play the game, or I'd lose, and sex was the only defense I had.

He'd made it very clear he didn't want to be his father. I'd made it very clear I didn't want to be his wife. But he'd proceeded anyway. So would I.

"But none of that means I'll fuck you against your will," he said with finality. "So leave. I have a lot of work to do. I'll fix your bandage in the morning."

Cristiano wanted me. It had been written on his face since before I'd even known it was his eyes I was looking into. Under Calavera face paint as he'd asked for a dance, his want had shown. It showed now, and it'd grown into *need*.

He had the strength and prowess of a lion. He could tear me apart. Perhaps he would.

He'd promised in the church that I'd bleed in other ways.

But at some point, I'd shifted from trepidation over that —to trepidation over what would happen if I *loved* it.

Even when I hadn't known what to call it, that fear had weighed on me from the moment he'd put his hands on me on the dancefloor and threatened to take me from my fiancé and make me his.

I untied my robe and let it drop. "I'm neither your property nor your wife until you claim me."

Dark, ravenous eyes raked over me, and I felt them like hands. "Claim you?" He nearly growled. "What happened to consummating the marriage?"

Exposing myself this way, I had to contain a shiver of fear while my nipples hardened with the hungry way he looked at me. "This isn't about that. I'm not doing this for Diego."

He walked forward until he towered over me. "Let me see my tattoo."

It took me a moment to register his meaning. *His* tattoo. He owned it, even when it was on my body. I wanted to tell him to go to hell, but I needed to control my reaction. Slapping him in the church had been satisfying, but it hadn't accomplished anything. Getting him to break down and fuck me against my will? *That* would be much more effective.

I turned, and he hovered his fingers over the ink. "I hope it serves as a strong enough reminder of who you are and where your loyalty belongs."

"I expect it will," I said, facing him again.

He raised my chin with his knuckles. "You're more exquisite, more finely drawn, than any piece of art I've collected over the years."

"I'm glad my body pleases you."

"As am I," he said, his voice deep enough to register in my mind as desire. My own craving for him reared its ugly head. "But it's more than that, my Natalia. *Mmm.* I do like the sound of that. My Natalia. What once was his is now *mine.*"

"I'm not thinking of Diego now," I said. "But you are."

"No. No more. He's an echo—and you, darling, are a symphony." He bent his head as if he might kiss me. "I sent you to your room out of anger, but also because seeing my name branded on your body gives me the most raging hard-on I've ever had. It's a dangerous combination. I haven't been in a situation where I didn't trust myself in years. I can't say how I'll react."

My heart pounded with his thinly veiled warning. I could already feel his hands on me, consuming every inch of my skin, charting new lands, conquering curves and valleys. I was the one in dangerous territory, though. I had to hold strong. He could have my body, but he would never possess my heart. That wasn't on the table. Diego had broken it, and Cristiano was the last man who could put it back together.

I turned my cheek as he leaned in to kiss me.

He stayed there a few moments, his breath warm on my cheek. "You're turning away from me?"

"No. My body is yours, Cristiano. But I won't kiss you."

"You've kissed me before."

And each time, I'd lost any sense of my surroundings, and that was why I couldn't let it happen again. Not until

I'd grown stronger and held more control. "I can lie back on the couch for you. What more do you want?"

"I want to know what it will take for you kiss me the way you did on our wedding day."

"I'll keep your secrets as I've promised. I will obey you as I swore before God. But I *won't* kiss you."

He pinched my chin and turned my face to his. "You are my wife. You will kiss me when I say."

A thrill ran through me. As I suspected, he only possessed so much willpower.

The same thought must've dawned on him because he released my face and picked up my robe. "Go to bed."

I put my hands over my breasts. "You're rejecting me?"

He held the robe open, and I reluctantly slipped into it. "You're on your period anyway," he said.

"You said that wouldn't stop you."

"And it won't." A wolfish grin spread across his face as he adjusted the shoulder of the robe so it didn't touch the tattoo. "With the life I've led, do you think a little blood scares me?"

"Then why are you sending me away?"

He tied my sash into a firm knot. "Do you have any idea what you're asking for?"

Disappointment seeped through me. My only weapon against him had failed me. "I'm not asking for anything," I said sharply. "I'm giving you what you need."

"And *I'm* not asking you to submit to the inevitable," he said. "Only that you come to me because you want to."

"That will never happen."

"Then I will never fuck you, because I am not a rapist." He walked around to my back, gathering my hair into a loose ponytail and freeing it from the collar of the robe. With his mouth at my ear, he said, "Don't get me wrong. I could bend your naked body over every flat surface of this office. I could chain your ankles to my bedpost and fuck you raw for days on end. I could push your tits up against the window and make you look down on everyone as I finger you with such restraint that you'd beg me to finish you off while your juices drip over my hand and run down the glass."

I couldn't breathe. My thighs shook, and it wasn't from fear. An entire *world* of possibility opened up to me—a frightening world in which I actually wanted to experience all the things Cristiano had just said. In which I craved to be humiliated, dominated, and *ruined* by the king himself.

"Nobody's stopping you, Cristiano," I said breathlessly.

"You know what's stopping me."

"You're not interested," I said to provoke him.

"Back up and feel how interested I am."

I did, closing the distance between us. My heart pounded as I pressed my ass against his hardness. I reached back to touch him, but he caught my wrist. "I could do all those things to you and more, Natalia. But it would mean nothing to me if you didn't want it. Go back upstairs and don't come to me again until your sweet pussy is so wet with need for me, that if you sat on my lap, I'd slide right in."

I opened my mouth, silently gasping from his words, from the tidal wave of arousal that washed over me. I wanted all of that. But his determination not to break spoke volumes.

Nothing scared a man as powerful as Cristiano. But *this* did. The fear of becoming his father ran deep in him. As deep as his cock was hard.

"Fly away, *mariposa*," he said heatedly in my ear. "I can picture exactly what I want to do with you first, and I'm dangerously close to giving in."

I drew back my shoulders triumphantly. "What do you want?"

"To see how far down your throat I can fit my cock."

I inhaled sharply, shocked, and yet the words were nothing to him. He tossed them between us like a bag of groceries, amused at how I stood there gaping.

"I have work to do." He turned his back. "Go."

He didn't have to tell me twice. The idea of a penis in my *throat* was enough to send me upstairs—but slowly. I could barely walk as desire mounted in me. Why? It was beyond wrong to be aroused at the idea of taking Cristiano so brutally in my mouth. If Diego had ever said such a thing to me, I might never have spoken to him again. But to hear Cristiano tell me what he wanted to do to me so resolutely, without apology, my instinct to kneel and let him push the boundaries of my comfort—and my body—was alarming. I was tempted to throw myself at his mercy and have him exert his ceaseless dominance over my mouth. And equal was my craving to get *him* to pass his limits and give in to his desires—so he could hate himself for it.

Something was changing, but it wasn't in him. It was in me.

Yet, perhaps *changing* was the wrong word. What if all along, I'd wanted those filthy things he'd said, but I'd been denying myself?

I'd known when he'd taken me in his arms at the costume party despite my refusal that my power came from his weakness for me.

I had failed tonight, yet it didn't feel like it. I'd tested the waters, and they were warm and inviting. Having something he wanted—to fuck me—and something he could never have—my devotion—emboldened me.

Just as much as my building desire for him terrified me.

18

NATALIA

I woke in the dead of night to a warm, soothing touch. I didn't remember falling asleep, only lying on my stomach, replaying Cristiano's filthy, arousing words over and over again. I'd had to resist from touching myself so he wouldn't walk in and catch me in the act. So he wouldn't see firsthand the effect he was having on me.

Cristiano cleaned my tattoo with a damp towel so gently that I closed my eyes and let him finish without protest.

Afterward, he cleared my hair from my neck and smoothed his hand over my back as my mother had done when I was small. "Marked but still flawless," he murmured.

I drifted. Maybe. I wasn't sure. He'd stopped touching me but still weighed down my side of the bed. I opened my eyes, blinking over my shoulder until he came into view, sitting with his head in his hands.

"What's wrong?" I whispered.

He shook his head. I didn't actually expect him to

confide in me, but he said, "A problem I can't solve. Every time I get close, I seem to end up further from the answer."

I sat up, pulling the sheet with me and tucking it under my arms to cover the cream negligee Jaz had packed for me. The raw emotion in his face made my heart do something funny. Something unwelcome. I didn't need to have spent much time with Cristiano to understand he wouldn't show this side of himself to many people. For any cartel leader, vulnerability could mean death. But for Cristiano, control was everything, and in this moment, I sensed he didn't have it.

"I'm sorry."

"Don't be sorry. Be useful."

Of course.

There was only one way he saw me as useful, and that was on my back. I was an idiot for offering my condolences. I started to lie back down to sleep when he spoke again. "Advise me."

"What?"

"Be useful and advise me on this issue," he said.

"You have men for that."

"They tell me to drop it." He shrugged one shoulder. "That I've been pursuing it too long. They don't see the payoff, only that I'm emotionally attached."

Having had the most emotional attachment possible severed—that between a mother and daughter—I understood. "There's no room for emotional attachments when you choose this life."

He stared at me as if he'd seen a ghost and his voice dropped so low I had to lean in to hear him. "Do you really believe that?"

"I don't know," I admitted. "They're dangerous. But I wouldn't want to know anyone who didn't have them—those attachments remind us that we're human."

Elbows on his knees, he bent his head and scrubbed his hands through his hair. "Despite what you may think, I *am* human. I do feel the loss of things I once had and crave those I never can, no matter how badly I want them."

"What things?" I asked.

"My needs aren't different just because I'm . . ." He gestured at himself. "This."

My heart tugged. Of course I'd known I didn't have to show Cristiano the monster inside himself. He knew his demons, as we all did.

"Never get attached," he said. "*Never.*"

I sensed he was speaking from experience—intimate experience. He'd learned that lesson the hard way. "Who taught you that?"

He hesitated, then looked over at me, both drinking me in and fighting himself. "My father. But I am attached. So, tell me, Natalia. What would you do in my position? I have a gut instinct I can't ignore. A theory I can't prove. A need that only this missing piece can meet."

He'd shown me carnal need earlier, but this one ran deeper. Why come to *me* for help? He was the one man in my life who shouldn't care about anything more than my body. And what he was asking here was no small thing— my opinion, my advice. On cartel business.

For that grave reason alone, I attempted to put aside my situation and walk in his shoes. He had more than a cartel in his care. He had an entire town, and most people in it had suffered in some form or another. They depended on him. He'd been described to me as a leader, provider, savior—even a guiding light. I hadn't believed any of it until I'd seen it with my own eyes. Most men would either buckle under the pressure or let that kind of authority go to their heads. Maybe he had done both, but he was still standing.

Or sitting, rather—at my bedside, so he could talk this through with *me*.

I shifted against the headboard. "What do you stand to lose?"

"There may *never* be payoff, but there will *always* be risk." He blew out a sigh, thinking. "My resources are better spent other places—commanding a business that allows me to keep the Badlands running. I'd be taking up resources that save lives."

Helping others was more than important to him. It was his way of life. I still wasn't sure why, or if he had ulterior motives, but if people were better off in the end, wasn't that for the best? "And what do you have to gain?"

He dropped his hands between his knees. "Peace of mind. And something I want very much. Suddenly, it's within reach—if I'm right and can prove my suspicions."

I inched a little closer. "Is it dangerous?"

His eyebrows cinched. "How so?"

"You traffic weapons. Is it something that will give you inexorable power over other cartels?"

"What if it was? Would you tell me to grab it before someone else could?"

I pulled my knees against my chest under the sheet. The right weapon in the wrong hands could be devastating. But to use it as an offense wasn't any better. Obliterating others to save myself was something I didn't think I could live with. "No."

"Smart girl. A weapon of mass destruction was a good guess," he said. "But wrong answer. We'll have to work on that."

I frowned, a sliver of dread twisting through me.

"This mission isn't just for me, but my reasons for pursuing it are selfish—"

"How?"

He blinked at me, moonlight bathing him. Even when I'd hated him fiercely, I hadn't been able to ignore how devastatingly handsome he was. But in this moment, with his pain showing, his beauty was a thing of wonder. "It's selfish because as someone who's had nothing, I recognize how much I have now," he said. "And I'm grateful for it. But I want more, Natalia."

"More?" I asked under a coat of goose bumps. "Power? Money?"

"It's not about money. I've already spent enough money and time pursuing it, only to come up empty-handed."

"Then why continue?"

He cupped one hand over the other, forming a fist nearly as big as a child's head. His knuckles whitened, and a familiar tremor moved through me. I'd seen this kind of contained fury before, and I'd missed it—in Diego.

"Revenge?" I asked.

He stared straight ahead. "When is it ever not about that?" he asked.

"But it's never only that." Cristiano, like his brother, had also witnessed his parents' death. It was a scene I'd envisioned many times, but for the first time, I saw him in the room, too—not just Diego. "Revenge stems from other things, like pain. Are you in pain?"

Slowly, to my surprise, he nodded, but to my even greater surprise, it broke my heart a little. They'd only been boys. *This* boy, in front of me, had experienced something from which he hadn't healed. And he was here now, asking for permission to find what he needed. Maybe even looking to me for more. That was a new kind of power, not sexual or physical, and not the kind of emotional we'd been dealing with up until this point. These wounds lived deep, amongst distrust and lost hope.

"I've been through this with Diego," I said. "If it's revenge you seek, leave it. If it's against me or my father, I beg you to see how we've already suffered."

"It's not against you, my lovely wife. I promised you earlier tonight, and I meant it—where you're concerned, I'm done scheming. But for you, I still want many things. Not just revenge, but closure, happiness, even love."

My throat threatened to close with the conviction in his voice. Revenge and closure. Those two things could tempt the devil. They fit easily into my life, but into many areas —revenge and closure for my mother. My father. Or against Diego. Cristiano, too. Happiness and love were murkier—and much scarier coming from Cristiano's mouth. "You're a formidable man. I don't need to tell you that."

"I am."

"So why can't you take this like you do everything else?"

"It can only be given."

An eerie feeling fell over me with the familiar words. *I* had been given to him. So was it a person? Was he trying to command the same loyalty, devotion, and fidelity from someone else that he'd tried to from me?

"I *have* tried taking it regardless," he said with resignation. "Now, what I wonder, is just how much I'd give up." He paused, running both hands over his face. "I have unmet needs. And a fierce desire for answers. I want to regain a sense of what I lost. I want . . ."

My heart pounded with the yearning to understand how *I* could give such a powerful man and equally broken boy what he wanted. Maybe even what he needed. "What?" I asked softly.

"If I go on, I may confront things I'm not sure I want to know. And in the end, there's no guarantee I'll get what

I want." His jaw firmed as if it was difficult to admit. "No guarantee I'll even meet those needs."

It was clear to me he had to do this. There was nothing Cristiano couldn't have if he set his mind to it. But I also knew Cristiano had to figure that out on his own—and I could help him get there.

"Not knowing the truth will drive me mad." Frustration seeped into his voice. "But if I keep looking for it, I may go mad before I get there."

"Then leave it," I said.

He pulled back, his eyes finding mine. "Just like that?"

"Could you get hurt?"

"Tell me you don't want me to, and I'll promise you I won't."

I bit my lip to hide a smile, thankful for darkness to conceal my pinkening cheeks. "Will it hurt others?" I asked.

"Only those who deserve it."

"Did those men tonight deserve it?"

"You tell me." The silhouette of his Adam's apple bobbed as he swallowed. "I don't need to explain where they meant to take Sandra and those girls—or what they meant to do."

I'd seen the bound-and-gagged with my own eyes. I'd seen more these past couple weeks than I had in a lifetime, beginning with the inside of a *sicario's* head. Papá had tried to keep me from witnessing the dark side of this world, and pretty much everything else—while Cristiano had made me watch him deliver death by machete.

Was he steeling me for things that may come my way? *Our* way? Protecting me by arming me? He'd put his body in front of mine more than once, and deep down, I knew he would again if I needed him to. But if ever the day came that he wasn't there, then what?

"My father and Diego never would've brought me along tonight," I said.

"It was risky," he admitted. "But such is life. The more you see, the less it will shock you if you ever encounter it. I can't have you puking every time you see blood and guts, or this marriage will never work."

My stomach protested, despite the fact that it was another attempt at a sinister joke.

"I wouldn't have brought you if I wasn't ninety-nine percent confident in my team," he said.

"And the one percent?"

"One-hundred percent confidence is a death wish. And if you weren't confident in *me*, you wouldn't have come. Were you scared?"

I stared back at him. "Yes. But I won't be as scared next time."

"And even less the time after that," he said with a nod of approval. "Do you see me differently now?"

I tilted my head. Contoured by shadows, his bicep flexed. I *did* see him differently. He had always been a man who could hurt me and innocent people. But now, he was *also* a man who could hurt others. Those who *weren't* innocent. The ones immune to the law. Sinners to which God had seemingly turned a blind eye. There were plenty of those around who were never made to pay for their crimes.

I had a very powerful husband, not just in physique, but in dominion. His reach was long, far, and unforgiving.

If I'd learned anything from my mother, it was that behind every powerful man stood a stronger woman.

And if I'd learned one thing from *Jazmín*, it was that I could *control* a powerful man with my mouth—and not by telling him what to do.

Indecision warred on his face. The dark, hauntingly

beautiful face that hid fears, grief, and heartbreak. I could tell with eyes like his that he'd seen things. He already knew the answer he was looking for, but he needed me to confirm it.

Would I let him suffer, or would I free him to pursue and conquer what ailed him?

I glanced at my hands and considered the best way to urge him forward. What came to mind was the universal currency around here—one we'd both been dealing in. Power, and it came in endless forms. "How much money do you have?" I asked.

His eyebrow rose at the brusque change in topic. "Enough," he said. "And more coming in every day. You'll never have to worry."

I peeled back the sheet, put one foot on the ground, and then the other. After rising from the bed, I stepped softly until I stood before him. He followed my every move with bottomless eyes, willing me closer so he could suck me into his universe.

He'd come to me for help, vulnerable and fighting himself.

The real domination would be harnessing the kind of power he wielded. Using his own weakness to turn him against himself, against everything he stood for. I'd wanted that for a while.

But I wanted other things, too, and not all of it made sense.

Now that his walls had begun to crumble, I wondered if I could achieve the impossible feat of filling such a man's voids and needs.

My more carnal desires surfaced, too, but what it all came down to was . . .

I wanted to get on my knees to see if I could bring the great Cristiano de la Rosa to *his*.

I kneeled between his legs with butterflies in my stomach and nothing but him in my vision.

"If I'd known money would be the thing to bring you to your knees," he said, "I would've bragged about my fortune relentlessly."

"I already know you have money. More than my father, and he's a multi-millionaire." I willed my hands steady as I reached up and opened his belt. "That's not why I asked."

"Why then?"

I slid the fine leather band through his pant loops and set it on the bed. "If money is no object," I said, "there's nothing you cannot buy."

"Nothing."

"This thing you want to find. Tell me, truly, why you want it. Maybe it becomes revenge or money or sex—but at your core, what is your unmet need?"

The lust in his eyes burned so hot, I suspected he wouldn't even be able to form a coherent answer. "I'm looking for the key that unlocks something I've wanted for a long time." He jutted out his chin. "Not something. *Everything.*"

Though my throat dried with the prospect of what I was about to do, my mouth watered. He'd said this was what he wanted tonight, but it was more of a need. And he seemed to think that I of all people could fill it. Had anyone ever reciprocated that kind of trust in me?

I had no keys to give—whatever he ultimately needed, it wasn't here tonight. But I was.

I sat back on my calves and lowered the zipper of his pants. "Why should a man like you ever have a need that isn't met?"

"I tend to agree."

Dark hair gathered like a storm cloud at the root of his hidden cock. There'd be no turning back once I freed him from his underwear. There was no need to be scared. I was in control here, and that was saying something. I'd heard about giving head plenty of times, just as I'd heard about receiving it—and that had been a more pleasant experience than I'd expected.

"Have you done this before?" Cristiano asked.

I stared at the bulge twitching to be liberated. "No."

"I'm glad. But tonight, I'm in no state to be your first." It was a warning, but not a refusal.

When I shifted my hand and brushed against him, he sucked in a breath. "Why not?" I asked.

"It took everything in me—and I mean everything—not to fuck you in your wedding dress in the church. I want to own you so badly, it scares even me. Now, seeing my cartel on your body for eternity . . . I've been tortured with need since the first ink touched your skin."

He was telling *me* he didn't want this? Or he was giving me an out. An opportunity to retreat. I didn't want to, and I didn't want to ask myself why that was. I'd been prepared to take all of him on my wedding night, and then again earlier when I'd gone to his office in my robe.

"What state *are* you in?" I asked.

"The one where I find your limits and push them. I'm fine to sit back and let you kiss on my dick for hours while you figure it out—one day. Not tonight. Tonight, I want to fuck something."

"There are lots of somethings downstairs."

"You're right. I don't want to fuck any of them. I want to fuck you."

I needed to get up. He was warning me. This had been my goal and my fear—to unleash his inner demons.

"I'm scarier than any monster," he'd told me as a child to chase away my nightmares.

But it was also my desire—to see his worst. I was

prepared to let him use me, because I was prepared to hate him.

I *wasn't* prepared for the alternative. To accept him, to crave him. To . . .

I pushed the thought away.

His own inner battle played out on his face. He was just as tortured as I was bewildered by my own desire to do this.

"This is my last attempt to scare you off." He took my jaw in his big hand and lifted my face to meet his gaze. "I will fuck this mouth. I will fill this throat, first with cock, then with cum. And you know what I'll do after that?"

I shook my head. I couldn't even conceive what more he *could* do.

"I will protect this mouth and this throat from any motherfucker who even looks at you wrong. Every part of your body will submit to me, and every inch of you will know the protection of a man who would lay down his life to keep each hair in place." He stood to his full height, doubling in size and menace. "No man will touch what's mine to suck and lick and fuck. No man will take what you give only to me."

Sitting on my heels, I had to tip my head back all the way to see him. Raw, throbbing desire replaced any fear his words should've inspired. "And does that work both ways?"

"You have my devotion in and out of my bed."

"*Diego* got a tattoo for me."

"You want me to reciprocate? I can. What would you like?" He cuffed my wrists in one hand and tugged me up onto my knees until I was face to face with his groin. With his free hand, he pulled out his cock. "Shall I get 'Property of Natalia' scrawled across it?"

I swallowed my gasp as the source of his confidence revealed itself. Had I never seen another penis, I still would've known it was larger than average, and equally intimidating in its girth.

It begged to be sucked. The engorged purple head asked for entry. Had I lost control of the situation? Or was I getting exactly what I wanted? Shackled by his hand, I was his prisoner. I was at his mercy. I was his. And I could've exploded for all my pent-up desire. We'd spoken of unmet needs? I had one. *Relief.* I could soothe and be soothed if I would let myself.

"Open," he said, "or go back to bed and stay away until you're ready."

I inhaled through my nose, wet my lips, and parted them. "I'm ready."

"Good girl," he rumbled. "Don't close until I say." He slid past my teeth without pretense, feeding himself into my mouth. "You have a lovely, wide mouth, Natalia. I noticed it instantly at the costume ball."

Unable to respond, I moved my tongue under the silky skin of a rigid, veiny shaft. He had promised to fill me, and he was a man of his word. He left no room for anything else. No thoughts in my head, nothing but his dark pubic hair and taut, godlike belt of muscles in my sight. Only my own saliva slickened the way.

"When I saw you," he continued, "I thought to myself —what a fucking woman Natalia has become. I wasn't ready for that." He kept pushing, approaching the back of my mouth. "But don't think that just because I was and am your protector that I'll treat you like you're breakable while you're in my bed." He stared down at me, his gaze menacing one moment and adoring the next as he tightened his one large hand around both of my wrists. "Even trapped and filled by me, you already know you're in charge here, don't you?"

As he thrust deeper, I swallowed to keep from choking.

In that moment, I knew nothing but the weight of a man's cock on my tongue and his tip begging entry to my throat. It stripped me of anything but pure satisfaction that I could pleasure him.

"That's it," he said, caressing his thumb on the inside of one of my wrists. "Open your throat, *mamacita*. Show me what you can do."

I had no idea what to do. All the talk in the world couldn't have prepared me for being dominated by a man of his size and prowess. My mind rejected this, told me to fight back, but my body, my instincts, my throat, yielded for him, welcomed him, and I found my pussy pulsing for how he demanded my submission.

"Breathe through your nose," he instructed. "Open. Take me deeper."

To feel him in my mouth was strange but natural, as if I were a creature made to receive him. But when he breached my throat, it took all of me not to push him out. I gagged and tears flooded my eyes. "There's no sight in the world like watching you try to take as much of my cock as possible."

I wanted it between my legs. I'd sworn to myself I wouldn't beg for it, but my body betrayed me, nearly shaking with longing to take him the one place I knew he'd truly possess me.

"*Qué bellísima*," he murmured. "Such a good girl has no reason to fear me."

He withdrew. Once the tip of his cock reached the tip of my tongue, he glided back in, but only partway. "Suck," he said, releasing me.

I hollowed my cheeks and did as he said, using my hands to cover what I couldn't reach with my mouth.

"*Sí, Natalia*," he said with a groan. "Now grip my hips and see how deep you can go on your own."

I dug my hands into his skin and tried but didn't make it nearly as far as he'd been able to push himself.

"Look at me, *mi amor*," he said. "It's one of the many things I'll demand of you, but perhaps the most important. Keep your eyes on me when my cock is in any of your holes—even when I take your ass."

Butterflies erupted in my stomach. He was so crass, and now that I was on my knees for him, ruled by arousal and desire, I could admit that I fucking loved it. I had been treated so carefully my entire life, with kid gloves and placating words. Cristiano was the opposite of all that— and unlike any man I'd ever met. I pulled back, panting for breath. "I will never let you do . . . *that*."

"You will. And I'll find a way to watch your face as I press every last inch of myself into the tightest hole on your body, until you think you're going to break in half."

I wiped saliva from my mouth, so turned on that I was nearly ready to agree to what sounded like the ultimate ruination.

"I didn't say you could stop." He cupped the back of my head, pulling me to him. "Flatten your tongue."

I didn't have to; he flattened it for me. When I forced it to relax, he took advantage, pushing even deeper down my throat. Once he was anchored there, he held my head in place and moved his hips, slowly at first and then faster. And now, I understood what it meant to have my face fucked.

When I gagged, he stopped. "Your virgin mouth can't take it, can it? You still need breaking in."

I blinked away the tears that had gathered as I'd choked on him. He was letting me put a stop to this, but I didn't want that. Not even close. I'd gotten on my knees willingly, and I was at his mercy, stripped emotionally bare.

Only honesty remained.

And the truth was, I needed this.

I loved the primal way he used me. The look of admiration that came with each "good girl." The sense that he'd do almost anything in his power to have me continue.

I drew his hips closer, pulling him marginally deeper into my mouth.

"Use your nails," he said.

When I dug them into his skin, he inhaled sharply. "Do exactly that if it's too much. I'm not going to ask again if you need a break. Use your nails and I'll stop. *¿Entiendes?*"

I nodded—as best I could with a mouthful of cock—that I understood.

He resumed his pillage and plunder. "Take it deep for me just a little longer, *mi amor*. You'll know it's the last time when I spill down your throat."

He pushed back as far as he could before I clawed his hips and came up coughing.

My heart pounded as I regained composure. I opened my mouth and he was back inside in a second, impaling me. As he fucked the opening of my throat into yielding for him, he looped his fingers into my hair, massaging the back of my head until I jerked away to catch my breath.

He pumped his fist over the monstrous length of him, my saliva glistening and dripping in the moonlight. "Enough?" he asked as the corner of his mouth lifted. "I can paint your face a pretty, pearly white instead and coat your throat another time. Just say the word."

I would not. This only scratched the surface of all the ways he was going to ruin me, but the same was true for him. He was at my mercy just as much as I was at his.

I leaned in. The tip of him was swollen and purple. I could practically read his need for release. He slowed his furious stroking as I put just the tip in my mouth, sucking on it like a lollipop then licking under the ridge.

His fingers curled against my scalp. *"Fuck."*

At the intensity of his curse, I darted my eyes to his face, wondering if I'd done something wrong. Instead, I met a half-lidded gaze that said I was doing everything right. This time, I slid my mouth along his shaft on my own, keeping my eyes up.

His lips parted for what would surely be another command, but then he clenched his jaw shut, glancing up at the ceiling. "God, that's so fucking good. *You're* so goddamn good."

This was control, and I understood why Cristiano wanted it so badly. It was heady to watch the face of such a powerful man screw up with need and desperation—all for *me*.

He took both sides of my face in a firm but gentle hold and used my mouth to finish himself off. He left my throat alone as he thrust hard and fast into my mouth, his fingers gripping tightly. "I'm coming." His massive body shook with his impending explosion. "Your mouth is too hot and sweet to resist. And now, it's finally mine."

He shoved to the back of my throat and shuddered as he came warm and sticky down my throat. The moment he pulled out, he towered over me, placing his hand under my jaw and angling it up. "Swallow me, Natalia." I started to cough, but he held me there. "Swallow."

I gulped him down, but it was more than I thought possible and some spilled over my chin. He stroked his cock slowly as it settled between his legs, as spent as I was.

As he walked away, I fell forward onto my palms, reorienting myself. It was oddly satisfying to work and be worked and to feel the result dripping down my throat and over my chin. Not once in my life had I ever been handled so ruthlessly, with such fervor, or been broken down and so relentlessly exposed.

"You're sufficiently ruined for one night," he said from somewhere in the dark, my thoughts apparently running through his mind as well.

I looked up. He was wholly naked now, his cock hanging between his legs, his thigh muscles working as he approached me barefoot and with a damp towel in his hand.

"That's what you wanted, wasn't it?" I asked hoarsely.

"For longer than I care to admit," he said. "I suspect you won't admit you wanted it, too."

I couldn't, not in that moment, but I wouldn't deny it, either. I reached for the towel, but he took my elbow and helped me up. He put his knuckle under my jaw to raise my head and look me in the eye as he smoothed the warm, damp towel over my chin. "You will learn to swallow every last drop," he said gently. "But I must say. You were *increíble*."

I smiled, then turned red, embarrassed by how good his praise felt. "You're only saying that so I'll do it again."

"Perhaps. Or perhaps it's the truth." His eyes scanned my face and landed on my lips. When he bent his head, I was tempted to lean in and meet him.

But that was enough to make me angle away.

A kiss was a different kind of submission. It was one thing to let myself enjoy how he handled my body, but my heart couldn't take the same beating.

Cristiano didn't move, hovering near my cheek. "Still no kiss?"

"I can't really stop you."

"As I've said, there's no joy in that for me. You were incredible just now because you wanted this as much as I did." His hot breath warmed my cheek, and he spoke with a thread of desperation. "Tell me why you won't kiss me."

"It should be obvious. Sex is sex, but a kiss is more."

"We haven't had sex."

"But we will. And you'll know exactly how to make me enjoy it. But that's my body, nothing more."

He turned my face back to his as he wet his full lips. He was a good kisser. He'd managed to draw me in for a few seconds amidst the horrors of our wedding day. He'd nearly convinced me on our wedding night that I wanted him. He cast a spell with his kiss, and I couldn't afford to stray from reality.

"You're wrong," he said, sounding almost amused. "This goes far beyond your body. You need things, and I can give them to you. I want to give them to you."

"Why?" I whispered.

He pressed his lips to the corner of my mouth. "Someday soon, maybe when you least expect it, I will repay what you did for me tonight."

"How?" I asked. "I have nothing down there to jam down your throat."

He smirked. "And *gracias a Dios* for that."

"Speak for yourself. I should like to see *you* suffer for *my* orgasm."

The corner of his mouth quirked. "I imagine I will." He touched his lips to the other corner of mine. "You took my cock like a champ. In return, I'll eat you like my life depends on it, and believe me, I value my life."

Oh my God. I was frustratingly aware of the throb between my legs. It had started in his office and hadn't subsided since.

"Unless you'd like to collect on my debt now?" he asked. "Just ask."

To be relieved of that ache was almost too good to pass up. Accepting his advances, or even submitting to them, was one thing. Asking for something felt wrong, though. I shook my head and forced myself to turn away before I changed my mind.

He took my elbow and pulled me back. "Kiss me once," he said. "In exchange, I won't lay so much as a finger on you for a while, not even if the kiss tempts you to more."

Disappointment at the loss of him struck me first followed quickly by horror. I didn't want to miss his touch or wander down that path. To cover up that confusing feeling, I quickly agreed. "Deal."

"I'll pretend you said that with a little less vigor." He frowned. "Would you like to think on it a moment?"

"No. How long is a while?"

"Days. Maybe even weeks, if I'm unlucky."

Weeks? He seemed to both keep his hands to himself and touch me non-stop. "And you won't touch me at all?"

"Not even to help you from the car."

"All right." I closed my eyes and waited, but nothing came. When I looked again, he was pulling back the sheets of his bed.

"*Ven aquí*," he said, lying down.

"We had a deal."

"Come here," he repeated.

I trudged back to my side of the bed, climbed in next to him, and curled into a ball with my back to him as I had every night.

After a moment, he tugged me close with a loose grip on my bicep. I glanced over my shoulder at him and met his eyes, dark with demands once again.

He ghosted a finger over the tattoo. "Mine," he said. "*Mi mariposita*. My rare and unusual, beautiful white monarch."

"You're wrong," I whispered. "He made the wings orange, not white."

He barely traced the outline of it. "The butterfly's orange color warns of its poison," he explained. "It's dangerous to be colorless. And you, my wife, are toxic to predators."

"This isn't just a reminder to me." I had suspected as much. "It's a warning to others."

"She is mine." He moved some of my hair behind my ear and pressed closed lips to my mouth. His hand tightened around my arm, but he stayed still, not yet pushing for more.

He angled his shoulder over me, cocooning me. His butterfly. It shouldn't have surprised me to feel him harden against the cushion of my ass. *I should like to be able to roll over and be inside you.* I tried to think of anything to keep from wanting that. To keep from falling into him as he slid his hand down my forearm, squeezed my wrist, caressed my hip and the curve of my ass.

I wanted him to keep going. To slip between my thighs and relieve me of the arousal he'd inspired, to chase my shame away without permission so I didn't have to face that I wanted it.

I had to think of anything else or I wouldn't just ask him for more—I would *beg* for it.

Out of habit, Diego came to mind. Had it felt like this to kiss him? Like I was standing at the edge of a black hole, and he was both pushing me over the edge and pulling me down into the dark? I'd always known that darkness was too easy to walk into, and now, Cristiano knew it, too. He'd drag me down, ruin and defile me, while Diego had wanted to keep me pristine.

No, the kiss with Diego hadn't been a magic spell like Cristiano's, because it wasn't just about sex. I believed Diego had loved me on some level, as much as he was capable. And that on some level, *I'd* known that what I'd had with Diego wasn't real.

Cristiano was real. Raw. His honesty could be brutal, but it left no room for pretense, and my body responded.

I moaned greedily and thrust my tongue into his mouth first, then gasped at my forwardness.

Cristiano smiled against my lips. "Goodnight. Sleep tight knowing you're safe from me for a time. And should you realize that isn't what you want, take comfort in the fact that this is far from our last kiss."

When I awoke next, it was to a dark and empty room, yet I sensed dawn had broken. I rose from the bed and opened blackout shades to find the sun rising in the distant desert.

Below, Cristiano carried his suitcase to a town car.

No wonder he'd promised not to touch me. The sneaky bastard was going somewhere.

Cristiano was a master of words and manipulation, and that wasn't news to me. But in place of the fear I'd been clinging to, I suddenly wondered if I could keep up with him. If I could learn to decipher the true meaning behind his words, thoughts, and actions—and play on his level. Something told me he wanted that, too.

And just like that, already, that small shift in mindset was working.

I knew without asking why he was leaving.

He was going in search of answers that would fill whatever void existed in him. Of the key that could unlock the something—the *everything*—he wanted.

Or he'd drive himself mad trying.

And where would that leave me?

19

NATALIA

A dark-haired, petite mirage of a girl wrung her hands in front of a dusty black SUV. I shielded my eyes from the sun as Alejandro took a beat-up suitcase from the trunk.

As I ran down the front steps, my flip-flops slapped against the stone. "*Pilar?*"

My best friend threw her arms around my neck. "*¡Dios mío, Natalia!*"

I took her by her shoulders so hard that she winced. Loosening my grip, I looked her over. "What are you doing here?"

Her crystal green eyes widened. "I have no idea."

I whirled around. "What the hell, Alejo?"

He shrugged. "Cristiano said you might be lonely while he was away."

"So he *took* my friend?"

"No." Alejandro winked at Pilar. "*I* did."

Her cheeks flushed as she glanced away, but *I* didn't. I scowled at Alejo and grasped Pilar's elbow to pull her up to the house. "What happened?"

"I was at the market getting milk," she said. "I was making *arroz con leche* for Manu, and—"

"For *Manu?*" I asked, leading her through the foyer. "You bake for your family's *panadería* for a living. Why are you making anyone anything when you aren't working?" I waved my hand. "Never mind. What happened next?"

"He,"—she nodded behind us at Alejandro—"told me to get in the car. I recognized him from . . ." She lowered her voice as if someone might be listening. "The wedding."

"And you got in?" I balked. "That's one of the first things we learn as kids. *Never* get in the car or you're as good as dead. He didn't hurt you, did he?"

She chewed her bottom lip. "You know me. I don't have to be ordered to do anything twice."

It was true. My sweet Pilar had no backbone, and she never had. I hated that Cristiano had dragged her into this, first by burdening her with being a witness to our wedding ceremony, and now by bringing her here. But I was glad Alejandro hadn't been forceful, and truthfully, I wouldn't actually think he'd be. "He brought you straight here?"

"My bag was already in the car when I got in. He packed it for me. I don't know when or how." Her eyebrows met in the middle of her forehead. "Now all the ingredients are just sitting on my kitchen counter."

"*Puta madre*, fucking domineering asshole—" When Pilar shuddered, I forced myself to calm down. I would deal with Cristiano later. "Don't worry." I attempted to soothe her as we approached the house's main room. "Alejandro is a good guy. I mean, as good as it gets around here."

"I've been worried sick for you," she said under her breath, then stopped at the grand dining table with brass candelabras. She took in the fireplace, wooden coffee table with wild dahlias, and the regal tapestry on the wall.

Turning in a circle, she surveyed the majestic room. "I didn't know what to expect. I thought it . . . I thought *you* would look . . . different."

She'd probably been expecting wreckage and devastation. I wrapped the slinky, colorful cover-up I'd found in one of my drawers over my bathing suit and pursed my lips. "Looks can be deceiving."

"*Vengan.*" In the doorway, Alejandro ordered us to follow and turned back for the staircase. "You'll be staying upstairs, Pilar."

"For how long?" I demanded.

I didn't expect an answer, and I didn't get one.

At the second floor, I left Pilar with Alejandro and promised her I'd be back in a moment. I continued up to Cristiano's bedroom and went to my nightstand. When I'd returned from *La Madrina* last weekend, I'd found a cell phone in the top drawer with only one number programmed in it. *His.*

I'd considered it some kind of annoying joke after our last encounter with a phone, but now, I prayed it actually made outgoing calls.

And that appeal was answered. He picked up on the first ring. "How are you, my beautiful bride?"

"You asshole."

"*Ah.* I assume Alejandro delivered Pilar." His shit-eating grin was unmistakable, even over the phone. "I thought you'd be pleased—you said you were bored."

"I didn't mean you should kidnap my friend."

"Relax. It's only for the weekend . . . unless she wants to stay longer, that is."

"She has a life. A fiancé and a family business. You can't just rip her out of it for no reason."

"Not for no reason," he said. "For you. I thought seeing your friend would make you happy."

Pilar was like a light in the dark, but I wasn't going to force this life on her for my own amusement. "She's scared half to death."

"So show her she has no reason to be," he said over some static on the line. "You have free rein of the house. All I ask is that you continue your lessons with Alejo—and bring Pilar with you. I get the feeling she couldn't tiptoe over an ant without shedding a few tears."

Pilar might be prone to trembling, but that didn't mean she wasn't tough in her own way. My nostrils flared. "You—"

"I know, I know. I'm horrible." He cleared his throat. "I'm also heading into a bad area, so I have to go."

"Bad?" I asked, straightening as alarm jolted me. I'd be surprised if whatever mission he'd left on was legal or safe —after all, if this thing he wanted so badly was easy to get, he'd have made it his a long time ago. But for someone in this life to consider an area *bad*, it had to be dangerous. "What do you mean bad?"

"Er—bad for reception," he clarified.

Surprisingly, relief passed over me—and with that, my irritation was free to return. Especially with myself over finding out that my gut reaction to Cristiano in danger wasn't joy, but . . . *concern*.

"Is there anything else, Natalia?"

"Yes," I said. "About a million things."

I thought I heard his breathy chuckle through the phone. "Will you call me tonight?"

"No."

"I like seeing your name light up my phone, *mi amor*. Call me when you're in bed, and tell me how it went with Pilar."

He hung up before I could protest.

I hurried down a floor and followed voices to one of

the bedrooms. Pilar stood at the foot of a bed, gaping at the ornate, four-poster frame, large window overlooking the water, and beamed ceiling. "Do you have a room like this?" she asked me as I entered. "There's a fireplace."

"Yes, I do," I muttered. "Cristiano's room."

"Oh . . ." Concern creased her forehead as understanding dawned. "Oh, no. I mean, of course. It makes sense, but—I'm sorry."

Alejandro, standing in the doorway of the walk-in closet, stared at us with one eyebrow arched as if we were speaking another language. "Jaz will unpack your things," he said.

"I spoke to Cristiano," I said, pursing my lips at Alejo before turning to my friend. "You're not stuck here forever —just for the weekend. Did you have plans?"

Pilar sat on the edge of the bed. "Well, Manu's *arroz con leche*—"

"Never mind the *arroz con leche*," I said, exasperated.

"He really likes it," she said slowly. "He expects it. When I don't bring it over, he won't be happy."

Alejandro typed something into his cell phone. "Manu's the fiancé?" he asked without looking up.

"If Manu has a problem, he can take it up with Cristiano," I said, ignoring Alejandro. What did *he* care?

"I don't know," Pilar hedged, sticking a fingernail between her front teeth. "Are you sure?"

"Don't worry. Any man in his right mind wouldn't challenge the Calavera cartel," I reassured Pilar and sighed. There was nothing really left to say. "Did you bring a bathing suit?"

"*No sé.*" She glanced at Alejandro. "Did I?"

"There's one in the closet," he said. "Cristiano gave me a list of things to pick up."

"And I was at the top of it," Pilar said.

Alejandro laughed heartily, while I just stared at her. She wasn't generally one to make jokes, especially in a tense situation. "Go change," I told her, tearing my glare from Alejandro. "We'll get in the pool. It's supposed to be especially warm today."

Alejandro tucked his phone back into his pocket, dipped his head, and left the room, closing the door after himself.

In the walk-in closet, Pilar's little suitcase sat in one corner, but I wasn't sure why Alejandro had bothered with it. We found ourselves staring at enough outfits to last her a month. "*Jesus*," I muttered to myself. "What, does Cristiano own a woman's clothing brand?"

"Is this stuff yours?" she asked me.

"I think it's for you." I shook my head. "Cristiano's doing."

She fingered a light, floral dress. "This is from that boutique you and I go to in the plaza at home. Do you think Alejandro went shopping for me?"

Alejandro was no Cristiano, but he was certainly a big, burly, scarred—and armed—guy who had no business shopping for women's apparel.

Pilar and I exchanged a look and despite myself, I laughed. Taking my cue, she also giggled.

At the dresser, I opened drawers until I found a couple bathing suits. "Imagine what the salesgirl thought when a man like him bought all this," I said, handing her the only one-piece. "There's even a sun hat."

"I think maybe she didn't notice," Pilar said, pretending to inspect the suit's fabric as she blushed.

"What does *that* mean?"

"Oh, come on. You didn't notice?" she asked. "His face is a *bit* distracting."

I lowered my voice. "He is handsome," I agreed. "And

he may be nice. But he's also dangerous, Pilar. All these guys are."

Her emerald eyes turned into big, sparkly gems. "I didn't mean—I was just saying . . . I don't mean that anything makes up for what Cristiano did. I'm sorry I laughed earlier."

"Don't be sorry," I said gently and pulled her into a hug. "Laughter is good. That's why Cristiano brought you here—he knew it would make me happy."

She drew back, her eyebrows cinched. "Really?"

"Yes." I needed to try to stay positive about him and my situation. It would be a lot easier on Pilar if she felt safe and realized I wasn't in any immediate danger.

I went to leave the closet—Pilar was as modest as it came and wouldn't even change in front of me—but she stopped me. "Are . . . are there cameras in the house?"

"Not in the bedrooms."

She mouthed, "Microphones?"

"No, at least I don't think so," I said, frowning. "The house isn't surveilled to spy on us. It's to protect us." I rolled my eyes inwardly. That was something Cristiano would say.

"But will you show me where the cameras are?" she asked, twisting the bathing suit through her hands. "I mean, if you even know. If you want. It makes me anxious to think I'm being watched."

I went back and kissed her cheek. "Of course," I said soothingly. "Don't be anxious. I'm the one he wants, not you."

"I still can't believe you're here," she said.

"Neither can I most days," I said as I left to give her privacy.

I had to admit, though—I was getting used to things. Cristiano had been gone almost a week, and I'd even been bored enough to miss him in a way—or at least his stimulating conversation. With him gone, what I looked forward to the most were the self-defense lessons I did once or twice a day. Solomon wasn't as afraid to get physical with me as Alejandro was, and he was more patient than my brutish husband. I could already feel my body getting stronger in small ways.

When Pilar came out of the closet, she took modesty to a whole new level. To go down to the pool, she'd pulled on drawstring pants and a navy cotton shirt with sleeves long enough to hide her hands. Since I could make out the shape of a swimsuit underneath, I didn't question her.

Downstairs, I walked her to the patio and down to the sparkling infinity pool set amongst the jungle and over-looking the ocean. I'd been spending my days there, too, since Cristiano had left. Even during intermittent showers, I'd sit under an umbrella with a book.

I almost felt a sense of pride as Pilar lifted her sleeved hands to her mouth and gasped, "Wow."

Navy-and-white striped lounge chairs and matching cabanas surrounded the pool with a swim-up bar. It sat at the edge of the world, facing the ocean. The thing that got me was that I couldn't imagine a *single* person in this house using the pool, least of all its master.

As I stripped down and tossed my cover-up on a chair, one of the staff who helped Jaz on occasion approached us with large, sweating glasses of water. "Would you and your friend like lunch, *señora?*" she asked.

"Are you hungry?" I asked Pilar.

Her face seemed set in a permanent expression of shock. "I guess?"

"Tell the chef to surprise us," I said.

"There's a *chef?*" Pilar whispered as the woman walked away.

"More than one." I set my water on a side table. "We have a lot to talk about."

Pilar removed her pants and perched on the edge of a chair cushion.

"Don't sit," I said. "Let's cool off in the pool."

"I can't swim," she said.

I furrowed my brows. "You've been in the pool at my house."

"I stayed in the shallow part, and there were always people around. I knew I'd be safe."

"There are people around now," I said, taking her hand and pulling her up. "Come on. We'll just go in to our waists. I shouldn't get my tattoo wet anyway."

"You have a *tattoo*?"

"Like I said, I've got a lot to share. Let's—"

She stopped, leaning back with all of her body weight. "Wait. Natalia—"

"What?" She wasn't afraid of water. We'd swum at my house and had been to the coast lots of times. I shielded my eyes and located Alejandro, standing—and most likely sweating   between the pool and patio. "As you can see, Alejandro is our shadow today." I called to him. "Can you swim, Alejo?"

"*Sí.*"

"There. See?" I told Pilar. "I promise, he won't let you drown."

"I've gained weight, and I'm self-conscious."

"You haven't gained a kilo since I've known you." I crossed my arms. "What's the matter?"

She hesitated, her posture wilting. "Nothing," she said and turned her back to peel off her shirt, revealing bruises up and down her arms and sides.

I gasped. "*Pila.* What . . .?"

"Please," she said softly, taking my hands. "Don't make a thing of this. They don't really hurt."

Anger burned through me, turning my vision spotted. No wonder she'd been trembling when she'd arrived. I whirled around, charging toward Alejandro. "You fucking *asshole*," I said.

Alejandro drew back, his eyebrows cinched. *"¿Qué?"*

"When I tell Cristiano about this, he'll skin you alive. And if he doesn't, my father will."

"What are you talking—"

"Natalia," Pilar called, her footsteps shuffling after me.

Alejandro's gaze shifted over my shoulder, and his brows dropped. "Are those bruises? *Hijo de la chingada*," he cursed. "I didn't do that, Natalia. I would never—I told you about my history."

As soon as he said it, I stopped short, knowing it was true. I started to apologize when the actual truth hit me. My scalp prickled, and I turned back to Pilar. "Manu did this?"

"The fiancé," Alejandro said through gritted teeth, staring daggers at the marks on her arm.

"Has this happened before?" I asked Pilar.

Absentmindedly, she scratched her shoulder. "It looks worse than it is."

She was uncomfortable with Alejandro here. He raised his eyes to meet mine, and a current of anger passed between us. I was so furious, I didn't even know what to say. Pilar had been promised to Manu for months by her parents, and they wouldn't hear her protests.

Well, fuck him. Manu had no idea who he was dealing with.

Alejandro seemed to follow my line of thinking. Slowly, he dipped his head in a nod. As he turned and walked away, he took his cell phone from his pocket, and I didn't need to ask who he was calling.

"I'm sorry," Pilar said. "I didn't want to say in front of Alejandro in case it got me in trouble . . ."

"Say what?" I linked my elbow in hers and guided her toward the shallow end of the pool. "Why would you get in trouble?"

"After your . . . ah, wedding . . . I was so scared for you, I ran straight to your house."

"Wow. You *must've* been scared," I said. "You're terrified of my father."

"I didn't go to him." We waded into the pool, and she sat on one of the steps, submerged to her chest. "I found Barto and told him about the wedding. He's always been nice to me."

Ah. I didn't need to imagine how Barto would react hearing the story from a terrified Pilar. No wonder he'd shown up here the next morning with such a chip on his shoulder. "What does that have to do with Manu?"

"Nothing yet. Barto helped calm me down. He wanted all the details, and I was having trouble getting them out, so he made me a drink."

"A *drink*?" I asked, as amused as I was shocked. "I've never seen him take a sip of alcohol."

"He didn't have one," she said quickly. "We started talking about life and other things until I was finally composed enough to relay what had happened in the church."

"Hmm." I leaned my back against the lip of the pool. "Barto's always been good in a crisis."

"He spoke really softly and tried to soothe me, but I could see him fuming on the inside. He really cares about you, Natalia."

"I know," I said. "I think he sees me as a kid sister."

"Anyway, afterward, Barto drove me home. My family and Manu's were at the house and had been looking for me since I hadn't come back from Mass."

I grimaced. "And you'd been drinking."

"Manu smelled the alcohol. Once Barto left, Manu exploded. He's still angry about it, which is why I was making him *arroz con leche*. He wants me to do more considerate things like that."

"Oh, God, what a fucking manipulative asshole," I said, rolling my eyes.

But my words hung in the air, taunting me. How come I could see Manu's manipulation so easily, but I'd missed every warning sign with Diego? And my own father? And now, I was in the grips of another controlling man. One I'd gotten on my knees for willingly—and had controlled right back, if only for a few minutes.

And yet, I couldn't imagine Cristiano guilting me into baking him treats like Manu.

In fact, I had a feeling if Cristiano thought, in any way, he was remotely responsible for Pilar's bruises since the wedding had started this—he'd harness that guilt into making it up to her.

"I'm so sorry," I said. "What about your parents?"

She shook her head. "They turn a blind eye, as you'd suspect. They just want this marriage to go through."

My heart sank, and suddenly, swimming in the sunshine in my expensive bikini while being waited on seemed like *the life*. Overindulgent, even. "Was this the first time he hurt you?"

"No."

Here, I'd been anticipating the worst from Cristiano while Pilar had been enduring it from Manu. "Why didn't you tell me?"

"What could you have done?"

"My father is one of the most powerful men in the country," I said. "We would've figured something out."

She tucked some hair behind her ear. "Barto said the same thing."

I watched her smile to herself as I stretched my arms along the pool's edge. "He knows about this?"

"Not the bruises, but he came by the house to check on me a few days later. I asked him not to do that again because Manu could get jealous. And we started talking about the whole arranged marriage thing . . ."

Barto wasn't much of a talker. At all. Thinking of him sitting and conversing with my friend not once but twice made me smile. "I take it he wasn't a fan?"

"No. He said if I ever needed help getting out of it, to come to him. He'd talk to your father."

Considering how Cristiano was going after Belmonte-Ruiz, I could only imagine how he'd receive this news . . . and what he and I would do to rectify it. "Well, now *we're* going to get you out," I promised.

She swallowed. "It's not possible, Natalia. Manu has been pursuing me for a year, and he comes from a good background. My parents want him as a son-in-law."

"But that doesn't mean it has to be."

"I can't exactly go home and tell them I won't do it. They'll throw me out, and then where will I go?"

Cristiano's invitation rang through my mind. It had frustrated me then, but now, it was a godsend. "You can stay here as long as you want," I said.

"Here?" she asked. "But Cristiano—"

"Would love to have you. Believe me, he'll be more supportive than you know. We have so much room."

We? I didn't blame her for looking confused. I was as well. This life had been forced upon me. I'd come into it kicking and screaming. And now, not even two weeks later,

I was inviting her into it? Referring to Cristiano and myself as *we*?

There may have been a world full of people with more freedom than me, but that didn't mean they were safer. Whether or not I wanted to be here, it hit me just how much worse off I could be.

"It's not . . ."

She waited for me to continue. "What?"

"It's not as bad as I thought it would be," I admitted and teased, "but if you tell Cristiano that, I will toss you in the deep end of the pool."

"I'm too scared to tell him *anything*." She fidgeted with the strap of her suit. "Are you just saying that so I won't worry about you?"

Ever since my arrival, I'd made the worst of my situation. Had I even *tried* to consider it as anything else? There had been more surprises than anything. I'd never imagined such a beautiful cage, eating the finest foods and sleeping in Egyptian cotton next to a man who made my body feel things I hadn't thought possible—and we hadn't even slept together. *That* was a surprise—the heady feeling of getting to my knees to comfort a man as stoic as Cristiano and actually enjoying it.

"You don't have to tell me what he's done to you," she continued, "but I'm here if you want to talk about it. Nessa went through something like this."

"Nessa?" I asked. "Your half-sister? I didn't know that."

"A guy she trusted, he . . . anyway, I've talked to her about it." Her posture lifted. "I mean, obviously it's not even *close* to what Cristiano has put you through—"

"He hasn't," I said, looking away. My gaze caught on the rings weighing down my hand. They were collars. Glittering splendors in the sunlight . . . and possibly even weapons.

"Hasn't what?" she prompted.

I sighed, turning back to her. "We haven't had sex."

Her jaw dropped nearly into the water. "How is that possible? Is he gay?"

I couldn't help laughing. I'd have given anything to see Cristiano's face if he'd heard that. "He's definitely not."

"How do you know?"

"He's . . . vocal about the things he wants to do. And we've, you know. . . done a little." God, I wasn't *that* shy about these things—I'd talked a lot with my friends in California. But it was Cristiano who made my cheeks heat. The wrongness of fooling around with him. Curiosity over what he'd do when he saw me next. The unsettling urge to call him tonight from our bed.

With my thumb, I spun the diamond on my ring finger. "The way he talks, it's just . . . it's filthy, and scary, and . . ."

Pilar waited. "Do you like it, Natalia?" she asked quietly. "Do you like *him*?"

"No," I said, stopping the horrifying thought in its tracks. "God, no."

"What if you did?" she asked. "It would make life here a lot easier."

"That's not a good reason to fall in love."

"I don't mean love. No, not at all. I mean, what if you find a way to . . ." She pulled her hair off her neck and fanned herself. "Never mind. It's dumb. I'm not the one in this situation."

"No, what?" I prompted. I hated when Pilar doubted herself, but if I was honest, I was more curious about what she had to say. I fought every day—against Cristiano, my situation, and sometimes even myself. To hear someone tell me I didn't have to could alleviate some of my guilt. "What if I find a way to accept this?" I asked. "Is that what you mean?"

"Or at least not hate it. Only until you get out of here. Maybe you can compartmentalize his past and the horrible things he does to others. For self-preservation."

"But he doesn't force me, Pilar. And I don't hate what he does to me. So I don't know what to think. To see him as anything other than the man who stormed my wedding and ruined my life . . ."

It would change everything. But I didn't *want* things to change. Cristiano had forced my hand in marriage—how could I ever forgive that? Especially while the reason behind my mother's death remained uncertain. To form any kind of attachment to Cristiano would mean I'd only have to sever it later.

"You said you haven't had sex, but you also say he's done things to you." Pilar crossed her arms over her stomach. "From what I know, Cristiano is really convincing, Natalia. You have to be careful. Go somewhere in your mind if you need to until you get out. But you can't ever *want* to stay."

"Of course not," I said. With a sinking feeling in my stomach, I knew that wasn't what I'd hoped she'd say. I waded away from the wall. "It's just that he's complex. It makes it hard to know how I feel about him. One minute, I think he's going to lock me away and strip me of everything, and the next, I learn that he's not *totally* the villain I thought he was."

"Has he done that?" she asked, her tone completely serious. "Locked you up?"

"No. Not unless you count staying in the house. I'm not allowed to leave the property."

"*You?* But you never let that stop you before. How many times has Barto wanted to ring your neck for slipping by him?"

I laughed. "When I was a kid? More than I can count."

She looked kindly at me. "You're laughing. I'm relieved, Natalia. I was so scared of what I'd find when I got here. I know it doesn't mean you're happy, but I'm just glad you're okay. For now."

For now.

She squinted ahead, seeming to process everything. "But he's always been the villain around our parts. Do you still think he killed your mom?"

"I can never let myself believe otherwise. What if months from now, I find out he *was* somehow involved? As long as I have doubt, I can't fall for him."

Pilar stayed seated but glided her arms through the water. "Wow. I didn't know love was on the table."

Fuck. I hadn't even realized what I'd said. "The heat must be getting to me. Falling for him was the wrong way of putting it, obviously. More like tolerating him."

"And Diego?" she asked. "What about him?"

I blanched. Once a prayer to me, his name sounded foreign now—I thought about Diego less and less each day. I blew out a breath. "Diego . . . is not who we thought he was. He can go to hell, actually."

"*What?*" Her eyebrows shot up. "You've been head over heels for him since I can remember."

"Things change fast around here," I said, pacing through the water. "This is going to sound crazy, but try to stay with me. First of all, Diego was the one who orchestrated all of this. The wedding to Cristiano was his idea, and he *tricked* me into showing up."

She chewed on her thumbnail. "How do you know that?"

"Cristiano told me."

"And you believe him? I don't understand," she said. "Two weeks ago, you *hated* Cristiano, and you were smiling ear to ear thinking you were going to marry Diego."

It would be nearly impossible to explain what the last couple weeks had been like. "It still hurts," I admitted. "Diego lied to me. I saw a future with him. I gave him my *virginity*, Pilar. I was smiling because I was on cloud nine."

"I remember."

"And then I find out he made the deal with Cristiano before we even had sex. Diego knew he and I weren't going to be together."

She looked at her hands under the water. "That doesn't sound like Diego."

"He *admitted* it."

"But what if he had to?" She raised her eyes again, concern clear in them. "Maybe Cristiano has something over him. Obviously you don't trust Cristiano, so why would you believe anything he says?"

I turned to pace the other way, glancing toward the house, maybe because of what I was about to admit. "I trust him more than Diego."

She gasped. "Your shoulder! That's the tattoo?"

I turned my head as she stood to get a better look. My butterfly was brighter out in the sun. I liked her more and more each day, but that stayed between me, myself, and I. Not only did I not want Cristiano to know, but I was also a little embarrassed to admit I didn't hate it when the circumstances around it had been so ugly.

Pilar frowned. "Does it say *Calavera Cartel?* With a skull?"

"Yes," I said, adding wryly, "A gift from Cristiano . . ."

She balled her fist at her mouth. "A *gift?* You didn't want that, did you?"

How did I explain that I could've stopped it? That I could've begged his forgiveness and let him spank me instead, but I'd chosen not to? How did I say, without sounding as if I were justifying it, that I *knew*, deep down—

if I'd truly not wanted it, Cristiano wouldn't have gone through with it?

It all sounded like defending an abuser to Pilar, someone who was actually living the life I'd feared I would. "I could've said no," I promised.

"Then why didn't you? That doesn't make any sense." Pilar's face contorted with concern. "Talia. If he'd force a tattoo on you, he'd do much worse. Believe me. Can't Diego get you out of here somehow?"

"Diego's all talk, Pilar. That's what I've been trying to tell you. I'm done with him." I went to the pool's infinity edge. On the horizon, the ocean seemed to touch the clouds. "He used to promise he'd come to California with me, but he was never going to."

Ever.

It was hard to believe he could've been so convincing. That I'd hardly questioned him.

Looking back with fresh perspective, though, there'd only been excuses, delays, and Diego entangling himself more and more in cartel life while promising me he was getting out.

Cristiano, on the other hand, had wanted what I had to offer so much that he hadn't let anything stand in his way. It was a twisted way of looking at things, but there was some comfort in it, I supposed. Diego and Cristiano had faced off. Cristiano had fought for me, and Diego . . . hadn't. So, if fate and fortune demanded I be with one of the brothers, maybe I'd somehow ended up with the right one.

I looked up at white-cotton clouds, wondering what the future had in store for me. "Cristiano says he never would've done what Diego did . . . and he never will. That he'd never let me go, let alone give me to another. Apparently, *my* prison sentence is *his* wedding vow."

"*Dios mío*," Pilar said.

At the small tremor in her voice, I swam back, hoping I hadn't frightened her. "Cristiano takes all this very seriously."

"I can see that." When I caught her looking at my ring, she lifted a slender shoulder. "It's blinding me, Natalia. But it's just jewelry. Don't let diamonds blind *you* from the truth. That's probably what he wants."

I spread my fingers, frowning at the rings. "I could care less about Cristiano's wealth." If anything distracted me about them, it was that he'd put actual thought into the design. It was such a kingpin move, matching my rings to a gun, but in its own way, it was sweet.

Sweet?

Cristiano?

Never before had the word been used to describe him, I was sure. He was rough around the edges, weather-beaten, a man who'd seen and done too much to have any sweetness remain intact. And yet with me, and only me, there was something there. He yielded. He showed vulnerability. He considered me where others hadn't . . .

I pushed the thoughts away.

That was dangerous thinking about a man who I could never care for.

"I'm getting out of this marriage," I said resolutely, as much to Pilar as to myself. "Without Diego, and without my father."

"What about Barto?" she asked.

"Nope. He's under Papá's control. I've got to do it on my own."

She leaned in, speaking softly. "How can you? You might be crafty enough to get by the guards, but it's not as simple as that."

"No, it isn't. Running away isn't an option." I chewed

the inside of my cheek. "Cristiano can hurt me the most without touching me."

"So how do you escape a man who has the means to find you wherever you go? You need help."

"Nobody can help me," I said. "I'm on my own, and I have a plan. The more I know about Cristiano and the Calavera cartel, the more power I have."

Admittedly, the plan didn't sound like much of one. Getting to know Cristiano had proved to be a wild ride. It seemed like every time he opened his mouth, something I didn't expect came out. And his actions were even more unpredictable.

But it all formed a bigger picture, and I had to believe once that revealed itself, I would understand what was best for me. That was my goal now—taking charge of *my* life as much as I could.

"I've learned so much already," I murmured. Not just about him, but about this world. And maybe even myself.

"Like what?" she asked.

"The Calaveras are nothing like they seem." I scratched my chin on my shoulder and glanced at my *mariposa*. "To be honest, this isn't the worst tattoo I could have. Calavera represents the opposite of what you'd think. The wings are almost symbolic."

Pilar's forehead creased—she looked like she was going to blow a gasket—and I realized how backward all of this sounded. I opened my mouth to clarify, but that would mean I was defending Cristiano. Explaining his actions. And the way Pilar looked at me, I felt like a sucker.

"Cristiano, unlike anyone I've known around here, evens the score," I said carefully. "He does good things as well as bad."

"The arms trafficking?" she asked.

"No, that's legit, but the profits he earns from that—

and they're considerable—he puts toward other . . . endeavors."

"The sex trade," she almost whispered. "I've been hearing that for years about this place."

I nodded. "Did you see anything when you drove in?"

She shook her head. "I had to wear a blindfold, but Alejandro was nice about it. He sort of gave me the option without really giving me an option, you know?"

I smiled a little. "I do, all too well." I paused, trying to think of how to word what I wanted to say. Since Cristiano had left the morning after we'd slept at *La Madrina*, I'd been asking myself what I believed and what I didn't. His story added up. But my feelings about it didn't. "I can't really say too much. But whatever you've heard about the Calavera cartel, there's another side of the story. A good side."

"Good?" She looked over her shoulder. "Not a single thing I've heard could be described that way."

I shielded my eyes against the sun reflecting on the water. "Just trust me."

"I do, Tali, but . . . that's the complete opposite of what everyone says." She blinked a few times. "I mean, how could some of it not to be true?"

"I'm not saying they're angels, believe me." I rubbed the inside corners of my eyes, knowing how it sounded— like I was excusing Cristiano's behavior. "Cristiano is still . . . he's . . ." I couldn't find the words, because I didn't know myself. I knew what I *wanted* to believe about him, but what I actually believed? Not the best but not the worst, either.

"He's scarier than any monster," I said quietly.

I'd let that soothe me as a child, but it wasn't until my mother's death that the words had taken on a negative meaning. On some level, as a young girl, I must've known something good in Cristiano.

And now . . . I wanted Cristiano on my side. He was the law in a lawless land, a dark hero for those who needed one. A protector.

Things I might've called him to his face, if only he'd been that for *me*.

And now, thanks to my guidance, he was out there searching for something that would only make him more powerful. That was all a man like Cristiano wanted. No matter what he'd divulged about his mission, it was the only thing he would pursue to the point of madness.

Power.

That was the *everything* he'd claimed was within grasp.

The everything he'd confront danger to get.

And that could either hurt or benefit me, depending on which Cristiano I was dealing with.

When he returned, it would most likely be as an even more powerful husband . . . or a more formidable captor.

NATALIA

C ristiano's bed was irritatingly comfortable and welcoming—nothing like what I'd expected riding to the Badlands with him.

I stared up at the ceiling, thankful Pilar was under the same roof as me and away from Manu. We'd actually managed to have a good time lunching by the pool, followed by popcorn and a movie, but I could tell she was anxious over Cristiano's return.

I was the one who should be anxious—yet my mind was occupied by my earlier conversation with Pilar. She was skeptical of his business, but I'd tried to defend it. Could I believe and respect him while despising what he'd done to me?

I reached over to the nightstand and took the cell phone he'd left me from the drawer. He'd told me to call, and there *were* things I wanted to discuss with him.

"I have to talk to you about Pilar," I said when the line clicked.

"Good evening to you, too," came Cristiano's familiar,

rumbling voice over a din of background chatter that sounded like a restaurant.

I flopped back onto my pillow and twirled my hair around my finger. "Good evening."

"I've already spoken with Alejandro," he said tersely.

"And?" I asked.

His voice went distant as he excused himself from wherever her was; he didn't speak again until the background quieted. "Tell me what you'd like me to do with him, Natalia. The fiancé."

Chills covered my skin. I'd never been asked to determine anyone's fate before, and if I knew Cristiano, he wasn't asking if I thought we should write Manu a threatening e-mail. "I don't know," I said.

"Yes, you do. Don't get shy on me. Don't you want justice for your friend?"

"Yes . . ." I counted the number of antlers in the chandelier to avoid asking myself what kind of justice seemed fair for a pig like Manu. Someone who'd beat on a woman half his size should feel that same wrath turned on him. And with my husband hanging on the line, I had the means to make that happen. "She's afraid of you. You beat up her cousin," I said. "She saw the whole thing."

"I remember. He was a thief. I should've killed him."

"For stealing?" I asked.

"No. For sexually abusing Pilar's half-sister."

My mouth fell open as the chandelier's faint, warm glow blurred. Pilar had mentioned supporting Nessa through that. "*That's* why you did it?"

"Costa didn't give me permission to kill him, even though I disagreed and told him so," Cristiano said. "Instead, I left him lacking in the one place that matters."

I shuddered. "You mean you . . ."

"No, but I'd be surprised if the thing between his legs could even twitch on its own."

"Oh my God."

"So about the ex-fiancé," he said almost cheerfully, ignoring the fact that he'd probably just scarred me with that mental image.

"Ex?" I asked, wrinkling my nose. "She won't leave him."

"Then he'll have to leave her."

I fell silent. I had some idea of what that meant, but I was afraid to ask for clarification. I wasn't sure it mattered what Cristiano intended to do to Manu, only that it would be bad enough to keep him away.

"It seems we don't even have to be in the same room for me to scare you," Cristiano said.

Manu deserved whatever was coming to him. All I had to do was order the punishment, and my husband would enforce it. Cristiano could deliver justice when everyone else Pilar cared about had failed her—but to feel pride over that posed a question I wasn't sure how to answer.

Did I belong in this world as Cristiano kept suggesting? Had I ever really left? Just because I'd been deaf, dumb, and blind to my father's business while in California didn't mean I could erase the years I'd been raised in the middle of it. It didn't mean I wasn't my father—or my mother's—daughter. Papá served justice, as Mamá had.

"I'm not afraid. But why would you do all that for Pilar?"

"She needs someone stronger than him in her corner. Now she has an army of us. But that's not what you're asking." With shuffling on the line, it got even quieter. "You're wondering why I should help her when you feel I've done the opposite for you."

My stomach rose with a deep inhale. Who was in my

corner? Who was stronger than Cristiano? Perhaps *I* could be. I was learning the ropes from the master himself, after all. "You can see why I'd think that."

He didn't respond right away, and when he did, I had to listen hard to catch his words. "I've asked myself the same." He cleared his throat. "All I can tell you is that I'd help Pilar regardless of your association with her, but the fact that she's your friend makes it all the more personal. I will handle this, Natalia. And I will take her under my protection if that's what she wants."

I shook my head, gratitude for his help and contempt for my situation warring inside me. "I don't know what to say."

"Say nothing. In any case, Alejo will be happy to handle this while I'm away. He seems overly concerned for a girl he hardly knows. Perhaps he's got a thing for her."

"It might be mutual," I said, allowing a small smile. "*Although* . . . she did speak about him the same way she did Barto."

"Barto?" Cristiano sounded annoyed. "What's he got to do with anything?"

"He helped her, too, after the wedding." I reached up and played with one of the bed's gauzy, white curtains. "I can't really blame her. They're both handsome men, Barto and Alejandro."

Cristiano growled. "You'd call them handsome, but your own husband, you treat like Quasimodo."

I laughed. Cristiano was the last man on Earth I'd think of as insecure, and perhaps the last man who had reason to be. He was beautiful in a way normal men could never touch. His own brother was strikingly handsome with clear green eyes, high cheekbones, and hair that begged to be touched. But there was still no comparison.

Paired with a face and body right from Mount Olympus, Cristiano's darkness devastated.

And I'd die before I admitted that to him, I thought willfully.

"Speaking of Alejandro, you need to let him spar with me," I said.

"No."

"Why not?" I asked.

"He could hurt you."

"So let me get hurt, Cristiano. You let me fight with Solomon. Is it because Alejandro's good-looking?"

"You're not helping your case."

I sighed. "If I don't practice what I'm learning, I'll be useless in a real fight."

"You're my wife, and I don't want him putting his hands on you." His anger fizzled with his words. Cristiano didn't truly believe Alejo would try anything. "Fine," he conceded. "I'll talk to him before tomorrow's lesson—but when I get back, you'd better be advanced enough to take me on."

"Thank you," I said, biting my lip as I tried not to entertain all the ways I could take him on. Silence settled over the line. "You should get back to your thing."

"What thing?" he asked. "I'm talking to my wife. That's my thing."

I stretched my legs under the covers, pointing my toes. "Have you found what you're looking for?"

"Eager for me to come home, eh? Or perhaps the opposite, in which case you'll be glad to learn I've had a setback."

"How?" I asked.

"The trail has turned cold. I wasted two days."

"Are you still in the country?"

"Yes."

"Have you asked my father for help?" I asked. "You

have a stronger worldwide network, but within México, Papá is well-connected."

"This is a matter I have to handle on my own," he said. "I don't want to tell Costa until I have every confidence that it's true."

"That what's true?" I asked, sitting up straighter. "Does it involve him?"

"Yes."

With a flurry of jitters, I spread my hand over my stomach. "How?"

"I would tell you, Natalia—I promised to answer your questions. But like with your father, I don't want to until I know more. Because it involves you, too."

I curled my hand into the sheets, intrigue rising in me and clashing with wariness. In this new world of mine, anything could happen. Nothing was off-limits. I'd been lucky in my situation so far, but that could change. "I don't know how many more surprises I can handle, Cristiano."

"You can handle a lot. I wouldn't have married you if I didn't think so. You prove it to yourself more every day."

I wasn't sure where his confidence in me came from, but he had a point. Almost two weeks at Cristiano's, and I was physically, emotionally, and mentally stronger than I'd been when I'd arrived.

"What if you don't find what you're after?"

"Then I suppose it will be some time before I return. I'll be tempted to come home for the same reason I have to press on, but I won't return empty-handed unless I have to."

A reason that involved me. Something that tempted him to come home—and also drove him. I tapped my chin, trying to piece it together but coming up short. "You are the most cryptic man I've ever met."

"I choose to find the compliment in that. I'm grateful

to have graduated from asshole, monster, and devil to 'cryptic.'"

I bit my cheek to hide my smile. "Wishful thinking. But if you do this for Pilar, then I promise to cross one of those off the list."

"Then I will do this for Pilar. And I will do it for you."

He still hadn't said *why* in any way I could fully comprehend. Why he'd handle everyone from Manu to the Belmonte-Ruiz cartel, and all the dangers in between, if it meant helping women. There was only one explanation for that.

It had to be personal.

And personal was exactly what I needed if I had any chance at even beginning to understand him. And to understand if escaping him was still the best thing for me.

"Have there been women you couldn't help?" I asked.

He went silent for so long, I wondered if he was still on the line. Maybe I shouldn't have pressed.

With a firm, sudden knock, I vaulted upright in the bed. "Someone's at the bedroom door."

"It'll be Jaz with my dry cleaning," he said.

"*Dry cleaning?*" I wondered aloud, picturing Cristiano in one of his pressed suits. Despite the nature of his business, he was almost always clean-shaven or neatly trimmed, sporting fine Italian loafers and Swiss watches, and his black, inky hair was never too short or too long. "What's the point?"

"Not every interaction I have ends with bloodshed," he said. "Are you decent?"

I glanced down at the silky red camisole and shorts that had one day appeared in my dresser drawer. "My mother instilled in me the importance of dressing as well for bed as I would for church," I told him. "Even when I'm alone."

"Mmm." I heard his contentment over the line. "Send Jaz away and tell me every last thing you're not wearing."

"*Cristiano.*"

"I promised I wouldn't touch you for a while—I never promised you wouldn't touch yourself."

While he *listened*? God, how obscene. And tempting. It was turning out that I loved the utter filth that spilled out of him when he got excited. With that thought, I shifted the phone from my mouth and called, "Come in, Jaz."

"Use my imagination, I guess," Cristiano grumbled to himself.

The door flew open and Jazmín breezed in with armfuls of suits and shirts sheathed in plastic. "Excuse me. I'll be quick."

"No rush," I said as she passed into the closet without even a glance in my direction. I moved back against the headboard and lowered my voice. "She hates me."

"Give her time."

Hangers scraped in the closet as Cristiano's line remained quiet. I checked the clock. It was almost nine. I wanted to ask where he was, and not just because it could be a clue as to why he was gone. I was curious about what he did outside these walls. About his life. About whether he was with anyone. Where he was, what he was doing.

About him.

Every layer I'd unpeeled had revealed something I hadn't expected. And with his promise to help Pilar, I felt myself opening to the idea that he could possibly be not just a hero to others, but to me—even if he wasn't one *for* me.

Did that mean I cared? Whether I wanted to admit it or not, my trepidation and hatred of him had been waning. Would other feelings rise in their absence? They had to. The only thing more improbable than falling in love with Cristiano would be indifference toward him.

"I'm sure you're needed at your party or whatever," I said, hoping he'd offer up something without me asking.

"Yes," he agreed, but made no move to get off the line. After a brief silence, he said, "Don't worry about Jaz. She hasn't known much kindness."

I was lucky that most of my life, I'd had an abundance of that, despite the betrayals and death I'd seen. There was still a wall between Jaz and me—more like every brick was still in place. But that didn't mean I hoped we wouldn't break it down. I could afford to show compassion.

I swung my legs over the side of the bed and prepared to say goodnight. Plastic wrap crinkled in the closet, then it went quiet. Nine o'clock wasn't late at all. Maybe Jaz and I could talk—even over a drink. It seemed as if Cristiano would welcome that more than he would mind.

Anticipating Cristiano would end the call, I stuck my head in the closet to address Jaz and nearly knocked my forehead into hers. She jumped back and the wood hangers in her hands fell, banging against each other.

Had she been *listening* to our conversation?

"Everything okay over there?" Cristiano asked.

"Um," I said, stalling as Jaz's eyes widened. I'd never caught her spying on me, but that didn't mean it was the first time. I wouldn't forget anytime soon how she'd ratted me out to Cristiano the night I'd arrived at the Badlands. When I'd been scared and alone. *She* looked scared now. I opened my mouth to respond, but nothing came.

I'd just decided to show her kindness, and I myself had sure as hell been caught eavesdropping on more than one occasion. Plus, whatever Jaz had against me, she was loyal to a fault to Cristiano, and I didn't want to give him reason to question that.

"Everything's fine," I told him, raising my brows at Jaz. "I dropped my hairbrush in the bathroom."

"I see."

"So, goodnight then," I said.

"Goodnight. I—uh . . ." He paused.

My heart missed a beat. Cristiano didn't stammer over his words, and that sent up a red flag in me. "What is it?" I asked, backing away from the closet, keeping Jaz in sight until I turned and walked onto the balcony for privacy.

"I'm only one man, Natalia," Cristiano said. "And there's a world full of evil to contend with."

My nerves calmed at the absence of alarm in Cristiano's voice. But the melancholy in it touched something deep inside me. It was hard to imagine a man as strong and tightly coiled as Cristiano feeling sad, so I never really wondered if he was.

I rested my elbows on the stucco wall, squinting out over the inky black ocean. "What's wrong, Cristiano?"

"When you say my name that way, nothing."

I had also sensed the shift in how I addressed him—I was starting to feel at ease, but I didn't necessarily want to admit that to him.

"You asked if there are ever women I can't help," he said. "I wish I had a different answer."

I remembered how I'd once peered over this wall and wondered if it could be a way out. My *only* way out.

Don't die. It was Cristiano's first rule.

I'd cheated death already, though, if that soothsayer from my father's party weeks ago was to be believed. I hadn't forgotten her prophecy about Diego and me. *You will die for him, your love.*

If she'd been so prescient, why hadn't she warned me about the kind of person Diego would turn out to be?

"You'd have to be a superhero to save them all," I told

Cristiano as a breeze sent a shiver down my bare shoulders. "And superheroes don't exist."

But you come close.

The unbidden thought scared me. It was true—for others. Not for me. Cristiano held the key to this tower. He could unlock the door and free me, but as long he'd put me here, he couldn't save me.

"I cannot describe to you, nor would I ever try, the things I have seen," he said slowly. "Things no man should ever witness. The sex trade runs so deep, and touches parts of the world, of the internet, and of men, that even the strongest army can't beat. But we can still fight." He paused as a gripping sorrow passed through the phone from him into me. Cristiano had taken on a beast that could never be killed. How did that feel for someone as mighty as him? "I'm sorry it's this way," he continued. "I do what I can. The people I care about, I will protect, and those I didn't, I will avenge."

My heart stopped a moment, and his grave words hung heavy over the line. I'd never doubted Cristiano had demons, only that he'd ever show them to me. Or anyone.

"Those you didn't?" I repeated softly. "Who?"

A beat passed, and then another. I thought he might actually answer until he said, "A story for another time, my love. Now, it's really time to say goodnight. Sleep well. I will, knowing you're one of the protected."

The line went dead, but I made no move except to raise my head to the stars twinkling above us. I was one of the protected, which meant he cared, and though that should've come as a surprise, it didn't. The tenderness in his voice didn't match the man I'd thought I'd married. This man had a past that I'd lived alongside him and which I still knew very little about. How could I, when I'd been so consumed with hating him?

Cristiano had lost people he'd cared about, but hadn't been able to protect, and he was trying to make that right by doing everything he could for strangers.

Unless it wasn't about strangers at all. Cristiano had lost my mother when it'd been his job to protect her. And perhaps he was trying to make *that* right . . . but how?

The answer sat on the tip of my tongue but also eluded me.

Silence fell over the night as the waves lulled. With a noise at my back, I spun around.

Framed by the clean, white arched doorway, Jazmín looked almost devilish with her dainty, sharp features and red hair. "What are you doing here?" she asked.

"*Me?*" My heart rate kicked up a notch. "This is my bedroom."

"I mean in the Badlands." She took a step toward me, narrowing her eyes. "You may think he's blind. That he's too wrapped up in you to see anything else, but *I* see everything."

"He's hardly wrapped up in me," I said, also stepping forward. "If you saw *anything*, you'd know that. Maybe you're the one who's blind."

Jaz made two tiny fists, her mouth sliding into a frown. "I meant what I said. If anything happens to him, you'll pay the price. If he doesn't come home, you'll have all of us to face."

"Why wouldn't he come h-home?" I asked, stumbling over the strange word. It wasn't the first time I'd referred to the Badlands that way, but it was the first time it felt . . . true. And the first time fear had *ever* entered my heart that Cristiano might not return.

"Every time he leaves these walls, he's in danger. But this time especially, and you don't even *appreciate* it." She shook her head up at the night sky. "He's wasting time and resources that could go to people who actually need it."

I wrinkled my nose, trying to make sense of her words. Cristiano was in search of something he desperately wanted. Something he needed. And he'd said it involved my father and me.

I'd thought power was the only thing that drove a man like Cristiano, but power was a fickle bitch that wore many masks.

Sex. Money. Revenge.

Cristiano had only hinted that it wasn't any of those, but he'd never confirmed anything. He *had* told me he was done scheming, though. What, then, could possibly drive him to put himself in harm's way? And why, when I'd spent the last few weeks wishing to be free of him, did the thought of him in danger inspire concern?

"I don't know what you're talking about, Jazmín," I said. "He didn't tell me where he was going. He barely said good-bye when he left."

"He went because of you. Because you told him to. Because even though he gives you *everything*,"—she gestured emphatically around the palatial room where I rested my head each night—"it's still not enough."

"I never asked for any of this," I said, my voice wavering until I reminded myself it was true. My cheeks warmed, my temper rising as I repeated, "I never asked for *any* of this."

"But you're lucky to have it, and have you ever *thanked* him? Ever returned any of the kindness he shows you?" As she took another step, I straightened. I was taller than her, but she possessed a scrappiness I never would, no matter how much I trained. "Out there, he's exposed. The deeper he gets into this, the more dangerous it is."

"What is *this*?" He'd said he'd look until he found what

he needed—or until it drove him mad. I'd told him to go, but I'd had no idea I was the force behind his search. "What's he looking for?"

"It's not my place to say—"

"You inserted yourself in this, now tell me what puts *my* husband in danger," I demanded.

Slowly, she crossed her thin arms, glaring back at me. After a moment, she gritted her teeth and looked out over the water. "He knows you'll never trust him, and never believe him, without proof." She turned back to me. "And even if he doesn't know it yet, he loves you too much to live with that."

Waves crashed against the shore as silence fell over each of us. Cristiano was controlling, dominant, aggressive, even cheeky at times, but was he loving? My heart answered with a skipped beat. I'd known from the beginning that Cristiano hadn't done any of this out of hatred or indifference—how did I not ever *once* consider it might be love? I wouldn't believe that unless I heard it from his mouth, but I realized there was a chance it was true.

As tempted as I was to explore that possibility, the first half of Jaz's thought demanded my attention. "Proof of what?" I asked.

"I've said too much." She shook her head as she retreated. "Tell him to come home. If he doesn't make it back, *you* won't make it out. We need him. This town needs him. We can never repay him for what he's done for us . . . but we'd all jump at the chance to."

Her threat was clear. Nobody would bat an eye if I paid the price for their hero's fall. But Jaz didn't intimidate me. Her concern only demonstrated how truly worried she and the others were. *That* scared me—the idea of losing Cristiano. For now, it was as much as I could admit in the privacy of my own thoughts.

There were people out there who wanted Cristiano dead. I'd known that when I'd told him to go. In my mind, he was invincible, but in my heart, I knew that wasn't true.

Cristiano was on a mission I'd sent him on. I didn't even care what he'd gone to find. There wasn't anything I could think of that was worth risking his life.

I could call him back.

But why did I care? Why would I tell him to retreat when I'd done nothing but try to think of ways to get away from him?

The people I care about, I will protect.

He had sworn me his protection, but he was out there now, unprotected.

And *my* care could bring him home—if I could allow myself to want that.

21

CRISTIANO

I'd traveled across the country, brought along two of my most trusted men, and worst of all, left behind my new bride—only to come up empty-handed. Now, I navigated a small crowd in a warmly lit hotel ballroom with chandeliers overhead, hit songs on the speakers, and a fresh mezcal in my hand.

Max, Daniel, and I had kicked up mud on our way through dirt-road towns, hitting up local bars and banging on doors to ask questions that put targets on our backs—all in an effort to excavate information from those who were willing to sell at the risk of their lives.

But the remaining members of the long-disbanded Valverde family were nowhere to be found since they'd changed their identities and gone into deep hiding. Either that or they were dead.

So I was hitting somewhere even more dangerous—the elite. Those who had more, demanded more, but also possessed an even greater weakness for money than the poverty-stricken towns we'd just come from. The right offer to the right person could produce information. But the wrong inquiry to the wrong one? These people had enough money and power to wipe anyone from existence.

Some—myself included—would call me a fool for trying to raise one rival from the dead when I already had another to contend with. Belmonte-Ruiz wanted my neck after the attack Sandra had helped us pull off, the most recent in a line of several. But the information the Valverde family possessed could be invaluable—proven by the fact that I was still trying to track them down.

Natalia had been right, though. What was all of this for if I couldn't have everything I wanted?

Tonight was my first politician's event. Everything I'd done up until now had been under the radar and cloak of anonymity. Every government and law enforcement official, judge, or ally of mine had been secured via a complicated but nearly impenetrable network that spanned the world.

Now that my identity had been revealed, I was coming to collect on years of staying clear of polite society.

I hadn't been invited, but that didn't matter. Senator Raúl Sanchez wouldn't dare turn me away knowing the influence—and capital—I had to offer.

The crowd was a thing to see, particularly the confused and anxious expressions of the state's elite when they recognized me. And, of course, as they took in disheveled, Russian Max and his glass eye, and my completely hairless associate Daniel.

"I hear congratulations are in order." Sanchez shook my hand, but I didn't miss his furtive glances. I was both a liability and an asset, the latter being the kind better kept in the wings.

"Thank you, Senator."

Coming up to my neck, he had a habit of looking at

my chin rather than into my eyes. "How are you finding your new bride?" he asked.

"Expensive." I adjusted the knot of my tie. "She has a credit card with her new name on it and nothing but time to kill."

"Welcome to married life." He clinked his drink with mine. "I hope she at least pays off the card both timely and *abundantly*."

"Do you think there's any woman who denies me?" I asked with a dismissive wave. "I have access to the best pussy in the world. The girl doesn't even come close. I needed the connection to her family—that's all."

"I've heard Costa's daughter is quite the beauty, though."

An ember of fire lit at the base of my chest. I breathed through my nose, calming my instinct to put him in his place. He should be so lucky to ever lay eyes on Natalia Cruz *de la Rosa*. I forced out the only acceptable response. "Exaggeration. She's a plain and boring brat."

"Nonetheless, she has brought you even greater fortune and power," he said with a sip. "I'm happy you could make it tonight."

"How happy?" I asked, ready to move on from the subject of Natalia. "I'm looking for the Valverde family."

"Now's not really the time, de la Rosa." With a tissue from inside his jacket, he patted his hairline. "Have you gotten a chance to visit the silent auction?"

"Now is exactly the time." I had a low tolerance for political smoke and shadows and would sooner be back at the hotel working than shoveling this bullshit, but I'd exhausted all other options. "The sooner I get what I need, the sooner I'll leave."

"I never had any association with Valverde," he said

out of the side of his mouth, "and that's the God's honest truth."

"Then give me the name of someone here who can help me."

"I haven't even heard the name *Valverde* in years. How would I know what you need?"

"Wrong answer. Try again, *compa*. Give me a name."

He forced a smile that couldn't even pass as an *attempt* at genuine and raised his cocktail across the room. To me, he spoke under his breath. "See the gentleman in the wheelchair to the left?"

I followed his gaze to a man in a bespoke suit with wrinkled skin and thinning gray hair. Despite his sunglasses, I knew the face underneath was hard as nails. It'd been years since I'd seen him, but I recognized him instantly. "*El Búho*," I said.

"Once wise and all-seeing."

"Now blind and senile," I said, frustrated by yet another useless lead.

I'd gone to The Owl as a twenty-something in need of help, and he and his family had done everything they could, but it hadn't been enough. I appreciated the man he'd been, but at almost a hundred years old, I'd heard through the grapevine that his mind was worthless now.

Sanchez clucked his tongue, shaking his head. "Not so fast. Those secrets are still in there, and he just might be out of it enough to share some." The senator shrugged. "But what's true and what's lies? You'll have to decide for yourself. He's your best bet at information here, though."

I started toward the old man, but Sanchez called me back. "He's on a tight leash. Family doesn't let him talk to anyone anymore."

Sure. But I wasn't anyone.

My phone buzzed in my shirt pocket. I slipped it out

and kept the screen close to my chest as Natalia's name flashed. *Well, well*. It wasn't the ideal place to talk, but the fact that she'd called at all was reason enough to pick up. I did love when she obeyed—almost as much as when she didn't.

I got Max's attention and nodded toward the man in the wheelchair. "Bring me *El Búho*. I need a few minutes alone with him."

I'd barely put the phone to my ear when Natalia blurted, "I have to talk to you about Pilar."

My free hand curled into a fist as lust rooted itself in me. Being called upon by Natalia for help was one of the sweetest things I'd experienced to date. It would be my perverse pleasure to hear Natalia ask me to deliver a certain fate to the woman-beating molester.

I smiled to myself then schooled my expression for anyone who might care enough to take note. "Good evening to you too," I responded.

I thought I detected a sigh as she said, "Good evening."

Recalling Alejandro's account of her best friend's bruises and the cowardly fiancé was enough to turn me from doting husband into Manu's personal nightmare. I tugged at my collar as my chest burned. "I've already spoken with Alejandro."

"And?"

I excused myself from the senator and made my way through the crowd with Daniel at my back. He opened the patio door for me, and I stepped out onto a balcony.

Two women in gowns smoked between sips of martinis. My presence was enough to get them to stub out their cigarettes and clear the area. I gave Daniel a nod, and he returned inside. I could speak freely to my wife knowing he was guarding the door.

Natalia had called for help, and I was more than happy to answer. My mind was already running through the ways I could make Manu pay. I tried my best to keep the growl out of my voice so as not to scare Natalia. Although, I'd quite enjoyed watching the evolution of her responses to my attempts to instill fear.

"Tell me what you'd like me to do with him, Natalia. The fiancé."

As she spoke, I listened with all the attention I had. It wasn't always easy, pretending she was nothing to me, but it was necessary. Even amongst my own townspeople. Natalia had taken it in stride the day we'd arrived at the Badlands, or perhaps she'd just been relieved I'd kept my distance. She was in enough danger as my wife—even the slightest suspicion that she meant anything to me put her even more in the line of fire.

Although, there was a flip side to that. Perhaps the best way to go about this marriage would be to show everyone just exactly how prized my new wife was. And let them even *think* about coming for her.

I preferred to stay on the line with Natalia, but once the conversation turned to the past, talking over the phone wasn't the way to go. I ended our call and glanced out over the balcony as I sipped my liquor, welcoming the burn down my throat. With Natalia around, I'd been thinking more and more of the life I'd had before all of this. Of my time at Costa's, of my parents and brother . . . of others I'd been unable to help. Of things I would go back and change if I could.

Things I should've prevented at all costs.

At a noise, I spun around. A small, white-haired woman looked over the balcony with her back to me. I glanced at the door, where Daniel still stood.

"*Oye.* How'd you get out here?"

She turned slowly, her black, beaded dress trickling like a waterfall. She had more pink lipstick on her teeth and on the mouthpiece of a long cigarette holder than she did on her lips. "What a handsome man," she said, her watchful eyes resting on me, "a beauty rivaled only by her."

Her? Who did she mean? It didn't matter. She'd listened to a private conversation between my wife and me. "Didn't anyone ever teach you not to sneak up on a man that way?"

"So toss me over. Isn't that what the cartels do?" She shrugged a thin shoulder and leaned against the balcony wall. "Nobody will see, and if they do, they won't challenge you over an old, faceless woman."

Whatever she'd meant by bringing up cartels, I didn't care for it. With an uneasy feeling, I said, "Leave."

"I'm not finished with my cigarette, my friend."

"Friend? You don't even know who I am—if you did, you'd do as I say."

"Ah, yes. You are well-known for your treatment of women." She sucked on the cigarette holder and set a frail elbow on the edge of the wall. "Despite the rumors and your cold demeanor, I can't help but think I'd be safer with you than anyone else at this party."

I took a step toward her, completely aware of how menacing it would seem. "Who are you?"

"You were wrong just now, my friend—I *do* know who you are," she said. "And what you want, who you love, and who you seek."

My jaw tingled, and not from the drink. I set the glass on a wall. "Then tell me how to find it."

"You're closer than you think."

"That's vague." I went to take a cigarette from my jacket, but I'd left the pack in the car. When I glanced up, the woman held one out to me. Cautiously, I stepped closer to accept it.

"Don't give up." She flicked a lighter open. The stacked, mixed metal rings on her fingers clinked as she cupped her hand around the flame for me. I had to bend considerably to reach her. Wrinkles deepened her leathery skin as she peered at me. "And when death strikes, don't fall down."

"I don't intend to."

"And know when to *back* down. You don't always need to fight—"

"I will *always* fight."

"Brains beat brawn, *señor*. You have both. But there's a time to throw a punch and a time to be patient. And calculating."

I tipped my head back and blew smoke at the sky. This cigarette was not an indulgence, but an attempt to ease my frustration, all the dead ends and false starts—and this cryptic old woman wasn't helping. "Give me something I can use," I said. "Is there someone here tonight who can help me?"

"You've spent a long time leading others. Someone here can lead *you*—if you let them."

"You," I deduced.

She grinned. "I'm just an old lady with a bad back."

"Tell me then. Without details, nothing you've said means anything to me."

"I can tell you the senile man is indeed wise, but that you'd be wiser than him if you left right now. Before your chat."

Senile man . . . The Owl. She might've nearby when I'd been speaking to Sanchez. I wasn't going anywhere until I spoke to *El Búho*.

"I can say that you were on the right path, but it's

about to split." She rubbed her teeth with her index finger, but the lipstick didn't budge. "And you'll have to decide how badly you want the prize."

My prize. Natalia got this look sometimes when she was suppressing a smile or laugh. She did it enough around me to signal that she thought feeling happiness in her situation was wrong. That would change, though. "Badly."

She sighed as if she'd done all she could to convince me otherwise. "Then you should value it more than life itself, because that will be the cost."

"Whose life?"

She shrugged. She didn't know. *Because she doesn't know* anything, I reminded myself. I almost *wanted* to listen to her, which showed how desperate I was. "Then at least tell me if I'll succeed in obtaining what I want."

"No." She put out her cigarette.

"No I won't, or no you won't tell me?"

She nodded at my mezcal on the wall. "I'd dump that out if I were you."

Alarmed, I inspected the glass. "Poisoned?"

"Drugged. But it's not doing your heartburn any favors, either."

I frowned at her, then burst into laughter—even as I asked myself how the fuck she'd known about my heartburn. I must've been rubbing my chest.

She winked at me and knocked on the glass door.

Daniel turned to open it, and his non-existent eyebrows rose as the woman pushed by him. "What the——"

"Don't ask," I said, shaking my head after her. She had balls of steel to corner me that way, then spout a bunch of bull. How had she even gotten out here? I looked to the balcony several floors up as if she'd been airdropped in like a package of canned goods.

I didn't have time to wonder, since Max wheeled the blind man in sunglasses through the doorway.

"*¿Quién está ahí?*" the ancient man asked before he was even all the way on the balcony.

"You're safe," I assured him. "I just have some questions I need answered."

"*Vete a la chingada.* Fuck off." He turned his head in every direction, looking remarkably like an owl. I half-expected him to *hoot*. "Where's my wife?"

"Dead," I said, ashing my cigarette. I nodded at Daniel and Max, who closed the door and resumed guarding the balcony.

"You may not remember me, but I'm a friend to your family," I said.

"Cristiano," he said.

I paused with my smoke halfway to my mouth. Pleased by his coherence, I nodded. "*Sí, señor.* You remember?"

"No. I can't remember. That's what they tell me. Can't see, either."

"I'm sorry. I thought the dementia was more advanced or I would've visited."

"Visited where?" he asked, a thread of panic in his voice. "Where am I?"

I scratched my eyebrow as he started to squirm. "It's me. Cristiano de la Rosa," I said. "I'm looking for the remaining members of the Valverde family from the northwest."

"Cristiano." He grumbled, shaking his head. "Your father's playing with fire."

"Not anymore," I said. "The fucker's dead. I'm with the Cruz cartel now, and we need to get in touch with the Valverdes."

"The Valverdes and the Cruzes are enemies," he

informed me. "Vicente and Costa are fighting over the old de la Rosa turf like vultures."

Once my parents had died, Vicente Valverde had pounced on their cartel's carcass, resulting in years of battling with the Cruzes over their narcotics territories.

The Owl was stuck in the past, but that might not be a bad thing. "Do you know who wins?" I asked.

Costa would, eventually. Largely because the Valverdes had vanished one day, practically into thin air. The Cruzes had absorbed all that remained of the fallen cartels. And when Costa had decided to trade risk for stability, he'd used some of those territories as currency to build out and focus on the shipping side of his business.

He gripped the arms of his wheelchair with knotty, spotted fingers. "I have to get home. My wife is waiting."

With a tap on the glass, I looked up and met familiar dark, sparkling eyes. *Tasha.* She arched a manicured, scolding eyebrow at me—*busted*. She'd caught me pumping her grandfather for intel.

Then again . . . could she and her smirking red lips get the old man to hoot?

I nodded at Daniel and Max to let her onto the patio.

Natasha Sokolov-Flores stepped out in strappy, cherry-colored heels and a matching dress that stopped just below the curve of her ass. Her curled auburn hair brushed her cleavage as she came toward me. "Cristiano. It's been a while."

22

CRISTIANO

All my hopes were pinned on a blind, senile man in a wheelchair. The closure and proof my wife needed to allow me to smash through the lies she'd been told currently lay with The Owl.

Tasha, his granddaughter and my old friend, leaned in to kiss me on both cheeks. "How've you been?"

I nodded once. "I didn't know you were in town."

Her red lips curled up at the corners. "Then I won't be offended you didn't call."

"Is that you, Tasha?" the old man asked.

"*Sí, abuelito*," she answered. "I'm right here."

"I recognized your perfume."

As did I. Tasha and I had hooked up enough times to turn me into a dog whose mouth watered at the hint of Chanel No. 5.

"*Tsk, tsk*, Cristiano," she said quietly to me. "What are you doing sneaking my grandfather into dark corners?"

Tasha had a powerful bloodline. Her mother—the daughter of a self-made, well-connected Russian mobster —had been married into a Mexican dynasty. Natasha—

Tasha or Tatia—had been born the baby of her family and was more interested in the spoils the arms and narcotics trade afforded her than the business itself. But she knew more than she let on. And she could be of use to me now.

Fleetingly, I wondered what my Natalia at home would think of me standing here with *Natasha*, the woman I'd teased her about in *La Madrina* weeks ago. I'd told my then-unknown future bride that Natasha had sucked my cock like it'd end in a mouthful of gold. And she had, but I'd said it to shock Natalia. What would my bride say about it now that she'd given me the gift of her beautiful mouth? I'd heard repressed tremors of jealousy in Natalia's voice before—over Jaz, Sandra, or just at the prospect of my infidelity. After I'd fought so hard for just the chance to earn Natalia's devotion, I gave in easily to the satisfying feeling that she might one day be possessive over me.

Or that maybe she already was.

Without thinking, I picked up my mezcal, then froze as the old woman's words from earlier filtered through my consciousness.

I'd dump that out if I were you.

Strange woman. And seemingly very intuitive. I didn't believe in clairvoyance but perhaps she'd seen something. I glanced into the dregs of the glass, feeling better than ever and tempted to finish it off. But I was too far from the safety of the Badlands' walls to take any chances.

I set it back down. "I'm looking for remaining members of the Valverde family," I told Tasha.

The Owl answered. "You want the locations of their gravesites?"

Tasha pursed her lips to suppress her smile. "There's your answer. Now, how about we get a drink?"

Not so fast. Clearly, the old man's mind wasn't *completely* gone. "I don't believe they're all dead," I said, though I'd been told they were plenty of times.

"They might as well be." Tasha crossed her bare arms. "They haven't been relevant in years."

I arched an eyebrow at her. "Then giving me information on them shouldn't be a problem."

With a sigh, she squatted at her grandfather's side. "Grandfather? What do you know about the Valverdes?"

"I know nothing about nothing," he said.

She glanced up at me as she spoke to him. "You know so much, though. It's me, Tasha. Are there still any living members of the Valverde family?"

"Who? What?"

"Listen to me, *abuelo*," she said firmly, and then repeated, "Where are the living members of the Valverde family now?"

"They're all dead. All of them . . . but there are men in the south who say otherwise."

Tasha covered his hand with hers. "Where in the south?"

"If you've hit Guatemala, you've gone too far."

I would've laughed if I wasn't desperate for this information, which could not only bring some peace to my world, but also get me where I was meant to be—back home. Running the Badlands. Unearthing things most thought were better left to rest. And teasing, learning about, and sleeping by my Natalia.

"Which town down south?" I pressed.

"Go fuck yourself," he said. "I know nothing about nothing. Where's Elena?"

"She's not with us anymore, *papi*," Tasha said. "You remember."

Perfect. I'd been reduced to getting information from,

first, an aging mystic-for-hire, and second, a once great man who now didn't know his own wife was six feet under.

Tasha shook her head and stood. "I think that's the best you'll get. 'I know nothing about nothing' is his mantra."

"I just need to know which town," I said.

She took my cigarette from my hand and placed it between her lips, staring at me as she took a drag. "Use that devious brain you're so famous for." She parted her lips, and smoke curled around us. "Where would *you* hide? If it were me, I'd look for either the deepest hole or the highest mountain."

I shifted my gaze behind her and nodded at Max. "Take him back."

When Tasha and I were alone, she set the cigarette on the ledge next to my drink, pressed a hand to my chest, and leaned in for a kiss.

I drew back. "I'm married now. Didn't you know?" I teased, since it was unlikely she'd heard.

One dark eyebrow rose almost imperceptibly. Though she'd grown up in the eye of the tornado that was this world and had perfected her mask, I could tell she wasn't deterred. "When? I didn't know you were looking for a wife."

"It's an arranged marriage," I said, showing her my ring. *Or more accurately*, I thought, *a forced one.*

"Who makes a more powerful alliance than me?"

"I didn't know *you* were looking for a *husband*," I pointed out.

"I'm not." She smiled a little. "But for the right cock, I might make an exception. And, baby, there's isn't a cock more right than yours."

I snorted. "My wife's is a different kind of alliance."

She played with one of the buttons of my shirt. "You

mean because her family offers some other vice we don't? Business is expanding, you know."

"No. Not that. I mean . . . they don't give me as much power as yours would have. But she brings other things to the table."

"Such as?"

"It's not something I can really put into words."

"I see." She licked her lips. "You love her?"

"No." I wanted that very clear to anyone around me, including Tasha, even if I did trust her.

"Who's the family?" she asked.

"The Cruzes."

"Ah. Bianca's daughter." Tasha eased back but kept her hand on my chest. "She's young."

"Twenty."

"I knew you when I was twenty," Tasha said. "I wasn't naïve enough to fall in love, but if I had been, I wouldn't have stood a chance against a man like you. She must be following you around like a lovesick puppy."

I grunted. *I* was the one constantly trailing *her*. Watching her. She was on my mind too much. I normally traveled with more men, but I'd left everyone except Max and Daniel behind with instructions to keep her safe.

Barto breaking in had shaken me. In my absence, I'd increased security tenfold around the Badlands, even if it meant traveling light. And I wouldn't relax again until I was back in her presence.

"This is an arrangement between her father and me," I explained. "She could care less what I do."

Tasha's button nose crinkled with a smile. "A shame. She doesn't know what she's missing . . . but I do. What does it matter if we spend one night together?"

I'd walked right into that one.

She pursed her plump, red mouth. A mouth that

sucked dick like a pro and enjoyed every minute. Her eyelids lowered as if she was also remembering her lipstick smeared all over me. But there was something even better about my wife's nubile, naked mouth tasting a man for the first time. Tasting *me*. And I was going to break in that pussy as a faithful husband.

And if I never gained Natalia's complete trust? If I came home empty-handed? What then? I'd be forced to choose between life as a celibate husband or an adulterous one.

It was a line of thinking I couldn't afford to follow. I'd press forward to the south as The Owl had suggested, and if I didn't find what I needed, I'd go deeper, harder, and more ruthlessly into the dark corners of this country, no matter the risk.

If I wanted Natalia to fall completely into me, without any reservations, then I had to be successful.

And I would be.

"It matters," I said.

"Because she gives you a different kind of power than anyone else could," Tasha concluded. "She's your past. The things you lost. The people you failed. That doesn't mean she can be your future, Cristiano. You should be careful."

A chill passed over me, despite the fact that it was a warm night. Her instincts hit too close to home, and I didn't like it. "You're warning me about my marriage?"

"If you're putting the pressure of the past on her and expecting her to fill those voids, you'll probably be disappointed. There are plenty of other women you could make a family with. Why does it have to be her?"

My heart thumped once. I'd asked myself the same thing over and over since Diego had begged for his life in my office.

Why did it have to be *Natalia*? Why couldn't I have let her go and stayed on course to bring my brother down? Why did I still feel drawn to her, and protective—even after she'd betrayed me and she continued to turn her head when I tried to kiss her?

In weak moments as a young man, I'd confided things in my friend Tasha. I hadn't seen her in at least a couple years and was surprised she could read me so easily. Then again, she'd been there from the start, when each side of her family had tapped their local and Eastern European connections to get me as close as possible to righting past wrongs. Wrongs that continued to plague me.

Was Tasha right? I missed the warmth and acceptance Bianca and Costa had given me after all I'd known was the dismissal of my own parents as they'd busied themselves playing with innocent lives.

I didn't expect that from Natalia now, but I could be a persistent motherfucker when I wanted something. And I wanted the home, the contented life I'd once had before I'd been forced to give it up.

"By seeking out the Valverde ghosts, you're plunging yourself into the past," Tasha warned. "Whatever you want them for, it must be connected to her."

I kept my mouth shut. I appreciated Tasha's help, but I wasn't about to share any more than I already had. "Enjoy the party," I said.

She rose onto the tips of her toes and pressed her lips to my cheek. "Are you sure I can't convince you to come back to my apartment?" She cupped her hand around my dick, and it twitched against her palm. "I'm wearing that invisible underwear you love so much."

It would be so easy to lose myself in her for tonight. I couldn't remember being so riled up in all my life as I was waiting for Natalia to invite me into her bed. Not even when I'd first fled the Cruz's home and had gone an embarrassing amount of time without a woman. I was crazed for Natalia, evidenced by the fact that I'd broken down and fucked her mouth when I'd promised myself I'd wait until I knew for sure it was what she wanted.

But in Natalia, I saw the potential for so much. As Tasha had just said—it was a lot to put on one person's shoulders, but I had faith. A night with another woman might not be much, especially around here, but to me, it was one small way of giving up hope in Natalia and me— and that, I wouldn't do. Not yet.

I removed Tasha's hand from my crotch. "I appreciate the offer, but I'm certain."

She pouted. "I lied earlier. Every other cock I've met is better than yours, simply because they didn't deny me."

I laughed. "If it makes you feel better, it's not my cock that denies you."

"Your heart?" she asked.

"No," I said. "The same thing that rules everything else —my reason."

"Very well," she said, backing away. "You know how to reach me if you change your mind."

I longed to bury myself somewhere warm and wet, but whereas in the past, any woman would have been good enough, now, only one would do.

Natalia was a conquest that would undoubtedly conquer me back.

I had seeds of hope that I might yet earn her devotion. That hope drove me. It was why I stood here now.

I walked back into the party, motioning for Max and Daniel.

"What now, boss?" Daniel asked, plucking a mint from a glass bowl on our way through the lobby.

"We head south," I said as we headed outside, passing under the bright lights of the hotel's awning. "Start gathering satellite images of the terrain and mountain ranges," I continued, stopping at the valet stand, "and putting out feelers for information from existing and potential sources." I glanced around for one of the parking attendants, eager to move. "We have plenty of contacts at the México-Guatemala border, which—*puta madre*," I cursed. "Why the fuck did they make us valet if nobody's working?"

Due to the high-profile nature of the event, we'd been forced to hand over the keys to the Suburban, but for such a high-end hotel in this city, the service was shit.

"I'm on it," Max said, sauntering into the small booth. He swiped our keys and took off running.

My phone buzzed, and I slipped it from my pocket to check the screen.

Natalia.

Twice in one night? Maybe one day, that would be the norm . . . but now, it wasn't right. And it set off warning bells.

With a quick glance at Daniel, I said, "Get ahold of Alejo. Check on things at the house, yeah?"

"You already had me do that hours ago," he said, snickering at my overprotectiveness of Natalia.

"Do it the fuck again or I'll leave you in that party," I threatened.

His eyes flew open. It was enough to get him on his phone. He stepped away to call Alejandro as I swiped my finger across the screen. "Natalia," I answered. "What is it?"

"Cristiano. I'm—I'm sorry to call again, and so late."

"It's not late." Surveying the space around me, I stuck a hand in my pocket and paced toward the lawn for privacy.

"Call me any hour of the night. I leave my phone on for you."

She took a breath, and with that small inhale, I sensed some hesitation. Was it possible to read her just through respiration—tiny, sexy gasps, light exhales, heavy pants? *Fuck*. Perhaps I was descending into madness already . . .

"What is it?" I repeated. "Is something wrong?"

"No," she said, but it wasn't as resolute as I'd have liked. She almost hedged on fearful. "Everything's fine. I just . . ."

With the ensuing silence, my hand sweat around the phone. Why the fuck was one damned call and a few simple words making my heart pound?

I felt . . . panicked. In a way I hadn't in a long time.

And the only explanation was Natalia. My attachment to her was fully formed now, and that was a problem for me.

It was weakness.

And it was a problem for her, too, if she never came around to the idea of me. Because I had no plans to let her go.

"You don't sound fine," I said.

She sighed. "Where are you?"

"Not far. If you need me, I can get on a helicopter, just . . . ask."

She wouldn't. What reason would she have? Things between us had shifted, but not to the place where she could ask me for something like that.

More silence. The longer it spread over the line, the more uneasy I felt. What was going on? An ache pulsed at my temples, my thoughts jumbling. I felt like I was in a snow globe that'd just been shaken. "Why are you asking?"

"It's just that you didn't tell me you were leaving, not explicitly. And you didn't say how far you were going. So I just feel like, as, you know, your . . . I should know where you are."

As my wife. No longer my captive? Finally, the SUV pulled up. I glanced over my shoulder as the valet got out of the driver's side. "Talk to me, *mi amor*," I said, turning forward again. "What's going on?"

"I've just been thinking a lot about our conversation at the nightclub last weekend," she said softly.

"Why didn't you bring it up earlier?"

"I didn't realize . . . well, you said you were looking for something, and it might be dangerous."

I racked my brain for what might cause Natalia to stumble over her words or beat around the bush. If she wasn't in trouble, could she possibly just be . . . shy?

"What are you trying to ask?" I firmed my tone in case she needed to be told. "Tell me now."

"I want to know if *you're* in danger—for real. Like actual, real danger. And if so, are you sure this mission is worth it?"

Ah. I leaned back on my heels as a soothing, unfamiliar warmth bloomed in my chest. She was concerned? For me? In these last weeks, she'd been resisting me at every turn. The last eleven *years*, she'd hated me for what she'd thought I'd done. Even the smallest inquiry about my life was a breakthrough—and here, she was actually checking in on my wellbeing. I couldn't help my small smile. "Natalia."

"Cristiano," she answered, and I heard her own smile over the phone. She knew she'd pleased me.

"Are you *worried* about me?" I asked.

"Well, if worrying about what the people here in your household, and in all of the Badlands would do without you . . . and if being concerned over the futures of the mistreated women and children your resources could help .

. . if all that means I'm worried about you, then I suppose I am."

I would take it. Every word of it. She couldn't say the things she wanted to—it was too early for that. But the meaning behind her concern came through. And I appreciated it.

"I'm not in too much danger," I said, downplaying the risk. Traveling farther and farther from my home would always expose me to enemies and potential threats.

"I don't believe that," she said, her voice rising to its normal tone.

"Any time I leave the Badlands, there's a chance something could go wrong," I admitted. "Especially since I've only got two men with me."

"Why didn't you take more?" she asked. "Is it because they're here with me?"

Realizing I'd been strolling around the lawn, I stopped and looked around for Daniel. Where *was* he anyway? And Max? My eyes landed on the Suburban as it idled by the valet stand, unattended. Had I seen that a valet had pulled it around? Max was the one with the keys.

"Where are you?" Natalia asked.

I frowned, still scanning the area. A wave of uneasiness weirdly similar to nausea hit me. "At a political event, but that's not important. I'm planning to go south from here."

"Why?"

It wasn't that I wanted to keep the details from Natalia, but I needed more information before I shared anything. If I told her what I was looking for and came up short, it could drive an even bigger wedge between us. And if my instincts about this were right, it could potentially break her heart—again. And like Costa, I didn't take that lightly. I'd vowed to protect her, but if my suspicions proved true, it would be a deeply emotional betrayal I couldn't shield her from. I wasn't going to breathe a word until I was one-hundred-goddamn-percent sure.

"Does it have to do with politics?" she asked.

"No."

"What then?" she asked. "Can't you give me any more hints as to what you're looking for?"

I shut my eyes briefly. *Closure.*

"I don't need it," she said immediately.

I blinked my eyes open against the awning's bright lights. I hadn't said the word aloud. Had I? What the fuck was wrong with me? Words never slipped out if I didn't mean them to.

"If you're doing all this to give me closure over something, don't," she practically pleaded.

Of course I was doing it for her—but I was no saint. I had my own selfish reasons, too. I turned back for the hotel and jogged up the steps to check the lobby for Daniel. "You don't even know what I'm trying to find."

"It doesn't *matter*, Cristiano."

"It does to me."

"But why?"

I massaged my jaw, thinking. "Tiny Dancer" played over the hotel speakers, and it was damn loud. When had I last put on a record and listened all the way through? And what kind of a thought was that right now? The song carried outside as I returned through the revolving doors and headed for the car.

If Natalia knew why I was gone and I came home empty-handed, she'd never fully open for me. Without this, there'd always be a part of her heart I'd never touch, no matter what happened. I knew it. *She* knew it. She was the one who'd sworn to me that without closure, she and I could never reach a level of complete trust.

"You don't have to do anything for me," she said. "Not if it, you know—not if you're not safe."

Her measured words spoke volumes. If Natalia didn't want me to put myself in danger, that meant on some level, however deeply buried—she might . . . *care* about me.

And not only was it hard for her to say, but after eleven years of seeing me as the worst man in her life, it was probably impossible.

I was moving from *monster* to the man she'd call *husband*.

But that alone wasn't enough. I wanted it all. I wanted her to *ask* for what she wanted. And I hoped what she *wanted*—was for me to come home. "Natalia. What are you trying to say?"

"I . . . I want you to—to—"

I missed the end of her sentence as my ears began to ring. I stretched my jaw, working it side to side . . . only to realize the sound was coming through the phone.

A piercing wail that drowned out Natalia as my spine went rod-straight.

My heart thudded in my chest as I strode to the car. I'd recognize that alarm anywhere.

"What *is* that?" Natalia yelled over what I knew was an earsplitting noise on her end.

"The house alarm. Where are you?"

"The bedroom—"

"Get down to the panic room, through the cellar—like Alejandro showed you, Natalia. Now!"

The ground under my feet turned to jelly, and I stumbled as I rushed to the Suburban.

When death strikes, don't fall down.

I righted myself, ignoring the way my head swam.

"Your car, *señor* de la Rosa." I turned and came face to face with one of the young valet parkers. I looked over his head for

Max at the same moment the kid lunged into me full force. My shoulder flew into the Suburban's side panel. Pain radiated from my bicep as I bounced off it, swung at him—and missed.

I never missed.

What the fuck?

Bright lights burned my vision. Whether the house alarm echoed in my ears or blared from my cell phone, I wasn't sure. *Natalia.*

My back slammed up against the car door as I was pummeled again. The valet did the best he could to get in my face while I towered over him. I could easily pick up two of him and crack both skulls together—but my reflexes had slowed to the point that I could barely even push him off.

My mezcal. It'd been fucking *drugged*. I gritted my teeth and tried to propel myself forward. I had many lives depending on me—including Natalia's.

With the bolstering thought, I managed to knee the valet in the balls, and a sharp pain burnt up my stomach to my chest.

He disappeared, but I couldn't move my head fast enough to get him in my sight.

My muscles fatigued, and I had to steady myself against the car or I'd fall. My phone, still in my hand, vibrated and lit up with Natalia's name for the third time in one night.

I stared at it, willing my hand to move so I could answer it. I swiped my finger across, but couldn't get the phone to my ear. "Natalia," I managed to grate out.

And her piercing screams answered.

No. Fuck! No. *The alarms. The cellar.* Was she in there? I tried forcing the question from my mouth.

With a flash of motion at my side, the valet threw

himself at me again. "A gift from Belmonte-Ruiz, *cabrón*," he said. "You've fucked with us for the last time."

Time slowed. I blinked against the blinding lights above the awning as they brightened and sharpened. Elton John's crooning slowed to a deep, lethargic warble. My head fell forward, and I caught sight of a bloodied knife in the valet's hand. Where was the blood coming from? And why was it dripping at my feet?

With a brutal thrust, he plunged it into my side, and searing pain followed.

As he withdrew it, I gasped for air and tried shooting out my hand to grab his neck, but exhaustion weighted my movements.

The world undulated around me. My ears tuned back into the screams.

Natalia's screams, as they mixed with the house alarm.

My vision blurred. I focused everything on getting the phone up to my ear.

I heard my name. I grasped for it. "Cristiano—" Her voice—small, terrified. "Cristiano!"

Get to the cellar. My knees buckled, and I fell onto them, but only one thing mattered—the shrieking of the woman I'd protected as a baby, a child, and now as my wife. They could not, *would not*, be the thing I heard as hell pulled me under. I couldn't go down in fear that she was being hurt. That another man had entered my bedroom. Cornered her when she needed me most. That he'd do all the unspeakable things I'd been fighting against. Put his *fucking* hands around the delicate throat I'd promised her only *I* would ever touch. My entire body burned at the thought that anyone would get close enough to her to broach the gates of Heaven—*my* goddamn Heaven—which I'd barely tasted and had never even breached.

Anger surged in me as the worst possibility of all hit

me. I forced myself to my feet with everything I had and managed to wrap my hands around the fucker's neck. Belmonte-Ruiz would not take my wife from the Badlands and into a worse hell than the one where I was headed.

I squeezed with the strength of a body that had faced death countless times and was still standing. A body that had taken down men three times the size of this scum. A body that had triumphed.

And then I reached into the depths of my reserves for even more—the reserves that had kept me alive in the past, the ones that I'd always fallen back on to save my own life. Now, I called on them for Natalia.

But the body I'd always depended on, which had stumbled but never fallen, that had racked up kill after kill—it failed me now. My vision darkened as I dropped him and fell back onto my knees, wheezing for breath.

I couldn't slip into the darkness. I fought against it. To lay my eyes on her and know she was okay, to kiss lips I'd barely begun to learn. To speak the things I couldn't imagine never saying . . .

I mouthed her name. I needed to return to her, to my . . . my . . . "*Natalia*—"

"Don't worry about Natalia." It took every effort to lift my head and meet the Belmonte-Ruiz member's eyes as he stood over me with his bloody dagger. His mouth slid into a menacing smile. "Your wife is next."

BOOK THREE IN THE
WHITE MONARCH SERIES:

———————

VIOLENT TRIUMPHS

———————

LEARN MORE AT
WWW.JESSICAHAWKINS.NET/WHITEMONARCH

ALSO BY JESSICA HAWKINS

LEARN MORE AT WWW.JESSICAHAWKINS.NET

White Monarch Trilogy

Violent Delights

Violent Ends

Violent Triumphs

Right Where I Want You

"An intelligently written, sexy, feel-good romance that packs an emotional punch…" (*USA Today*)

A witty workplace romance filled with heart, sexual tension, and smart enemies-to-lovers banter.

Something in the Way Series

"A tale of forbidden love in epic proportion… Brilliant" (New York Times bestselling author Corinne Michaels)

Lake Kaplan falls for a handsome older man — but then her sister sets her sights on him too.

Something in the Way

Somebody Else's Sky

Move the Stars

Lake + Manning

Slip of the Tongue Series

"Addictive. Painful. Captivating…an authentic, raw, and emotionally gripping must-read." (Angie's Dreamy Reads)

Her husband doesn't want her anymore. The man next door would give up everything to have her.

Slip of the Tongue

The First Taste

Yours to Bare

Explicitly Yours Series

"*Pretty Woman* meets *Indecent Proposal*...a seductive series." (*USA Today* Bestselling Author Louise Bay)

What if one night with her isn't enough? A red-hot collection.

Possession

Domination

Provocation

Obsession

The Cityscape Series

Olivia has the perfect life—but something is missing. Handsome playboy David Dylan awakens a passion that she thought she'd lost a long time ago. Can she keep their combustible lust from spilling over into love?

Come Undone

Come Alive

Come Together

ACKNOWLEDGMENTS

Many thanks to:
My editor, Elizabeth London Editing
My beta, Underline This Editing
My proofreader, Paige Maroney Smith
My sensitivity readers, Chayo Ramón and Maria D.
My release PA, Serena McDonald
Cover Designed by Najla Qamber Designs
Cover Photographed by Perrywinkle Photography

ABOUT THE AUTHOR

Jessica Hawkins is a *USA Today* bestselling author known for her "emotionally gripping" and "off-the-charts hot" romance. Dubbed "queen of angst" by both peers and readers for her smart and provocative work, she's garnered a cult-like following of fans who love to be torn apart...and put back together.

She writes romance both at home in New York and around the world, a coffee shop traveler who bounces from café to café with just a laptop, headphones, and a coffee cup. She loves to keep in close touch with her readers, mostly via Facebook, Instagram, and her mailing list.

Stay updated:
www.jessicahawkins.net/mailing-list
www.amazon.com/author/jessicahawkins

www.jessicahawkins.net
jessicahawkinsauthor@gmail.com